Generation 7

Ross Richdale

On the planet of Delpe, eighty light years from Earth, 1300 human settlers, descended from a stranded starship crew, have been at war with the crucnon, the native intelligent species of insect creatures, for seven generations.

When a flying female named Jaddig Qarte crashes in human territory she is befriended by human, Holly Jurjevics, Generation 7 Leader. Holly finds the clicker (as humans call them) a compassionate creature with high moral values, not the ruthless killer expected.

Later, it is discovered that Jaddig is genetically related to Holly but how can this be so? And why has this information been suppressed by earlier human generations?

Who are the crucks, a new species who attack both the human settlement and the Crucnon? How will the humans survive after being squeezed between two enemies? Will the long lost Earth bases and shuttle craft, their one hope of leaving the planet, be found?

And what of Jaddig and the thousands of her hybrid species? Where do they belong?

National Library of New Zealand Cataloguing-in-Publication Data

Richdale, Ross, 1941-
Generation 7 / Ross Richdale.
Previously pub.: Lost generations / Wayne South. 1998. (e-book).
ISBN 978-1-877438-28-8
I. Title. II. South, Wayne. Lost generations. III. Title: Lost generations.
NZ823.3—dc 22

Published by
Purrbooks
Palmerston North
New Zealand

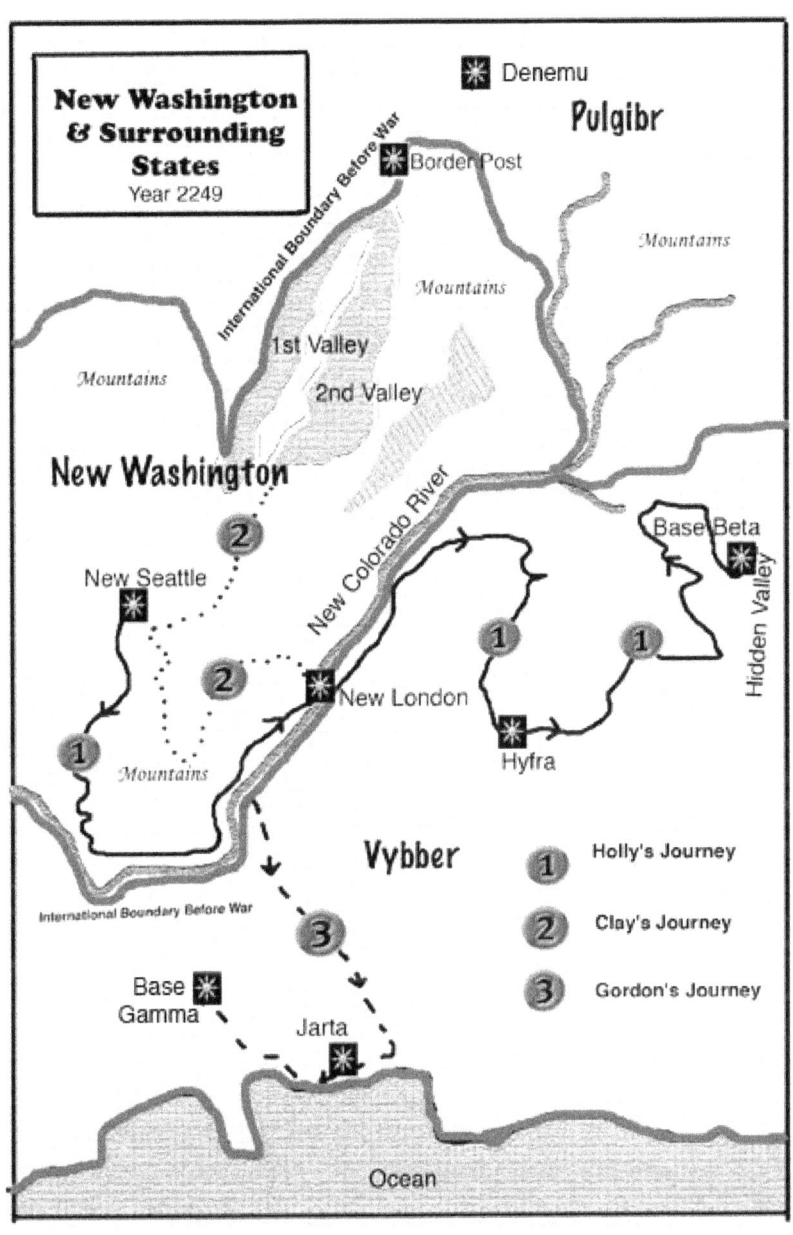

Purrbooks

Science Fiction and Fantasy by Ross Richdale

Anu Factor

Arising Magic

Armlet

Crystal Souls

Emerald Eyes Destiny

Emerald Eyes Mist

Emerald Eyes Pyramid

Into the Wormhole

Omega Seed

Time Genes

Time Portal

Transmigration

Lulu Publishers

Beyond Infinity

http://www.cyberread.com/info/12123/ross_richdale/ross_richdale/arising_magic/

Bumblebee Publishers

Time Ripple

*

CHAPTER 1

The wooden fort that crouched on a hillside overlooking the snow covered valley could have been in the American Wild West in the nineteenth century rather than the twenty-third. It could have even have been Washington or perhaps north of the border in British Columbia, Canada with the towering mountains stretching across the horizon but was neither.

New Seattle, the fortified village of a little over a thousand humans was so far removed in distance and time that, except for Jordan Wittenburg and the handful of Generation 4 centenarians, the inhabitants had forgotten their ancestry. They didn't know the significance of the flag that blew from the corners of the fort's four-metre high log walls. It was a light blue with white circle of symbols around the centre, the long forgotten United Nations. The history of it had been purposely withheld from Generation 5 eighty years earlier by the unanimous vote in the Survival of Humanity Protocol.

But the flag survived to represent the last bastion of humanity on the entire planet of Delpe, hundreds of light years from their ancestors' Earth, Information about this planet was also withheld from the younger generations.

On this 16th day of February 2248, True Time, the inhabitants had more pressing problems on their minds. A scout had returned with important information. The clickers were already across the international boundary at the New Colorado River. Over the summer and autumn, the lower plains had been evacuated as the enemy had moved through the human state. Worse, though, were the creatures' new body suits that were equipped with thermal heating so their cold blood could remain functional in the winter climate that normally froze them into immobility. It was also believed twenty or more flying females were assembling behind the front line. This was unusual as these females were normally only used for reproduction of the species.

The native inhabitants of the planet were only slightly shorter than a human and stood on two legs with the other four limbs used like human arms. In intelligence, they were equal to the humans but lacked any kind of morality or conscience to go with it. Old Jordan Wittenburg called them giant ants, another word lost in antiquity, but to the succeeding generations they were simply clickers because of the sound they supposedly made when they were annoyed or surprised. Most Generation 6 and 7 humans could speak Crucnon but preferred to converse in English, the language of their ancestors. The alphabet the enemy used was identical to theirs but the theory was that clickers had stolen it more than a century earlier to replace less functional hieroglyphics. Nobody, though, could give a reason why the structure of both languages were similar, in fact Crucnon was closer in syntax to English than Russian, another Earth language that had been phased out two generations earlier.

However, more practical problems were being discussed in the besieged village that day. Proctor Andrea Jurjevics, dressed in her usual blue jeans and red woollen pullover, sat in the underground council chambers and frowned.

"What else have you found out, Ron?" she asked.

The Generation 6 man wiped a somewhat dirty hand across his brow and grimaced. "They have mechanical vehicles with gigantic wheels that can travel up our highway from the river in a few hours. The ones we saw can hold twenty or more clickers and have reinforced bars at the front. I believe they intend to batter our walls down or perhaps surround New Seattle and starve us into surrendering."

"Have they learned to manufacture gunpowder in sufficient quantities to make explosive weapons, yet?"

"I don't believe so," Ron Cotterell replied. "The mechanical vehicles have been seen pulling gigantic catapults on skids. I earnestly believe they are preparing for one last attack on our walls. By attacking in mid-winter they are hoping to catch us with our defences down."

"I see," muttered Commander Toby Evans, the tall grey-headed officer who was head of the village's Defence and Police Force, colloquially called the DPF. "This supports other information I have gathered."

Andrea glanced up but refrained from inquiring how Commander Evans gained his information. It was believed he had contact with an underground clickers' movement that supported coexistence on the planet with humans. She, instead, glanced around at the members of the Inner Council and spoke in a hushed voice.

"It appears we have little time, fellow councillors," she said. "We may need to prepare to evacuate New Seattle and withdraw to the caves beneath the mountains."

"But how long will we last there?" grumbled Councillor Malone Davidson. "They merely have to wait and starve us out. Without access to our farms in spring we will be out of food before October."

"So what do we do?" snapped Andrea. This councillor was quick to criticize but never bothered to offer constructive help. "Become their slaves or be wiped out? We all know what happened whenever any of our ancestors attempted to reason with the clickers?"

"Yes," supported Ron solemnly. "Records show the few humans that ventured into their lands were never heard of again. That was eighty years back."

"That's my point," Malone added with her own voice raised in anger. "The clickers are a much more advanced society now. They may agree to speak to us."

"Only the Blue Watch will," Toby replied. "They're small in number, young and really just a student protest group with no power."

The proctor sighed. They had survived four attacks over the last summer with their farms wiped out and domesticated animals slaughtered. Now there were barely enough cattle, dairy cows or sheep to supply the village, the conditions in these northern latitudes were too cold to grow wheat and even the native vegetables really needed a warmer climate. Each year became more desperate and, with the clickers now capable of mounting a winter offensive, it seemed their days were numbered.

The Inner Council discussed the situation throughout the day and into the evening without really solving the problem. Withdrawal to the underground tunnels seemed the only solution if clickers broke through the outer defences.

"I'll consult with Jordan Wittenburg and the elders," Andrea finally suggested.

"Those stupid old fools who live in dream of a far world somewhere out there," Malone waved her hands out in exasperation, "They think there is a great silver flying machine to take us away to the heavens. It's all fantasy, I tell you!"

"We all know your opinions, Malone but there may be some fact behind the legends." Andrea stood up and fixed the other woman with an icy glare. "I'll speak to Jordan. It will do no harm."

"Not much good, either," Melanie muttered as she gathered up her papers, nodded at the flag attached to the front wall and strutted out of the chamber.

*

The attack on New Seattle came at dawn the following Monday, when, without warning, thirty flying female clickers appeared out of the predawn darkness to attack the outer walls of the village. Before the lookouts could even sound the siren the attackers were overhead with huge canisters clasped in their four arms. These were dropped on the south wall and burst in thunderclaps of explosion after explosion. The wooden logs simply disintegrated in the onslaught and more than two dozen defenders were killed.

"My stars, they do have explosives!" Commander Evans gasped as he stared out the smoking gap to where the field outside could be seen. Line after line of suited clickers marched towards the gap to the ominous beat of a drum.

But the chief of the DPF was not about to give up easily. "Right flank, form a semicircle outside the breach!" he roared above the roar of the flames. "Left flank. Fire duties."

Fifty young men and women, all with shields, swords and crossbows leapt outside through the flames to meet the incoming foe while fifty more were already bathing the wood with high pressure water hoses.

"Flying clickers heading for the north wall," a lookout screamed through a loud speaker. "At least a dozen."

This time, though, the humans were ready. Their own firearms came into action. Twenty mortars exploded and hurled a wall of stones at the incoming flight of female clickers. Five were hit and crashed to the ground to be killed by the explosives still held in their arms, another two dropped the bombs harmlessly beyond the outer perimeter. Four, however, reached the wall. Again, there was a discharge of explosions and a four-metre gap was blasted in the fence line.

"Lower and fire at will," Commander Evans ordered.

He smiled grimly as one clicker disintegrated in the air above him while a second tipped and plummeted to earth inside the compound.

*

The clicker lay gasping on the ground with terrified eyes as a youth ran up with his sword drawn.

"Please!" she cried out in well-spoken English. "Please have mercy." Four three fingered hands covered her face in defence.

"Insect!" screamed the youth and was about to stab the clicker with his sword when a young woman rushed up and grabbed his arm.

"No, we do not kill in cold blood," she hissed and glowered at the youth.

"Why, Holly?" the youth replied but hesitated. After all, Holly Jurjevics was the Proctor's daughter and held considerable powers with humans as Generation 7 Leader.

The young woman swished a strand of red hair out of her eyes and stared down at the wounded clicker. Like the entire enemy, this female was dressed in a blue coverall; gloves, boots and Perspex like helmet that covered all except the yellow eyes and almost human shaped mouth. Her

8

four wings were folded beneath her with the two left ones bleeding thick yellow blood.

The eyes, though, looked directly at Holly and tears of emotion appeared in their corners. "I had no choice," the creature gasped, again in English. "We must obey orders.

"Crap!" snarled the youth and lifted his sword again.

"You will withdraw, Hilton Foster," Holly said in a soft voice. "We are under military law today so that is an order."

Hilton stared at the angry face of his colleague but knew to disobey an order in an emergency was a serious offence. Holly outranked him by three stars.

"Watch her sting," he snorted but stood back.

"Crucnon do not have stings," the clicker gasped. Her eyes turned to Holly. "You must be Holly, Proctor Andrea Jurjevics" daughter," she continued. "Thank you for sparing my life Holly Jurjevics. I am your slave and will seek your permission to ritually assassinate myself so I am not a burden to the Vybber Nation nor the biped enemy." Tears once again appeared in the yellow eyes. "We have a poison capsule to bite on."

"I see," Holly replied and squatted beside the female. She had never been this close to a clicker before but had studied numerous photographs of them. This one would be no older than her own twenty-three years. "What is your name and rank, Crucnon?"

She had studied clicker military law at college and knew this young female had failed in her duty and was expected to commit suicide in disgrace. She also knew, though, the ritual of becoming a slave. Any Crucnon, as the clickers' real name was, had the right to surrender as a slave to an enemy. This was usually to their kind and flying females would be sent to a concubine to reproduce the victor's offspring. Usually this amounted to a life of misery and death within months of the capture. In most cases suicide was the more pleasant alternative.

"Third Class Mother Jaddig Qarte, seconded to the First Fighting Wing of Northern Command's 27th Fighting Brigade as a Flying Bombardier." She spoke in her own language without removing her eyes from Holly.

"Have you any offspring?" Holly asked in the same language.

"I have not yet been prepared for mating," the creature replied and, for the first time diverted her eyes. "I was called up for military service instead."

"I see," Holly continued. "So under the protocols of war you are now under my orders?"

"That is correct. Shall I bite the poison capsule, Holly Jurjevics?" There was a tremble in the voice, which made Holly frown. Clickers were meant to be entirely devoid of emotions, totally regimented and also without pity. This wounded female was different than she expected.

The eyes looking at her were pleading and full of emotion.

Before she could reply, a swordsman who walked up interrupted Holly. "The clickers have stopped advancing, Generation 7 Leader Jurjevics," he said and tried to ignore the clicker lying on the ground. "Your platoons are on stand down unless there is a rally call."

"Thank you," Holly replied and gave the man a brief smile. The sudden attention to her rank annoyed her. She turned back to the clicker. "I order you to spit out the poison and surrender any weapons," she commanded.

"But you can't!" snapped Hilton Foster. "Let the creature kill herself."

Holly glowered at Foster but said nothing. Instead she turned to the wounded female and snapped. "Do it!"

Jaddig Qarte's mouth quivered but she nodded and spat a tiny red capsule out, reached to a small pocket inside of her body suit, removed a stiletto type knife and placed it on the ground beside her. "I have never had contact with humans." She trembled as her eyes switched to Hilton standing a metre behind Holly. "I have heard the males are particularly aggressive."

"They can be," Holly retorted. "We are not barbarians, though." She next quoted a phrase learned at Military Academy. Its origin was, like many other things, unknown but the meaning was real. "Under the Geneva Convention, you are a prisoner of war and shall be treated for your wounds."

"I have heard of this convention," Jaddig Qarte muttered, still in her own language. "A cowardly protocol that our military forces do not recognize."

Holly looked into the yellow eyes. "Perhaps that is why we're human and you're Crucnon." she whispered and looked up at Hilton. "Get a stretcher and take Jaddig Qarte to the infirmary," she ordered.

"Yes, Generation 7 Leader Jurjevics," he muttered and walked away.

*

New Seattle was, in reality, a village built with defence and security utmost in the architects' minds. All security buildings were in four underground levels with dormitories and storage areas further down still. When first started a generation earlier, a gigantic limestone cave had been used as the basis of the village. As well, entrance corridors had vacuum doors with a no-man's corridor between that could be filled with freezing carbon dioxide within seconds. Of course, the defences could now be of little value when the clickers wore their thermal heated body suits.

The infirmary was off 2nd Avenue, the long walkway two levels below the surface and reached by zigzag ramps. No elevators were installed as the small electrical generating plants only had the capacity to provide lighting and a few other essential services.

When Holly let the stretcher party through, citizens in the access route stood aside with varying expressions on their faces from curiosity to outright abhorrence. However, the young woman's standing in the small human outpost was high so no comment was made as the wounded clicker was wheeled past.

The hospital was filled with burn victims and warriors suffering from cuts from the brief but ferocious fight before the humans drove the advancing enemy back by sending thousands of arrows into them. Dozens of young men and women were wounded but hundreds of the enemy lay dead around the village.

"We cannot give you blood as we have none of your type," Doctor Martin McLean stated in a quiet voice as he examined Jaddig. "We will, however, patch up your wings and stitch those nasty wounds in your shoulder and thorax. It is twenty degrees Celsius in here so you can remove your body suit without fear of losing mobility."

The young female's normally tanned face turned a dull grey. "Female Crucnon do not undress in front of males," she replied in English and turned her pleading eyes to Holly. "Surely you understand that?"

Holly smiled. This was another unexpected response from this creature. "We can get Doctor Sandy Boydell to examine you," she replied. "She is female."

"Thank you," replied Jaddig. "I know I am a non creature now with no rights but..."

"You have the same rights as everyone else here and that includes the right to privacy." She turned to Doctor McLean. "You don't mind, do you?"

"Of course not," he replied and nodded to a nurse "You can take Ms...." he looked at the card in his hand, "Qarte through to that side room and I'll get Sandy."

"You humans are kind," the clicker stuttered. "We were told..." She never completed the sentence but caught Holly's eyes. Even though the clicker had no eyebrows or eyelids she managed to show her innermost thoughts through a facial expression.

"I think both creatures on this world have been told untruths about each other," Holly replied and briskly added. "I know I was."

A short dumpy woman appeared and without even a moment's hesitation began examining her patient. "We will give you a penicillin injection," she said. "I know your species respond to this antibiotic."

The young Crucnon stared at the hypodermic needle but didn't object when the doctor injected her upper arm. The pale, almost human face relaxed and she lapsed into a peaceful sleep. "I forgot to tell her I added morphine," Sandra added. "She was in considerable pain but her species has some system of blocking off the signal. Unfortunately this does not cure the injury and often adds to the damage."

"You know about clicker anatomy?" Holly grimaced.

"Yes, like their language at school, it is a compulsory subject at our medical training centre. I think everyone hopes that, one day, we can be allies," She nodded. "Perhaps this is a first step on a long journey."

"Could be," Holly replied. "I know I learned something today."

*

Holly was sitting in a chair with a book in her hands when Jaddig awoke , stared around and sat up on the bed in alarm.

"It's okay," Holly said quietly. "Nobody will hurt you."

"What time is it?" the clicker girl asked.

"Three hundred hours," Holly added.

"Thank Sun God!" Jaddig gasped. "Quick, you must raise the alarm!"

"Why?" replied Holly. "Your forces have retreated. The battle is over."

"No it isn't! You don't understand."

Holly frowned. "Understand what, Jaddig?" She bent forward and gazed into the yellow eyes. There was something this young female was worried about.

"You have two hours," gasped the clicker. "At five, our mechanical machines arrive. They have drilling equipment and tanks of testra."

"Testra. What's that?"

"A deadly nerve gas," Jaddig Qarte replied. Her eyes expanded perfectly round to over three centimetres in diameter, "They're going to pump it into here. One whiff is enough to kill a person. Within half an hour you'll all be dead. Our army has plans of your whole underground city. They know where the main ventilation pipes are. Everything!" She reached out with both right hands and gripped Holly. The grip was cold but the young human woman knew the warning was genuine.

"Right," Holly whispered and walked to the telephone on the wall. Four digits were punched in and she cursed as she waited for Commander Evans to answer.

"Commander. It's Holly," she said when his sleepy voice answered. "Code Red. We must evacuate everyone immediately and seal the city. This is not a bluff. My emergency authority number is Triple 8, 59, double 7."

"Explain!"

Holly repeated Jaddig's warning.

"Can you trust this Crucnon?"

"I believe so. She has nothing to gain by lying."

"Okay. Evacuate the infirmary to Emergency Exit 76. Go into the maze. Left, straight then right. You'll find Airlock 774. Repeat please," he added in a crisp voice.

Holly did and Evans continued. "Through the airlock is a reception room. Wait there for further instructions. I'll do everything else."

"We're evacuating," Holly told her patient as a siren began to wail through out the room and a mechanical voice filled the air. "Condition Red. Emergency Evacuation. This is not a drill. Please proceed to your nearest Red Exit sign. Repeat. This is not a practice. Please proceed to your nearest Red Exit. All military personnel are ordered to find the children and Generation 4 citizens on your personal list and escort them to the exit doors. Condition Red..." the message was repeated.

Holly checked her notepad and found it contained the names of ten hospital patients in her immediate vicinity.

"Can you walk?" she asked Jaddig and received a nod.

"I can also push a bed." the clicker replied as she slipped out of bed, grabbed her body suit and proceeded to put it on.

"Come on," Holly said to a young soldier with multiple burns in the next room. "You heard the speaker. Do you mind if Jaddig pushes your bed?"

"No." The young man chuckled. "I often wondered what a female clicker looked like. Almost as beautiful as you, Holly."

"Watch it, Douglas," she replied with a tiny grin and moved to the next bed.

It took an hour but by four fifteen, New Seattle was like a ghost town, electronic detonations were set and the last troops turned off and isolated the main ventilation shafts before they opened the secret emergency ventilation. The entrances to the maze were sealed behind them and citizens gathered in the reception room where a roll call was in operation.

*

At five, exactly as Jaddig Qarte had said, twenty mechanical vehicles rolled in through the gaps in the fence followed by hundreds of ground troops. There was no resistance. The mechanical monsters drove to pre-selected sites and raised steel drills similar to oilrigs. But they never began operating.

Hundreds of metres below the surface, Andrea Jurjevics gave the order and three councillors entered their codes into a computer, Toby Evans nodded and pulled the self-destruct lever down.

Above, New Seattle disappeared in high explosive, smoke, flames and debris as fifty charges detonated simultaneously. Five thousand living beings died that morning but one thousand three hundred and fifteen humans and one clicker survived the earthquake that shook their reinforced bomb shelter below. The emergency evacuation that had been built sixty years earlier worked perfectly. Now there was a ten-kilometre journey through underground tunnels to caves in the mountains, the last retreat for humankind on the planet of Delpe.

*

CHAPTER 2

After the evacuation into the tunnels began, Andrea Jurjevics walked up and waited while Holly tended to Jaddig's wounds. She exchanged a few brief comments with the clicker and drew Holly aside.

"Jordan Wittenburg wishes to speak to you urgently, Holly, " she said. "He is quite depressed by the destruction of New Seattle but I believe he has more to say than just the ramblings of an old man."

Holly grimaced. She knew Jordan of course but had not really had a lot to do with him.

"Okay, Mum," she sighed. "Where is he."

"Here my child," a raspy voice interrupted and Holly glanced up to see the elder standing at a small side entrance. "I need to speak to you alone."

Holly nodded, gave her mother a brief grimace and followed him through the crowded main auditorium until they came to another alcove lit by one weak light bulb.

"This is a poor substitute for my apartment but will have to do," Jordan began. "Please sit if you wish."

Holly smiled and sat on the dry ground with her back against the wall. Shadows from the one swinging bulb gave the cave a surreal appearance and the voices in the main cave became a faint hum in the distance.

Jacob took a small bottle and two mugs from his jacket pocket, poured a small amount of liquid in each and handed one to Holly.

"A little wine?" he asked.

"Thank you," Holly politely sipped the drink. It tasted tart but was relaxing on the lips.

"I noticed what you did for the Crucnon," the centenarian began with a crinkled smile and wave of a shaky hand. "Somehow, it reflects everything we stand for."

"And what is that, Jordan?"

"Humanity and compassion? That young Crucnon was dropping death and devastation on our village but you did not rush in with a sword and pierce the creature's heart like that youth wanted to do. Instead you offered her help. " His watery eyes found hers. "You turned an enemy into a possible friend."

"I could not leave her to die," Holly replied in a soft voice. "As it worked out I found she was forced into fighting us. She had no choice."

"Exactly," the old man continued. "Human history is filled with accounts of behaviour no different than that of the ruling Crucnon. Historically, our kind is no better than hers."

"How do you know, Jordan?" Holly replied.

Jordan Wittenburg sighed. "Have you heard of the Survival of Humanity Protocol?"

"Yes," Holly replied. "Eighty years ago our ancestors set out a course for us to follow."

"When it was discussed I was your age, Holly and the junior representative on the committee that proposed it." Jordan sighed, sat down beside her, lifted his knees and folded his arms around them. There seemed to be a glow in his eyes and his old body appeared to shed the years. "It was more than a vision of the future. It was a decision to hide the past from future generations."

"But why?" Holly whispered.

"So we would not cling to a faint hope of something that might never happen."

"And what was that?"

The old man's eyes moved across to seize her own, "We are not of this world, Holly. Our ancestors came here in a starship but were stranded on this planet. The first generations thought they would be rescued but the years went by until we realized that it would not happen. We wanted our children and children's children to be free of this faint hope of rescue, hence the Survival of Humanity Protocol. It was agreed to withhold information about our past from our children and up until this day, it has worked."

"So why are you telling me, Jacob? Surely this knowledge will only depress our people?"

"True," Jordan sighed. "Except for one last subclause in the protocol, which I am now invoking."

Holly bit on her lip but said nothing.

"Like it or not young lady, you are, through your age and democratic choice, leader of the Generation 7 that goes from your 23 years down to John Garret born but three weeks ago. Your child, when you chose to have one, could be one of the first of Generation 8, but I digress." He stopped and sipped his wine before continuing. "Subclause 63.7 of the Survival of Humanity Protocol gives me the right; no commands me to hand to the leader of the last adult generation the final orders. That, Holly Jurjevics is you." His old leathery face twisted into a thin smile. "I am glad it is you and not that whippersnapper hothead Hilton Foster."

16

"He almost beat me in the election for Generation 7 Leader," Holly replied modestly.

"If you can call ninety percent of the female vote and sixty of the male vote close," Jordan chortled. "I've followed you closely, My Dear, and are proud you are my great grand daughter."

"Am I?" Holly gasped. "I didn't know."

The old man shrugged. "Another Survival of Humanity Protocol," he added. "We wanted to stop any inter-family rivalry so from that date, all children were given their mother's surname. This stopped trying to trace the father and inter-sibling rivalry between half brothers and sisters." He grunted. "It worked well, too."

Holly frowned. "What happened before that?" she asked.

"Children took the father's surname."

"How stupid!" she whispered.

"Yes, it does seem so now, I agree but eighty years ago attitudes were different. Many wanted to cling to the old ways." He stopped again and gave a nostalgic sigh. "My wife, Christina had your red hair, Holly. Her Irish ancestry, she used to say."

Holly frowned again. Irish! She'd never heard the word. All she knew was that she was one of very few red haired humans and had often wished she had blonde or dark hair like most of the people. She thought of her fellow humans. As well as hair colouring and style, they were often quite different in skin colour and appearance.

She was slim, a metre eighty-three tall, weighed seventy odd kilograms and took pride in her fitness. However, most males towered above her. Every generation, it seemed, was taller than the one before it.

"Anyway," Jordan continued and took a crumpled yellowing document out of his pocket. "This is the Survival of Humanity Protocol in its entirety. I now officially hand it on to you to care for and preserve for future generations. You are our leader, Holly."

"What about Mum?" the girl protested.

"She is the present. You are the future. Do you understand the difference?"

Holly hesitated for a moment before nodding. "I think so," she added in a whisper.

"Good. Now the information." Jordan smiled.

The elder spoke in a clear voice for an hour with frequent references to the old document. Holly's eyes opened wide in astonishment at the knowledge being passed onto her. She felt proud and humble, if it was possible to be both at the same time, as she listened, asked a few questions or read extracts from the document.

"Does Mum know this information?" she finally asked.

"Yes," Jordan replied, along with Commander Evans and two members of the Inner Council. They have all taken the vow of secrecy, something you will not have to do."

"Why?" the young woman asked again.

"The time has come to tell our peoples about their past, Holly. That will be your job; not mine or Andrea's but yours, as shall be the decision as what to do with the information you now know. Discuss it with your mother, the Inner Council but the final decision is yours."

"Yeah I know," Holly grunted. "It's what the Survival of Humanity Protocol directs."

"True," smiled the old man. "Your ancestors as well as living compatriots depend on you. As I said at the beginning of our conversation; like it or not, you're it, Holly."

Holly's body shook as Jordan Wittenburg reached out and gave her a brief hug. Her mind was in a spin. Information she received was almost too much to comprehend. Their ancestors did come from another world and, perhaps even more important, the starship was still out there orbiting Planet Delpe. All they had to do was to get to it.

*

That evening the Inner Council had a special meeting to discuss the fate of the their kind and, as well as the usual members, Holly and Jordan were in attendance.

Andrea stood, nodded gravely at the members and glanced across the small table that almost filled the side cave.

"Today, we reached a turning point in our society," she stated. "We are here deep under the ground, our homes have gone, our supplies are finite and we are at war with an enemy who wants to exterminate us but why?" She paused. "We are no threat to them, a little over a thousand souls compared with hundreds of thousands, if not millions of the Crucnon on this planet. In 2098, ninety-eight Earthlings, fifty women and forty-eight men landed on Delpe due to an emergency deep in space.

It is now 2248, True Time. Due to the orbit of this planet we have thirty one years for every thirty two on Earth," She grinned. "On Earth I'd be almost two years older. We have been here one hundred and fifty years, Fellow Councillors; seven generations and we are still the aliens. We are still no accepted. We are still hunted down like animals and killed." Andrea's voice became louder before she stopped and continued in a whisper. "That's the trouble, I guess. We are animals, mammals to be precise, whereas the Crucnon are insects… " Andrea hesitated when she heard a faint cough and saw Holly's eyes attracting her attention.

"Can I speak please, Mother," the younger Jurjevics asked. Her white frock shone in the artificial light. She stood, acknowledged her mother's slight nod and began to speak.

"It is not the Crucnon who are the ruthless killers," she began and hoped her nervousness did not show. "It is their government. I learned a lot in the last two days. I met my first Crucnon yesterday, a woman my age. Sure she has no hair or warm blood. She has four arms and four wings but she also has intelligence and compassion." Holly stopped and glanced at each councillor in turn. "She also saved our lives, every one of us. She could have remained silent and let her army pump nerve gas into our shelter, but she didn't Ladies and Gentlemen..." Holly's voice continued and grew in confidence as she told the small elite group everything about Jaddig Qarte.

"But how does it help us?" muttered Malone Davidson. "Her kind have us trapped. All they need to do is wait. We have food for three months then we starve or surrender. It's as simple as that."

"Or we find the shuttle craft our ancestors used," Jordan Wittenburg interjected. "It is sitting four hundred kilometres from here, secure and safe, ready to rise to the heavens to the mother craft in orbit."

"A fantasy," scoffed Davidson.

"No," said the old man. "It has been waiting while breeder cells slowly replenished the oxygen supply in the mother craft and solar energy replenished battery power. This took a hundred and twenty five years. The space ship has been is ready to receive us for eighty years, now."

"Rubbish!" shouted an elderly man to the right of Andrea.

Jordan Wittenburg smiled. "I have proof," he said and placed a small television receiver on the table. "An old video disc," he said and slid a tape in the side. "I got this one working." He grinned at Holly. "Plug it in my girl."

Holly took the cord, reached up with a handkerchief in her hand, took out the light bulb and plunged the room into reflected light from the main cave around a half corner. She screwed in the plug and watched the monitor light up. "We're ready, Jordan," she said.

"The old man thanked her, pressed a remote button and the screen lit up to show a line of people dressed in silver suits waving at the audience. Behind was a gigantic rocket with a shuttlecraft perched on top.

"The journey to the stars is about to begin..." the commentary started.

For two hours the disc played and traced the story of Inter-galatical Starship 7. It showed the one hundred and five astronauts entering deep freeze chambers where they were put in suspended animation before the starship switched to light speed. There was a brief display of static until the next scenes came into view. A planet, all blue, green and white dangled in the black sky. This was Delpe where the computers had brought them after Inter-galatical Starship 7 had been hit by a rogue meteorite the size of a tennis ball. An external view showed astronauts repairing Star Ship 7's fractured outer hull as a stream of white condensation poured out. The commentary noted that ninety percent of the craft's oxygen was lost. Finally a spherical shuttlecraft shuttled the ninety-eight survivors of the deep space journey to the planet below.

"It is Wednesday, the 17th of August 2098 and we are stranded," an astronaut spoke to the screen. "We cannot leave but perhaps, one day, our ancestors will. Our signals will take seventy years or more to reach Earth at light speed so there is no hope of rescue. This is Admiral Leonard Jurjevics, leader of this fated expedition signing off."

The screen turned to static again, Holly replaced the light bulb and strained faces stared, speechless, at each other.

"My ancestor," Jordan muttered, "Andrea and young Holly's, too. They landed in a temperate zone believing it was the best place but were driven further and further north by the Crucnon. New Seattle was once a hundred kilometres north of the nearest clicker outpost as the winter weather was too sever for their metabolism, so for two generations our peoples lived in peace." The old man shrugged. "I think the clickers chose to ignore us as long as we never moved south of the river we call New Columbia."

"Why did it change?" Holly broke the silence that followed.

"They were invaded by another clicker nation," Jordan continued. "The invaders had a program of mass annihilation but were beaten back. Afterwards the Crucnon had a surplus of weapons and turned their attention to us. We could fend for ourselves until they began to use these modern weapons. You all know the rest of the story." He shrugged. "I am too old to leave this world but you people here, our leaders, are not."

Suddenly everyone began speaking at once as they grasp at the truth and tried to comprehend how the lives of the thousand settlers in the outside cave would be affected.

Holly glanced at her mother and found tears in her eyes as they reached out and hugged each other. "You knew all along, didn't you Mum?" Holly sniffed.

"I did Sweetheart," Andrea replied and hugged her daughter again.

*

An air of despondency hung over the community as the settlers attempted to sleep in the tunnels and natural caves beyond. Grieving relations reflected on the seven warriors killed in the battle while nurses and

20

doctors cared for the two dozen more wounded survivors. Stretchers and bunks were allocated to elderly citizens and children while blankets were distributed to everyone else who had to sleep wherever there was space available.

The small but dedicated police force remained vigilant and arguments or fights were stopped before they could become a problem. An attack on two teenage girls by five youths was interrupted when the girls' screams from a remote corner brought their plight to attention.

After almost forcing her daughter to lie down and rest, Andrea made no attempt to sleep herself but walked through the crowded tunnels, talking to settlers, offering to feed a crying baby, consoling a grieved parent over a lost son, and generally helping anyone and everyone in need.

By four hundred hours, the tunnels were almost quiet and the proctor made her way back to the small area allocated to her immediate family. This was now only Holly; her husband had died five years previously and her parents before that. She was about to slip into a sleeping bag when a man in dressed in a white jacket approached.

"Proctor Jurjevics," he said in a serious voice. "I am afraid I have some bad news."

Andrea's heart raced and her face drained of colour. Visions of the enemy rushing into their retreat and slaughtering humans rushed into her mind. "Tell me, Martin!" she gasped and fixed the doctor with an apprehensive stare.

Doctor Martin McLean placed a hand on Andrea's shoulder. "It's Jordan Wittenburg," he stated in a hushed voice. "I am afraid he hasn't made it."

"What do you mean?"

"I checked on him a few minutes ago and found he had died in his sleep. Two hours ago he was speaking to me and he dropped off to sleep and just didn't wake up. There was no pain. His old heart just stopped. It was as if he had done his duty and was confident in your ability to carry on to lead our people. I am sorry, Andrea. We all loved him." His eyes dropped.

"I see," Andrea replied. "Thank you, Martin. Does anyone else know?"

The doctor shook his head. "I came straight to you," he whispered.

"Have there been any other deaths over the night?"

"No," the man replied. "Only our warriors killed in battle after the initial attack. All the wounded are responding to treatment and are out of danger."

"Have you had any sleep?"

"No less than you, Andrea." The man sighed. "There are too few doctors or medics left now." He shrugged. "Mind you, the youngsters of Holly's generation are very willing and capable. Within a few years they'll more than replace the Generation 5 and 6s who are reaching retirement."

"If we have a few years," Andrea added sadly. She stood up. "I shall come and see Jordan for one last time. I appreciate you coming straight to me. He would have liked it that way. He was my grandfather, you know."

"Yes, and mine." The doctor gave a tiny smile. "I guess we're all related by now."

"Probably," Andrea replied, "but I'm glad the Survival of Humanity Protocol attempted to stop fragmentation of our society into family units."

She placed a coat over her crumpled clothes and followed the doctor through the dim tunnel lit by an occasional orange security light. Everywhere were the sounds of close packed humanity as the refugees had finally succumbed to the sanctuary of sleep.

*

Customs steeped in antiquity from before the Survival of Humanity Protocol were used in the funerals for the swordsmen, warriors and Elder Jordan Wittenburg. Fifteen wooden coffins draped in the blue flags of the United Nations were carried by DPF officers of both genders to a corner of the underground cave beside where a small underground stream.

Proctor Andrea Jurjevics and Commander Toby Evans spoke briefly on the lives of the deceased and a bugle played the haunting *Last Post*. Citizens filed by, dropped a symbolic handful of soil into the graves and stood in silence as the leaders of each generation, including Holly, said a few brief words. The graves were covered and topped with small semicircular stones on which their names had been carved.

Amazingly, it was Jaddig Qarte who was one of the most moved. The Crucnon stood at the rear of the humans trying to remain inconspicuous but everyone knew she was there and most appreciated it.

"What are the collared pieces of cloth?" she asked Holly.

"Our flag," Holly replied. "It represents our community. I do not know who designed it."

"And the name stones?"

"They are a symbol of remembrance. Before the Survival of Humanity Protocol there were different symbols but it was decided the stone best represents our life on Delpe." Holly noticed the young insect creature was almost in tears. "What do your people do to when someone dies? Is there a special ceremony?"

"No," answered Jaddig in her precise English. "When a Crucnon dies the body is cremated and they are forgotten as if they never were. It is a law that they are never mentioned again."

"Oh how awful!" Holly gasped.

"I know," Jaddig continued, "but we can still remember in our minds. I had a brother called Glyka who was killed in a training exercise." Tears appeared in her eyes as she remembered.

"How were you told of his death then?" Holly asked in a quiet tone.

"We were visited by an officer who said, 'There is no Glyka Qarte. His brain does not function'. That meant he was dead." Jaddig sighed. "I like your system better. Glyka and I were from the same batch, had the same mother, and were very close" Her yellow eyes turned to Holly. "Even to cry is considered a weakness but I do; all the time."

"And so you should," Holly answered. "We do not consider it a weakness. My Mum had tears rolling down her face a few moments ago. She is one of the strongest people here and I am proud of her."

"I noticed both her tears and your pride," the young Crucnon answered. She took a handkerchief from her body suit, wiped her eyes and blew her nose, smaller in size than human noses but also just above the mouth. "Thank you for letting me attend this moving ceremony for your deceased but I must return to the infirmary. I promised the nurse I'd help wash some bloodstained sheets in the underground stream."

Holly was deep in thought as she studied her companion. "I'll walk back with you, Jaddig," she whispered.

The tall human girl was a head taller than the Crucnon and perhaps for the first time on that planet, the two intelligent species walked and chatted as friends. Stranger still, though, was that not one human near them showed any objection but Holly noticed four teenage youths staring at her.

As she walked by, Holly heard Commander Evans, reprimanded the youths.

"If you have nothing better to do except goggle at your leader with eyes of lust, I would recommend three hours of heavy chores," the commander snapped. "We need the water containers filled from the underground stream and distributed. If you hurry you may get it done in two hours."

"Yes Sir," the youths stuttered, glanced at each other and headed for a pile of jerricans nearby.

Holly grinned. When you are fourteen; to be reprimanded by the Commander can be quite scary.

*

CHAPTER 3

While Proctor Jurjevics and the other councillors watched with pursed lips and heavy frowns, Commander Toby Evans leaned over the table and ran his finger over the map unrolled in front of the Inner Circle. "The river valley to the south where we used to have our farms has been annexed by the enemy," he said. "Clicker settlers are moving in and using our farm houses to live in..."

Andrea frowned. Once again she had no idea how Toby gathered his information but had no doubt what-so-ever as to its authenticity.

"... New Seattle has gone," Evans continued, "and New London is occupied by clickers." His finger pointed to the only other human village on the banks of the New Columbia, a hundred and fifty kilometres to the southwest. This was the former boundary between human and clicker territories. "The landing shuttle landed four hundred kilometres south of Vybber, as the clickers call their land. Ancient records say it is hidden in a cave similar to this one and protected by a force field."

"What's that?" Ron Cotterell asked, his face wrinkled in concentration

"An invisible wall of electricity nothing can get through. This one also hides the craft from view. Anyone walking into the cave would merely see a clay wall."

"Of course," muttered Malone Davidson with sarcasm in her voice.

"Hush up, Malone," Andrea retorted.

"Our maps of Vybber are very basic and, I'm afraid, not very helpful," the commander continued. "However, we know the southern coastal area to is heavily populated with really one metropolis leading into another."

"Why don't we ask Jaddig Qarte to bring us up to date?" Andrea asked.

"The enemy!" Malone Davidson cut in. "Why don't we just walk out and surrender and save all the fuss. That insect should be immediately executed."

"That's it!" Andrea Jurjevics felt her anger rise as she stood and leaned forward on her hands so knuckles showed white. "You are totally negative, Councillor Davidson. Every day we tolerate your innuendoes and sarcasm. Not once, though, have you offered a constructive solution to our problems." She bore her eyes into the other woman. "As Proctor of New

Washington, I invoke Clause 473 of the Survival of Humanity Protocol. You are hereby dismissed as representative of New London. An election for your successor shall be called within the statutory thirty days. You do have the right to seek re-election, if you so desire."

"You can't do that!" the woman retorted but looked a shade paler.

"She can, I'm afraid." Ron Cotterell, the lawyer of the Inner Council stroked his black beard and replied in a firm voice. "Under the present emergency conditions, it is completely within her rights."

"Thank you, Ron," Andrea said quietly. "The former councillor will please leave our chambers."

"Dictator!" the woman's face contorted in fury. She stood, flung her head back in disgust, glared around the alcove and stalked out.

Andrea flushed and, for a moment, hesitated before she noticed Toby grin.

"If you didn't do it, Andrea," he said. "I would have."

The other members all nodded and broke into spontaneous applause.

"We're with you, Andrea," William Van Schaik, the normally dour old Generation 5 representative, added and reached across to shake her hand. "I place the proposal on the table that we consult Jaddig Qarte so the map of Vybber can be updated"

"I'll second that," Toby said.

The result was unanimous so within five minutes Jaddig was standing before them with a nervous twitch on her lips.

Andrea discretely studied the native of their planet who had removed her body suit. The clicker now wore clothes borrowed from Holly; jeans that covered the minute abdomen her species had and a woollen jersey with holes cut for her lower arms and wings folded, almost invisible across her back. With no breasts, her body appeared masculine but the face was very feminine. Except for being hairless and with tiny centimetre high hearing antennae replacing a human's eyebrows, the face was remarkably human looking with eyes, tiny nose and lips painted with a shade of lipstick.

"The cave is a constant twenty five degrees Celsius so I can function outside my thermal body suit," Jaddig explained in a shy voice. "Holly was kind enough to loan me some of her clothes and make up. I would have changed back if I had time but was told it was urgent to be here." Like a human she sucked on an upper lip to try to cover her nervousness. "I hope you don't think I look stupid."

"Not at all," Andrea remarked and grinned to herself. It seemed this young woman and her daughter had much in common. She coughed and returned to the matter in hand.

Jaddig nodded and, within moments, was bending over the map "There is a highway that travels to the river you call the New Columbia," she said and drew a pencil line across the map. "It follows the river and..." her voice continued on with a detailed description of her homeland.

Andrea grinned and gave Tory a dig on the leg. He nodded and followed her eyes. Jaddig was right handed but used both right hands with equal dexterity. At one point, her upper hand was sketching in a city boundary while her lower one was writing words in neat English block capitals.

The Crucnon looked up, saw their expressions and stopped. Her face drained white in embarrassment. "Have I done something wrong?" she stuttered.

"No, far from it." Andrea smiled. "We're impressed with your neat writing and the ability to write two things at once, that's all."

"I learned English at school and Double Write at University," the Crucnon explained. "It is difficult at first but speeds our work up. Most of our kind only use one hand."

"We are amazed, actually," Ron added, "But please continue, Jaddig. Your information is vital."

Jaddig smiled in return and glanced back at the map. "The safest way through our land is via the outer lands here..." She pointed to the right of the map. "The east is high country, cold for our peoples and lightly populated. The journey would be longer by about twenty weddens, that's a hundred of your kilometres, but far safer." Once again the young woman and the councillors began to see her as that; not an alien insect creature, sketched detail after detail on the map.

The paper was soon covered in her neat printing and sketches. "I took typography, too," Jaddig added modestly. "That was before I was ordered into motherhood and my studies cancelled."

"What's that? "Andrea asked in a quiet voice.

The clicker flushed again. "Most females are neuters, proper females but ones that cannot reproduce offspring. If selected for motherhood we undergo..." She shrugged. "How would you say it in English? It is hormonal treatment, our wings develop and we can fly. It is considered an honour. In our land we are not given a choice. If told to do something, one does it." She shrugged. "My female friends and I did not know it at the time but we were really wanted as flying warriors, not mothers. By the time I found out, it was too late."

"I'm sorry." Toby added. "You are obviously an intelligent young Crucnon. May I thank you for all your help here? "

"I want to be of assistance," Jaddig answered in a whisper. "In my homeland I am already classified as dead and would be executed for failing in my duty if I returned." Her eyes found Andrea's. "I've also found I like you humans." She gave a tiny giggle. "Do you know what the Crucnon call you?"

Commander Evans raised an eyebrow. "Biped-rats, I believe. Rats that walk on two legs."

"Why yes!" Jaddig seemed surprised at the commander's knowledge. "Rats are one of the few mammals we have. It is believed you humans brought them to Delpe. They are considered a pest and a menace in our cities, something to be exterminated without mercy."

"Like us," Andrea replied.

"I'm afraid so." Jaddig looked up. "But our people are wrong. I realize that, now."

"…And perhaps always surmised," Andrea added.

"Yes," whispered the clicker, "but there are too few of us freedom thinkers; far too few."

*

It was late and the settlers' second evening in the caves. Holly was losing her third game of chess against Jaddig.

"Oh Holly," said the clicker girl as she moved her Bishop. "You do leave yourself wide open. Check!"

"What?" gasped the human with a slight twinge of anger. "How can it be?"

She did check but every possible move was covered. The game had been going only forty minutes. She looked across at the intense yellow eyes and slight smile. "Okay, I resign." She gave a laugh. "I reached our inter-generation quarter finals last year but admit that you're too good for me."

"I believe the game was brought here by your ancestors," Jaddig added. "You did have me worried four moves back."

"Yeah." Holly grinned. "I bet." She glanced up as her mother entered their section of the tunnel "Hi Mum, care to challenge Jaddig at chess? She is one mean competitor."

"I can't even beat you Holly," Andrea sounded casual but looked worried. "Can I speak to you a moment, Sweetheart?"

"Sure Mum," Holly replied.

"I'll slip away and see if there is a shower available," Jaddig stood, smiled and walked out.

"Mum," retorted Holly. "You didn't have to be rude to her."

"Sweetheart, listen please," her mother replied with a frown. "We have some grave news that concerns Jaddig."

Holly nodded and saw that Commander Evans had appeared. He sat down and cast sad eyes across to her. "Would you call Jaddig a friend?" he asked in a harsh whisper.

"I guess," the young woman replied with a frown. "I never really thought about it that way. Why?"

"Jaddig will need a friend right now." He sighed and glanced at Andrea who continued.

"The Crucnon found out Jaddig surrendered to us instead of committing suicide as she was obliged to do, Sweetheart," she began. "We believe there is a spy amongst us who passed the information back to them."

"So?" Holly gasped but knew something more serious was still to be told.

"It concerns her life brothers and sisters," Toby continued. "The Crucnon are hatched in batches of thirty or more but are adopted out at birth into families of non egg bearing families to be raised.

"Yes, Jaddig told me..." Holly studied the commander.

"Her mother and the other four children in her family were executed and their family home in Gygnonypy burnt to the ground. Two servants and a family pet were also killed."

"Oh my stars!" Holly gasped. She blinked back tears forming in her wide eyes. "Because she is with us?"

"That's right," Andrea replied. "They are a ruthless race."

"How do you know?" Holly swung around and grabbed the commander's arms. "It could be just a story!"

"I am afraid not," Toby replied. He took a hexagonal shaped piece of cardboard out of his pocket and Holly recognized the Crucnon printing on it.

"This is a message written by a young Crucnon called Birobi Osyjil. We believe he was Jaddig's partner before she became a fertile female."

"But not now?"

"The mothers are fertilized by the ruling class, usually older males high in the military or government. The fertile females are virtual prisoners who are expected to service dozens of males and expected to lay eggs by the hundred for up to five years. After that, if they survive the ordeal they lose their wings and can become ordinary neuters again. Most die of exhaustion and deprivation. Ordinary males are not permitted to mate with the winged females but lives with other females are carried on in much the same way as we live except that there are no offspring," He grimaced. "Jaddig was lucky in one way. She was wanted to fly bombs in the war and had not been placed in a concubine."

28

"How terrible!" Holly gasped. "But she is so intelligent. My stars she slaughters me at chess, she went to university and has feelings, compassion, and honesty. Everything! How can she be like this and the rest be so cruel?"

"They aren't," Toby continued "There are many like her and, from what I found out, this Birobi is one. They are the ones I have contact with." He gave a slight smile. "They are my spies in their world."

"Will you tell Jaddig the tragic news, Sweetheart or would you like us to?" Andrea asked.

"I will," Holly whispered.

"One thing," Toby said. "Tell her before you bring the hexagonal letter into view. The hexagon has special significance to the Crucnon. As soon as she sees it she will realize something tragic has happened."

"I see," Holly bit on her lip and wiped her eyes. She tucked the strange shaped cardboard in her jacket pocket and stood up. "I might as well get it over with. Thanks for asking me Mum, Toby. Jaddig is a friend, you know. Strange isn't it?"

"No Sweetheart, I don't think so," Andrea replied.

*

The clicker girl had just changed into another set of clothes provided for her when Holly walked in.

"At least I don't have hair to wash," Jaddig chatted away, turned and must have noticed her ashen face. "What is it, Holly?" she whispered. "It's my family, isn't it?"

Holly had prepared everything to say but was unnerved by the remark. "Yes," she whispered. "I told Mum I was your friend and would tell you."

"Go on..." the voice was soft and choked with emotion. "Tell me everything, Holly. Don't hold anything back."

"It's just that..." Holly swallowed and repeated everything her mother and Commander Evans had told her.

Jaddig stood like a ghostly statue and just stared at her for two or more minutes before two massive tears rolled out the corners of her eyes and plopped into the wooden floor of the shower block. The two turned to four; eight and the slim body shuddered into emotional howls of anguish.

Holly stepped forward and wrapped her warm arms around the four cold ones of her friend and pulled her in close. Jaddig buried her head in the nap of her neck and cried.

"How did the Commander know?" she finally sobbed.

"He has contact with The Blue Watch. I have news from Birobi."

"What!" screamed the Crucnon. "How do you know about him?"

"He's your partner, isn't he?" Holly asked in an empathic voice.

"Was!" Jaddig cried. "If he ever came near me now, he'd be killed. And that was even before I surrendered to you humans! Breeding females are reserved for the dirty old males who run the place." She stared up at Holly again. "I would not have survived, Holly. I never wanted to become a winged female. They actually arrested me and forced me to take the hormones. I only bombed of your village as I thought it might keep me our of the concubine and perhaps back to Birobi." She sniffed back the last tears and stopped short. "You said you had news of him! Has he been executed too!" she howled.

"No," Holly smiled for the first time. He wrote you a letter.

"What! " screamed the almost hysterical clicker.

Holly took the hexagonal note from her pocket and handed it to Jaddig. She sat down with an arm still around her companion and watched as the alien woman read the letter.

"He's all right," sobbed Jaddig. "Birobi told me about my family just as you said but he is alive and safe. He's back in the reserves so is not even having to fight," She shrugged. "Not that there is anything to fight against now. Your lands have been annexed. He's back at university and says that if I write back, Commander Evans will get the letter to him."

"And the hexagon shape? Toby said it had a meaning."

"Our eggs are laid in hexagon shaped cells. The hexagon stands for life and death. If you had shown it to me, I would have realized something tragic had happened to my family." She signed. "It was expected, I guess."

"But someone here told them," Holly cried. "A human here is a spy. We don't know who it is."

"Then we'll have to be extremely careful," Jaddig said with her tears replaced by determination. "But with Birobi and the Blue Watch out there, we are not alone, Holly. I have a strange premonition we are going to survive." She blinked and smiled. "I'm talking like a human, aren't I?"

"Yes," Holly replied, "an honorary human and I'm proud to call you my friend."

"And one day you might even beat me at chess," Jaddig gave the slightest of smiles before the tears began again. "Would your mother and the Inner Council object if I had the names of my family carved on a stone and placed next to Jordan Wittenburg's one?"

"We'd be proud, Jaddig." Holly whispered. "You write their names down and I'll get it done."

Later, back in their sleeping area, Jaddig talked about her family. It was alien in many ways to Holly while in others it appeared similar. Her mother had adopted her as an infant and she never knew the flying female who had laid the egg she was hatched from. Jaddig remembered her father as an elderly civil servant who worshipped her mother. He died when she was ten.

"My mother was still living in the same house where we were brought up," Jaddig sighed. "The boys had left home but Silaw and Trief, my sisters were still at home. They were all neuters." She sniffed away another tear.

"I think I understand," Holly replied in a quiet voice.

"What, Holly?"

"Your society is so regimented and ruthless with little or no individual rights, yet you have families and are so, oh I don't know... human."

"A human with four arms, cold blood, wings and no hair."

Holly pouted. "I guess I sound arrogant but I didn't mean it that way."

"I know you didn't Holly," Jaddig answered softly. "Thank you. I know what you mean." She broke into a smile. "Do you want to hear about Birobi?"

"You know, I think I do." Holly smiled, tucked her knees up under her blanket and listened to Jaddig's story.

*

The memorial service the following evening was attended by hundreds of settlers who had heard of the tragedy. The flag flew at half-mast; another custom steeped in antiquity, as the Commander and Proctor both spoke while Jaddig Qarte stood at rigid attention in her neatly pressed body suit. It was only when Andrea switched to the Crucnon native language and the bugle played that the tears began to roll down her face.

It was a time when that lonely figure shared her grief for her family in that alien city across the New Columbia River, in a way perhaps never done by her species before.

"I shall remember this outpouring of friendship for ever. Thank you all." Jaddig's dozen trembling words were heard and believed by the hushed people at the conclusion of the service.

As the young Crucnon with one hand gripping Holly's walked back to her quarters, the crowd parted and hundreds of hands reached out and touched her in affection. A member of the hated species they shared the planet with had become a friend.

*

CHAPTER 4

Though barely mid afternoon, a harsh twilight settled over New Washington. Snow had been falling for two days and was still drifting down to cover the lonely land with its blanket of whiteness. Even the harsh remains of New Seattle were obliterated by metre deep snow. A few blackened buildings that contrasted with the world of white had their vision softened by the snow covering them. The land was still and hushed. No lights shone, no figures moved for there was nothing there. Even the tracks of vehicles had been obliterated.

Behind the bombed out village, two men dressed in bulky white cover suits lay on a hill crest beneath a grove of pines and surveyed their former home below.

"I'd say the clickers have withdrawn, Sarge," Bowman Clay Farrell muttered. His breath puffed out clouds of condensation into the frigid air. The young Generation 7 man swished snow off the tuft of brown hair protruding from his fur lined Balaclava, wriggled forward through the snow and focused his field glasses on the valley below.

"Aye, Clay but come spring and they'll be back with vengeance." a grizzled fifty year old replied. "Come on, we've completed our patrol. Let's head back to the warmth of the tunnels."

Clay grunted and made one last sweep of the valley; sighed at the desolation of the only place he had ever known and swung back to inspect the opposite direction. He stopped, adjusted the focus and stared again. "George," he said. "What do you make of that movement just outside the village?"

Sergeant George Bereano took the instrument from him and stared at the object in question. "There's someone there all right, Clay. Two or three clickers. Let's get closer."

Their white camouflaged uniforms were invisible from a mere fifteen meters away in the conditions so the pair managed to reach a position behind an embankment and within bow shot range of the enemy without being noticed. It appeared the clickers had more on their mind than the possibility of a human patrol being around.

"My stars," Clay whispered when he saw the reason for the clicker's activity. "One of those mechanical vehicles. Looks as though it slid off the road into that snow bank."

As they watched, one of the clickers opened the cab door of the massive vehicle and disappeared inside. There was a faint whir and the motor burst into life. Clouds of evil smelling black fumes belched skyward from a chimney behind the cab as a mechanical roar punctured the air. Two of the enemy had placed logs beneath the six massive balloon tyres and a guttural command was called.

The motor accelerated, wheels churned and pieces of wood, sludge and ice squirted in all directions. The vehicle lurched forward for a few metres before it crunched down on the logs and sent fragments flying through the air. There was a roar of machinery before the motor noise slowed to a deep rumble and the wheels stopped spinning.

More shouts were heard, the driver flung his four arms up in agitation, jumped down and another clicker took his place. The motor roared again, black smoke shot into the air and the vehicle's tyres spun. Blue smoke competed with the flying sludge to cover the clickers pushing from the rear. A tyre gripped one log but instead of just pushing it down as had been happening, the massive vehicle shuddered and lifted slightly.

There was a shout of approval and the vehicle moved slowly forward. The clickers slung more logs in front of the turning wheels and, with another shudder the, vehicle moved again, tyres gripped and vehicle accelerated.

"They're almost out, Sarge," muttered Clay.

"And our chance to get a set of wheels, Lad. Much better than horses and sledges any day, wouldn't you say?"

Clay stared at the older man who took an ugly double-headed arrow and fitted it into his bow. He grimaced and did the same.

"Your eyes are better than mine, Clay. You get the driver. On three. Okay!"

It was over within moments. The driver hardly gave a grunt as his throat was pierced with the steel arrow and he slumped over the instrument panel. The two outside met a similar fate with George's arrows penetrating the centre of their thorax chest, a vulnerable spot known to the seasoned human DPF bowmen.

The vehicle rumbled forward with no driver in control, stopped, jerked and stalled. Silence returned to the snow covered land!

"Right," grunted the Sergeant. "There may be others around. Let's check the road. You go up, I'll go down. See you back here in ten minutes."

The valley, though, was deserted.

"Now, if we can get this contraption moving and get it back to the cave," Bereano muttered after the pair had removed the clicker bodies and climbed into the cab. It had three seats across the front behind a vertical glass windshield. Two rubber wipers were swishing back and forth scraping snow from the glass.

Clay sat in the seat they'd dragged the driver from and inspected the strange objects that obviously controlled the vehicle. In front was a row of hexagonal shaped dials and six protruding levers. There were also two foot pedals. Three dashboard lights flashed green and blue. "Have you any idea how it operates Sarge?" he muttered.

"Nope," the older man retorted. "But those levers are obviously the main controls. See how those outside ones are worn shiny. I guess they manipulate them together to provide power."

Clay pushed his foot on one of the pedals and jumped in alarm as the motor roared to life and screeched in a high-pitched howl. However, nothing else happened; just the screaming motor as clouds of fumes belched out of the chimney behind them.

"Lift your foot!" roared the sergeant.

Clay did and the howl dropped back to a quieter rumble. When Clay pushed the right pedal again, the speed of the motor increased but the wheels remained stationery. He pulled one of the levers down but nothing appeared to happen.

"Do it again, Clay," George ordered and glared out an opened window. "The front wheels turned slightly."

By experimenting, Clay found the outermost left lever turned the two front wheels to the left, the right did the opposite so by holding them both half way back, the tyres straightened. The next levers in did the same with the centre set of wheels but the pair at the back did not turn.

When the inner levers were pulled there was a high-pitched scream of components but still the vehicle didn't move forward. For twenty minutes the pair continued to fiddle around unsuccessfully until Clay touched a small hexagonal button, the lights went off and the motor ground to a halt.

"Oh hell!" muttered George. "At least horses know how to move when ordered. This mechanical monstrosity is bloody hopeless."

"I know," said Clay. "We'll get Jaddig. Even if she can't drive this contraption, she should be able to explain how the controls work."

George grimaced. "Okay," he said. "Look, you slip back, tell the commander we need some more warriors up here and suggest we ask Jaddig to come. She's a damn good sort," he grunted. "For a clicker, that is."

"And you've known hundreds of them have you, Sergeant?" Clay replied with a smile.

The older man shrugged. "I've spoken to a few, Lad but none like her. The males seem totally arrogant bastards, even at neutral meeting places on the old border." He snarled. "After the bastards invaded last year I swore I'd never trust one of their kind again."

"Then Jaddig Qarte turned up."

"Okay," muttered Sergeant George Bereano with a shrug of his shoulders "She's different, I admit. But get going. The enemy could return to look for their lost vehicle. In the meantime, I'll remove those body suits from those corpses. They could be useful for Jaddig to wear."

*

An hour later, Jaddig, dressed once again in her body suit so she could operated in the cold conditions, stood beside Holly and grinned at the dozen DPF personnel swarming over the enemy vehicle. It was still partly off the road and nobody had managed to move it.

"Want a ride in the combo?" she stated in a serious voice.

"The combo?" Holly stared apprehensively at the gigantic vehicle. The six wheels were at shoulder level and the cab towered above them.

"Yes. We have smaller versions called cars back in Vybber," Jaddig replied. "They're easy to drive. I own one." She shrugged. "Or did before the trouble began." She turned to the sergeant. "Get your warriors out of the way, George. The wheels could spin a little."

Holly walked around to the passenger side, climbed the steel ladder bolted to the bulkhead, swung the door above her head up and stared nervously inside. The interior was very utilitarian, all steel and brown synthetic material. There was another handhold; two actually, designed for four hands and beings slightly smaller than she was. She wriggled inside and squeezed her long legs under the dashboard, as Jaddig called the panel. Behind the front seats, the interior was packed with military equipment. Everything, though, smelt clean and warm and Holly grinned as she reached up to a leather strap dangling from the door. She pulled it and the steel and glass "L" shaped door crashed down with a solid clunk.

Jaddig smiled, placed her four hands on the row of levers poking out from the dashboard and pressed a button. There was a faint rumble as the motor started; rubber wipers swished and two powerful lights burst on to flood the road in light. Outside, it had stopped snowing but sludge covered the road in front of the combo.

Three DPFs watching them waved and retreated to a safe distance. Holly gripped one of the two handholds in front of her, her eyes stared ahead and white teeth bit down on her lower lip in anxiety.

"Relax!" Jaddig said. Her hands and feet worked in a whir. Holly had no idea what-so-ever what they were doing but the combo's wheels turned slowly and they were moving!

"Oh hell!" she muttered as she bounced up and banged her head on the window.

"There's a safety strap to click on," Jaddig advised. She didn't look at Holly, but concentrated on the small rise in front while her hands and feet worked in unison. It was as if she had become part of this ferocious monster. Somewhere in front, the motor roared like a furnace and everything shook.

But the young female clicker was in control. Wheels gripped the gravel beneath the layer of snow; the vehicle jerked up the last remaining part of the bank at such a steep angle that Holly could only see the mountaintops and the sky. Higher and higher the combo went, the motor howled and tyres swished water and stones against the metal under their feet. Just when she was about to scream, the combo levelled and crashed down on its front wheels. They gripped, fought the sludge and pulled the gigantic machine forward.

Jaddig stopped the heavy vehicle a few metres up the road, let the motor drop to a deep rumble and ignored the dirty brown fumes that belched into the air from the exhaust pipe. "Who wants a ride back?" she shouted out the window. "There's a door at the back. Pile in."

George ran his hand over grey stubble and studied the combo idling quietly beside him. "How does she do it?" he muttered up at Holly.

"Beats me," she answered. "Reckons it's dead easy, though."

"Yeah, if you have four hands," retorted the sergeant.

Holly saw him walk around the back where someone had already opened the door and personnel were climbing in the strange craft. Twelve warriors fitted in with ease and stared apprehensively at each other as Jaddig told everyone to hold on. After a few shudders as the tyres slipped on the slush, they moved forward at a speed totally unknown to Holly.

"My stars!" she screamed as the combo rumbled ahead. The view out the side windows was a blur of whiteness and slush that splashed up beside them. Suddenly there was a bend in the road and was a bank immediately in front. "Jaddig. Watch out!"

But Jaddig knew what to do. A foot moved across a pedal, brakes were applied, a lever was depressed and lower gear selected. Levers were expertly moved ever so slightly and the four steering wheels turned the combo around the ninety-degree corner with metres to spare. Behind Holly and the driver, passengers clung on and didn't know whether to scream in fright or congratulate the driver. Most did neither but just stared straight ahead as if they were scared out of their senses.

Ten minutes later the Crucnon drove through an opened doorway in a cliff, slowed to a crawl and drove down a steep zigzag track into the bowls of the earth. At the bottom they were met by forty or fifty DPF warriors and bowmen armed to the teeth and ready to fight the hated enemy.

Commander Evans, somewhat sheepishly ordered arms to be lowered when Holly waved at him from the cab. He would have also recognized Jaddig in the driver's seat.

Even Andrea appeared white faced but gave a tiny smile when she saw Holly behind the windshield of the gigantic vehicle that stopped with a hiss beside her. Jaddig turned the motor off and the belching fumes from the exhaust dissipated.

"Like our new acquisition, Mum?" Holly called down. "Jaddig said she's going teach me to drive."

"Don't do this to me!" her mother snapped back in the silence that followed. "We were certain we were under attack. You're lucky the bowmen didn't shoot first and ask questions afterwards."

"Oh Mum, They're too disciplined for that."

"We spend an hour trying to figure out how to work this contraption," Sergeant George Bereano muttered from behind the proctor, "Then young Jaddig here jumps in and tears over the snow faster than a young filly can gallop. I was shit scared, I admit." He grinned up at Jaddig. "You have my respect Ma'am," he continued. "I think this is a valuable piece of equipment we've managed to capture."

"We'll probably need fuel if we want to use it," Jaddig replied in a monotone but her yellow eyes smiled in appreciation at the compliment. "The fuel gauge is hovering on empty."

Holly had no idea what her friend was talking about and it was the commander who nodded. "I'll get a patrol back up there," he acknowledged. "There must be a storage depot somewhere. The enemy has retreated but there's equipment everywhere. They're coming back. That's a certainty."

*

Andrea sat at her makeshift desk, wiped her weary eyes and glanced at the watch that showed almost twenty five hundred hours, midnight. She was exhausted but still wanted to read through the latest reports from the surface. She sipped the last dregs of the hot spice drink they called coffifake and sighed.

"Can I have a chat?" interrupted a soft voice.

"Oh, hello Toby. You're still up, I see. I thought everyone except the guards would be asleep."

The commander smiled. "I'm like you, I guess, Andrea. I relish this quiet time in the middle of the night and do much of my work after everyone else is asleep."

"The coffifake is still hot if you'd like a mug." the proctor replied. She smiled. "I could do with a bit of company at the moment. "She glanced at the documents in her hand. "From your report it seems we have a little more time."

"Could be," the commander replied, "but I wouldn't depend on it. My contacts inform me the enemy will be back before spring. We need to be out of here within a week."

"So soon." Andrea replied. "But how can we? There are too many elderly people and children, not to mention the wounded warriors from the last battle."

"We carry them on stretchers," the commander replied. "I'll get it organized." He stopped, poured his drink and fixed his eyes on Andrea.

"We need to be careful," he continued. "I believe an Inner Circle Councillor is our spy."

"But who? "Andrea gasped. "Malone Davidson?"

"No," sighed the commander. "She's just ignorant. Our spy is too clever to be openly hostile. I have three suspects but no proof any way. The only way to stop information getting out at the moment is to lay a false trail for the enemy."

"How?"

"You know the tunnels lead into the caves that go kilometres back under the mountains. I don't think they've ever been completely explored. Our original intention was to take the high entrance out to the mountain pass and travel up to our food storage at Base Four."

"Go on," Andrea whispered.

"The clickers are waiting there for us," the commander said, "However, I want to tell the Inner Council That's where we're going. However, instead we'll head south and out a new entrance into a parallel mountain pass. Base 7 Food Base has been set up there. It is in the next valley and, I believe unknown to the enemy."

"And from there!"

"The travel east through the second valley between the mountains. It's quite a trek but ends up in a different country," He grimaced. "It's called The Confederation of Pulgibr."

"Clickers?"

"Yes, but they speak a different language and are know enemies of the Vybber clickers."

"So! They're still insect creatures and there is no reason they'll be any friendlier towards us than the locals. They could even be worse."

"I know, That's why we should seriously think of the alternative and try to find that shuttle craft. It is really our only hope."

"But we talked about it at the Inner Council. If our spy is the slightest bit efficient, the clickers will have the site surrounded and be waiting there, too."

"All they'll find is a homing signal. The actual ship is a hundred kilometres in the other direction."

"You are devious, Toby," Andrea smiled.

"Unfortunately, it's still in the deep in Vybber territory and four hundred kilometres away. Now with that combo we captured, the journey there could take days instead of weeks."

Andrea rubbed her chin. "And who goes? The Special Security Force?"

"No. I want your daughter and the Jaddig to go."

"What! I won't allow it," snapped the woman.

"Think of it Andrea. Holly is as capable as any Generation 7 we have, male or female. We can pitch a story that she is part of an advance group heading to Base 4. We need Jaddig to drive the combo and the two trust each other."

"But can Jaddig be trusted? She is still a clicker, you know."

"It's a risk but a minute one. She is one dead clicker if she ever appears back at her home, I know that and her despair at the deaths of her family was genuine."

"Okay, I'm inclined to believe that but we can't send just two of them off."

"We won't. I'd say more should go but too many will be a hindrance. I believe we should ask Holly who she wants to accompany them."

Andrea frowned. "You've already mentioned this to her, haven't you Commander?"

"It was her suggestion," the man replied, "and I took some convincing before I agreed on one condition."

"And that was?"

"You approved, Proctor. You have the power of veto. If you say no, Holly doesn't go."

"Thanks," Andrea's voice turned hard. "If I agreed, what would her chances be, Toby?"

"About the same as the rest of us, I'd say, perhaps even higher. Six or so people are easier to feed and move compared with over a thousand."

"If she goes I want to as well," Andrea snapped.

"No," Commander Evans replied. "You're needed to lead our people here, Andrea. If you disappeared, the community would break up; of that, I am certain." He sipped the last of his coffifake and reached over to squeeze her hand. "These are grave times, Proctor, but your daughter and that young Crucnon girl have a better chance than anyone of finding that craft of our ancestors."

"But she is all I have," Andrea whispered.

"I know," the man replied with sympathy in his voice. "That is why if you say no, I shall abide by your wishes." He stood up. "Good night, Andrea. Try to have a good night's sleep."

The proctor nodded but did not reply.

*

"Jaddig is prepared to make the journey, "Holly told her mother the next lunchtime, "and even though she hasn't said anything, I think she would be highly nervous if I wasn't with her."

Andrea sighed. "It is your decision, Sweetheart and I shall not influence you."

"Then I'll go, Mum," the younger woman replied. "I've had discussions with Toby about who should accompany us and we both agreed on the following people. What do you think?" She handed her mother a sheet of paper.

The list included George Bereano, Clay Farrell and a Graham Whitmore, all respected DPF members probably selected by the commander. Also on the list was a Doctor Suzi Yu, the surname was familiar to the proctor but she could not recall the woman.

"Yes you do, Mum," Holly replied. "That dark haired woman in the research laboratory. She's about the youngest of your generation but is only a few years older that me."

"Of course," Andrea replied. "If I can remember she is very introverted." She frowned. "Why did you pick her, Sweetheart?"

"She's our top scientist and has studied all the old records on electronics and such like. It would be useless finding the shuttlecraft and not being able to operate it. Graham is pretty well up in that field too. They should make a good pair. "

*

After telling the community their group was an advanced expedition heading out to check the mountain pass snow conditions, Holly and her companions slipped back through a service tunnel and up to the surface where the renovated combo stood waiting.

The DPF, under Jaddig's guidance, had painted out the recognition marks on the vehicle and substituted others. Crucnon writing on the roof and sides now said Security Command Unit, the feared military police of the

Vybber Empire. The interior of "Charlie", as they had decided to call their combo, had been stripped of unwanted gear and fitted out with survival equipment and food. Four, hundred litre drums filled with evil smelling fuel called diesel had been stolen from an enemy base so, in George's estimate, they had enough to reach the secret landing site but not to return again.

Finally, Graham Whitmore had manufactured clamps for the back steering wheels to lock them so humans could drive, using two steering levers instead of four. Trials had been held with Holly and Graham becoming reasonably good at driving Charlie, if it was necessary.

Dawn broke over the bleak countryside of melting snow as Jaddig drove Charlie down the valley. Their journey had begun.

*

"Nervous?" Holly asked Jaddig and hour later as they crawled up a steep windy road towards the summit of the last range in human territory.

Jaddig glanced sideways at her front seat passenger and nodded. "Very!" She replied in a hushed voice, "but I feel we can do it, Holly."

She changed gears and swung Charlie around a tight bend. They had reached the top with the road now following the ridge for several kilometres before descending the other side. Below, in the hazy distance far below, the New Columbia River flowed like a wriggling line of silver from horizon to horizon across the mighty plains.

This expanse of water had to be crossed and the only place was a pontoon bridge the clickers had built when they first invaded New Washington. If the crossing was successful, they would turn east, try to avoid the populated cities and travel through the high country before descending to the valley where the shuttlecraft was hidden.

"Bloody good driving, Jaddig" George called from behind the driver's seat and handed her a mug of steaming coffifake. "I added honey to keep the adrenaline supplied."

*

CHAPTER 5

Suzi Yu. was a slight person who barely reached Holly's shoulders in height, had short dark hair and the features of her Asian ancestors. She also spoke accentless Vybber language; something Holly and the others had failed to manage, and, even better, was the only human on that expedition who could fit into a clicker survival suit. Her tiny pinch of a nose was also closer to Jaddig's in shape than any of the others.

"You look great, Suzi," Jaddig chuckled as she helped the scientist into the suit. "With the bottom arms padded out and a pair of dark snow glasses over your eyes, I'll make you an honorary Crucnon. You'll need gloves to hide your five fingers, though."

It was noon and, after crossing the mountain pass through snow covered countryside; they drove Charlie down to a fertile valley north of the New Columbia River and parked in a deserted barn behind one of the human farms. The property, like two others they had visited, had been stripped of everything. Human animals, dairy cows, cattle, sheep and pigs along with chickens were highly prized by the clickers and had been transported back to Vybber to stock farms. Like the Crucnon, the planet's original farm creatures were also six legged and cold blooded such as the aphrin, a green creature farmed and milked for its honey type liquid that was the stable died of the clickers. Likewise, the hideous but docile three-metre krinton was farmed for its meat that the humans found tasted like rich beef. Since there was no native equivalent to sheep, over the years the clickers had bred thousands of them from the first few stolen from New Washington.

The rear of Charlie had been fitted out with a fake pile of timber, all glued together to fit the interior of the back door. This timber, though, was only twenty centimetres long and hid the passengers behind. A similar wall at the front hinged down behind the driving compartment. Small circular windows along the side provided light and the ventilation system was excellent. If they were stopped for inspection, they had wooden panels to cover the windows, and hopefully, would escape discovery.

"You'll have to drive if we come to any of my kind," Jaddig informed Suzi. "A winged female would not be driving a Security Command Unit vehicle but could easily be travelling in one. She tapped her four golden hexagonal emblems across her chest. "That's why I promoted myself to

Marshal Jaddig Qarte. Hopefully, any military police will be too nervous of my rank to make a thorough inspection of Charlie."

"Well, we're prepared," George grumbled. "If we want to be at the river and cross in the dark hours we'd better get moving."

Holly grinned. Even though she was the official leader she didn't mind the old sergeant's abruptness to keep them all on their toes.

*

Their thoroughness paid off only minutes later. Jaddig was still at the wheel and had slowed Charlie to a crawl around a tight bend when a gigantic sign appeared on a cliff face where it could not be missed.

The clicker girl paled.

"What does it say?" Holly asked.

"You are leaving the restricted zone and entering the New Territories of Vybber. Vehicles are subject to inspection. All unauthorized or stolen equipment must be surrendered." she read.

"New Territories?" Holly frowned.

Jaddig turned and stared at her friend. "The annexed territory is larger than I anticipated. It means they're moving our people into your lands instead of moving the animals and stolen things out. There are going to be my people everywhere."

She pulled to the side of the road and turned her eyes to Suzi. "Are you ready?" she asked.

"So soon," Suzi whispered and glanced at the five other people. "I know I've driven Charlie on a straight road but these tight bends…"

"You'll be fine," encouraged Holly. "Just go slowly."

"Okay," Suzi replied. She hitched her two fake arms into a folded position, fixed on the helmet and dark glasses and stared at the group. "How do I look?"

"The fake antennae wouldn't pass close inspection but everything else is fine," George muttered. "Remember you're the chauffeur for a very important Security Marshal. Act arrogant if you're asked anything. Snap a reply and don't look nervous."

"I'll try," Suzi flicked a tongue over dry lips, grinned at her companions and climbed into the driver's seat. Holly slid into the rear beside Graham and Clay who raised the back timber wall.

"They're our flaw," Bowman Clay Farrell muttered. "Why would a Marshal be carrying a load of timber?"

Holly nodded. "I know," she whispered. "If the clickers insist on a close inspection we are in real trouble."

Clay took a bow down off a hook, fitted an arrow and grimaced at the two other DPF men. George looked grim and said nothing but Graham gave Holly a confident smile.

"If it came to a fight, I have installed a few nasties on board," he said in a quiet voice.

*

In spite of her worries, Suzi drove Charlie well and only hesitated when, without warning, another combo appeared at the end of a short straight and headed straight towards them.

"Head directly at it," hissed Jaddig. "On a narrow road, a security vehicle has the right of way. " She stared white faced at her companion. "Use your siren and accelerate."

"Where?" Suzi gasped but Jaddig had already pushed in a small blue button and a terrible scream howled from the roof above.

"Bloody hell!" George's oath filled the air but the two in the cab had more to worry about than how their sergeant felt.

"Go!" screamed Jaddig. "If you need to pull aside, remember we drive on the left in Vybber.

Suzi gulped, gripped the steering levers with one hand and used the other to push the hand throttle. Without the modifications, it would have been impossible but her reflexes were excellent. Charlie accelerated and the siren wailed.

In its haste to move aside, the oncoming combo skidded off the road into a snow bank and stalled. Suzi stared straight ahead and headed for the gap. My stars, it was narrow. Would there be enough room?

"Don't slow!" Jaddig screamed. "It's a sign of nervousness to slow and they'll know we aren't the security force."

"Shit!" the scientist, who never swore, cursed as the gap narrowed.

Jaddig could see two faces staring at them from the other vehicle, Charlie wobbled as Suzi changed down a gear, the six wheels gripped slush beneath and they swung right towards the other combo! Jagged screamed and her four hands gripped handles.

They were going to hit!

At the last moment, though, Suzi swung left, scrapped past the stationary combo and splattered it with mud. Charlie's inside wheels hit the opposite side of the road and, for a second, the left of the vehicle lifted off the ground. Tyres groaned, the motor roared but the expected crash did not eventuate. Instead, the inside wheels crunched down but instead of braking, Suzi accelerated.

"Okay, I know I said speed up but I didn't expect you to go crazy!" Jaddig exclaimed as they reached a corner and the opposing vehicle disappeared from sight. She reached up and turned the siren off.

The fake wall behind them hinged down and Holly's white face appeared. "Did you see the clickers in the other combo?" she shouted, realized her voice was too loud now the siren was off and flushed.

"Never had time," Jaddig retorted. "Why?"

Holly's face relaxed and broke into a smile. "The last we saw, they were standing by their vehicle saluting but their faces showed utter terror, I'm sure they thought we were going to run them down."

"That's discipline for you," George added. "Shit scared but still managing to salute an officer."

"If they only knew," Jaddig gasped. Now the emergency was over she was shaking like a leaf.

Suzi, though, seemed confident. She smiled at the others and accelerated. "I know what to do next time," she grunted then cursed again. "Damn these fake arms," she retorted. "They keep getting in the way."

Holly's eyes caught Jaddig's and they both grinned. It seemed as if Suzi was going to be a real asset to their party, not just a docile academic they though she might have been when they selected her.

*

Traffic thickened over the next hour but, in every case, no sooner did Suzi turn on Charlie's siren or flash the lights when the opposing vehicle pulled aside and let them by. By fourteen hundred hours they were in a valley beside the river, the road had widened and the snow turned to a steady downpour of rain.

Then the foot soldiers arrived, hundreds of clickers marching in single file up both sides of the road, heads straight ahead and four arms swinging.

"They've got rifles," Jaddig groaned. "That's unexpected."

"What are they?" Graham asked.

"Weapons that fire a bullet with an explosive charge. Your arrows would be useless against them. The soldiers can just stand back a hundred metres or more and fire at you. A bullet is like a tiny arrow but is flying a hundred times the speed. If it hits you it goes clean through and will probably kill you."

"Our ancestors had them," Suzi explained. "They were banned in the Survival of Humanity Protocol as being too dangerous. Up until now, it was a good idea."

"I see," Holly replied in a grim voice. "So, for example, if the clickers were on a cliff top in a mountain pass, they could kill our people below without our arrows even reaching them?"

"Yes," the scientist replied. "In that case we wouldn't stand a chance. I believe we have some of our own in the secret vaults below the food caves. Your mother would have access to them. From what I remember, there are about thirty weapons of this sort and also the more advanced ray guns that fire a beam of concentrated light."

Holly shuddered. The thought of these ghastly weapons frightened her. "We need to tell the Commander but how can we get a message back?"

"I'll go," Clay volunteered. "If you let me out, I can slip into the hills and take one of the forest tracks. It should only take a couple of days. I've done it in exercises before the clickers invaded."

"If you aren't caught," George retorted. "It's too dangerous to go alone."

Holly stared at the sergeant. "You go too, George," she said. "I think this is too important to ignore."

"But I can't," muttered the man. "I promised your mother..."

"That's an order, Sergeant," Holly interrupted. "You and Bowman Farrell are ordered to report to Commander Evans and the proctor. They are not due to leave New Seattle until the day after tomorrow. If they've gone when you arrive you are ordered to follow and catch the settlers up."

"But Holly!" the man protested.

"We'll be okay, Sergeant," Holly's voice softened. "Graham will remain with us and we aren't helpless, you know."

"Put it in writing," snapped the sergeant. "Otherwise your mother will skin me alive."

"There are more immediate problems ahead," Suzi interjected. "A barrier is across the road and traffic on our side is not moving."

"Oh hell" George snapped.

As Suzi slowed Charlie down, Holly who had been sitting in the middle front seat, gave Jaddig a quick glance, dived through to the back and the fake wall was swung up. Suzi and Jaddig were on their own.

"Act confident," hissed Jaddig as they ground to a halt behind a row of vehicles.

"Right," Suzi whispered with determination that overrode her nervousness. She pulled the helmet lower on her face, slipped dark glasses on and juggled the fake arms so they appeared to be gripping the inner steering levers.

When a grim faced officer approached, Suzi slid down at the driver's window and snapped, "I have Marshal Mother Vinalon, hexagon clearance aboard, Guard Leader. We demand to know the reason for the delay." Her

46

voice was accentless with that ring of authority but she did not turn her head.

The male clicker glowered until he saw the insignia on Jaddig's chest and also wings folded neatly across her back. Suddenly he was all attention. "My apologies, Marshal Mother," he snapped. "I was not informed you were on this side of the river."

"I wanted to visit the front line myself, Guard Leader err..." she glanced at his body suit name tag, "... Mooren. I believe the biped-rats have not been eliminated."

"No, Marshal Mother. They blew up their own town and disappeared. No doubt you have the report."

"I do," Jaddig snapped. She turned and stared at the officer, "and more. It is urgent I get back to headquarters. Is it still on the Vybber side of the river?"

"Yes, Mother Marshal," the clicker replied. "Half our troops are there, too. The river's in flood and we cannot risk heavy vehicles on the pontoon bridge. At the moment only foot traffic are crossing."

In the darkened rear, Holly heart sank. She could hear the whole conversation through gaps in the timber but could see nobody. If they couldn't cross the river, they were doomed.

But it was Suzi who used her initiative. "One vehicle can make it, Guard Leader." She turned to face Jaddig. "I am prepared to drive across, Mother Marshal, if that is your order."

"Why yes," Jaddig replied. For a second her nerve had failed but now she swallowed and glanced back at the officer. "Can you arrange for an escort, Guard Leader Mooren?"

"Certainly, Ma'am," the clicker replied, "As soon as our routine inspection of your combo is made."

Again Holly's heart thumped.

Jaddig, though, was ready. "Of course, Guard Leader," she smiled sweetly. "I assume you have hexagonal level search clearance."

The man hesitated. "No Mother Marshal," he snapped. "Only Colonel Apnhil has that clearance. Will pentagonal clearance be sufficient?"

"You had better find your colonel then, Mooren." Her voice turned to ice. "We have top security equipment aboard."

"What's she doing?" George hissed in a hoarse whisper to Holly. "The damn fool girl is going to blow it."

"Bluffing, Sergeant," Holly whispered back, "and it seems to be working."

The guard leader stared at Jaddig but her eyes bore into him without a flicker. "Well, Guard Leader," she snapped. "Are you getting him?"

"It will take an hour, Mother Marshal. He is up in the forbidden zone."

"Where I came from," snorted Jaddig. "I'm sorry I missed him but I cannot wait."

The clicker officer grimaced but came to a decision. "I'll clear a path." He snapped to attention and saluted both right arms.

"Thank you, Group Leader and may I commend you on your vigilance. If you had not insisted on searching my vehicle I would have had you up on charges."

"Thank you, Ma'am," the relieved clicker replied. "It's a pleasure being at your service."

"Jaddig certainly knows how the clicker military hierarchy works," Graham whispered. "She must have nerves of steel."

Holly nodded and hung on as Charlie moved slowly forward. She wriggled to the side window and moved the wooden panel a slither so she could see. Outside, the rain was still pouring down but they were moving forward on the wrong side of the road. Clicker foot soldiers were standing at attention as they swished past. The guardhouse, with a raised barrier flashed by and, afterwards they drove by a row of combos exactly the same design as Charlie. The backs were open and every vehicle was filled with troops, hundreds of them.

She turned to a grim George who was peeping out the next window "Well, you can't get out here anyway, sergeant," she said. "We might have to keep you with us after all."

George nodded. "What I can't understand is why they have so many troops here. There must be more in their mind than just flushing us out of the caves."

"You're right," Holly replied. "Perhaps Jaddig can give us a reason."

*

In the cab, Suzi stared through the swishing wipers that could barely cope with the downpour and gasped. "I can't do it," she chortled.

Jaddig stared at the pontoon bridge in front. The structure floating on the bloated river bucked and rocked as clicker foot soldiers poured off the end.

"Stop Charlie," hissed the Crucnon. "I'll drive. The rain is so heavy no-one will notice us."

Suzi nodded and slowed to a crawl. "Are you ready?" she cried, eyes met and there was a brief nod.

"Open the wall," Jaddig called and banged on the structure. It hinged down and Holly was there.

"Right," Suzi snapped. She braked and found two sets of arms grabbing her. Graham and Clay had her into the rear in seconds. At the same time, Jaddig bounded across the cab and grabbed the throttle, Holly leaped into the passenger seat and the vehicle began to roll.

The bucking bridge, mere centimetres wider than their combo seemed to disappear into choppy dirty water that blended with the rain to form a wall of mist in front. Jaddig edged sideways so the driving wheels almost touched the slightly raised edge of the bridge while a clicker shouted instructions that were wrenched away by the wind.

"Check out your side!" she yelled.

"My hair!" screamed Holly. "If I put my head out they'll see I have hair."

"Here put this on," George tapped Holly on the shoulder and yelled in her ear. She turned and saw his grinning face and a Balaclava in his hand. She ducked and the man pulled the black woollen object over her hair. In seconds she had her hair tucked under and head out the window. Rain hit like nails and all she could see was water, but no, through the mist and spray below was a log bolted to the bridge edge. Water was lapping over it so the surface was one mass of water.

"Jaddig has half a metre," she called back.

George heard, passed the message on and Holly felt Charlie shift over. But as the wheels turned, water from the wide snow tyres now sent an arch of water directly into her face. There was a bump and the front wheel began to mount the side log.

"Too far!" she shrieked.

Unknown to her, the others were also helping as best they could. Graham yelled instructions from directly behind Jaddig while Suzi came back to the middle seat and was peering through the windshield wipers.

*

Jaddig eyes were riveted ahead at the bucking river. She realized something new; the current had carried the middle of the bridge downstream so the bridge was crescent shaped. It was useless just keeping the wheels straight!

"Fit in the gap between the retainer logs," George advised. "They'll hold the wheels inside and on the decking. Don't fight the steering."

Jaddig nodded and realized her four hands had the steering levers gripped so hard her fingers ached but she was scared to relax her hold. It would only take one wheel to mount a log for their whole vehicle to topple into the river.

"George is right," Suzi's calm voice penetrated Jaddig's brain. "Relax the steering and concentrate on maintaining a steady speed."

Jaddig swallowed and ever so slightly relaxed her grip on the outer levers, the ones that controlled the front wheels. There was a slight shudder as a tyre rubbed the right log but it worked! The lever moved a few millimetres as the wheel slipped away from the log. Jaddig noticed that the other steering wheels were locked for the human drivers and followed the front ones. She relaxed her hold further and maintained a steady crawler speed.

"We're following the curve of the bridge," Holly called back at George. "Oh hell!"

"What?" screamed George?

"The river is flowing over the log. I think the weight of the combo is holding the deck down."

"Right," the sergeant snapped and turned to Jaddig. "I'm new to these mechanical monsters but I reckon you should increase speed," he advised. "Just go that wee bit faster."

Jaddig never argued but edged the hand throttle up, the motor roared and they surged forward. Water from the wheels was now arching as high as the cab. Suddenly a howling gale filled the enclosed space.

"What happened?" Jaddig screeched.

"It's Clay," Graham yelled back. "Said he'd see us back at New Seattle and leapt out the back."

"The idiot!" George snarled.

"He's all right," Graham continued. "He waved. My stars, he dived in the river!"

"He'll be fine," George replied. "He's a strong swimmer. If he lets the river carry him down steam past the clickers he'll be safe. If he doesn't freeze, that is." The sergeant's eyes swept around the confined space. "Well I'll be off, too."

"What're you doing?" cried Holly.

"Your orders Generation 7 Leader," George replied with a slight grin.

"Don't be bloody silly!" Holly snapped. She glanced up. "Shut the back door."

"You'd better do it, lad," George said to Graham. "Orders, you know."

"Men!" snorted Holly and stuck her head back out the window into the stream of water arching up from Charlie's tyres.

*

"You know," Jaddig muttered, her eyes still riveted straight ahead. "I believe the logs were designed to guide the combo's wheels. I hardly have to hold the steering levers."

"Good," Suzi said. "Holly said the inside is fine."

"...And I believe the end is coming up," Jaddig replied. "You'd better get in the back and shut the flap, Holly."

Charlie rumbled on through the final section of the bridge, up the incline where the pontoons were anchored to the shore and onto the road. Rain still poured down and darkness had arrived. Jaddig switched the headlights on. They shone across a wide paved road running at right angles to the bridge. Water was everywhere with half the road flooded but Jaddig didn't care. The place was empty. Not one of her kind was in sight.

*

CHAPTER 6

Holly clung on but couldn't keep her eyes off the speed dial as Jaddig turned *Charlie* upstream and continued up a familiar sealed highway with the powerful front lights carving a tunnel of light through the darkness. The needle was pointing to twenty wedden and she mentally converted this to a hundred kilometres an hour. In these conditions, this was almost flying. Light reflected back at them from the wet road surface while rain still banged on the metal roof. Jaddig accelerated and the heavy tread of the tyres screamed.

"We have to get into the foothills before dawn," Jaddig explained. "That's over hundred of your kilometres," She yawned and rubbed her eyes.

"And you're exhausted," Holly replied. "Pull over and I'll drive."

After a brief protest, Jaddig relented so *Charlie* was soon humming along at a more leisurely eighty kilometres an hour with Holly at the wheel. Jaddig was sound asleep beside her and gentle snores came from the rear passengers but they were not all asleep.

"I'll keep you company," Graham whispered and slipped over into the middle seat with a thermos of hot coffifake in his hand and handed it to Holly. He tucked a blanket around Jaddig and stared through the swishing wipers at the diagonal lines of rain cutting through the vehicle's lights.

"You okay?" he asked.

"Not bad," Holly replied. "A bit stiff and tired. It's Jaddig and Susi who have done all of the driving."

"I wonder if there are other clickers like her. She acts human," He shrugged. "You know, she has feelings, concern for others and is not a cruel killing machine we've always been told clickers are like."

"I know," Holly replied and glanced at her companion. His usual clean shaven face had stubble growing and the unkempt short hair seemed to compliment his tanned features. He'd be slightly taller than her but heavier, probably close to ninety kilograms. "I've been amazed since I've got to know her. The clickers executed her family, you know."

"No I didn't," Graham replied with concern in his quiet voice. "Why?"

Holly repeated everything she knew. "I told the Inner Circle I believe the ruthlessness comes from their rulers, not because an intelligent species evolved from insects is incapable of human values. Jaddig seems to have every emotion we have; loyalty, honour, care for others..." She shrugged.

"She even has a partner that she appears to be in love with." Holly continued speaking while Graham added a brief comment or question every so often but mainly listened. "What was a hated enemy is now a friend sleeping across the cab from us," she concluded and smiled at the man beside her. "I do get carried away, don't I?"

"Not at all. I agree with everything you say." Graham stared out at the damp road before continuing. "Our ancestors were no better. When I was little, my grandfather used to tell me stories passed onto him. Our family lived in a continent called Europe and every twenty or thirty years, it seemed there was a war somewhere with cruelty and mass killings and that was between humans. There were no clickers on the planet."

"Perhaps if the situation was reversed, humans would be the same," Holly changed a gear and slowed at a corner.

Graham frowned. "What do you mean, Holly?"

"Perhaps our kind back where we came from are as bad as the clickers. What would they do if a hundred clickers landed a spaceship and began to build a strange town with krintons and aphrins replacing the cattle and cows? Would they ruthlessly try to eliminate them like the clickers have attempted to do with us?"

"But we aren't as cruel with no regard for individual rights. Look at Jaddig here. You said she was forced to become a egg producer and only the war stopped her being imprisoned like a sex slave." He shuddered.

"Are humans really any better?"

"I don't really know. There's too little information. The Survival of Humanity Protocol was good at binding us together but I think those earlier generations suppressed too much information about where we came from and who we were."

"So you think it is time for it to be updated, a sort of Survival of Humanity Protocol, but don't forget where we came from, document."

"Exactly," replied Graham.

"We think alike, Graham Whitmore," Holly replied. Somehow her male companion made her feel warm inside. Their eyes met in the darkness and he smiled at her.

"I'll drive soon," he offered. "You must be tired. "

"Do you know how?"

"I know as much as you."

Holly laughed. "Give me half and hour."

Outside the lights of various farm buildings became more spaced out. Ahead, according to Jaddig, was hill country similar to that around New Seattle. Holly's thoughts became sad. The only place she had known was now gone and they were deep in enemy territory chasing what could just be a dream.

She glanced at Graham who had become quiet. She noticed he had gone to sleep with an arm around the sleeping clicker whose head had flopped into his chest. Holly grinned and reached for the thermos sitting in a metal box on the dashboard. She was sure there was some coffifake left. The rain outside had stopped but water still swished up from the tyres and the motor had become a rumble in the background as if *Charlie* was at peace with the world.

She drove for an hour until, with her eyelids heavy, she opened a vent so cool air kept her awake, but it was becoming harder. The flat country had gone and they were now driving through black hills.

"My turn," said a voice that made her jump.

She turned to see Graham smiling at her.

"Okay," she answered, pulled over and opened the door. A cold breeze hit her face but that was what she needed. In a deft movement she climbed down onto the road and glanced around. There were dark trees opposite and the sweet smell of pines whiffed by her nose. The place was like home.

"Climb in through the driver's side so we don't awaken Jaddig," Graham said and Holly realized he was standing next to her.

"Yes, sure," she muttered, the spell broke, and she scrambled back in the cab and across to the middle seat beside her friend.

Graham followed and soon they were on their way again. Holly tried to chat but sleep caught up and she found herself in a dream of childhood. She was ten and it was her birthday…Warm memories helped her body relax and prepare for what was to come in the morning.

*

Jaddig awoke, all stiff and lethargic to silence. She frowned, shook her head and stared around. The combo's motor had stopped and it was dawn. They were in a forest clearing with a small building tucked under the trees. The crucnon smiled for she knew where they were. *Charlie* was parked in one of the campgrounds that littered her country and the building was an ablution block.

She felt cold and checked a small gauge on her lower right wrist. The body suit's battery had run low. No wonder she was so slow. Without more warmth she could barely function.

"Are you okay, Jaddig?" Holly's face appeared beside her. "You look terrible."

"It's just our species," Jaddig replied. "If our body temperature drops below fifteen degrees of your Celsius temperature we begin to slow down; below about five we go into suspended sleep. That's why we need the body suit in the colder climates. When I put the new one on, I'll be fine. It should have a charged battery. We usually recharge our suits every three days or so."

Holly nodded, crawled over the back and returned with a neatly packed body suit. "It was cleaned and repaired back home," she said, handed it to Jaddig and gazed at the building. "I'm impressed with the facilities here. There was even hot water and showers."

"Good," Jaddig grinned. "I'll have one. As soon as I warm up, I'll be fine." She staggered out and waved to the others who were painting out the security signs on *Charlie*. Now they were in the country an ordinary vehicle would arouse less suspicion.

"You ill, Girl?" George queried in his usual blunt manner and grunted when she re-examined her metabolism.

"Does that affect your wings, too?" The man added. "They look droopy."

"You are observant," Jaddig appeared embarrassed. "No. I'm a winged female who hasn't mated. If this continues my body reverts back to its original status and I lose my ability to fly"

"And your wings?"

"They drop off."

"Yuck," George replied, "Is that painful?"

"No more than you cutting your hair every morning." She grinned at his clean- face. "Tell me, why do males grow hair on the bottom of their faces and females don't?"

George shrugged. "That's just us, I guess. Men and women have different bodies."

"Exactly," Jaddig replied. "Crucnon are the same. When I lose my wings, I'll still be female but won't be an egg layer." She sighed. "I can't wait. Males often subject winged females to violent attacks for mating purposes while ordinary females are usually left alone. "

She smiled and continued her slow walk to the ablution block.

*

After a rejuvenated Jaddig returned in the heated suit and a hot breakfast was appreciated by all, *Charlie*'s fuel tank was filled and they were on their way again. Within a few kilometres, the windy road straightened out on a plateau but the forest continued with all views hidden except a strip of grey sky above. In the first hour they passed only three vehicles, square shaped like *Charlie* but smaller in size and painted bright colours.

"Cars," Jaddig, who was driving, muttered as she waved at the vehicle that roared pass. "Farmers going to town for supplies. I guess the war doesn't mean much up here."

Without warning, a screaming whistle filled the air and the ground ahead erupted in an explosion. Soil, grass and gigantic flames shot in the air to be followed, microseconds later by the discharge of thunder and a blast of hot stinking gas. Screams rent the air as Jaddig braked and managed to halt their vehicle before it reached the sheet of flames bellowing higher than the trees.

Time seemed to freeze! The initial explosion was followed by a whoosh of air being sucked in, the flames died as quickly as they began and replaced by stinking black smoke and a shower of debris which crashed around the stalled combo. A winged clicker could be seen flying away beyond the havoc.

"Another one's coming!" screamed Graham.

Holly stared up and saw another clicker flapping in towards them with a long cylinder clutched in her four arms.

"Drive into the forest!" George yelled but Jaddig had a different idea. She stared at Holly and yelled. "Take over!"

The combo stopped, the driver's door flung open and Jaddig stood up so only her legs could be seen.

"No!" screamed Holly but it was too late. Jaddig flapped her wings and rose into the air just as the second winged clicker dropped her bomb.

A terrible scream followed and another gigantic explosion followed fifty metres back. Once again, the ground erupted and noise made the human's ears ring. A second deluge of earth and paving stone pelted *Charlie*'s roof but no other harm was done.

George frowned and stared at Holly. "How could she have missed?" he barked.

"Hell, I don't know," Holly replied.

She had taken over the driving and bumped *Charlie* off the road. She scraped in between two trees and stalled the motor again; doors flung open and the four humans aboard evacuated. After a mad scramble, they arrived in a tiny dip behind a patch of scrub together.

"Where's Jaddig?" Holly panted.

Everyone peeped out above the foliage. The second bomb had torn a gigantic hole in the road. Flames and black smoke poured out while the first, only metres away was now just a hot crater of burnt grass and blackened soil.

"I don't know," Graham muttered. "There are three of them circling around up there. One's Jaddig but they're too similar to tell who is who."

George rose to a crouch and used his hand to shade the sun from his eyes as he stared at the three clickers flying like gigantic dragonflies above the trees. "It's all wrong," he muttered.

"For star's sake!" snapped Holly. "What are you going on about, George?" Her face was taut and expression wild.

"Look at those bomb craters," the sergeant replied. "One only had to be near *Charlie* and we would have been done for. With that power and *Charlie*'s tanks exploding, there was no way we would have survived. Yet, not one but both bombs were well away from us."

"Perhaps they're just poor at aiming," Graham suggested.

"With the training clickers give their troops," George snorted. "No way!"

Holly could now see George's reasoning. In theory they should all be dead in the smoking hulk of the bombed out vehicle. "You mean, they missed on purpose?" she asked.

"I'd say so," George replied. "And look at those clickers up there. Are they fighting?"

Everyone focused on the three creatures above. It was still impossible to tell which one was Jaddig but they certainly didn't seem to be attacking or defending one another.

"They're flying in circles," Suzi observed. "Surely the attackers would fly away or attack Jaddig." She stood up. "I'll go and get the binoculars out of the combo. We need a closer look."

*

When Jaddig flew up from the combo her one aim was to attack the incoming bombardier. If the bomb landed near *Charlie* all her human friends would be killed. There was no chance for them. Within seconds she was above the trees but still below the incoming female when the second bomb was released.

"You bastard!" Jaddig screamed in her own language but the explosion cut off her words. Superheated flames hit her a second later and propelled her straight up, rolled her over and flung her sideways like a twig in a storm. Hot gas pelted her skin and she couldn't breathe, her eyes smarted and tears streamed down her face. The world below blurred and she felt herself dropping. The young winged Crucnon almost lost consciousness but her mind fought to maintain control.

"I must fly," she groaned to herself and began to flap. Her wings ached and spasms of pain jolted her slim body but, just before plummeting into the firs below, she gained momentum, her body levelled off and slowly, ever so slowly, she began to rise.

She was terrified. There was two of her kind around. One quick kick in the head or thorax and she'd crash. She regretted her stupid reaction to fly but it was too late now. She blinked tears from her eyes and flapped harder. Something was wrong! Excruciating pain, like she'd never felt before, almost incapacitated her.

"You're burnt," a soft voice called from nearby. "Go into a glide and you'll be okay."

Jaddig stared sideways and gasped in alarm. A winged female was flying beside her but unexpectedly she did not look aggressive. In fact, the face showed concern. As Jaddig gained control over her emotions and body something else totally unexpected happened. The female flew close, poked a small hexagonal card in her hand and retreated flew a few metres away.

A hexagon, the sign for danger!

Though still suffering from spasms of agony, Jaddig managed to glance down and read the writing. *We are your friends and have come to warn you of danger,"* the note read. *Please do not talk but wave if you are Jaddig Qarte.*

Jaddig frowned and glanced around. She was about fifty metres above the firs and could see *Charlie* partly hidden below. Closer, though, both females were keeping pace with her but there was no sign of aggression. She swallowed and gave a brief wave.

The first female smiled and pointed to the ground. They wanted her to land. Jaddig frowned. Oh well, she was as safe on the ground as up here. Probably safer! But no, there could be males waiting in the forest to attack her.

She was about to speak but remembered the note, shook her head and pointed towards the combo. At the same time she altered her wing angle and dipped around so she was heading back. She could see her friends in a gully and the sun flashed off something. Of course, someone was using binoculars to watch them. She waved, gave a timid smile and continued down. Every nerve in her body, though, was on edge and she still expected to be attacked from behind; but it didn't come.

One female flew away but the second, the one who had handed her the note, followed her down.

Jaddig landed beside *Charlie* to see the humans, all armed with vicious crossbows ready to fire at the strangers. "I am okay," she called as her feet touched soft grass.

"Like hell you are," Holly retorted. "You're burnt!"

She rushed up, Jaddig felt warm human arms around her and someone else tucked a blanket over her wings and shoulders. She stared into Holly's fearful eyes and, without speaking handed the hexagonal card to her. Holly glowered and handed it on to Suzi who frowned as she mentally digested the contents.

Meanwhile, the stranger stood with her wings folded and arms held wide while Graham had his crossbow aimed directly at her and George searched the sky for the second winged female.

Suzi reached in her pocket, extracted a pen, wrote some Vybber words down and handed it to the stranger who nodded and wrote another note on the back. Suzi nodded and walked away, turned and indicated the others they should follow.

Graham remained to guard the female while the others gathered around Suzi back at the Combo. "She says your body suit is wired so everything you say is transmitted back to their headquarters by radio," Suzi whispered.

"A radio?" Holly asked with a frown. "What's that?"

"A top secret device that sends voices electronically through the air," George explained. "Our ancestors had them."

"The suit I am wearing is not mine," Jaddig gasped. "I changed this morning. Do they all have radios?"

"I don't know," Suzi replied, "but where is your suit."

"In the dirty clothes basket."

Holly grunted. "I'll remove it," she snapped. "Go and write our visitor another note asking if all suits have this radio thing in them."

Suzi and Jaddig nodded and walked back to where the scared but dignified stranger sat on the ground. Jaddig smiled and handed her the note.

"No, they are not," the Crucnon replied. "Mine is disconnected. It is safe to talk as long as we are away from the wired suit."

"I think it is safe," Holly said to Graham. "Keep an eye out just in case."

"Right," the bowman replied. His stance was professional and tone serious. The crossbow lowered but the arrow remained in place. Eyes bore into the visitor.

"My name is Bikut Kegning," the female began. In appearance she was similar to Jaddig but smaller and probably younger with a face like that of a human teenager. "I am sorry about the bombing but were ordered to destroy your combo. We needed to attract your attention so dropped our bombs close."

"You managed to do that very successfully but what's all this bit about the radio," Jaddig retorted

All flying females have their body suits wired with a built-in radio. Everything said is transmitted back to security headquarters. That is how they knew you had surrendered to the humans."

"So there was no spy," Holly gasped.

"And I was the reason my family was executed," Jaddig whispered.

"I am afraid so," replied Bikut. "All conversations you had while wearing your body suit would have been overheard. I have fitted a device to mine to turn it off when I don't want my voice transmitted."

Jaddig frowned. "Why are you risking this?" she asked.

"The Blue Watch," Bikut said in a whisper. "I have not met your friend, Birobi Osyjil, but was approached by an acquaintance of his to help when we were brought in to assassinate you all." She grimaced. "You were lucky at the river. The Military Security Command was ten minutes behind you when the pontoon bridge blew up stranding them on your country's side. "

"Clay!" gasped Holly.

George who had joined the group nodded. "I thought he might manage to get it blown," he muttered.

Bikut nodded grimly. "They executed the colonel who let you through for failing in his duty. He was a family friend."

"I'm sorry," Holy replied.

"As Jaddig knows, our rulers are ruthless" the clicker replied. "This morning we were sent out to find you and we did." She grimaced. "You'd be dead if we'd wanted it so."

"I know," George muttered.

"Thank you," Holly said, "but what happens now."

"We report back and say we hit you. You must destroy your suit, though, Jaddig so the radio stops transmitting. Also, you must get off this road. There is a village about fifteen minutes ahead with military police waiting. That was another reason we had to stop you."

"I see," Holly replied. "Have you any suggestions?"

"About two wedden back is a local side road. It serves some farms but leads across to the next highway. From there, you're on your own, I'm afraid." Bikut turned to George. "You are thorough. I notice the military marks painted out. That's good. We almost missed you. It was only when we saw your hair, Holly, we knew this was the combo we were after."

"Is it safe to continue using this vehicle?" George snapped.

"Probably," Bikut replied. "Many Farmers use them. Perhaps later you could paint it red or blue. The locals tend to use these colours." She turned to Jaddig and reached out her arms. "I must return. Ognje, my friend flying up there, will be worried and we can't be late reporting back to base. Make sure you get your wounds seen to."

"Thank you," Jaddig whispered. "With all my heart I thank you."

"That is from us all," Holly added. She smiled into the opposite yellow eyes.

"I have never been near a human before," Bikut replied in a soft voice. "Our help was for Jaddig and not yourselves. Her reputation is spreading throughout our land and the Blue Watch is recruiting more members because of her bravery. We have our own struggle but one day perhaps our two species can be friends. Take care Generation 7 Leader Holly Jurjevics. Your mother and yourself are highly respected by the Blue Watch. Perhaps we will meet again some day."

Her wings unfolded and she rose vertically, smiled once and disappeared above the trees. There was a brief glimpse of the other winged female joining her and the pair were gone.

"Right, we now need to get some treatment for your burns, Young lady," George snapped. He turned to Graham. "The boss left that suit over by the trees. I want it destroyed, Bowman?"

"Right away, Sarge." Graham grinned at Holly's nod and walked away.

*

CHAPTER 7

Jaddig never mentioned the extent of her injuries but it soon became obvious that her two left arms and torso were burnt. As well, her wings were torn with the scaly tissue curling up. The victim screwed her eyes shut and set her lips in a thin line as she diverted her mind to cut off pain signals. This helped but did not cure anything.

"It is beyond us," Suzi confirmed a few minutes later. "Jaddig cannot suppress the pain for ever. We can give her a morphine injection but I am hesitant about undoing her body suit. If we pulled a layer of burnt skin off with the material, shock could set in."

"I'll be all right," muttered Jaddig. "There is nowhere to go. You must head across that country road Bikut mentioned."

"Yes there is," muttered George. "That highway the side road leads into must continue to a bigger centre that has a hospital."

"There is a small city called Hyfra about sixty kilometres away but we can't risk it," Jaddig protested. "I'm okay. There could be a few scars maybe but, what the hell!"

"Speaks English well and lies like a trooper," Graham commented.

"We vote," Holly said with that air of stubborn authority. "Either we stay on back roads or take the highway and find a hospital."

The vote was four to find a hospital to Jaddig's one. The Crucnon stared at everyone with tears in her eyes. "You can't," she sobbed. "There's too much to lose."

"We have voted," Holly replied. "If the vote had gone the other way, you would not have objected." She gave a smile. "It's called democracy, Jaddig, something the Blue Watch wants. In a democracy, you are sometimes on the losing side."

"And if we plan our moves, we'll be fine," George insisted.

*

Hyfra was a rural service city built beside a small river that meandered through a broad valley. It was mid afternoon when *Charlie*, with the fake timber back in place so the interior couldn't be seen, was driven down the one main street. As well, mud had been plastered over the front windows to hinder any view of the interior.

George was holding a blanket around a shivering Jaddig at the back while Suzi sat pinch lipped in the third body suit. Fake arms had been made into a permanent fold across her waist and a bandage covered her human nose and eyebrows. A helmet hid her hair. Holly was driving the combo and Graham sat beside her gazing at a map Jaddig had sketched of the town.

"The emergency hospital sign looks like three intersecting triangles and the word is grutnaut," he said, "It will be painted green."

They were stopped in a line of traffic at an intersection. A light in front shone a bright yellow triangle. Suddenly, without warning, the black sides of the yellow slipped out so the shape became a rectangle.

"Go," hissed Graham but Holly was ready and *Charlie* moved forward. "Middle lane. I see a green sign pointing right... That's it. Watch out there's another stop signal."

Holly was perspiring but, so far, all had gone well. Except for being bigger, the road and buildings around could have easily been in New Seattle. She changed gears and passed another intersection until another green sign appeared. There was a left turn, easier because it was on her side of the road and another two blocks of travelling before a large three storey building appeared set back from the road in trim lawns and a garden of red and blue flowers. *Grutnaut Hyfra Nkypg*, a massive sign stated.

" It says Hyfra Women's Hospital," Suzi translated

"The emergency entrance sign looks like a hexagon," Graham explained. "That seems to be their main emergency or danger symbol. There it is," he gasped and pointed to where the road divided into two.

"Right," Holly replied and pulled in beside another combo parked by an opened door. "She turned to Suzi, "It's up to you now. Best of luck."

George squeezed Suzi's hand and held the back door open so she could help Jaddig out. After a brief thanks the Crucnon grabbed an overnight bag and stepped out.

"They've gone. You'd better find a parking space," George whispered as he clicked the door shut. "We're too conspicuous here."

Holly nodded, reversed around and made her way up the other driveway to a half-filled car park. Now was the worse part. The waiting!

*

The hospital interior was unexpected. A cream corridor with a hexagonal shaped ceiling disappeared around a corner twenty metres away and that was it! There was no entrance foyer, counter seats or even signs.

"You go," gasped Jaddig who could barely stand and screwed her eyes up. "Don't risk being recognized." She bit on her lip in a failed attempt to suppress the pain.

"No," Suzi retorted. "I'll stay until I find out what we have to do."

She stared around, they were at the hospital but, in the haste, the humans had not really thought beyond the fact. If Jaddig had to spend a long time in care, what should they do? She could not just be abandoned and left... Thoughts ran through the scientist's mind. "Come on," she whispered and placed an arm around her friend.

Jaddig grinned, reached out for Suzi's fake arm and pulled it out so it appeared two arms were holding her. "Don't worry," she grimaced. "You look a perfect Crucnon."

The pair walked forward up the silent corridor to a forty-five degree corner and followed it around. At the other end of this section, a wingless female clicker dressed in a green uniform stood staring at them. Suzi stopped and gulped. This was it!

"Not another one!" snapped the clicker and glared at Suzi. "And what happened to you, Miss?"

Suzi frowned and remembered the bandages to hide her human face. "There was a car accident," she muttered in her accentless Vybber. "I got cut up a bit."

"More like another coming out party," snorted the female clicker. "You young ones never learn." She glared at Jaddig and shrugged. "It isn't right. The military have a lot to answer for."

Jaddig stared across at Suzi and shrugged. Neither of them had any idea what the angry Crucnon was going on about.

"Well, get along to the winged female ward," the nurse continued. "Second ward to the left." She fixed Suzi with another gaze. "Got a hangover, too, Miss?" she said in a slightly more reconciliatory tone.

"Me...err not really," Suzi muttered.

"Fair enough," the clicker retorted. "I wondered about the dark glasses." She smiled for the first time. "I guess I was young once. Some coming out party, aye?"

They followed the nurse along until they came to a door that slid aside as they approached.

The scene inside was a complete contrast to the empty corridor. The ward was filled with about thirty iron beds and clickers just like Jaddig occupied almost every one. They were all young winged females and some were screaming, others moaning in agony while others again just sobbed. The loudest noise came from a curtained off bed where a high-pitched shriek filled the air.

"Take the third bed," the nurse ordered. "I'll get you a sedative." She switched her eyes onto Suzi and frowned. "Were you one, too?"

"No," Suzi whispered.

"Then you're lucky," the nurse pulled back the bed blankets and nodded at Jaddig. "Off with your body suit, Miss and slip into that hospital gown on the bed."

She was about to walk away when Suzi decided she'd better take the initiative. "Err Nurse," she said.

"Senior Sister, if you please," the clicker stood back and glowered. "There's no respect for authority these days."

"I'm sorry, Senior Sister," Suzi began to regain her confidence. "Do we have to sign any admission forms or anything?"

"For this!" The senior sister laughed and waved two right hands around the ward. "Are you going to wait for your friend?"

Suzi frowned. She had visions of Jaddig having a long stay. Another scream filled the air from the female in the adjacent bed. "How long?" she asked.

The senior sister's face softened again. "Come back in an hour," she said. "At least your friend can control her pain, not like some of the young madams here. The worst is already over for her."

"An hour!" gasped Suzi.

"Yes. What did you expect; ten minutes."

"No, of course not. I'll be back to see her then."

She turned to Jaddig and, in spite of herself, shuddered. Her friend was just slipping into a yellow gown and Suzi glimpsed at her shoulders and back. Jaddig's whole left side was covered in bloated red skin with a long layer hanging down like human sunburn peeling off but a hundred times worse. Her wings hung limp and tattered.

"I'll be right," Jaddig whispered. .

"Yes," Suzi gulped. She was horrified at her friend's disfigurement. The blast of the explosion must have completely engulfed her.

The senior sister began to pull a curtain around the bed. "You might as well wait," she said. "I reckon your ten minutes will be closer than my hour. There's a seat at the end of the ward."

Suzi nodded, reached out, squeezed Jaddig's hand and walked past the screams, sobs and shrieks to a small wooden seat. Every so often a smiling wingless female would go up and thank the senior sister or a nurse then disappear. The minutes ticked by. Suzi, deep in thought, placed the overnight bag she was still holding on the floor and tried to make sense of the situation. She was a scientist but had allowed emotion to cloud her mind. There must be some logical reason for all the winged females screaming in agony around the room. A fireball wouldn't have hit them all.

A shriek filled the air and it was from Jaddig's bed. Suzi's face drained white and she stood up with trembling hands. She wanted to run in to help her friend but held herself back.

The senior sister returned. "I see you have brought a change of clothes," she said and reached for the overnight bag. "Most of the girls don't bother. Give us a few more moments."

Ten minutes later, almost to a second, Suzi heard a cough and glanced up. Jaddig stood there smiling. She was dressed in her woollen blue jersey and jeans and looked perfect. The bloated skin on the side of her face was gone. Her friend held up her jersey and showed a bare tummy, slightly tanned and perfect. More amazing, though, something else made Suzi gasp. There were no wings; not even stubble.

"Retro-metamorphosis," the Crucnon explained with a grin. "My problems weren't caused by the explosion at all. They never told us losing our wings would be so painful. Come on. Let's go."

"You mean…"stuttered Suzi.

"Yes, I'm fine," Jaddig grabbed the human's arms. "I really am."

Just as they walked out, the senior sister strolled up with a grim determined expression and touched Suzi's cheek.

"Warm blood, just as I thought," she whispered. "Take care, human girl, some of my colleagues are not as liberal as I am. Look after yourself." Eyes flicked at the patient she had just helped. "You, too Jaddig Qarte," she muttered. "You were either very brave or very foolish to come here. Take the advice of a cynical old nurse and use the old highway south. Under no circumstances should you attempt to cross the river or try to return to the hills. Everyone is looking for you."

There was a thin smile and the pair found themselves alone in the corridor.

"She knew!" gasped Suzi.

"Yeah," Jaddig replied. "It was a pretty pathetic disguise, you know." She frowned. "But how did she know me, I wonder?"

Suzi shrugged. "Come on, Holly and the men must be worried."

*

The rain outside had reduced to misty drizzle but it took a few moments to find *Charlie* as all the vehicles were square shaped with six wheels and varied only in colour and size.

"There it is," gasped Suzi. "Tucked in the corner by the hedge."

Jaddig grinned, walked up to *Charlie* and flung the driver's door open. "Going to let me drive?" she snapped.

Holly swung around in fright and stared at the wingless clicker smiling at her. It took a few seconds for her to realize who it was. "Jaddig!" she exclaimed. "My stars, you look wonderful. What happened?"

It was Suzi who explained, in graphic detail, what had happened. "It was like a torture chamber with moaning and screaming everywhere," she added. "Poor old Jaddig. I thought she was seriously injured."

"We all did," Graham grinned.

"Yeah, and now you almost look human," George grunted.

"Thanks," smiled Jaddig. "I'll take that as a compliment."

"We swapped number plates with another combo," Graham said. "That's why we were over here by the hedge. In this weather nobody came near us."

"Good," replied Jaddig. "If all of you get behind our fake wall I'll drive. Without wings, I'll just be an ordinary farmer heading home with a pile of timber." She stared around the untidy cab. "We'd better remove everything human from the front, though. Even on the old highway the sister told us about, we may be stopped." She grinned again and held up a tiny plastic card. "A credit card," she added. "I stole from a bag of a screaming female next to me in hospital. With luck, it'll be hours before she realises it's gone."

"Is that money?" Holly asked.

"More or less," Jaddig answered. "If you all don't mind being cramped in the back for another hour or so, I'll get us some fresh food and other supplies."

"Go to it, Girl." George chortled and reached across to give her an affectionate hug.

By late afternoon, with *Charlie* refuelled and restocked, they headed out of Hyfra. Jaddig had bought a map of the city and surrounding hinterland and found the old highway more or less headed in their direction for twenty kilometres before rejoining the main highway outside the urban area.

*

Ten minutes later they arrived at a roadblock.

"Get out!" snapped the officer after the combo ground to a halt.

Jaddig stared at four soldiers lined up with weapons raised and climbed down from *Charlie*, slung her arms away as the male reached for her and walked across the road. She stopped and swung around.

"You do not touch females. Do it and I'll report you to your division headquarters, Junior Guardsman Doropen!" she snapped after reading the clicker's nametag.

"Why are you driving a military vehicle?" Doropen eyeballed her without a flinch.

"It's army surplus," Jaddig replied haughtily. Though her heart raced she was determined not let the soldiers intimidate her. The situation was precarious, she knew lone females were often attacked and civilians forced into military service or, worse still, just disappeared. Of course, that had already happened to her when she was dragged out of her university bed those months before and forced to take the hormone treatment.

An uncontrolled shiver passed through her body. She glanced up and saw three soldiers swarming over *Charlie*. The three doors were all open as well as the hood. She could see the timber and a soldier attempting to wiggle a bit out. He grunted for a moment and moved on.

Jaddig's eyes shifted to a circular side window. The wood behind had shifted just a fraction and something shiny showed. It was an arrowhead and she knew her human friends were waiting and ready. That small sign of support gave her the confidence to continue.

"Your papers!" Junior Guardsman Doropen demanded.

Jaddig reached in a pocket and extracted a small pentagonal card, stolen with the credit card from the hospital. She had no idea of the name, occupation or address written on it. If they asked her to repeat the details, she was doomed. However, the guard sniffed and handed it back to her. Meanwhile, clickers were crawling under their vehicle and examining behind the tyres.

"All clean, Junior Guardsman," a soldier reported. "Do you want the timber unloaded?"

Jaddig froze but she realized Doropen's eyes watched every move she made. One false eye flicker and he would know something was amiss. "I hope you put every bit back," she snapped with her tone controlled so it did not reflect the turmoil inside. "It took half an hour to load."

"These are dangerous roads for a lone female," Junior Guardsman Doropen answered and turned to the other clicker. "Leave it," he ordered. "Start on the next combo. We're getting behind time."

He handed Jaddig a yellow stamped card, and saluted. "Show this at the next road block and you will not need to go through the same rigorous inspection."

"Thank you Junior Guardsman Doropen," she replied and gazed into his eyes. "Tell me, what are the road conditions like?"

"Some flooding by the river but not too bad," he answered in a more cordial voice. "I don't think you'll have any trouble."

Jaddig gave a flash of a smile, climbed aboard *Charlie* and drove slowly forward beneath the raised barrier. When they were safely down the highway, the hinged wall came down and Holly slipped over to the front seat beside her.

"You're so cool and confident," she complimented. "How do you do it?"

"Sheer survival instincts, Holly," Jaddig replied with a nervous glance at her friend. "I'm all honey inside."

"You mean sweet and tasty?"

"No," explained the clicker. "It means all stuck up and scared."

"We call it butterflies in the tummy." Holly smiled. "You know, George and Graham were all ready to rush out and rescue you if things had gone wrong back there."

"I know," Jaddig replied in a sombre voice. She turned briefly and smiled at the others behind. "Thank you, my friends."

She changed up a gear and they continued their journey through rolling farmlands. The afternoon sun appeared from behind a cloud for the first time that day and bathed them in light. Perhaps this was an optimistic sign. Jaddig grimaced; or maybe it was just a brief lapse before further storm clouds drifted in.

*

The following afternoon, after taking turns to drive and passing two more check points, several towns that became smaller the further they went, and a mountain pass with the return of snow conditions, George drove the reliable *Charlie* into a broad and lonely valley near their destination. The last diesel had been emptied into the combo's tanks and food was getting low.

More worrying, though, was Jaddig who had fallen asleep ten hours earlier. Whether it was the cold temperatures or a natural reaction to her retro-metamorphosis, nobody knew, though attempts to awaken her had been unsuccessful.

"I am inclined to think it is a natural occurrence because her heartbeat is steady. If we gave her a stimulant it could do more harm than good," Suzi said. "It's been pretty cold up in those higher roads and she has only been wearing ordinary clothes."

"I hope so," Holly replied and cast a worried eye over her friend lying at the back. "It's the uncertainty and not knowing what's best for her that is frustrating. "

"I know," Suzi replied. She glanced out the window where dust was now blowing up behind them. "It's warm outside now. If she doesn't wake up before this evening I'll risk using one of our drugs."

Graham turned around from the front seat and smiled at them. "I'm sure she'll be fine," he said. "Look at her face. There's eye movement that wasn't there in the middle of the night. I'd lay odds to say shell be awake by the time we arrive." He turned to the map brought from home that was placed on his knees. "The original note says we have to find a rock face that looks like a human hand, I guess that means it has five fingers."

"Then what?" muttered George. He cursed as *Charlie* shuddered when he attempted to change to a lower gear. "Can't get used to these damn controls," he cursed. "I need Jaddig's four hands."

In spite of his muttering, the sergeant proved to be an excellent driver and had done most of the hard driving over the narrow trails, they couldn't be called roads, since Jaddig had fallen asleep.

"South of the rock is a small blind valley we have to go up. We need to find a cliff where a cave entrance is hidden," Graham continued. "That's it! I guess there is a sign of some sort there."

"After seven generations?" Holly grumbled. "It could have been obliterated by the weather decades ago."

Now they were close to their destination, the remote land depressed her. It was almost better in the clicker towns. Here, if they had an accident or *Charlie* broke down they had no way of getting help. They'd driven around the last clicker settlement, a small military outpost marking the border of Vybber, two hours and one mountain pass earlier and were in forbidden territory. Not that this meant a lot. The Vybber maps called all the land outside their own country that and the neighbouring country of Pulgibr wasn't even recognized.

"There it is!" Suzi called and pointed through the windscreen.

"Where?" snorted George. "I can't see anything that looks remotely like a hand."

"Look up," Suzi said with excitement in her voice. "That high hill above the trees."

Holly squinted in the direction indicated. Yes, there was a jagged rock there but it didn't look like anything.

"It's pointing down with folded fingers, not up," Suzi persisted. "See! That horizontal rock could be the thumb, that tipped over bit the forefinger and three bumps beneath, folded fingers."

"You're right," Graham supported. "See it, Holly?"

Holly couldn't really but gave a tiny grin of encouragement.

"My oath, you're right," George suddenly burst out. "The trouble was we were all expecting fingers pointing upwards or along. Good on yah, Suzi."

He grinned, changed gears and accelerated. "You know," he added. "This trail has been cut in the hillside. There's been a slip and it's overgrown but look at the sides. They're cut straight and the ground below is level. I doubt if a natural formation would be like this."

Holly stared out and, almost in spite of herself, felt a twang of excitement. It did look like an old road. There were even patches of smooth gravel poking out from the grass covering.

"That's not gravel," George exclaimed. "Bits are cracked and broken but I'm sure it is concrete. I'll have a look."

He stopped the combo and the four humans climbed out to examine the trail. Graham kicked a strip of mossy grass aside, crouched down and pulled a clump with his hand. It lifted off like a large strip of carpet to reveal a blackened smooth surface beneath. "You're right, George," he said in wonder. "This is concrete all right. Look how smooth it is."

The next bend proved to be even more exciting. The remains of a stone building stood tucked in beside the trail. It was covered in creeper, there were no windows or roof but it was distinctly human looking with rectangular walls and doors and not a pentagon or hexagon in sight. When they stopped in front of the ruin, the hand on the far off cliff appeared to be directly above it.

"It's pointing," Suzi gasped. "That must be the way to the valley."

"Not according to my map," George mumbled.

"Oh George," Suzi laughed. "Turn the map upside down and look again."

George did and a slow grin came over his face. "Bloody scientists," he said. "Do you always have to be right?"

"Not always," the young woman replied. "We deal in facts but sometimes one has to think laterally."

"It's fifteen hundred hours," Holly added, "so we should have about three hours of daylight. Shall we keep going or look around here?"

"Keep going," interrupted a sleepy voice. Everyone turned and saw Jaddig grinning at them from under the opened back door of the combo. "I guess I overslept."

"You could say that," Holly grumbled but relief showed in her voice. "Sixteen hours. You're constantly surprising us, Jaddig."

"I'm sorry," the clicker girl replied. "The sister at the hospital did mutter something about sleeping it off but I wasn't expecting it to be this a length of time." She yawned. "I'm hungry," she added and reached for the bag of fruit she'd bought at the clicker town just before her long sleep.

*

71

CHAPTER 8

When Bowman Clay Farrell leapt from *Charlie*'s rear door as it crossed the pontoon bridge, he was prepared for a buffeting but not the icy wind that cut into his cheeks and wrenched his breath away. Seconds later, he saw Graham's white face staring at him. He waved and dived off the upstream side of the bridge, a move he calculated would sweep him under the pontoons and out of sight before any enemy would see him. The water did but also sucked him under. He gasped! It was as if a million needles penetrated, not just his skin but the very bones and organs beneath. His eyes couldn't focus and pain slashed across his lungs. With super human effort, he lashed out with his arms, found a piece of framework and held on. The battle with the elements continued as the natural enemy tried to sweep him away, drown and freeze him, all in one fatal move. Even though only seconds had slipped by, Clay realized his battle to survive would be lost if he did not act immediately.

He found the surface and another immediate problem. His head hit the underside of the wooden decking so hard, stars flashed across his vision. He gasped, spat out water, opened his eyes and realized his right foot was lopped through a metal grid connected to the pontoon. The force of the water tore at his body and the metal cut into his skin but Clay clung on and managed to bring one leg up the grid and take the pressure off his foot. Panting and close to exhaustion, he used his left hand to pass a strap of the canvas bag he had inside his jacket through the grid.

The bag held three cylinders of high explosive. With trembling frozen fingers he knotted the strap to anchor the bag. Now, though, it had to be armed. Thank stars it wasn't a fuse that needed to be physically lit. He clung on with one hand and used the other to grab the small mechanical clock attached to the explosive. Back home the method was easy. There were two test tubes jointed to the clock hands. The minute hand of the clock shifted one tube up so the liquid inside tipped, ran down to the second test tube and, when the chemicals mixed, exploded.

However, here in the choppy water the test tubes were almost impossible to set up. It only took a few drops of the opposing chemicals to splash through the connecting tube and there would be a premature explosion that would kill him, and possibly those in the combo above, instantly. Clay gritted his teeth and kicked so his shivering arms and chest were out of the water. He removed the first cork stopper, fitted a rubber hose on it and looped it over to the other test tube. The device was now armed but where was he going to secure it? He reached up and felt along the underside of the decking until he found what he was needed, a small gap between the grid and wood above. Barely aware that his teeth were chattering, fingers numb and legs stiff, he tucked the metal clock handle through and secured it with a piece of twine. The whole contraption hung down mere centimetres above the raging flood. With luck, the chemicals would not mix for fifteen minutes. Clay grimaced, checked to see the main explosive was secure, let go and was swept away.

After five minutes of being tossed in the raging torrent, his frozen fingers grabbed an overhanging branch and he managed to haul himself up a muddy bank. He was safe for the moment.

A small tree covered bank stretched up above him and beyond, unknown territory. Clay's chest heaved as he gulped in still more freezing air and let the rain clean his mud-splattered face. Finally, after his pounding heart returned to a more regular beat, he wedged himself behind a small tree trunk, wiped his eyes and focused on the river. The combo, silhouetted against overhead electric lights, could be seen driving off the pontoon bridge on the opposite shore.

"Good on you, Jaddig!" Clay muttered through chattering teeth. "Well, bridge, you can blow whenever you like."

Now all he had to do was get past the clicker army, over the ranges and back to New Seattle. The task seemed impossible but Clay was a bowman, a human and the lives of a thousand souls could depend on him getting his message through. But priority one was to get warm. He was out of the freezing water but with soaked clothes and numb limbs he could still fall victim to hypothermia. He glanced around and wondered how he could get warmth back into his frozen body and screaming lungs.

*

The bush clad river bank led up to the highway that was thick with traffic and pedestrians, mainly foot soldiers marching in single file along the road edge. Worse, though, were the powerful electric lights that flooded everything in a harsh glare. Clay knew the area, as it was once the human border town of New London where, for years, the so-called peace talks were held with the clicker empire. When occupied by humans, the village consisted of half a dozen roads and a collection of wooden buildings to service the population of less than two hundred. Now, by what they'd seen on the way through in *Charlie*, thousands of clickers were encamped in the vicinity.

Clay wiped freezing water from his eyebrows and blew a cloud of condensation on his frozen hands. Though his clinging clothes warmed his body a little all his fingers had turned white. He studied the immediate area and noticed a muddy track almost obliterated by encroaching foliage that followed the river.

"Well, here goes," he muttered and brushed through the bushes in the direction away from the bridge.

The track was slippery and wet. Every tree or scrub seemed to cascade him with icy water that added to the discomfort of the murky drizzle but Clay continued on. Gradually his body heated the damp clothes and his teeth stopped their monotonous chatter. His limbs were still numb, as were his cheekbones, nose and lips. He pulled the woollen beanie down over his ears and forehead so only his eyes and lower face was exposed to the biting wind. Though wet, it provided warmth and helped his blood circulate.

Five minutes later there was a sudden clap of thunder behind and Clay grinned when he saw the bright orange flash above the trees from the direction of the bridge. In the flash he saw a small shed a few metres ahead. He stumbled up to it, made light work of the feeble lock and pushed into the musty darkness. The shed appeared to be empty but as Clay's eyes adjusted to the dim light he saw the outline of a small window opposite and a row of lumpy sacks stacked along beneath it. He opened the first sack and found it filled with pinecones. Probably this was a boat shed and the owner had brought back a supply for winter fires.

The contents were of little use but by tipping the pinecones out; Clay soon had a pile of dry sacks. He returned to the door and used some twine still in his pocket to tie it shut. Next he removed his outer clothes and hung them on a protruding nail. It was cold and dark but the sacks seemed as luxurious as a tavern bed to lie on.

Thoughts turned to the combo and his companions. Their journey into the unknown was more dangerous than his, he reckoned. Once he was beyond the township, he was certain the journey over the ranges would be free of enemy. They didn't like the snow and it would still be lying in the high country. He took a bar of cheese from his pocket, nibbled on it and, for the first time since leaving *Charlie*, began to feel warm. The half a dozen pinecone sacks he lay under scratched and tickled but they were dry.

Clay intended to stay only an hour in that little boat shed but it didn't work out that way. Without even realizing, his body succumbed to the snugness and he fell into a long asleep of exhaustion and natural tiredness. The last he remembered was the rain drumming on the roof above and the wind rattling one loose sheet of iron.

*

A cold but soft hand covered his mouth when Clay jerked awake from the middle of a dream.

"Quiet human," whispered a highly accented voice in English. "Just listen."

Adrenaline rose and Clay's first reaction was to lash out at the intruder but he realized the hand on his mouth was not tight, another hand was holding his shoulder and a small blue light was shining. Whoever the clicker was, at the moment it meant him no harm so he nodded and wriggled up into a sitting position.

A clicker was crouched beside him with a concerned look in its eyes. Clay had no idea of its sex. Except for the winged females, of course, the two genders looked similar. This one was dressed in the usual body suit that looked black in the blue light.

"I listening," Clay whispered.

"My name is Wunep and I saw you come out of the river just before it blew up…"

"What's the time?" the bowman asked as he orientated himself. He felt cold and stiff but noticed the rain had stopped beating on the roof.

"A little after three hundred hours. You've been asleep six hours but the time has come to move. By daylight this shed will be searched by the security patrols. The place is alive with military police trying to find those responsible for the sabotage." Wunep's eyes looked green in the light.

"So why are you here and not calling in the police? I'm sure there would be a nice reward for finding a dreaded biped-rat?" Clay could see only one clicker and knew, if it was necessary he could overpower it. But common sense prevailed. There could be an army waiting outside the door and, even if there wasn't where could he go?

This question was answered with another one. "Do you know Jaddig Qarte?"

"Yes," Clay replied cautiously. "She is safe with my people."

"And you did not torture and kill her?"

"We don't do that to prisoners," Clay retorted. "Nor do we assassinate family members of our kind just because they fall into enemy hands."

"You heard about that?" the clicker continued with a sigh. "Forgive me but I had to ask."

"It was a somewhat futile question, if I must say," Clay continued. His aim now was to play for time. The clicker had let him go and was crouched a metre away. "If we had killed her, do you think I would have admitted it?" He shrugged. "You have all the advantages. Why don't you just come out and tell me why you are talking to me. After all, it is not a pleasant Sunday afternoon chat in a tavern, now is it?"

"I do have ulterior motives," the clicker replied. "My friend Snimel is in need of help and..." the clicker's face in the reflected light looked sad, almost desperate as he switched to his own language. "I saw you and you're in as precarious situation as we are." He stopped and changed back to English. "I'm sorry," he muttered and glanced away.

"I understand Crucnon," Clay replied in that language. "Who is Snimel and what are his problem?"

"Like Jaddig, Snimel is a female, my partner, I guess you humans would call her. She was called up to take the treatment."

"To become a winged female?" Clay asked and mentally shrugged. So Wunep was a male clicker! He seemed no larger in size than Jaddig but he'd heard that male and female clickers were of similar size.

"Exactly. Instead we decided to leave the university together. The story of Jaddig is everywhere. The government's story is she was a traitor who went across to the enemy but was killed by them, anyway. However, unofficial stories are circulating that she is safe and well. They say you humans are looking after her and will treat any Crucnon with compassion." The eyes of the young male clicker, amazingly human in appearance, were filled with emotion. "We had nothing to lose. If Snimel reported for duty, I would never see her again. We heard that more and more winged females are being called up for an all out attack on your country. Those not killed are afterwards sent to concubines to become egg layers." He stopped and blew his nose. "Nobody survives those places."

"I had heard," Clay nodded. "So where is she now?"

"In my car."

"You have a car!" Clay gasped.

Wunep nodded miserably. "I'm almost out of fuel and, with the bridge gone, trapped on this side of the river. There are military police everywhere and the road up to the forbidden zone is banned to all civilian traffic." His frown broke into a grin. "Actually, we were one of those vehicles that pulled aside to let you through. I thought I saw a human through the back window of your combo and attempted to follow you. However, our car was turned back at the bridge. We saw your combo drive on and I tried to carry Snimel across after you. I pretended she needed urgent medical treatment at the hospital on the Vybber side. The police said if I was crazy enough to walk across, good luck to me. I was about twenty metres away when you dived into the river and I realized the conditions were too dangerous. Later, I found you here." He shrugged. "That's basically my story."

"And where's your car, now?"

76

Wunep stared at Clay for a moment, sucked on his bottom lip as if he had come to a decision and nodded. "Come with me," he replied and disappeared outside. Clay struggled into his damp stiff clothes and followed the clicker outside. As he had suspected, the rain had stopped but a cold breeze blew up off the river. Wunep stood half way up the bank waiting. "Don't worry," he called back in a hash whisper. "If someone was about to attack you, they would have done it by now."

"I guess," Clay shrugged and made his way up a set of small steps to the road above. It was deserted and the street lighting had been turned off. Only a glow in the distance showed signs of the enemy occupation force.

Wunep walked to a small vehicle parked a few metres away and lifted the back door up. An interior light glowed and Clay glanced in over this companion's shoulder. A sleeping clicker was slumped unconscious under a blanket on the back seat.

"Snimel's bodysuit had a malfunction and she's in hibernation. She'll wake up when it gets warmer," Wunep explained. "Shall we get in the car?"

Clay nodded and opened the passenger door. Once again a light came on to reveal the interior that, except for being smaller, looked identical to *Charlie*. Wunep slipped into the driver's seat and they were plunged back into darkness. "It's better not to be seen," he muttered and turned to face Clay. "That glow ahead is the new road block on the edge of town. That's the trouble, there's really nowhere we can go."

Clay frowned. "How about Old Coach Road?" he asked.

The clicker stared across the vehicle. "I know of no road of that name," he said.

"The original road to New Seattle," Clay explained. "It's really just a trail and I doubt if this car will get through. That's the way I was going to walk."

"Where is it?"

"You follow the river about three kilometres upstream past the bridge, then head straight in. It's pretty steep but was kept maintained until the invasion." He grinned. "We purposely kept this end rough so your lot wouldn't realize it's an alternative route. The top ridges will probably still be snowbound, though."

"You humans are resourceful," Wunep responded. "I need to replenish the tanks and get supplies." He gave a whisk of a smile. "A bit of bribery should do it. That's how we got this far." He stared at Clay. "If we lift Snimel over to the front you can conceal yourself under the blanket."

Clay still wasn't entirely happy about trusting this clicker but could see no alternative. Even if he managed to overwhelm him and steal the car how far would he get with no fuel? Also, Wunep's story fitted in with

Jaddig's experience. He glanced around the road but everything was deserted so he shrugged and climbed into the warm vehicle.

His trust was soon vindicated. By eight hundred and thirty hours, Wunep had completed a successful sojourn around various depots and proved to be very resourceful. Soon they had a full tank of diesel as well as food and supplies for several days.

Clay could not help comparing this young clicker with Jaddig. Both seemed to have an independent streak and grim determination that spoke well of their species. If more were like them perhaps there may have never been a war. He shrugged and gave the driver directions out of town. Luckily, there weren't any roadblocks in their direction so it appeared the clicker military still regarded the northern exit from New London a dead end road.

*

After a torturous ride through what was really a walking trail, the three arrived in dense forest country and a well-maintained gravel road. The overhead foliage was a perfect camouflage and Clay doubted if even flying females could see the road from above. The foothills turned into a steep range that they wound up until they came to a ridge of tussock where snow still clung to shady corners. After several kilometres the road plunged down a steep zigzag into another valley filled with more forest.

"Sorry," said Wunep when he noticed his companion's perspiring face. He reached over and turned the heater down "I'm trying to get the temperature up so Snimel will wake up."

Clay grinned and removed his jacket. "My clothes are filthy but at least they're dry now," he replied and glanced back at the sleeping clicker who had been placed back in the rear. "Is it my imagination but is there eye movement?"

Wunep smiled. "She should be awake soon and what a surprise it'll be with a human travelling along with us. I doubt if she's ever been close to one before."

"Yeah, a dirty scruffy one," Clay grinned as he passed a hand over his stubble. "I hope I don't frighten her."

At the top of the second ridge they again travelled through tussock that stretched across a broad plateau. The snow was thicker but at the slushy melting stage with the gravel of the road damp with moisture. Overhead it was a cloudless spring morning, mountains stretched across the horizon to the west while, in the opposite direction, the New Columbia could be seen like a silver snake winding through green farm land.

"Look!" grunted Clay and pointed out his window.

Way below, the main highway could be seen. Vehicles, looking no bigger than matchboxes appeared to be bumper to bumper in a gigantic convoy several kilometres long. Beside the combos the moving black dots could only be foot soldiers. There were hundreds of them!

"The invading army," Wunep sighed. "I wouldn't want to run into that lot."

"We should have blown the stop banks," Clay snorted and explained when his companion asked about the structures. "That's why this road was built," he said "The other route was once all swamp that flooded two or three times a year. Apparently it took years to build the stop banks and drain the swamps into two major canals that flow into the New Columbia." He waved out at the rectangles of green with a straight line of water bisecting them. "That's the Baby Panama Canal. If you look carefully you may even see the stop banks. After the lowland route was opened this road fell into disrepair. It was only reopened a few years back when we feared war was imminent."

"Damn pity," the clicker replied. "So what will happen to the human's now?"

"I don't know," Clay replied.

The pair chatted for a while before lapsing into silence while Wunep concentrated on driving through a particularly windy section. After half an hour they were in the security of another forested area and Clay offered to drive. The clicker grinned, pulled over and watched in interest as the human managed the four steering levers quite successfully by expanding his hands to operate two at once.

"Five fingers are almost as good as two right hands," the clicker commented, leaned back, shut his eyes and was fast asleep in an instant.

Clay smiled. He was pretty weary himself but, by concentrating on driving, managed to keep awake. Thoughts drifted to the events of the last few days and, without really thinking about it, he began to whistle of one of the old tunes he remembered from High School. The road outside came into another valley on the opposite side of the hill so all views of the enemy army were out of sight. He could have been alone in the world, the motor purred, the sun shone and little clouds of evaporating water hung across the road. It was beautiful country with the deciduous trees just beginning to bud and even a few flowers blooming. Many of them had been brought to the planet by his ancestors but he wasn't sure what ones.

It seemed strange but Clay felt he was being watched. It was not that ominous feeling that sent shivers up one's back but more like the feel of a friend. He stopped whistling glanced sideways but Wunep was snoring peacefully. The bowman shrugged and began his tune again but he still felt as if eyes were on him.

He turned and realized they were! Two enormous blue eyes, as blue as he had ever seen were staring directly into him and they belonged to the female Crucnon in the back seat. She noticed him catch her eyes and glanced away.

"Who are you and why is a human driving our car?" she whispered in her own language. Her voice was curious rather than angry or nervous.

"My name is Clay Farrell, one of the humans who helped Jaddig Qarte," he explained, "and you're Snimel. Wunep has told me everything about you. We're heading for New Seattle and trying to contact my kind. "

The blue eyes bore back at him as the female sat up and blew her nose with a tiny handkerchief. "We were at a road block heading for the forbidden territory when I fell asleep," she said in controlled precise English almost as clear as Jaddig's. "I would like to know how you happen to be here."

"Wunep found me," Clay replied. Those blue eyes were quite distracting with the slit pupils rather than round human ones, the tiny nose and very human looking lips. Of course, she had make up with light red lipstick and a touch of eye shadow.

Suddenly Snimel broke into a smile. "Forgive me," she said, still in English. "I've never spoken to a human male before, any human, actually. If Wunep has befriended you, that is good enough for me. She leaped up and squeezed through to the front, plunked herself, like an excited human girl in the little middle seat and did a strange thing. She smiled at Wunep and bent across and kissed him affectionately on the lips then turned her eyes back to Clay.

"Do human's kiss their partners?" she asked.

"Yes, all the time," Clay said. "

"I'm glad," she replied. We were told male humans"... She coughed and sort of flushed except her cheeks went white instead of red. "... Well, you know!"

"We've been told half truths about your species, too," Clay said. "Since I met Jaddig and today you two, I've realized that."

Snimel turned to Clay and her face turned serious. "I've never met Jaddig but everyone at the varsity heard about her family being executed. She's become well known."

The bowman smiled at his newest companion. She was the third clicker he'd met and, once again, this young female was so like a human to talk with it was uncanny. She was probably younger than Jaddig and akin to a human teenager. She slipped off her body suit helmet and Clay though that, with a head of hair, her face could easily be that of a human woman.

Snimel chatted away as she followed their progress out the windscreen. "In fact, by being so ruthless, the government has done the opposite to what they wanted. There are protest groups everywhere but they are unorganized and ruthlessly suppressed." She stared down at the forest in a valley below. "Humans are blamed for everything from new diseases to the rising crime rate. We've been told you need to be hunted down and executed on sight; once humans are gone we will all have rich full lives again and the human lands will be balloted out to Crucnon families." She frowned. "It's all lies, of course. If you humans are beaten, the lands will go to the government and military. Ordinary Crucnon will get nothing." She glanced at Clay. "I'm sorry, I do go on a little, I know."

"No, I'm interested," Clay replied. "Jaddig has similar views to you. I can't help feeling that both humans and Crucnon have been victims of propaganda aimed at making us enemies. We were told you had no sense of morality or emotions at all and were just ruthless killers who can talk." He switched his eyes across at the sleeping Wunep. "Yet you two, along with Jaddig, are the complete opposite."

"And we were told humans would hunt us down and slaughter us for a food supply," Snimel added. "We were told winged females would be caged and forced to lay hundreds of Crucnon eggs that are a stable human diet."

"We do eat eggs but they're hen or duck eggs." Clay replied, " I doubt if a human has even seen a Crucnon egg, let alone eaten one."

"We have hens, too," Snimel added. "They're birds and their eggs are in shells. "

She added no more and Clay didn't like to press the subject. The conversation drifted onto other topics before they reached another ridge and Snimel offered to drive. Clay nodded and insisted on sitting in the back. However, once they started again he found his eyelids grow heavy and he dozed off.

*

Snimel grinned at the two sleeping males in the car but her thoughts turned serious. She noticed the fuel gauge was below the half full mark. She gave Wunep a nervous glance and wondered what would happen if the army was at the human village when they arrived. They both knew that like Jaddig they could never go back. If caught, they'd both be executed. Standing orders stated trials were not even necessary in a war zone. Anybody fraternizing with the enemy was to be executed on the spot.

*

CHAPTER 9

Enormous black clouds appeared behind the summit of the next ridge and a few large snowflakes fluttered down on the vehicle Clay and his two companions were in. Seconds later the skies opened and the snow tumbled down, thick and furious. The windscreen wipers could not cope and all Snimel, who was still driving, could do was pull to the side and stop.

Both the clickers stared engrossed as the world turned to white. "I've never seen snow," Snimel said excitedly. "How cold will it be out there?"

In spite of his worry about their progressed being hindered, Clay grinned. "It's pretty cold on the hands but if you cover up I'm sure a short time out in it won't do any harm."

"Oh we never come to any harm in cold weather," Snimel added with a shrug. "We just slow down and fall asleep, that's all."

"Remember, your body suit isn't working," Wunep warned. "If you fall asleep we may not be able to wake you in these temperatures."

"Look who's talking," the female laughed. "Sleeping away until ten minutes ago and leaving me at the mercy of this ferocious human." She winked at Clay. "Anything could have happened."

"It did," Clay replied and continued when Wunep raised a hairless eyebrow. "Snimel kissed you."

"Clay!" Snimel retorted. "You didn't have to tell him that."

She grabbed her helmet, slid it on and opened the door. Seconds later she stood by the front of the car, waving the other two out.

Wunep grinned. "Did she wear you out with her chatter?" he asked.

"Not at all," Clay replied. "We just brought each other up to date on everything."

Wunep nodded but turned serious. "So what do we do now, Clay?"

"With the snow this thick, I'd say it will also be snowing on the low country. That should hold the army up. We have one more range to cross and a steep road down to New Seattle. It will be impossible to get through in these conditions so I guess we find a sheltered spot and wait until morning. " He frowned. "Does the engine run the heater?"

"Yes," Wunep replied.

"We'll need to bundle up, then It's going to be a cold night. Perhaps I could keep you both warm."

"How?" the clicker replied.

"If we crowd together under the blankets, my warm blood should help you two. In cold conditions, humans often crowd together for warmth."

"And if you begin to freeze?" Wunep asked.

"We don't hibernate," Clay replied. "If the conditions are really bad and our body temperature drops too much, it can kill us. We freeze to death."

The clicker looked shocked. "I've got a lot to learn about your kind," he said. "We can sleep for a month or more without any harm to our system."

Suddenly the door flung open, a scurry of snow blew in and Snimel dived back inside.

"It's fun," she laughed, "but so cold I felt myself slowing down. I've come back to warm up." She peeled off her four gloves and held cold hands in front of the heater. "And you softies just sat here gossiping," she added and poked Wunep affectionately in the stomach.

"Just stay inside for a while and I'll try to find shelter," Wunep replied. He slipped into the driver's seat and moved the vehicle forward at a walking speed through bellowing snow until they came to a relatively sheltered cutting away from the prevailing winds.

The heat disappeared within thirty minutes of the engine being turned off and Clay's attempt to keep his companions awake by using his body warmth and the blanket was only partly successful. Just as darkness fell over that lonely hillside both clickers fell asleep. The bowman followed Wunep's instructions and turned their body suits down. In their hibernated state they were safe, perhaps safer than he was but neither of them would awaken until the temperature rose. He covered them both in the only blanket available and went out in the storm to try to find wood for a fire.

A small grove of deciduous trees growing in a slight dip opposite proved to be a rich source of dry wood with one uprooted tree littered with branches and twigs. Clay gathered several armloads and soon had a blazing fire crackling a few metres from the car. As the heat built up the hiss of melting snow was accompanied by flickering firelight. White smoke punctured the air with hundreds of orange sparks that curled into the outer limits of the ring of light and disappeared. Clay hoped the falling snow would obliterate the light of the fire from unwelcome eyes in the valleys below but was not too concerned. As far as he remembered, they were in totally isolated territory.

He sat down with his back in a tiny alcove of the cliff, sipped a steaming mug of coffifake and munched on an energy bar from Wunep's supplies. The cracking of the fire was the only noise in this silent world of flickering light backed by inky blackness. By twenty hundred hours the snowstorm had moved on and stars came out, so bright and crisp that Clay felt he could reach out and touch them.

One white streak of light moved across the northern heavens and caused him to reminisce. As a teenager he had scoffed when one of his teachers who had insisted that that particular star was artificial and was, in fact, the orbiting spacecraft that had brought their ancestors to Delpe. He remembered he had had quite an argument with Karlina, a girl he had a crush on at the time, who told him it could be true and if he was foolish enough to ridicule the teacher she wanted nothing more to do with him.

Poor Karlina was killed a couple of years later in a climbing accident. Clay grimaced. It was funny how her face flashed back into his memory from a decade ago. He glanced back at the sky but the falling star had gone. Perhaps they were right and that was the orbiting spaceship Holly was trying to contact. Clay tossed another log on the fire and coughed with tears streaming out of his eyes when the smoke curled back and engulfed him but at least he was warmer now.

*

The next day was a time of waiting. Fifty centimetres of snow blanketed the road and, as far as Clay could see, the landscape everywhere was covered in snow. The temperature rose and by noon the snow began to melt. Clay spent the time finding more wood and seeing that his sleeping companions were comfortable but he became bored and decided to trudge back along the road to see if he could find a view to the west. However, every bend just showed another one so after half an hour he gave up and retreated. He laughed at his original idea to walk home from the river. It was fortunate Wunep had found him in that boat shed.

The car appeared again and a sudden movement beyond the smouldering fire caught his eyes. One of the clickers must have awoken. Clay grinned in anticipation of their company.

But something wasn't quite right! The bowman frowned, slipped back around the bend, dropped to his knees and crept forward so he could observe without being seen. A moving object was hovering in the air half a dozen metres above the car. He could make out beating wings and six limbs hanging down. It was a flying clicker, Jaddig perhaps!

Clay's military training, though, made him hesitate and size the situation up. The fire smoke visible from many kilometres away would have attracted the incoming flying female. He crept forward, found a snow free area beneath some trees and ran silently forward so he was close to the vehicle but still out of sight.

The flying female's flight was erratic. She seemed to dip to the right, stagger in the air and correct her movement. In the short time Clay observed her, this happened several times then a noise came through the air like a child crying; long pitiful sobs of someone in pain. The clicker rose in the air, fluttered almost in a circle and dropped.

My stars, it was Jaddig and she was wounded!

Clay slopped through the melting snow towards the crumpled shape on the ground. He reached the clicker and saw she was still awake and attempting to rise to her feet. It wasn't Jaddig but a stranger but the sight of her made him clench his fist in fury. The clicker was young; more like Snimel than Jaddig but the face was a pulpy mass of swollen flesh and the rest of her body looked no better. One wing drooped and an arm hung limp at a weird angle. She wore a body suit but there was a rip up one side and yellow clicker blood oozed out.

Clay's footfalls must have attracted her attention for she looked up and made a brave attempt to smile. "My name is Bikut Kegning. Help me, please," she sobbed. "I was beaten and shot."

"Hang in there, Bikut." Clay replied and scooped her into his arms. She was light, barely forty kilograms and gasped in agony when a wounded arm brushed his chest but she sniffed back tears as he carried her to the fire and sat her beside a sheltering rock.

"You're bleeding," he said and made a quick dash to the car, fussed around for a moment and returned with a first aid kit found in Wunep's supplies.

He carefully cut the rubber off Bikut's lower left arm and examined the wound below. A small black pellet could be seen at the base of a gaping wound.

"It's the bullet," the female gasped. "I was shot when I attempted to escape."

"Why?" Clay replied as he held a cloth soaked in disinfectant on the wound.

"For not killing your friends," Bikut replied. "Ognje Lannak, my so called friend, reported me when we returned to base." She pouted. "I guess I shouldn't blame her. She was terrified when we were told someone had seen me communicating with Jaddig. ..."

"Jaddig?" Clay interrupted. "How do you know about her?"

Bikut gave a tiny grin and news of her finding *Charlie* came tumbling out.

"Do you know how Jaddig is now?" Clay asked.

"The retro-metamorphosis was a success and, the last I heard, they had avoided capture and left Hyfra," the flying female replied. "That was yesterday."

Clay didn't understand all of Bikut's statement but the news sounded good. "Thank the stars and how is it you are so badly hurt. You have suffered more than a bullet wound."

"One of the Mother Matrons beat me up for failing in my duty." She pulled back as Clay dabbed some ointment on her face. "They're as cruel as the male officers. I was due to be court marshalled today but some dumb guard guessed I was too wounded to fly, allowed me out of my cell for exercise and I flew over the wall." She grimaced. "Almost made it, too, but a bullet sliced my arm. I knew I'd never find Jaddig so decided to head for your human village.

I flew for most of the night but was forced down by the snowstorm, saw your fire on a distant hillside and waited until now to investigate. I almost fell asleep but I guess the pain of my wounds kept me conscious." She gave a tiny smile. "I was terrified because I thought it was a Crucnon military vehicle but was too exhausted to fly away. When I saw your hairy face and realized you were a human."

Clay nodded and continued to bathe Bikut's wounds. "If that bullet is anything like a steel arrow head it will have to come out," he said. "Otherwise it will poison your system."

"Do it!" Bikut replied without hesitation.

"It may hurt a little."

"I can cope," she answered.

"Okay," the bowman replied and found a small razor sharp instrument in the first aid kit. He held the slim arm and positioned himself. Their eyes met and the Crucnon just smiled, Clay swallowed and dug into the white flesh, there was a gush of yellow blood and he felt the knife tip touch a hard object. "Almost there," he whispered and dug deeper.

The arm quivered slightly and the girl's eyes shut. He thought of her as a girl, not a clicker as he gave the instrument a slight twist under the pellet and edged the blade up. It worked! A minute piece of blackened metal came out in his hand.

"Got it, Bikut," he whispered. "Now we need to get your wound bound."

"Thank you," she replied and sat gazing at the fire embers in front of them while he returned to the car.

"Here, put this on," Clay said when he returned and handed her one of Snimel's sweaters.

She frowned but reached for it.

"I have two Crucnon friends asleep in the car," he explained. "I'm sure Snimel won't mind you borrowing her jersey."

"Snimel!" gasped Bikut. "Not Snimel Trati?"

"I think that's her last name. Do you know her?"

"We went to high school together." Bikut's eyes lit up. "Where is she?"

Clay nodded at the car and grinned when the Crucnon girl almost ran to the vehicle and peered in. She turned. "I knew she was going with Wunep but heard she was called up like I was," Her lips dropped when she noticed her friend had no wings. "But I guess she wasn't."

"She was but decided not to go."

"Snimel always had that independent streak," the clicker whispered. "I was too scared not to report. You don't know what it's like if you disobey orders."

"I'm learning," the bowman answered, "and I reckon you are as brave as the others. Flying out of jail takes a bit of nerve."

"No," Bikut stuttered. "The opportunity arose and I was too terrified to stay, that's all."

"Well, I think you're all courageous," Clay complimented, "I'll get the fire stoked and some food heated up before you fall asleep, too. I get lonely just talking to myself. ."

*

Clay and his clicker companions spent the night on that snowbound road where, in spite of her determination, Bikut also fell in the deep hibernation sleep her species were susceptible to in low temperatures. After breakfast the bowman examined the snowbound road and decided to drive on. It was a difficult start but, after finding a low ratio change box and tying the steering levers on each side together, he managed to move the spinning, groaning vehicle through the snow. The road surface was impossible to see in the conditions so Clay aimed straight down the middle of the smooth section of snow between the lumpy parts on each side where the vegetation was covered.

The heater was extremely efficient and Clay kept it on full in an attempt to get the interior up to a temperature necessary for his companions to wake up.

"Who's the visitor?" Snimel's voice filled the cabin a few minutes later and she leaned over to the front where Bikut was slumped against the door. "My stars, I know her. That's Bikut Kegning but how did she get here?" Her face stared at Clay with concern. "And look at her. What happened?"

"She was trying to fly to our lines and saw the fire during the night," Clay explained. "The military beat her up and shot her when she escaped."

"The poor thing," whispered Snimel. "At school she was such a quiet conscientious sort who never did anything wrong."

She tumbled over into the middle front seat and began to make herself useful "Her other arm has been dislocated," she snorted and with one deft movement, pulled the dangling arm out, there was a sickening clunk but it slid back into it's socket. "I learned to do that at school. Our limbs are easily dislocated." She grimaced. "It's a favourite form of punishment in the services. If they are not put back within a few hours the injury becomes permanent. However, I think Bikut will be okay." She turned the slumped companion around and very methodically examined the wings before smiling back at the driver. "For a human, you patched her up remarkably well, Clay. Thank you."

"Anyone would have helped," he replied.

"If the Crucnon army had found her she would be dead by now after the males had all gratified themselves," Snimel shuddered. Her blue eyes flashed with fear. "Don't let them catch us, will you, Clay?"

"I won't," he replied. "That's a promise."

Minutes later and within a few seconds of each other, the other two woke up. Greetings, hugs and explanations flowed. Everyone chattered at once in his or her own language. Clay attempted to keep up with the flow of words but soon abandoned the attempt and concentrated on driving through the snow. The jabbering voices and beautiful scenery outside, though, made him feel somehow content and he wished it could go on forever and the imminent battle would just disappear.

Snimel noticed and squeezed his leg with her hand. "I'm sorry, Clay," she said in English. "We're being so rude. "

"It's okay," said Clay. "I know Vybber but must admit I was a little left behind."

"Don't be modest," scolded Bikut. "You speak our language well."

Wunep in the back seat grinned. "They can talk, can't they, Clay?" he grunted. "I haven't managed to complete a sentence without…"

"… Being interrupted," Snimel flung her head around and grinned at her partner. "Come on, Wunep, we aren't too bad. I haven't seen Bikut for years and we have so much to catch up on."

Wunep's eyes met Clay's in the rear vision mirror. "Told you so, didn't I?" he chuckled and ducked as two well-aimed hands hit his shoulder.

*

An hour later they were at the highest point on the ridge, an area where there was a panoramic view of New Washington. To the south were the low lands with the New Columbia a thin line in the distance. Closer, the snow almost hid the clicker army that seemed to be stalled. Everywhere along the edge of the brown road, almost free of melting snow, were lines of dark green tents and campfires. The smoke rose vertical like columns in an ancient cathedral before intertwining to form a layer of cloud above the army.

Bikut stood beside Clay and reached out so one tiny hand was holding his and the second gripped his arm just above the wrist. "There's so many, Clay," she whispered. "I'm so sorry. You have every reason to hate us all."

"I never knew you," Clay replied. "Humans and clickers only tolerated each other over the last hundred years by remaining apart and pretending they were not sharing this wonderful land with another intelligent species."

Bikut looked up at him. "Why do you call us clickers?" she asked.

"Your language, I guess. I don't mean to be disrespectful."

"I'm not offended," Bikut smiled. "It's not as bad as biped-rats, is it?"

"No," Clay admitted and turned east.

Here, the ranges spread out like three long fingers with deep-forested valleys between them. The middle distance was covered in purple haze while further back, mountains, glistening with white snow, towered to the sky. Behind, the sky was a deep blue with one faint line of clouds.

"It is a beautiful land," Snimel, who had stepped in behind them, sighed. "If only we could just stay here."

Clay smiled. "Funny, I was thinking the very same thing a while ago."

"So where do we go," Wunep interrupted.

Clay frowned. "The original idea of the settlers was to come out in that first valley and follow it to a mountain pass but your army know that route. I think they now intend to take an underground cave system through to the second valley. The pass there is higher but safer."

"And how will you know where your people are?"

"They were not due to leave for two days or more so I had hoped to catch them before the main evacuation. I'm sure a rear guard will remain a few more days. The plans were secret because of fear of spies."

"But that was the radio," Bikut burst out. "I told Jaddig that."

"I know but my people don't," Clay replied. "They also don't know how large your invading army is." He shrugged. "Mind you the Proctor, that's Holly's mother, and Commander Evans are no fools. They may have even discovered the army is returning to New Seattle."

"I doubt if we can reach your village before the army," Wunep continued. "Wouldn't it be better to head for one of those valleys and work our way back?"

"True but there's no road," replied Clay, "This is probably the closest point to the valleys, the road swings back now and goes down the western side of this plateau to New Seattle. It meets the highway first."

"Where the army will be," Snimel added. "We'll be trapped and not be able to help anyone."

Clay sighed and glanced down. Bikut's hand was still in his. She smiled up at him and withdrew it. "You feel so warm," she commented. "Like a heater. I hope you don't mind being touched by a clicker."

"I'm honoured," he replied in a quiet voice. Somehow, the respect of this flying female seemed important.

*

"Go on!" screamed Bikut from the driver's seat.

The three others were behind the vehicle trying to push it out of a mud hole. It was late afternoon and they were away from the road and heading towards the second valley. The snow on the lower slopes had been replaced by mud and the walking trail had become so narrow the outside wheels of the combo reached over the side. The present problem occurred when the back wheels had sunk in mud.

Bikut pushed the hand throttle and let out the clutch but the four driving wheels merely spun. Mud flew up off the end and splattered the unfortunate Wunep full in the face. His entire body suit was caked in the smelly gunk. He reached up, wiped it away from his eyes and grinned across at Clay on the opposite side and Snimel in the middle.

"I'm sure it gripped a little," he gasped. "How about placing more pine needles under the wheels."

Clay stood up and placed a hand on his aching back. Perspiration ran down his face and the black undershirt and shorts he was down to wearing were both ringing wet. "At least you lot don't sweat," he grunted. "The warmer you get the faster you work. With me, it's the opposite."

"Come on, Clay. Once more," Snimel encouraged. "We need your strength."

"Okay," Clay grunted. "I'll try to lift while you two push."

"Are you lazy lot ready?" Bikut yelled back above the throb of the idling motor. She glanced back, saw Wunep's mud splattered body and burst into laughter.

"I'll swap jobs, if you like," he retorted.

Clay threw an armload of pine needles under the four driving wheels and grabbed the back bumper bar. "Right," he grunted. "I'm ready."

He lifted, the other two pushed and Bikut accelerated. Black fumes belched out the vertical exhaust pipe, more mud splattered Wunep, Snimel screamed when a turning wheel sent an arch of the black moisture over her but the vehicle jerked, gripped and screamed forward to leave the three sitting in the mud.

"Keep going!" screamed Wunep as the car seesawed along the trail. Mud splashed everywhere but the wheels continued to grip. The outside ones found hard ground and the whole vehicle jerked up and ran forward twenty metres into the pine forest and a dry soil. They were out!

"Pile in," Bikut yelled out her opened door.

The muddy individuals tumbled in the filthy vehicle and they were off, bouncing over protruding roots but on a clear trail through the pines.

Fifteen minutes later they met a wider road on the valley floor. It was muddy and covered in thousands of footprints, horse hooves and narrow wheeled tracks, all leading towards the mountains.

"They've been through here," Clay gasped and broke into a smile of relief.

The three Crucnon stared at the evidence of hundreds of tramping feet, human feet and glanced at each other.

Snimel gave a tiny embarrassed cough and repeated what was on all their minds. "So what now, Clay?" she asked. Her blue eyes stared at the bowman but the twinkle of the last day had been replaced by concern. "The last thing your kind will want is three of the enemy arriving in your midst."

*

CHAPTER 10

On that same day but hundreds of kilometres to the east, Holly and her party were close to their destination. A vertical slap of rock towered on the left of the narrow pass while the outer edge dipped into a gorge below. Jaddig had resumed driving with the steering clamps removed so she had full manoeuvrability. On this particular corner they were trying to navigate, it was necessary as were the four humans spaced out in front and behind *Charlie* to help guide the driver.

"There's room closer to the edge," Holly hollowed. "A good metre."

Jaddig waved an acknowledgment and, using all her hands, moved the four steering levers just a fraction. The vehicle was in a crawler gear that the others didn't even realize was available, and swung out a good metre over the edge before the front wheel turned and ran parallel to the abyss.

Holly gasped when she noticed the outer edge of the massive tyre was over nothing but air.

"You're too far over!" she screamed and waved at the same time but Jaddig knew what she was doing.

The central wheel turned at almost a right angle so, for a moment, *Charlie* moved sideways away from the edge. The cab followed while the rear wheels manoeuvred the vehicle around the bend with the rear section now overhanging the canyon below.

George grunted as the inside slid past the vertical cliff with centimetres to spare. The familiar diesel fumes belched into the air, wheels straightened and Jaddig accelerated beyond walking speed. A few metres ahead where the trail widened, she braked and changed the rumbling motor to neutral.

"All aboard!" she shouted and grinned as three humans scrambled in. Graham, who was further up the trail, waved Jaddig forward to the next ninety-degree bend. Though appearing just as difficult, the combo tackled it with ease. Jaddig waited while Graham jumped aboard, and drove into a valley surrounded by steep forested hills.

"My stars girl!" George muttered. "I'm glad you decided to wake up. We would have had to walk, I reckon."

Jaddig smiled, "You or Holly would have managed," she replied in a modest voice but looked pleased at the compliment.

Charlie rumbled forward to make light work of the two-metre high scrub that the tyres flattened and snapped like matchwood while the chassis bounced and swayed. Inside, the passengers clung to the shaking framework and let the driver concentrate. Jaddig was cool and calm in control, a tiny smile glued to her faced and yellow eyes fixed ahead as hands and feet twisted and jabbed in unison. For a second only blue sky could be seen as the combo rose high, mounted a rock and plunked down the other side.

Graham stuck his chin up from the map on his knees. "We should just about be there," he advised. "Not that this map shows a lot."

Now there was only scrub in view and, seconds later, the gigantic cliff face blotted out the landscape.

"We're here!" Holly exclaimed. "Look!"

The valley opened into a wide, almost square shaped grass area large enough for *Charlie* to turn with ease. At the end was a vertical cliff, so high that the summit gave the illusion of moving towards them. The top was still in the setting sunlight while dark shadows covered the explorers below.

Jaddig turned *Charlie* parallel to the cliff and switched the motor off. She wiped two hands over her face and waited. Holly leaped out the passenger door with Graham directly behind. She felt her heart racing inside and welcomed two warm hands that held her waist from behind.

"Our destiny, do you think?" Graham said in a quiet voice.

"It had better be," Holly sighed. "After all the trouble getting here I hope we find something."

Suzi, looking serious but confident, joined them while George who, always the military man, stepped behind *Charlie* and searched the trail with the binoculars.

"We're alone but I'll maintain a lookout." He reached for his crossbow and glanced at Jaddig. "Some of your winged compatriots could fly by. I'm sure we haven't been forgotten."

"Thanks George," Holly replied but her mind was on the cliff ahead.

They stepped forward under the towering bluff that seemed to shimmer in the sunlight above as, higher still, flakes of white clouds raced across the sky.

Holly frowned and stretched her neck back. The sunlit section was shimmering. It was not an illusion. "Careful," she warned. "Something's not right."

Suzi stopped and her eyes followed Holly's. She frowned and stepped back but the other two continued forward. "You two stop!" she screamed.

*

Graham looked back, grinned and was about to continue when a high-pitched whistle filled the air. He stopped and glanced around.

"Hear it, Jaddig?" he muttered.

She stared back at him with horror on her face. "Your arm!" she shrieked.

Graham looked down. His arm was in front of him but there was no hand, just nothing. He frowned and stepped back in alarm. His hand appeared, the whistling stopped and his senses returned to normal.

"What is it?" Holly asked.

Graham turned with wide eyes and opened mouth. "The whistle and my hand. It's all pins and needles. I suddenly felt giddy."

"What whistle?" Holly asked.

"I heard a strange whistling noise..." Something was very wrong!

"...And his hand disappeared," Jaddig added.

"Don't move," Suzi ordered. "I'll check."

She searched around until she found a spindly tree, snapped off a long branch and held it in front at arm's length. With infinite slowness, she moved forward to where the front pair had stepped back. When she reached Graham's former position the bushy front part of the branch vanished.

"I hear the whistle," she whispered and jerked the branch back. "I think we have found our force field."

Everyone gathered around while Graham explained how he felt. "It was like a minute electric shock," he explained. "Almost like a warning."

"How do you feel now?" Suzi asked.

Graham shrugged, "Normal. As soon as I stepped back, the whistling and dizziness stopped. I wouldn't want to keep going, though."

"Let's follow it sideways," George suggested. "The controls must be somewhere."

"Good idea," Suzi answered and took the lead. When it came to anything scientific she was the expert.

*

They followed the invisible force field fifty metres along the cliff face with Suzi poking the branch in every ten paces or so. Every time the branch end disappeared she reported a faint whistling noise. They were almost at the edge where the grass became a barrier of closely growing forest, vines and dense undergrowth when Suzi stopped in front of a massive tree trunk.

"That tree trunk is artificial," she stated in a neutral voice.

Holly frowned and stared. It looked perfect to her, all knotty bark towering up to branches spread high above their heads. "How do you know, Suzi?" She asked.

"Look at the adjacent tree," the scientist said, "It has moss growing on the shady side of the trunk. The next one has, too but this trunk is as clean as if someone had washed it down with a high-pressure hose. See, it is wet but the water is trickling off and not soaking in."

She reached forward with the branch until it touched the trunk in question. Nothing happened so she touched the tree with her hand. "No force field," she muttered.

A brief but thorough check soon revealed that the force field circled behind the tree, changed direction a few metres on and stopped at the cliff face. Suzi returned to the tree and ran her hand across the surface of the trunk, gave a grunt of a satisfaction and pulled a piece of bark. It lifted to reveal a small red button with *Push* written on it in English.

"Do we?" she asked Holly.

Holly nodded and waited. Suzi slipped a rubber glove on her hand gripped the branch and used that to push the button. Immediately, a section slid aside to reveal a rectangle of frosted glass about the size of a double hand spread.

"I think I know what this is," she whispered and placed her open hand on the glass.

It immediately turned black but when Suzi removed her hand her white handprint was left behind.

Holly bend forward, gasped and was about to say something when a metallic voice echoed through the air. She jumped in fright and stared at the others whose faces reflected their own surprise.

"You have Class Three Classification," a voice announced. "Classification Five is necessary to enter. Please report to a superior officer."

The hand image disappeared and glass appeared frosted again. "You try it," Suzi whispered to Holly.

"You have Class Four Classification," the metallic voice announced after Holly's handprint was examined. "Classification Five is necessary to enter. Please report to a superior officer."

Every other human was Classification Three and the voice repeated the same monotonous reply.

"What about me?" Jaddig said after the disappointed human's discussed what could be done. Before anybody could object she placed her upper right hand on the glass. Her three-fingered hand appeared tiny when the handprint appeared and George looked as if he was about to make a cynical remark when the voice spoke again.

"Your identification is being checked," the voice said. "One moment please."

"You fooled the bastard," George retorted.

"A D.N.A check is necessary," the voice continued ten seconds later. "Please place a strand of hair in the receptacle."

A small drawer like an opened matchbox slid out under the glass.

"Hair. I have no hair!" muttered Jaddig in a disappointed voice.

"Anything from your body will do," Suzi replied in an intense voice. She fixed her eyes on Jaddig and appeared deep in thought. "A piece of fingernail or flake of skin or, better still, a drop of blood."

Jaddig met Suzi's eyes. "What does it mean?" she stuttered.

"I have a theory but we'll see what happens first, shall we?" the scientist replied.

Jaddig frowned and lifted her hand up where three immaculate kept fingernails almost shone in the evening twilight. "Well here goes," she said and, watched by the humans, placed a finger in her very human looking mouth and bit a tiny bit off. She held the minute piece up for Suzi to examine. "I hate doing this," she complained, "Is that enough?"

"It should be," Suzi replied. "Place it in the box and push it in."

"I'm scared," Jaddig said. "I'm not a human."

"Perhaps this is a clicker force field," George suggested.

"No, it was designed by our ancestors," Suzi replied. "I'm certain of that."

"But how?" Holly's forehead creased into a frown.

"Go on, Jaddig, place it in.," Suzi encouraged. "Nothing will happen to you. The worse will be that rejection voice."

The Crucnon nodded and dropped the tiny piece of fingernail in the receptacle and pushed it in.

Everyone waited; five seconds, ten before the voice returned.

"You have Class Six Classification," it announced. "Welcome to Hanger Base Beta. Your companions and yourself have ten Earth minutes to enter before the force field is reinstated. Have a nice day."

A grinding sound sounded and the cliff face immediately behind the tree shimmered for a second and disappeared.

"Holly shit!" George muttered. In front of them was a doorway made of a black marble. It was as large as the side of a house and slid open to reveal a cavity inside lit by electric lights.

"The cave!" Holly gasped.

"Get inside," George snapped. "I'll go and bring *Charlie* in."

He turned and ran back while the others just stood in shocked silence gazing at each other.

"You heard the man," Suzi broke the silence. "There's only nine minutes left."

They arrived at the entrance of a natural cave. The difference was that it was lit by electricity and adjacent to a wall was a long building, a very human looking building with five windows, a tiny veranda and door.

Everyone seemed overwhelmed by the sudden events as George drove the combo in. The deep-throated roar of the motor echoed in the confined space and was followed by an eerie silence when the motor was switched off. George climbed down and broke into a broad grin at the sight of Suzi's serious faraway look.

Graham grabbed Holly in a massive hug and deposited a kiss on her cheek. "I always wanted to do that but never had a reason before." He stopped and looked embarrassed. "I hope you don't mind."

Holly met his eyes and smiled. "I don't mind Graham," she whispered. "Why should I?"

Two metres away Jaddig stood as white as a ghost with her tiny chin quivering. She glanced around and grabbed Suzi's arm.

"What does it mean?" she whispered. Her yellow eyes looked terrified. "Why could my fingernail activate the door?"

Suzi's expression changed to a warm smile. "It means, Jaddig that we are related. You have human D.N.A genes in you and those genes came from one of the leaders of the original space ship. The computer diagnosed your D.N.A, found this relationship, assumed you were this person and opened the door."

*

The building was divided into two main parts with one end being a workshop and storeroom, filled with electronic equipment, weapons, and pile after pile of rations and survival gear. The other half brought a smile to weary faces. It was a living quarters with living and sleeping accommodation for a dozen people. As well as electricity there was piped hot and cold water. Everything was unexpectedly clean and tidy.

"There must be some sort of automatic maintenance program," George noted as he poked his head in the workshop. "Look at the stuff, here, Graham. It's a regular armoury."

"Yes." Graham picked up a strange looking pistol, examined it and placed it back. "The place appears to be set up as a defence post; everything is self contained. I'd say one could live here quite happily for a month."

The two men walked out and around the back of the building to where a narrow stairway disappeared up through a diagonal tunnel. "Let's have a peep," George said.

The stairs led up to a mezzanine floor along the top of the now closed main entrance door and was littered with equipment covered in dust, grime and cobwebs.

"Nothing important here, " George coughed in the dust filled air.

Graham, though, made his way through the junk to another door. After a couple of heaves he pushed it open, smiled as sunlight cut across the floor and stared out.

"It leads out to a natural ledge along the cliff face, " he called back to George. "It must have originally been an observation deck. There's a stone protection wall and I can see right up the valley where we came in."

"This could be handy," George replied after he joined his companion. "I wonder if that force field functions up here. I can't remember noticing any ledge from the ground." He gazed down about thirty metres to where *Charlie*'s tracks and crushed grass showed where they'd been. "My stars, we might as well have left directions on a sign post," he snorted.

Graham shrugged and gazed at the sergeant. "Do you think we were followed?" he asked.

"I think so. After the roadblock, our journey was too easy. I can't believe a country on high military alert would let us slip away as they did. Now, if they were trying to find this cave, wouldn't it be easier to just follow us from a discrete distance?" He wiped a hand over his chin. "There were two high flying females around, earlier."

"You never said anything," Graham replied.

George shrugged. "Everyone was worried about our young friend and her long sleep. We couldn't do anything about them so I decided it wasn't worth adding to the problems."

"But shouldn't you tell Holly?"

"I did," George replied. "That young woman has her head screwed on. She agreed that it wouldn't help to..." He stopped mid sentence and grabbed Graham's arm. "Talk of the devil," he muttered and pointed.

Three winged females were flying up the valley in an arrow formation.

"Get down," hissed the sergeant. "We don't know whether we are hidden by the force field or not."

The clickers flew closer until they were directly above the wider section of the valley. For a moment they circled and passed mere metres in front and slightly below the observers. Graham could see the flapping wings, green body suits similar to the one Jaddig had worn except for the colour, and searching yellow eyes. Even a faint cry could be heard as one of the females pointed to the ground. Two glided down to land by *Charlie*'s tracks while the third disappeared out of sight above the ledge.

"Good military tactics," George commented. "Now we'll see how good our ancestor's force field is. If we found that fake tree, they will."

"They haven't seen us," Graham whispered. He heard a sound and turned to see Holly standing by the open door.

"The enemy didn't take long," she commented and joined the two men. "Are we hidden?"

"I believe so," Graham replied.

The two winged females below followed the crushed grass up to where Graham had first touched the force field. One jerked back in alarm and could be seen gazing at her hands.

"She got zapped," George whispered.

Like the humans less than an hour earlier, the clickers tested the invisible barrier before following the trail made for them by the humans until they were out of sight near the fake tree.

Only the patrolling clicker continued flying above them in lazy circles. Either they were invisible or she had nerves of steel for she gave no indication that their ledge was seen.

Five minutes later there was a sharp bang like a clap of thunder and a cloud of white smoke burst up through trees. A clicker staggered out to the clearing supporting her companion.

"Well, they can't be related to Jaddig," George commented dryly.

Holly stared at him and paled slightly. "Of course," she exclaimed. "If Jaddig had the genes to access the force field, others could, too."

"Yes," George replied. "Perhaps they were only Class Three Classification like us."

"And now they've found us, we could be in trouble," Graham added.

"Could be," Holly said as she stared down into the valley. "But it looks as if our visitors have decided to retreat."

After a wobbly start, the wounded female managed to gain altitude, there was one more circle of the area and the trio disappeared back up the valley.

"Well, we won't be driving *Charlie* out," George muttered. "Come tomorrow and the place will be swarming with clickers."

"So we'd better find the shuttle craft, hadn't we?" Holly replied with her lips pursed. "I don't like this situation one bit."

*

In the living quarters below, Jaddig and Suzi were trying to piece together the puzzle of the clicker's ability to access the human computer. Suzi's attempt to put a scientific slant on the conversation was overwhelmed by the emotions the clicker girl had subjected herself to.

"How can it be, Suzi?" she asked for the third time. "Our species have nothing in common, absolutely nothing!"

"Hold a hand up," the scientist said in a quiet voice.

Jaddig did so and grimaced as Suzi placed her own one beside it. Five fingers lined up with three but the thumbs were similar and the fingers, too.

"Now show me your claws."

"What claws?" snorted the clicker. "I have no claws."

"I believe you got sun burnt last summer." Suzi ignored the reply and continued, "and your new skin is quite red."

"So!"

"Your mouth and teeth?"

Jaddig glowered. "What are you getting at, Suzi?"

"For a species based on what we called insects, you have some remarkably interesting mammal like features, not to mention your inner qualities; compassion, modesty..."

Jaddig slumped down in a soft chair. "But how? There are hundreds of thousands of us."

"This is just a theory, Jaddig. Your offspring are a product of eggs laid by winged females rather than human births?"

"Right."

"Let's say a batch of these eggs had human D.N.A injected into them or original D.N.A replaced by a human variety. The offspring would be different. Evolution that takes millions of years naturally could be perfected within a few generations. Lets pretend there were a thousand eggs. Even if only five percent survived and half of these were deficient for some reason the few left could be isolated and raised. If you had continued as a winged female, how many eggs would you have produced?"

"Most laying females have a thousand or more offspring," Jaddig replied in a hushed whisper.

"Let's say fifteen of this original thousand were egg layers; by generation two there would be fifteen thousand. With hormonal treatment most females could become egg producers, say ten thousand by generation three. It was humans of Generation Three and Four who brought in the Survival of Humanity Protocol. Perhaps they were more than interested in human survival. Perhaps they wanted to hide mistakes made by their ancestors.

Meanwhile the new species replaced the original one through assimilation or annihilation and continued to breed at a phenomenal rate until we reach today; the evolution of a million years in a century and a half."

"So Crucnon are half human?"

"No," Suzi replied. "More like twenty percent. Tell me, have you ever met a Crucnon from Pulgibr?"

"No. A law bans us from having anything to do with them. In school we were told they were sub-Crucnon, worse than humans. Most of our border wars were against them, not you."

"So perhaps they are the pure Crucnon and your race is a hybrid species," the scientist continued.

"But my kind are ruthless killers."

"Are you?"

"Well, no…" Jaddig bit on her bottom lip.

"Humans have a history of being ruthless killers, too. I've researched human history, especially the old records suppressed by the Survival of Humanity Protocol. Our species were, and perhaps still are, as barbaric and cruel as your kind. It took us thousands of years to develop the traits we are proud of." She sighed. "It was only a few generations before our ancestors arrived here that people like myself were discriminated against because of our eye shape and skin colouring. Perhaps the genes your species were given from humans were the reason for your government's aggression. Perhaps the original Crucnon were docile friendly creatures. That could be why the Pulgibr retreated over the mountains and let your ancestors take control."

"A theory is it?" Jaddig said in a slow voice.

Scientists deal in facts, Jaddig. I really don't have a lot of them so could be very wrong."

"But one fact is I must have human genes?"

"Or the computer program was altered. Another theory I have is that your ancestors accessed the computer here and changed the memory banks to recognize your kind."

"But that is unlikely?"

"I don't know but the probability is low."

"Oh, Suzi, you are a scientist, aren't you?" Jaddig grinned." It gives me something to think about, though. Perhaps that was why losing my wings was so painful. The human pain genes were working overtime."

"Could be," Suzi glanced around and frowned. "Where are the others? They've been gone for ages."

"Holly went to find them," Jaddig replied. "She mentioned something about a staircase around the back. Shall we go and have a look?"

"Why not?" Suzi replied. She grabbed a jersey from her bag, placed it on and followed her clicker friend out into the main cave. Floodlights snapped on as they walked out and the interior lights went off. "Efficient computer," she commented. "I wonder if your ancestors or mine designed it."

"Ours," replied Jaddig without even a smile.

*

CHAPTER 11

Holly stared out from the ledge and shivered. Dawn had arrived, the sky up the valley was red and already the outline of the encampment below could be seen. When she'd taken over guard duties from Graham at three hundred hours he'd told her the enemy were moving in below. In the three hours since he'd gone off for a well-earned sleep, hardly a light shone and there was not a sound, not even the usual twittering of birds they heard every morning. But the ledge constantly shook, sometimes quite violently like a series of ongoing earthquakes.

Now, as darkness disappeared Holly could see what she knew was there. The small area was full. Six combos stood in a line facing the cliff. Two were equipped with drilling rigs similar to those back in New Seattle and already a trench sloped down into the soil. Beyond them, thirty or more black tents had been erected and clickers, more than the human woman could count, were everywhere. Fires were lit and food being cooked. Holly realized one other sense wasn't operating. As well as hearing nothing, she could not smell the campfire smoke

"Suzi's computer override must have worked. They found they couldn't access the force field and are attempting to go under it." The familiar voice behind Holly still made her jump.

"George!" she snapped. "Do you always have to sneak up on me?"

"Go and have a clean up before breakfast," the sergeant replied. "You look exhausted."

However Holly didn't move. "How long will we have, George?" she asked in a hushed voice.

"If their drilling is successful, it'll be all over by lunch time," he grunted, "But I want to try something."

He walked back to the door and lugged out a monstrous weapon. It had a barrel two metres long by fifteen centimetres wide and an electronic control panel attached to the side. "The biggest in the armoury," he snorted. "This should curb their spontaneity a little."

He rested the front onto the stone wall and pulled out three telescopic legs so it stood on the rock ledge.

"What about the force field?" Holly warned. "Couldn't whatever it fires bounce back and explode in our faces."

"Could but I doubt it." The sergeant sniffed. "Our ancestors designed this place to be defended. Everything coming has been stopped otherwise we would have been blasted by now but I am pretty sure we can fire out through it." He nodded at two combos below armed with ugly looking guns aimed directly at them. "Look down."

Holly bit on her lip and leaned out over the wall so she could see the ground close to where she knew the force field was. The area was littered with blackened holes, scorched vegetation and clicker bodies lying at grotesque angles. The scene made her feel sick. "They already tried," she whispered.

"About midnight," George replied. "I was here with Graham when all hell broke loose."

"What happened and why didn't we hear it?" Holly retorted.

"The projectiles hit the force field, dropped to the ground and exploded. We felt the ground shake but there was no sound. I think the force field repeals sound waves. That's also why we can't smell their fires."

"And you're just going to fire that monstrosity at them?" Holly gasped. "What if your theory doesn't work?"

"We die three hours earlier than when the clickers dig through," George retorted. "What do you suggest? Use our crossbows?"

"Okay, you don't need to be sarcastic," Holly snapped back. "But couldn't we just explore the cave again. If the shuttle is here…"

"It isn't," George replied in a low sympathetic voice. "You know that. We searched and the cave is empty."

Holly's thoughts reflected the disappointment and frustration of the evening before. They had searched the cave from end to end. It went back into the hill a mere fifty metres and stopped at a clay wall. There was nothing except the building there so it appeared their journey had been futile.

"And Suzi agreed it would probably work?" Holly asked.

"No," George snorted. "You know her. She weighs everything up and…"

"Okay, George," Holly answered. "So that is why you're here now. I could order you to stop, you know."

The old sergeant cast his eyes at her. "If you did, I would obey," he said in a firm voice. "I may be an intolerant old fool but I am a military man and DPF member for thirty five years; since I was sixteen, Lassie. You order me to stop and I'll return this weapon downstairs." He stopped and continued to receive her intense gaze with hardly a blink. "But think of the alternative, Holly," he added in words so quiet she hardly heard them.

Holly turned and watched the silent activity below. A hundred clickers were lining up in traditional attack squads, three deep, shoulder to shoulder. Everyone held a rifle or similar vicious weapon. They were ruthless and, she knew, would show no mercy. She thought of Jaddig and how she would be tortured, Suzi their delicate scientist and Graham's cool confidence.

"Hit the drilling rigs first!" she hissed.

George gave a grunt, pressed a switch on the side of his weapon and a monitor lit up. Neither of the humans had seen a television screen before and stared in amazement at the picture on the screen of the valley below. George moved the weapon and the scene changed. He pushed a tiny lever and the monitor magnified objects. Suddenly words appeared.

Choose targets the words flashed and a red circle appeared in the middle of the screen.

"What now?" grunted George. There seemed to be no other controls.

"How about that drilling combo," Holly said and touched it's picture on the screen.

Immediately the red circle jumped to the place she'd touched and the words *Target One* appeared in the circle.

"My stars, you've got it, Lassie!" George exclaimed and touched the screen above the second drilling machine.

Target two. The words appeared then a sentence rolled across the screen bottom. *Do you wish to select more targets?* George grinned and touched the *Yes* ,

All the combos were targeted before George pressed *No.*

Immediately the screen blanked out and the words. *Fire Power* appeared and underneath was a row of numbers from one to five. George selected three then pressed the words, *Automatic Fire*

Once again the screen blacked out and two words appeared *Fire* and "*Abort*".

"Let me," Holly gasped. She noticed their machine moved on its own accord and, while she watched, the rear telescopic leg raised itself and the barrel front lowered.

With shaking fingers she reached up and touched *Fire* .

Even the grizzled old sergeant leaped in fright at the machine's response in the next twenty seconds while Holly held her hands to her mouth to suppress a scream. There was a whir of machinery and the weapon moved, a hiss followed and a long line of red light pulsed out of the barrel. The ray hit the first drilling combo, which glowed bright red for a second and imploded, if that was the word. For one second it was there and in the next there was a puddle of white hot metal slithering along the ground. Two clickers standing beside the combo also disappeared. Combo two disappeared two seconds later, followed by every target, one after the other in the order they had been programmed in.

Finally the gun, stopped and the monitor came on. *Targets Destroyed,* the words stated in a clinical fashion.

"Oh my stars!" Holly whispered while George just stared at the silent devastation below. Clickers dived for cover, ran back up the valley and all sense of military discipline had vanished. Where the combos had been were puddles of liquid metal frothing and steaming. Several nearby corpses lay blackened on the ground.

"I'll get the bastards," George snarled at the panicking clickers and reached for the monitor.

"No," Holly grabbed his arm. "We do not kill for the sake of killing, George. Let them be."

George caught her intense gaze. "Okay, Holly." He shrugged." You're the boss."

"Holly, come quickly!" another voice pierced the silence.

Holly glanced up and saw Graham with his face flushed with excitement. He rushed up and grabbed her hands, was about to explain when his eyes saw the scene below. Still with an arm around her, he gaped and looked again; rubbed his eyes and turned back to Holly.

"Why is there no sound?" was all he could mutter.

"It's just that..." she replied but emotions took over. Tears began to roll down her check and she felt Graham pull her in close.

"It's okay," he said tenderly and stroked her hair. "It's just fine."

Somehow his muscular arms around her felt right. Their eyes met and Holly smiled. "You were about to tell me something?" she said.

"There's a flying craft in the cave," he replied. "The back wall was a fake. Jaddig said something and another door opened," He reached down and kissed her lightly on the lips. "Come and look."

"You go," said George. He grinned. "I'll keep an eye out here."

"Fire at anyone who approaches the force field, Sergeant," she ordered and added. "Also any vehicles that come into sight. Nothing else."

"Right, Generation Seven Leader," the sergeant replied and winked at Graham. "Look after our leader, Lad." he said.

Holly was about to snort she was perfectly capable of looking after herself, thank you, when she saw the sergeant's expression. The old blue eyes seemed strangely sad, different from any expression she remembered. She turned and also saw Graham's eyes. They were different, too, in a strange sort of way. She frowned. Perhaps she was the one who had changed. "Thanks George," she said, left her hand in Graham's and led him downstairs.

Suzi and Jaddig both were waiting at the bottom of the stairs.

"Look, Holly!" Jaddig gasped, her voice tingling with excitement.

Lit by a bank of floodlights at the back of the cave was a gigantic metal flying machine at least forty metres long and so high a vertical tail fin touched the cave roof. Triangular wings reached out another twenty metres, and a row of over thirty round windows was spaced along the side. The smooth streamlined surface was just about everything *Charlie* wasn't. A tricycle undercarriage with ten wheels held it up while, at the rear, a ramp hinged down to the ground.

"My stars, it's massive. We could drive *Charlie* inside," Holly gasped and walked around to peer up the ramp. The interior looked like a barley silo turned sideways with a curved framework and a smooth steel floor with clamps in tiny recesses every few metres.

"Have you been in?" she added.

"No," Jaddig replied. "I was playing with a control panel in the kitchen, heard a grinding noise outside and there it was. Graham rushed straight up to get you."

"Well," Holly said. "Let's have a look, shall we?"

She led the way up the ramp and inside. Stretched along each side wall were seats, forty or more, each with its own arm rests and safety straps. A faint hum greeted her and the darkened interior lit up to show a circular front wall with a door in the middle. Holly walked forward and reached for the silver door handle.

"Place your hand on the identification panel," a voice cackled from out of nowhere and Holly shuddered in fright. She searched around and saw a small screen light up on the wall.

"Oh hell, here we go again," she grumbled and turned to Jaddig standing by her shoulder. "I'll probably need you again."

However, when she placed her hand on it, the door slid back to reveal a control room with a large windscreen. Four comfortable seats were arranged in two rows. Monitors, levers and gauges were under and above the windscreen and between the front seats.

"The driving controls," Graham said. "It's a bit bigger than *Charlie*, isn't it?"

Holly turned and smiled. "You could say that," she whispered and sat in one of the front seats. They were facing the cave front, level with the mezzanine floor. The windscreen was three metres high and five wide. In front was a circular steel wheel that Holly reached for.

As with the door, as soon as she touched the wheel, a screen lit up and the voice asked for hand print identification.

"Well, I know what to do," Holly grunted, reached forward and placed her hand on the monitor. Immediately the computer began a long monotonous report on the condition of the aircraft. It was highly technical and meant little to her or the others. When it finally stopped the voice asked if other information was required.

Holly glanced at Jaddig who had seated herself in the other front seat, and frowned. "What qualifications or experience does one need to operate this craft?" she asked.

"All authorized personnel can operate the FanWarrior."

"FanWarrior?"

"This aircraft is a FanWarrior HT. That stands for Heavy Transport. It is used for transportation of equipment or personnel within the atmosphere of this planet but also has the ability to protect itself in a hostile environment.

"Can it fly into space?" interrupted Holly. There was disappointment in her voice.

"No, only the shuttle craft at Base Alpha can leave the atmosphere."

"Where is that?" Holly again cut in.

"On Pacifica Island, three hours flying time south of this continent."

"I see," Holly continued and fixed Jaddig with a quizzical gaze. "Am I permitted to fly this FanWarrior?"

"With your commander's permission."

Jaddig grinned and placed her hand on the panel on her side of the cabin. "I give my permission," she caught Holly's eyes with a cheeky look.

"Thank you, Admiral," the computer replied.

"Call me Jaddig," the clicker girl replied. "All the personnel here today have permission to operate the FanWarrior."

"They need to place their hands on the monitor..."

It took a while to get the computer to speak in an almost normal voice. After some trial and error, the group discovered a Lightshield engine drove the FanWarrior, whatever that was, and had power to fly for an almost limitless time before the two engines needed recharging. The flying controls were automated with only a destination being required. The pilot or co-pilot's voice could override these. Other controls of interest were search and rendezvous modes.

"And who is the pilot?" Holly asked.

"The authorized person seated where you are now, is the pilot. The pilot's name at the moment is Generation 7 Leader Holly Jurjevics and the co-pilot, Admiral Jaddig Qarte. Doctor Suzi Yu and Bowman Graham Whitmore seated in the rear most seats of this cockpit are the navigator and communications officers while Sergeant George Bereano, not present on this aircraft, still has to have his hand print analysed for authorization."

"So if we wanted to leave, how is it done?" Holly continued.

"Go into lift off mode and open the hanger doors."

"How?" Holly persisted.

"I do it on your command, Generation 7 Leader Holly Jurjevics."

"I see, "she replied. "How do I turn you off and on."

"Call out Plato, my name, when you're in the cockpit or you can operate the remote. I recognize all authorized personnel. I shut down to the *Sign Off* command."

"The remote?"

"There are two attached to the control panel. They are black cubes, twenty-seven cubic centimetres in volume. I advise that the admiral and yourself to keep one on your persons or in a secure place."

Holly gazed around and found the objects in question. They looked like a smooth black marble cube. She reached over, handed one to Jaddig and placed the other in a zipped pocket of her jacket.

"Sign Off," she finally said and received an ovation from her friends as the green monitors went blank and the FanWarrior became silent.

*

Up on the ledge, George Bereano was fascinated with their new weapon. He set the controls to five and programmed in a section of forest with devastating results. Not only were the trees vaporized but the rocks and soil disappeared as well, to form a massive crater twenty metres deep.

"So that's the maximum," he muttered to himself, adjusted the control to one and aimed it at a line of clickers who insisted on marching directly into the force field. Every time they were greeted with a flash of electrical energy and slumped, unconscious to the ground, only to be walked over by another wave of marching comrades. The minimum setting blasted the incoming clickers but appeared to merely stun rather that pulverize them. The result was, in reality, similar to the power of the force field.

"Interesting," George muttered and aimed the weapon at three incoming flying clickers carrying bombs in their arms just like Jaddig in the original attack on New Seattle. Even though on the minimum setting, the result was spectacular. The ray exploded the bombs and the winged females disappeared in a mass of flaming debris.

George hesitated and regretted his last action. They could have been young females just like Jaddig or that Bikut Kegning who had helped them on the highway. Three more flying females approached but this time, George only watched as they flapped in high above the cliff. Three cylinders tumbled slowly down and exploded in a sheet of orange a hundred metres above the sergeant. Debris appeared to slide off an invisible wall and land on the ground below to add to the scene of devastation.

George grunted when he saw the winged females circle away, unhurt. "I guess that's something," he muttered, again to himself but smiled as Graham appeared.

"I'm to relieve you. Holly needs you downstairs" Graham said then noticed the changed scene below. "My stars, Sergeant. What have you been doing?"

"Just trying out the ray gun," George grinned. "I got a bit carried away. I was quite intrigued with the settings. The lowest is really just a stun mode. It could be handy."

"Holly will be mad," Graham grumbled.

George stared at him. "You like her a lot, don't you, Lad," he remarked.

"Me?" flushed the younger man." Of course, we all do."

"But it's more than that, isn't it? I've seen you watching her. Now, if I was twenty years younger I'd be dragging her between the sheets. She's one curvy redhead."

"George," Graham stuttered. "Shut up. This is not the time…"

"Why?" The old sergeant grinned. "Personally, I reckon this is as good a time as any. She's a lonely young woman, you know."

"Oh hell, George, what would she see in me? There must be a score of males back home of more interest to her."

"Possibly," the old sergeant muttered and slapped his companion on the shoulders. "But you're here, Lad, and so is she."

*

Just behind the opened door but out of sight, Holly had hesitated when she heard the men's voices. It was unintentional but everything had been heard. She reddened at George's colourful comments but smiled to herself at Graham's reply. Once again her stomach gave a flutter as she retreated downstairs without making her presence known.

*

That evening the five had an intense discussion about their next move. They now had fast safe transport but were no closer to providing the humans on the planet with a safe place to live.

"We have no idea what has happened at home or where the settlers are." Holly continued, ""

"The FanWarrior can trace them," Jaddig added.

"How do you know?" Suzi interrupted.

"I asked Plato," Jaddig said. "There are tracking devices on board that are sensitive to warm blooded creatures."

"But what if they're still underground in the cave complex?" Suzi added.

"I don't know," Jaddig admitted.

"Well, I reckon we should cram the Fan Warrior with as much of the emergency food and medical supplies we can and go looking for the settlers," George added. "Once they are found, we can then discuss our next move. Rushing off to this island could be a waste of time."

"Perhaps the island will be a safe area to evacuate the settlers to," Graham added.

"I doubt it," Suzi answered. "Otherwise, why did the our ancestors leave it in the first place?"

Holly nodded. "I take it, therefore, that we all agree we should find where the settlers are. If they're still under New Seattle in the caves they could be in danger from the invading clickers. Clay may never have got back to warn them and they may have decided to stay put."

"I think we should find them," George replied and the others nodded. "Also, we should take as many supplies as we can."

"That's a good idea, George. The food supplies at home must be getting low by now and with the farms gone even with spring approaching, there is little hope of growing more. We could load *Charlie* up and drive it aboard. I'm sure the Plato will tell us when we become overloaded."

"The next question is when we leave," Suzi added.

"I thought in the morning," Holly said.

"It might be better to leave in the dark," Suzi added. "That could give us an advantage over the enemy."

"They'll hear us," Graham added.

"No," Suzi replied. "The Fan Warrior has a silent motor. There's only the rush of air and something called a sonic boom if we go over a thousand kilometres and hour."

"Oh, my stars," grumbled George. "You've been talking to the damn computer, too."

"Why not?" Suzi retorted.

"I just hate the idea of my life being controlled by a bundle of wires," George replied with a shrug, "Though, I must admit, it's a pity our ancestors decided to keep all this technology from us." He turned to Holly. "How about leaving in the predawn darkness?"

Their leader glanced around at everyone's nods. "Okay," she said. "It's agreed then but let's be sure we select the very best supplies to take back with us."

Her eyes caught Graham's warm smile, her own nervous feelings disappeared and were replaced by a cautious optimism.

*

CHAPTER 12

Lieutenant Jay Johnston was a human female; not that this was unusual. Half the rear guard bowmen assembled on both sides of the forested valley were of her gender. She glanced up from the view of the valley below as a mud splattered male bowman slid in beside her.

"A vehicle is approaching, Lieutenant," he hissed. "It's similar to the one Holly Jurjevics went off in but is smaller. Clickers are inside."

"My stars! That didn't take them long," Johnston grunted. "When will they be here, Don?"

Bowman Don Torrey glanced at his watch. "It took us half an hour to get back over the hill, Jay but they have to access the ridge into this valley. They're in mud and travelling pretty slowly."

"How long, Bowman?" Johnston glowered.

"Thirty minutes at the outside."

"Any other troops or vehicles?"

"None. Just a lone vehicle. I was on the summit and had a view right along the valley."

"Right, Don. You did well. Go and have some breakfast." She turned to another bowman beside her. "Get back to base and report this information to Commander Evans, Bryce. Tell him we'll send a second runner when more information comes through."

"Yes lieutenant," the man replied and disappeared through the foliage.

The officer reached for a long flagpole and assembled eight coloured flags of differing shapes and raised them out from the trees. The other bowmen read the signal and, in six positions along the valley, flags rose in acknowledgment then disappeared again. To a casual observer the forest was empty but thirty powerful crossbows were armed and ready.

Johnston issued orders to six personnel around and the group made their way towards the road.

*

Wunep glanced at his car's fuel gauge hovering in the empty zone and grunted. "If we get to the summit we can perhaps roll down the other side, Clay," he said. "I guess we're damn lucky to get this far."

They'd been driving since before dawn after camping the night below the snow line. The signs of the human refugees continued but there were no actual sightings, only the footprints and tracks and one flattened area by a stream where the remains of a camp had been found.

Clay, who had been asleep in the rear after being on guard duty most of the night, gave the two girls a quick grin and slid into the front by the driver. "We mustn't be far away now. That camp site would only be a day or two old and thirteen hundred people can't travel very fast." He glanced out at the crisp morning sunshine. "At least the weather is fine and we're below the snow line."

Five minutes later they reached the summit and Wunep pulled off the road where they had a view up the long valley ahead. The road curved down before disappearing in a straight line through a thickly forested area.

"A long way, if we have to walk," Snimel commented.

"The settlers could be in there and we'd never see them," Clay added and rubbed his chin.

"I'll fly ahead and look," Bikut offered.

"No," replied Clay. "Your wing is still on the mend and if you are attacked up there we cannot help you. The settlers will regard you as the enemy, too. We stay together as we agreed last night."

"Okay Clay," the flying female replied and gave him a smile of appreciation.

After they had found the settlers' trail, the three Crucnon suggested Clay went ahead on his own but he had flatly refused and his gesture further enhanced the bond of friendship between them. That morning he had also spent ages dressing and rebinding Bikut's wounds. Her arm wound where the bullet had been removed was still tender but clean while her face had come out in a massive purple bruise with one eye barely open. Her relocated arm and damaged wings had repaired themselves at a phenomenal speed and that morning she had flown in a brief circle above their camp. After she landed there was a worried expression on her face. Nothing was said but Clay realized but the short flight had exhausted her.

After they reached the summit, Wunep drove the car down the road to the valley below where he pulled a lever and restarted the motor. "The reserve tank," he said. "I reckon we have enough fuel for about twenty kilometres."

Clay nodded but said nothing. Everything looked deserted but in this dense forest an army could be hidden in the trees. It was almost too quiet. He knew the settlers would have their backs covered and was worried they could attack their vehicle without warning. Perhaps a sign was necessary. He turned to the others. "Have any of you got white clothing or anything white?" he asked.

"My old blouse," Snimel replied. "But why?"

"Just an idea," Clay replied. "Could I borrow it, please."

A few moments later the car had a makeshift flagpole attached to the roof with the white blouse flying. The wind caught the four sleeves and it bellowed out like a balloon as they drove along at a steady thirty kilometres an hour. Clay wound down his window and turned to the others.

"If there's a human patrol around, they'll hesitate with the white flag and my hairy face out the window," he grunted. "At least, I hope they do."

"And if there's Crucnon out there," cautioned Bikut.

"I duck," grunted Clay and stood up so his head and shoulders were outside being buffeted in the wind. "Just keep driving at a steady speed as if we don't have a care in the world."

"If you say," Wunep answered but the apprehension on his face showed.

*

"They're diving like hell and waving a white flag, Lieutenant," a sergeant, who could have been George's brother, reported. "They'll be here in a few minutes."

"Right," Johnston replied. "Bring the tree down across the road. I want only three bowmen in sight and everyone ready. Nobody is to fire unless I order."

There was the sound of chopping the groan of timbers and a large pine tree crashed across the road with a splash of mud and dust. The new roadblock was strategically placed twenty metres from a corner so the vehicle wouldn't have a warning but should have time to stop without hurting the passengers.

"Here it comes," a young bowman sitting half way up a tree called out.

For the conditions, the car was speeding; mud spun out from the six tyres and the front wobbled as the driver sort to keep control. It came to the corner and bore down on the tree. For the first few seconds the spectators thought the vehicle was going to hit at full speed but there was a high-pitched scream of brakes and the smell of burning rubber. The rear end slid around and mud sliced through the air like rain. Metal hit dirt and the cab lifted, wobbled and crashed down before the car embedded itself into the branches and lurched to a stop with steam hissing from the crumpled front radiator.

"Oh hell," muttered the sergeant.

Lieutenant Johnston signalled for the others to maintain position and moved forward. She pulled a branch aside, reached for the driver's door and wrenched it open.

"Everyone out!" she commanded in Vybber. "This is the New Washington DPF. Your vehicle is surrounded. Any hostile act will be stopped with force."

Wunep stared at the hostile eyes and held his four arms wide. "We are refugees," he replied in English. "If you weren't so bloody efficient, Clay would have vouched for us."

Jay Johnson frowned and bent down to inspect the interior. Her eyes caught those of two terrified clickers in the back, one a winged female. She turned and suppressed a tiny gasp. An unconscious and bleeding human was slumped across the far side of the cab.

"Get out!" she barked and, without taking her eyes off Wunep, gave another command. "Sergeant, could you lift Bowman Farrell from the vehicle. He managed to knock himself out."

*

Clay woke up with a throbbing head and the view of flickering green canvas above him. It was dark and a small lamp provided the only light. His eyes focused on Proctor Andrea Jurjevics' slight smile then shifted to where a distressed Bikut and Snimel were sitting on canvas seats.

"Your fellow passengers from the vehicle refused to leave your side," the proctor stated in a quiet voice. "Wunep is bringing Commander Evans up to date on the enemy's troop movements."

"All the Crucnon with me are friends," Clay gasped. "They are to be treated with respect."

"We have been," Snimel leaned forward and fixed the bowman with blue eyes while Bikut gave a shy nod. "You have been unconscious all day. We've been worried."

"Yeah," Clay replied and broke into a smile. "I guess I should have worn my seat belt."

"From the reports I received, you're lucky you weren't thrown out of the vehicle and run over," Andrea chastised but her expression softened into another smile. "You did well, Clay. The information your friends gave us will be of great value. The inner council met an hour ago and has granted political asylum to Snimel, Bikut and Wunep. That means they are under our protection. I'll leave you all to chat in peace. A meal will arrive shortly." The proctor squeezed Clay's arm, smiled at the two clickers and departed.

"Oh, Clay," Bikut bit on her lip and immediately started talking. "The humans couldn't have been kinder to us but we were scared for you. There was blood all over your face and down your shirt."

"Apart from a terrible headache, I'm fine," Clay replied.

"Headache?" Snimel asked. "What's that?"

"A pain in my skull," Clay replied and turned to Bikut. "Your face bruise has gone down a lot. How are you?"

"I was terrified when we crashed but now..."She smiled and continued in a whisper. "I'm glad we came."

*

News of Clay and the Crucnon's arrival passed through the camp but, like all events, it became distorted and exaggerated as each version of their presence just added that wee slither of personal prejudice, most positive but some negative. It was early afternoon when the incident happened.

For the first time since their arrival, Wunep was separated from his companions through the simple call of nature. There were ablutions block spread throughout the forest under which most of the tents were erected and the male block was a hundred metres across a small clearing from the ones the females used.

After refreshing himself and ignoring the sullen glare of the couple of men in the sacking enclosed facility, Wunep slung his towel around his shoulders and headed back across the grassed area towards a newly erected tent they had been given for their use. At first, he never noticed the half dozen youths walking slowly behind him but their attitude soon became obvious when he stopped and turned.

The youths stopped too and just glared at him with hands on their hips. Wunep gave a slight smile and continued his walk but four more human males appeared in front.

"My, what do we have here, a cold-blooded bald freak with spare arms," a tall muscular youth with an attempt at a beard growing from his chin, muttered.

Wunep stared directly at the youth and swallowed. Trouble was certain but pride was at stake. "Why don't you go, have a shave and be a real man like the bowmen protecting the village," he hissed in his own language.

"Oh, the insect can speak," a redheaded youth adjacent to the first male spat. "If you can call those grunts and clicks talk."

"Then why do you learn our language at school?" Wunep glowered as he stretched his four arms in a wide stance.

He knew both these humans outweighed him by twenty kilograms and in physical strength his light frame would be no match for them. He was, though, no coward and a skilled self-defence expert in kiwwyf, a popular sport back home.

"Look at him Clive," the whiskered youth, who spoke first, snickered. "He wants to surrender."

"Yeah, David. Just like the rest of his kind, I'd say. All very good when there's hundreds of them to protect each other but yellow to the belly on their own." He reached out and flicked a finger under Wunep's chin. "Where are the two girlfriends to protect you, insect."

Wunep stepped back slightly but realized the humans behind had close in. "I'm going to my tent," he muttered and stepped forward. "My advice is to save your energies for the battle ahead."

"We don't take advice from insects," David, who appeared to be the leader of this particular group, whispered. His powerful arm reached out to grab the clicker's shoulder. But the shoulder wasn't there. In a blur, Wunep had crouched, bent sideways and caught the advancing wrist. The ninety-five kilogram youth found himself over Wunep's bent shoulder and on his back. He gasped for breath as the thump of the landing forced air from his lungs. The youth thrashed around, his face purple and froth pouring from his mouth before he staggered on his hands and knees and vomited on the grass.

"Don't just stand there, you bastards," he coughed and spluttered. Tears streamed from his blotchy eyes. "Get the prick."

Clive went next, in a repeat performance and also lay gasping on the ground. However, as in all gangs, the youths gave up all pretence of fair play and moved en mass towards Wunep. Four grabbed his arms and another put his face into that of the defiant Crucnon.

"You're going to wish you never did that, clicker boy," he snarled and brought a clenched fist back to strike the firmly held victim.

Wunep glared at the human and thought how they stunk of perspiration when aggravated. He struggled but his arms and even legs were pinned were forced back, almost to breaking position.

Suddenly there was whir. The youth with the clenched fist staggered and looked in amazement at his shoulder where a metal headed arrow had entered his body. The arrowhead was protruding out the back of his shoulder while the feathered shaft vibrated at the front. Blood began to squirt!

"The next one who moves more than a finger gets the next arrow!" Bowman Clay Farrell stated in an enforced calm voice. He stood on a small rise at the edge of the clearing; his crossbow rearmed and face red. Eyes, glaring with fury, flicked from one youth to the next. Beside him stood the two clicker girls, their own faces dark with the terror of the situation.

The males, there were more than a dozen now, stopped; the punctured youth staggered several steps and collapsed, whimpering to the ground in a pool of blood but Wunep didn't move. Hands holding him let go as the solemn males stepped back.

"You do not treat our guests like that," Clay glowered through clenched teeth. Everybody could see his right fist clenching and unclenching and the tanned muscles on his arms bulging as anger raked his body.

"It was just a bit of fun, Clay," David muttered but couldn't look the angry bowman in the eyes.

"You, David O'Brien and you also, Clive Wilson, will place yourselves on report. The rest of you will take Daniel Sanders to the infirmary." He glowered at the whimpering youth with the arrow through his shoulder. "Every one of you will apologize personally to Wunep before the hour is out or also go on report." He stared at the group now standing self-consciously in a semicircle. "I know every one of you snivelling little runts."

For a second, not a soul moved.

"Do it!" the bowman screamed. He very purposely placed the crossbow across his back and placed and arm around Bikut and Snimel. Both were shaking in fear. He continued in a quieter voice that was as hard as steel. "And if any of you as much as says one rude word to our friends, you are answerable to me… personally."

Several youths slunk away but three muttered a brief apology to Wunep and one shook his hand.

"Don't take it personally, Wunep," he said in a whisper.

Wunep met the young man's eyes. "I haven't," he said, turned and walked to his tent.

*

Two hours later the two clicker girls looked up from where they were resting in their tent. They were expecting Wunep who was about to return from a meeting with Commander Evans but smiled when Clay walked in.

"Did you get into trouble?" Bikut queried.

"Not really," Clay gave a slow smile. "Commander Evans told me I shouldn't try to do everything myself and…" He stopped and flushed a bright red.

"Go on," Snimel laughed. There was something he wanted to tell them.

117

"They made me a sergeant," Clay muttered and held out two cloth insignia, each containing three stripes. "I wondered if you would like to sew them on for me."

"Yes, Sergeant, " Snimel chuckled and gave a grandiose salute with her two right arms.

Clay grinned, "Humans only salute officers but a hand shake will do."

"But we aren't human," Bikut replied. She stood and tucked her arms under his "In the Crucnon army everyone salutes anyone above their station." Her eyes met his. "Thank you," she said and kissed his cheek, "…for everything."

"That's fine, Bikut." the embarrassed sergeant replied. "Oh yes, the proctor would like to see you. I was asked to take you across to her tent." He gave her a tight hug and glanced at her companion. "You, too, Snimel," he added.

*

Holly stared at the illuminated monitors of the aircraft and gave Jaddig a nervous grin. "Well, here goes," she said. "Plato, I want you to start the engines."

There was a whine as two starter motors hummed and two panels slid back in the middle of the stubby wings. Inside were eight bladed propellers that began to twirl. The speed increased and, with seconds the whole craft was shaking. George and Graham, who had remained outside to guide Holly, were buffeted by a howling wind.

"Slow it down!" screamed Graham as the whole gigantic craft began to lift slightly so the wheels just touched the ground.

Inside, Holly was almost in a panic. "Slow down!" she screamed as she felt the FanWarrior wobble on a cushion of air.

"Command not understood," the computer's deadpan voice announced. The engines if anything went faster and they rose higher into the air. Dust and debris flew everywhere and George, the only one in sight, ducked for cover before he was blown over by the onslaught of air.

"Graham is signalling the wheels are off the ground," Suzi reported from other side of the aircraft.

"Cannot proceed without opening the hanger doors," the computer announced.

"Oh hell!" gasped Holly. She grasped the steering wheel with perspiring hands and wondered what to do next.

"Geographical destination not understood. Aircraft is at take off velocity. Do you require the hanger doors opened? Cannot proceed in a confined space."

"This is only an engine test," Jaddig interrupted. "Please switch off."

The result was spectacular. The engines gave a sort of ping, the massive propellers swung in ever decreasing speeds and the massive craft dropped a metre to the ground where gigantic shock absorbers above the wheels groaned and compressed. The wheels flattened before returning to their original shape but they held the craft. However, without warning there was a horrendous crash of metal on earth from the rear.

"The back ramp," Suzi gasped. "It was still open and hit the ground."

"Shit!" Holly exclaimed as the spinning propellers stopped and the panels slipped over to cover them. She stared, wide eyed, at Jaddig and Suzi. "So much for trying to get this monstrosity to turn around."

"Try it again," Suzi said.

"What!" Holly almost screamed.

"Think of your instructions and do it again."

Holly sighed. "Okay," she said and placed her hand on the monitor. "Start the engines at a very slow speed," she instructed.

"Do not understand the word *very*," the computer replied. "Please reissue instructions."

"Start the engines but leave the aircraft in neutral," Holly said using a term she had learned from driving *Charlie*.

"Are you nuts!" George screamed from outside when the engines spluttered, the wing panels slid back and the propellers spun to life.

This time, though, the engines throbbed quietly without even shaking the fuselage. Holly grinned nervously at her companions and shrugged.

Suzi screwed her nose up, leaned over Holly, placed her hand on the identity monitor and spoke. "We want to move the FanWarrior one hundred and eighty degrees so the cargo door is facing the building. Please acknowledge if you understand."

"This can be done using only the wheels," Plato responded. "Do you wish to use the main drive?"

"Use only the wheels to turn the FanWarrior around," Suzi continued. "Travel at crawler speed. Acknowledge if you understand but do not begin."

"Command understood. Waiting for commence command."

Suzi glanced at Holly. "Tell the men to get out of the way," she said.

"Right," Holly replied and slid open the side window. "Move away!" she yelled and flapped her hand in a sideways movement but saw that George was trying to tell her something.

"The ramp!" his voice reached her. "Shut the bloody ramp."

Holly grinned and a minute later the end of the ram lifted up into the aircraft to form a smooth underside of the fuselage. The eight wheels under the wings began to turn on an angle and roll. At a speed little beyond that of

119

a walker the gigantic aeroplane rolled around. The cave must have been excavated to fit it because the wings slid by the walls with a metre to spare and finally the cockpit faced the blank back wall and the tail; the shed.

"Lower the ramp and switch off," Holly ordered and turned to her friends after the craft did exactly what she ordered. "My stars, between us we did it. Thanks. I just about lost my nerve."

"I don't think there was any danger," Suzi replied. "I'm sure safety controls would override any incorrect commands."

"You'll be a better flyer than I was." Jaddig grinned and stared out the side window. "George has started up *Charlie* and is driving it aboard."

They heard the rumble of the diesel motor and felt the aircraft sink a little as the combo drove up the ramp and into the FanWarrior. George, with Graham guiding, eased the vehicle forward into the cargo bay of the aircraft, drove almost to the front and halted. There was just enough room for him to open the driver's door and squeeze out. He grinned at Holly.

"Bloody good show," he said. "Now I guess we tie old *Charlie* here down and load everything else around it."

Graham squeezed through the side of the vehicle, walked up to Holly and slid his hands on her waist. "For a moment I thought you were about to leave George and me behind," he chuckled, "but once you got the idea of using the wheels it worked well."

"That was Suzi," Holly replied. "I was like a bag of jelly and my mind froze."

"She didn't," Jaddig broke in. "We all worked well together."

"I agree," Suzi added. "It's just a matter of using a logical sequence."

"Damn scientist," George grunted but he was grinning. "Now, I reckon we should have some supper then finish loading so we came leave before dawn as we had agreed." He turned to his companion "Give us a hand with that ray gun, Graham. We may need it tomorrow."

Holly caught Jaddig's eyes and grimaced. It was like a big game to the sergeant but she was worried about more serious consequences.

*

CHAPTER 13

Proctor Andrea Jurjevics studied Bikut and Snimel with curious but kind eyes after they were shown into her tent.

"I hear you were beaten and wounded while trying to escape from a detention centre," she said to Bikut after waving them both into a seat. "Sergeant Farrell speaks highly of you both and has filled me in on your experiences but I'd like to hear everything in your own words." She reached across the table and filled three glasses from a tumbler. "Please, have some wine."

Bikut sipped the wine and gazed at her companion before switching her attention to the human woman. Proctor, Jurjevics seated behind an unpretentious foldout table, was dressed in a warm jersey, jacket and slacks and, with a touch of makeup, was different than expected. There were no signs of her rank at all on her person or in the tent around. Only a guard standing silently by the door flap gave any indication of authority.

After a hesitant start, Bikut relaxed to the gentle probing of the Proctor and their stories came tumbling out.

"I see," Andrea said in a soft voice a few moments later. "How many of your kind are like yourselves and dissatisfied with your government?"

Snimel, who had done most of the talking, shrugged. "I don't know," she admitted. "Everyone keeps their opinions to themselves. There are agents and secret police everywhere to report on malcontents and traitors, as they call anyone who opposes the government "

"That's what's happened to me," Bikut continued. "I was arrested for talking to the enemy." She grimaced. "I had never seen a human before but found you are different..." She stopped and her eyes gazed over the proctor's shoulder.

"How, Bikut?"

"You're like us," Bikut blurted out and flushed white as Crucnon do. "We're physically different, of course, but I mean how we feel. When I first came across the combo and met Clay I was terrified. But he..." She stopped and tears sprung into her eyes. "He treated me with kindness and respect. In my whole life, except when I was with some friends at school, I have never been made to feel wanted." She sniffed back tears and glanced back at the human woman gazing into her eyes. "You too, Proctor Jurjevics..." She stopped again as if she couldn't form the words to convey her innermost feelings. "I know those human males attacked Wunep but you should have

121

seen Clay come to his aid. When we saw what was about to happen we were frightened and went to Clay for help…"

"…And he did not even hesitate," Snimel continued. "If three humans were in a Crucnon camp, that would not have happened."

Andrea smiled and sipped her wine. "If there are other Crucnon like Wunep, Jaddig and yourselves, and I believe there are, I'm sure they would have. In fact it already has happened."

"How?" Snimel asked.

"Your partner rescued Clay didn't he? Without your help and use of the vehicle there was no way he could have made it back to our lines."

"But if our army captures this base all humans will be slaughtered," Bikut gasped. "It's standing orders."

"So we'd better see that doesn't happen," Andrea replied. She gazed at Bikut. "That's why I'm going to ask for your help." She gave a slight cough. "Let me say two things, though. Sergeant Clay Fennel is opposed to what I am about to ask and stated firmly that it was not fair on you. Secondly, it is a request. If you feel you cannot do what I ask, please tell me and I shall respect your wishes. "

"Go on, Proctor," Bikut replied in a hushed voice.

"The pass a few kilometres east of this camp is as far west as humans have gone. We have no idea what is beyond and very scant knowledge of the Pulgibr Crucnon." Her face creased into a frown. "Three attempts to contact them have failed and six of our people who attempted to make contact with the inhabitants are missing and assumed dead."

"They're different from us," Snimel hissed. "You cannot ask Bikut to visit them, if that is what you're thinking. They will kill her just as your humans have been killed."

"No, we were not thinking that," Andrea replied. "We would though, like you, Bikut, to fly up over the mountain pass and report back on what you see east of the mountains. You will not even have to land."

"She can't do it!" snapped Snimel. She stood up and glared at the human "Look at her, Proctor! She is still recovering from her injuries, her wings are covered in scar tissue and the wound where the bullet was removed is still to heal. She can barely fly."

Bikut placed two hands on her friend's arms and looked into the Proctor's steady eyes. "I'll do it but promise nothing." she whispered.

"Thank you," Andrea replied and turned to Bikut's friend. "Your concerns are appreciated, Snimel," she replied, "I assure you we will do everything to make her journey safe. Our scientists have already made a better heating and breathing suit for you to wear and we have a patrol waiting at the pass who are under orders to enter Pulgibr territory if Bikut needs assistance."

122

"I have one request," the flying female asked.

"And that is?"

"I want to do it today," Bikut replied in a whisper. "As soon as possible; before I lose my nerve."

*

A hand painted sign told it all. *You are leaving the State of New Washington Next tavern 12 000 km.*

The last human observation post at the top of the pass consisted of a small DPF hut that sat on a rocky knob with a panoramic view of the remote valley below. The road ended at the hut without even a trail on the Pulgibr side, only the pass that dropped steeply between towering mountains and disappeared into a pine forest hundreds of metres below.

In spite of her new body suit, Bikut shivered as she stepped from their faithful car refuelled from a barrel of diesel Commander Evans had produced from stores. Snow crunched under her feet and the DPF lieutenant's breath made a small cloud of white as he saluted the commander and grinned at Clay and herself.

"The weather report is for cold clear conditions with sixty percent cloud cover, Sir," Lieutenant Kelvin Pope reported. "It snowed over night."

Toby Evans grimaced zipped his jacket up and glanced at his watch. It was just after noon.

"Okay, Bikut," he said. "You know how all the controls work?"

"I do, Commander Evans," she replied.

Her eyes caught Clay's and he stepped in and wrapped his arms around her. Snimel and Wunep hugged her next before she snapped down the glass goggles and tested the oxygen supply. It hissed slightly and warm air circulated around her mouth. Only her wings were exposed but she knew that once she was flying the movement would keep her blood in circulation.

"See you in a couple of hours," her muffled voice said, eyes met Clay again and in a blur of flapping wings, she rose above the remote outpost

Once she was on her way, Bikut found her nerves calmed and she began to enjoy the exhilaration of flight. The new suit made her remote from the freezing air temperature with even her wings kept warm and comfortable. Below, the pass filled with blue, green pine forests topped by a layers of snow gave the delusion of serenity, as did the fluffy white peaks on either side of the pass.

She navigated automatically with an inborn confidence and veered left behind the last mountain on human soil before the first change was noticed. The pass below had a wide brown line dissecting it that seemed, by the absence of snow, either a well-travelled road or one artificially cleared of snow.

Bikut frowned and made a backwards loop, another automatic movement flying females used when they wished to make a quick observation of the scene above, below and behind. The sky was empty. She contemplated flying down to the road but decided it could be done on the return journey, if necessary. Instead, she increased height in a defensive move. Most flying females stayed below a hundred metres altitude to maintain warmth and breathable air but, with her suit, she was not hindered by this restriction. Also, if any enemy were flying around it was better to be above them.

Fog enveloped her for a few moments before she came out above the cloud layer into a world of mountain peaks and fluffy clouds. The sun seemed larger up here somehow and the deep blue sky darker, too. It was beautiful and she had the advantage that she would be unseen from the ground. Of course, she also had her own vision restricted. Bikut glanced at her watch. Twenty-five minutes had already slipped by and another ten minutes above the clouds should be sufficient time for the pass to open into a valley or plateau.

Ten minutes later, with all senses on high alert, she glided down through the cloudbank into the enemy country below into clear skies above a wide plateau. But it wasn't the natural surroundings that made her gasp in consternation it was the activity.

Crucnon, thousands of them were assembled in lines, a hundred wide, stretched back as far as she could see. All were dressed in brown battle fatigues and carried weapons similar to those used in the Vybber army.

Through the centre of the assembled troops two lines of motorized vehicles, once again similar to Vybber combos but with ominous barrels poking out the front, stood waiting bumper to bumper. Bikut's heart pounded but she knew this was her one chance to find more about this assembled army. She continued on until she was above a tent city erected behind the army. Hundreds of brown tents were placed in squares with lanes between them. Smaller vehicles, not unlike Wunep's car, darted back and forth and pedestrians ambled around in almost complete contrast to the assembled battalions nearby.

Something caught Bikut's eyes. A flash of orange erupted below. Someone was firing a weapon at her. It was time to leave! She thrust down with her four wings and propelled her self upwards towards the cloud layer but, just before they surrounded her in their protective haze she noticed a line of black shapes immediately below. Flying females, at least a dozen of them, were circling up towards her!

Bikut came out above the clouds at a speed she would not be able to maintain and saw the peak that led home. However, the flying females that appeared out of the clouds had already halved the distance between them. Bikut gasped! There was no way she could reach safety before they overtook her.

"If in danger, go high," she remembered Commander Evans' instructions. "Your suit is far superior to your old one, you have heat for three hours and oxygen for six. If you are attacked don't try to fight back but use your emergency pack." Bikut concentrated and tried to remember the instructions "Face the sky, make sure you are clear of obstacles and pull the lever," the commander had continued. "It is our latest invention, a sky rocket adapted to take your weight."

She stared around and cried out in alarm. Three flying females were coming straight for her from above and out of the sun. This was in addition to the ones below. How long they had been there, she had no idea but they were closing in fast.

Her hand reached to a small pack attached to her chest and fingers found an oval latch, which a finger could fit through.

"I hope your rocket works, Commander," Bikut said in a controlled voice and pulled.

There was a faint hiss and all hell broke loose! A sheet of flame roared across her legs from below her wings and she found herself propelled upwards at a phenomenal speed. Her hearing antennae ringed at the screaming howl and the world below just dropped away. In seconds she was above the mountains, the clouds, everything. In fact the horizon was curved, not level, the sky a deep purple and stars could be seen yet the sun was still there blazing away above her.

Seconds later the screaming roar stopped, there was a slight shudder and she felt something fall from her body. One of the backpacks she wore detached itself and fell to Earth. Then she realized she had reached the apex of her flight and was also heading earthward and the mountain peaks far below were now racing towards her.

She flapped her wings but they felt heavy and unresponsive. What could be wrong? One quick sideways glance showed that the outer surface of her wings was coated in a layer of white ice. It was below freezing at this height. Bikut almost lost her composure and a state of panic threatened to take control. Her body began a slow tumble and began dropping vertically and the peaks below zoomed closer by the microsecond.

She blinked, clamped her teeth together and forced her thoughts to review the situation. The flying females were gone, left hundreds of metres below her, she could breathe and her warmed body sent heated blood through to her wings. They were heavy but not impossible to operate.

Furthermore, the two peaks below were ones on the border. Her friends were close and almost directly below her. She had vital news that had to be brought back. Commander Evans, the Proctor and her friends were relying on her.

She grimaced when her wing muscles protested at her attempts to move them. Agonizing cramp shot through her body but she did not hesitate any longer. She ignored the pain, flapped her wings again and again with ever increasing speed. A scrapping noise reached her hearing antennae and her whole body flipped sideways. A slither of ice like a pane of glass had fallen off her left wings. The sun must have melted the skin's surface. She gave her offside wings a violent shake and smiled as another pane of ice slid off and floated down from her body. Her wings were back to normal. She had control!

*

Snimel gripped Wunep's hands and stared in horror as a line of orange flame shot through the sky beyond the southernmost peak. Two seconds later a clap of thunder rumbled through the air like a banshee from hell while a white arc curved up beyond the cloud layer.

"What's wrong!" she gasped.

Commander Evans cast a grim face over his petite companions. "Bikut has fired the rocket," he explained. "There must be something out there she is escaping from."

"Will she be hurt?" Snimel trembled.

"I doubt it," the officer replied, "but we'll get prepared." He turned to the DPF squad who waited with dour expressions as they watched the thin white cloud trail above the mountain began to expand and flatten out. "I want every crossbow ready, Lieutenant," he snapped. "All the positions are to be manned so Bikut Kegning has protection if she is pursued on her way back. Also keep the pass covered with your binoculars. She may be wounded and crash on the other side of the border."

"All the bowmen are in place and the mortar gun is ready to fire, Sir," Lieutenant Pope replied. "If it works as well as that rocket did we should have no problems with any flying enemy," he added.

"Don't depend on it, Lieutenant," Evans retorted. "A well placed crossbow arrow could be all we need."

They waited!

Wunep tried to console Snimel but was so nervous the reverse was really the case while Commander Evans stood sweeping the sky above the southern peak his own binoculars. Lieutenant Pope walked up to a high outcrop of frock above the hut, muttered some orders to the three bowmen in position there and returned to the others.

Suddenly a blue diamond shaped flag flew from the opposite side of the valley. "A sighting, Sir," the lieutenant said and Evans trained his binoculars on his men and read the hand signals to the others.

"Eight flying objects are coming in," he muttered. "One is flying well above the others but the main force is keeping pace directly below. Bikut must be the higher one."

He barked an order and reached for his crossbow.

*

Bikut knew she was above the pass, a kilometre out from the border and still at a height where she was safe … for the moment. However, to get back to the human outpost she had to descend through a line of enemy flying females who were pacing her a hundred metres below. Two had attempted to reach her on several occasions but failed and indescribable words in a foreign language, hash and angry filtered through the cold air. Far below was a tiny brown cube topped in white, placed on a snow-covered rock, the DPF hut.

"Well, my friends, here I come," she cried out.

She put a hand on the controls around her waist, folded her wings and dropped like a stone to reach terminal velocity, something like four hundred kilometres an hour, within seconds. One unfortunate creature was directly beneath when Bikut plundered into her. For several seconds their bodies and limbs were entangled before being flung apart. Bikut stretched her wings to slow her fall while shivers of doubt swept through her mind. But there was not the time for felling sorry for oneself; action was necessary.

Her outstretched wings caught the air so she slowed and twisted into a glide with her slender body now horizontal. Her wings beat the air in a blur, once again pain from the effort obliterated other thoughts from her mind but she kept pumping her wings. She had to keep them moving so she wouldn't stall and plummet to the debts below. The pinnacle of rock loomed up in front of her to become the focus or her attention but the small shed flashed by. She was too far out and had to fly back up to reach safety.

A scream, so close she jerked in fright, sounded behind her and something sharp like a knife tore across her back. It wasn't one knife, though. It was three! Three claw-like objects scratched across her back before Bikut twisted and slashed out with her tiny fists. There was a curse in that foreign language and the attacker was knocked aside.

Bikut blinked away tears of agony and realized the hut was directly in front. Two clickers and a tall muscular human were standing in front of the hut waving her in. She could see their faces of concern and hear shouts; friendly encouraging sounds penetrate the air.

But the enemy did not withdraw. She was attacked again but this time the approach was different. Two of the enemy grabbed her arms in a grip so tight she cried out in agony. There was no strength left to fight them off.

"You're coming with us, Crucnon," a voice hissed in the Vybber language. "Your earth-bound friends can't help you."

But they did!

When the enemy female who had confronted her turned away to speak with her cohorts there was a whiz. A crossbow arrow quivered in the creature's throat, she gurgled, caught Bikut's eyes in an expression of sheer loathing and dropped. The second Pulgibr holding Bikut also shrieked in anguish as an arrow pierced her wing. Her hold relaxed and Bikut fought the creature with her fists. Another arrow hit the creature in the chest. It howled and released Bikut's arms.

A third enemy swooped towards Bikut with a scream of aggression. However, this turned to despair as not one, but three arrows punctured the black body suit.

A voice reached Bikut's exhausted mind. "You can make it, my beauty. A few metres and I'll have you." She looked out and saw Clay on the rock. His hands were stretched out over a void. Behind Snimel and Wunep were holding him so he would not fall. Further behind were four grim faced humans, all firing crossbows. Their eyes were not on her but concentrated on the enemy around.

Four arrows fired while in the same instant there was a roar of thunder and the area above the hut erupted in a cloud of smoke; a rocket like the one she'd used earlier in her flight roared out and exploded at close range a sheet of orange explosive. The concussion buffeted Bikut but she felt a strong hand grab her, two hands. Warm hands! She was in Clay's arms. He had her. She was safe!

More arrows filled the air as the last enemy female gave a defiant scream of frustration and flashed over their heads. Of the attacking force, four had crashed into the valley below but one lay in a crumpled heap beside the car.

"You're safe, Bikut," Clay's voice, pitched with emotion, filled the air.

She stared up into his wide eyes of compassion and burst into long heart rendering sobs.

*

Moments latter, Clay reluctantly let his bleeding distraught friend go into the care of a medic. She was covered in blood from deep wounds down her back and her scarred wing had the wound reopened and clear blood was oozing out.

"I'll look after her, Clay." The young woman squeezed Clay's arm. "The wounds look bad but are superficial."

The sergeant nodded and stared up at Commander Evens. "She goes on no more flights, Sir. I don't care if the proctor or you order it. She has suffered enough!"

"I agree," Toby Evans replied in a soft voice. "Our young friend has done her duty for both humans and Crucnon, I believe."

Clay frowned. "The Crucnon's, Sir? Surely they are..."

"Come with me, Clay," the commander said and led Clay over to the car where the dead female lay face down in the snow.

"Turn it over, Bowman," the commander ordered the woman standing by the corpse.

The young woman's face was white but she nodded and reached out.

Clay gasped. The creature had four arms and four wings the same as the clickers they knew but there were no hands, no gentle face, and no soft skin. Instead the limbs were joined to clasping claws like an eagle's with five-centimetre long claws; the mouth had no lips but pinched mandibles. There was no skin but layers of bony brown scales. Long jointed antennae thirty centimetres in length and two centimetres thick at the base replaced the tiny hearing antennae of the clickers. The slumped body had an abdomen three ties the size of the tiny bump on the clicker's posterior.

"The Pulgibr are indeed different than the Crucnon," the commander observed in a hushed voice. "I'd say they are a completely different species, as different from the clickers as the clickers are from humans."

Another voice spoke and Bikut looked up from where she had also been examining the body. "We were told they were different but I never realized how much," she whispered and turned to face Toby Evans. "There are tens of thousands of them assembled in the valley below, Commander," she explained. "There is an army all set to invade us and I believe they'll be coming soon . . . possibly even today!"

*

CHAPTER 14

When Proctor Andrea Jurjevics heard the car brake in a slush of mud she went straight to the vehicle and assisted Bikut out. "Thank you, Bikut," she began. "My signals officer read the flags and your brave actions are appreciated by us all. We'll get you to the infirmary to have your wounds seen to."

"But what will you do, Proctor?" Bikut gasped. Her torn body suit and patched wounds as well as a wide bandage across her torn wings only partly showed her stress and exhaustion. Black rings bagged under hollow eyes and there was a yellow hue around her tiny mouth. "There are thousands of them. I saw dozens of motorized vehicles armed with cannons, Proctor. Your arrows or even explosives will be useless against them."

Andrea smiled and placed an arm around the clicker's slumped shoulders. "Your warning has given us time, Bikut; valuable time that will be used by my peoples. We shall retreat to the catacombs."

The young clicker girl frowned. "The catacombs?" she queried. "I do not understand that English word."

"Our human ancestors planned these bases with great forethought, Bikut," Andrea replied. "Beneath our feet is a massive cave system that still has never been completely explored. It is believed that your ancestors artificially created many sections thousands of years ago. Apparently they lead all the way back to the ones we used under New Seattle and even beyond the New Columbia. We have only explored and used the eastern end. There are underground streams, room for us all to fit, and supplies for many weeks." She frowned. "But not, of course, for ever."

Bikut nodded and waited for her friends to climb out of the car. Clay fell in beside her and glanced at Andrea. "Unless I'm needed for other duties, Proctor, I'd like permission to stay with Bikut, Snimel and Wunep." He coughed and looked embarrassed. "After that episode with those youths they may still need my protection."

"I was about to suggest it, Sergeant," Andrea replied. "All of you need to have a meal and change into dry clothes." She placed a hand on Clay's shoulder. "Have you looked at yourself in the mirror, Clay?"

Clay glanced down at his soaked muddy clothes and grinned. "I can't say I have, Proctor," he replied. "There were more important things on my mind."

*

Everything throughout the camp appeared to be in chaos but, in reality, there was an urgent but well planned evacuation. The tents had almost all disappeared and wagons, each hitched to a huge placid draught-horse, were being loaded with supplies and led off through the forest in a westerly direction. Meanwhile two platoons of troops headed up the valley with more horses loaded with long sacks.

"Explosives," one bowman explained to the three clickers when he saw their inquiring looks. The news of Bikut's discovery of an unknown enemy had enhanced the Crucnon's standing with the humans and her walk through the camp brought forth smiles and kind words from all directions. "We're going to blow the pass up at the border. A few thousand tons of rock may hinder that invasion force a little."

"I hope so," Snimel replied, "but what of the Vybber forces?"

The bowman shrugged. "We have patrols out," he said." The remains of New Seattle is occupied again but they aren't in this valley yet."

Clay and the three Crucnon continued onto the caves. DPF officers were everywhere and large yellow arrows attached to the limestone walls directed them to the infirmary. After twisting and turning in narrow tunnels lit by weak electric bulbs, they came into an immense natural cavity, so large the floodlights tied around stalactites hanging like icicles out of the inky darkness only created circles of light on the crumpled dust below. Voices and other sounds echoed and re-echoed to create an eerie rumble of vibrating sounds in the still air. When they reached their destination, a white uniformed nurse directed Bikut to one of a line of iron beds, all empty and ominously waiting for future casualties.

"Just lay down," she ordered and pulled back the sheets. "It looks as if the medics up at the border did a good job at patching you up but we'll have another look, shall we?"

"I don't want to stay in a bed," Bikut replied with a defiant tone. "I want to help, not just lie around."

The nurse smiled. "Fine," she replied. "I'll get the doctor to examine you and we'll see." The nurse glanced at Clay and Wunep. "If you men don't mind leaving us for a few minutes, we'd like to give your friend a thorough examination." She turned to Snimel. "You can stay and assist if you wish Ms … "

"Trati, but call me Snimel. I would like to stay with Bikut, thank you."

"These are more than wounds from fingernails," the nurse commented.

131

"They had claws," Bikut whispered and stared at Snimel. "They were not like us. At school we were told Pulgibrians were our natural enemies but nothing else..." Her face contorted into a scowl.

"Yeah," Snimel, who had sat herself on the end of the bed, interrupted. "We were also told humans were our enemy with rat faces and stinking skin. I believe our teachers hid the truth from us in just about everything."

"But these creatures are hideous." Bikut shuddered and spoke in her own language so she could express her innermost feelings to her friend. She gave described the flying females who had attacked her in minute detail. "The mere sight of them terrified me. They seemed utterly without remorse," she concluded in a hushed voice. "I don't think the commander or Proctor Jurjevics really believe me."

"They do," Snimel fixed her friend with an affectionate look. "That, I am sure of and because of you, there will not now be a surprise attack. We are all proud of you."

Bikut nodded but her face remained serious as she stared into the darkness above the lights. She doubted if even these caves would save her new human friends from the debacle she was sure would arrive.

*

At fifteen hundred hours, exact to the second, the invasion began. Flying females in waves of ten, like gigantic arrowheads with a leader followed by two behind, three and finally four, pounded the human camp with firebombs. Following waves flew in at exactly three-minute intervals. Their navigation was exact and the forest burst into flames with clouds of dirty brown smoke curling into the air. By the fifth wave, there was little else to hit so the road above and below the camp was fire bombed. Fifty-three DPF bowmen and officers on the surface at the time were killed but one thousand, three hundred other humans were safe in the caves thanks to the advanced warning of one lone flying female Crucnon.

At sixteen hundred hours the Pulgibr army crossed the border in a pulsing mass of moving bodies. The border hut disappeared in an explosion after only one round was fired from the cannon of the armoured vehicle grinding up the slope. But no defenders were in the hut. Twenty engineers hundreds of metres up each side of the valley had connected the charges, set timers before they sneaked along ridges into the forest from where they could see the valley below. At sixteen hundred and ten hours the mountainsides blew. A faint rumble of the initial charge echoed through the valley but this was only the forerunner for the main explosion.

When it came, even the human engineers were amazed by the power of the lines of explosives. Thousands of tons of rock and soil shot hundreds of metres into the air before dropping back into the steep valley below. The ruptured ground groaned and cracked while both hillsides shook in an artificially induced earthquake. Cracks appeared below the forest floor and two mountainsides moved. The momentum was slow at first but the built up until millions of tons of rocks, forest, soil and snow cascaded into the valley below. After the debris, smoke and clouds of dust cleared there was neither valley nor front line as the enemy army, including dozens of armoured vehicles were buried.

Commander Evans grunted in satisfaction when he studied the devastation with his binoculars. The army behind the landslides ground to a halt. Thousands had been buried alive but he only had to shift his view a few degrees to see into Pulgibr territory. Tens of thousands of the creatures were there, every bit as bad, if not worse than Bikut had warned. The landslides had slowed the invading army but the Commander Evans doubted if it would stop them.

"There is little more we can do here," he said. "I want three bowmen to remain as observers and the rest are to return to the caves with me."

"I'll stay," Lieutenant Jay Johnston volunteered.

"Right," Toby Evans replied. "Pick two of your best signal officers and don't show yourselves. The enemy are deadly accurate with their weapons." He grimaced. "Take care, Lieutenant Johnston. We cannot afford to lose officers of your calibre."

"I shall, Sir," she answered in a whisper.

Evans glanced down through the trees at the enemy that were already attempting to find a way up the wall of rock and slush. Two lines of marchers zigzagged relentlessly forward, higher and higher up the dangerous slopes. Many fell but the creatures appeared to have little regard for life. Fallen foot soldiers were ignored and replaced as the front moved forward. In half an hour they had already reached half way up what would normally be an impregnable slope.

Further down, motorized vehicles with steel blades in front were smoothing a trail in the rock but were being hindered by slushy mud than flowed back over every spot they cleared.

Evans turned to the lieutenant next to him. "Signal that the enemy will be at the base by eighteen hundred hours," he ordered. "I suggest the entrances are blown and the settlers retreat back to the lower caves."

*

They were running late but at five twenty hours, the fully laden FanWarrior rose above Hanger Base Beta with Holly at the controls and her companions seated in the cockpit; George had moved a fifth seat between the two rear seats so they could all be together.

"Altitude is a thousand metres," Plato announced after the aircraft shot vertically up at a speed that left Holly gasping and her stomach still catching up. "Follow the New Columbia River inland and search for a large group of humans." she directed as she cast a nervous eye over at Jaddig who was sitting in the co-pilot's seat.

"The terms of reference are unknown," the computer replied. "Please make a grid reference on the monitor map."

"I guess many of the places weren't named when the FanWarrior was mothballed," Graham suggested from the navigator's seat behind Holly's. He stared at the monitor in front of him; identical to the pilot's but three times the size. All the physical features of the land they knew were shown but there were no towns or roads. "That's the New Columbia," he muttered and ran his finger along the map.

"Grid reference; Latitude, north forty eight degrees, sixteen minutes; Longitude, one hundred and forty one degrees, Delpe measurement which is ninety five point five three percentage of Earth size with a variation of..." the computer responded.

"Okay," Graham interrupted. "Follow the river from the west to north east."

"Confirm please, Holly," Plato responded

"Orders confirmed," Holly grinned back at Graham while the computer reeled off another complicated report that she couldn't understand about speed, altitude and velocity in comparison with relative fuel consumption, the temperature and weather conditions.

"Oh my stars," she hissed as she stared outside. The wing panels slid over the interior propellers, there was a rumble from the rear and they began to accelerate forward.

"Lightshield engines engaged and forward thrust begun. Estimated time of arrival will be five minutes after sunrise at ground zero," the computer reported

The humans and even Jaddig who had, of course experienced being above rather than on the Earth, stared out the windscreen at the world below. The eastern horizon was red and yellow above the still hidden sun while, ahead, millions of lights lit up the landscape.

"Our country," Jaddig commented without emotion. "Those big squares of concentrated light are the cities. To the south is the ocean" She pointed at some red lights bobbing in the distance. "That'll be a ship of some sort." She swung around. "That darkness ahead will be the forests we travelled through in *Charlie*."

"The mountains," Suzi gasped. "I never dreamed I would ever look down on mountains."

"And you're the scientist," Jaddig laughed.

In front, the mountains almost glowed as their snow-capped peaks reflect the dawn light. Everything looked a peaceful fairyland rather than the real world. Stars above the mountains seemed to switch off as the black sky changed to grey above a slither of silver bound by electric lights that stretched across their view.

"The New Columbia River, I believe," George commented.

"Do you wish to save the name New Columbia for the river at latitude…"

"Yes," Holly replied. "Please start searching for humans."

"The only warm-blooded creatures in range are farm animals," Plato reported. "The FanWarrior shall change course in two minutes to follow the New Columbia upstream."

Five minutes later the scene below differed. A mountain valley appeared with a line of flickering orange light stretched across it in a crescent.

"What is it?" Holly asked and glanced at Jaddig but it was Plato who replied.

"There is a large forest fire and the residue of explosive material present. The heat being discharged interferes with the aircraft's infrared body seeking material. Will switch to movement mode, if you wish."

"What will that do?" Holly asked.

"Record all movement of creatures below? "

"Do it?" Holly replied.

The computer rambled on. "In the vicinity of the forest fire there are seventeen thousand, four hundred and twenty three living creatures. They are concentrated at grid points…"

It was Suzi who paled. "How many?" she asked.

"Seventeen thousand, four hundred and twenty three."

"What species are they?" she continued while Holly stared at her.

"Do you require a view of a specimen?"

"Yes," Suzi answered.

Immediately, three of the monitors in the cabin flickered and a moving picture replaced the map. A creature dressed, like Jaddig in a body suit appeared. It was walking along a road in front of burning pine trees. For a second Holly thought it was a clicker until the light was adjusted and the creature turned and stared directly at them."

"Oh hell!" George muttered. Huge antennae flickered and mandibles crunched into something the creature was eating.

"The hands!" Holly gasped. "Look at the hands."

Four claws twisted and ripped into what looked like a small forest creature.

Jaddig paled. "I think I know what that is," she said. "It's a native of Pulgibr." She stared at her companions. "I believe that is what my ancestors were like before we had human D.N.A added to our genes."

Suzi grimaced. "Of course," she exclaimed. "That would fit into my theory."

"But what are they doing in that valley?" Graham asked.

The creature on the monitor stopped and stepped back as a vehicle even larger than *Charlie* drove by.

"Bloody hell!" George snapped. "That thing has a gun on it. That's an army on the move."

"But it's in New Washington," Suzi added after she checked another monitor that lit up the creature's position on a contour map of the area.

"A different species has been sighted," Plato reported in his usual monotone and the scene changed to show the more familiar armed Crucnon soldiers.

"The two species are five kilometres apart with a range of hills between them," the computer reported. "At their present speed, the two species should meet within forty three minutes."

"But where are the humans?" Holly gasped.

"There are three in the vicinity of the first species," Plato reported.

"Show me, please." Holly ordered.

The vision changed once again and a human woman appeared. She was standing on a hillside gazing at the valley below through binoculars then, like the first creature they saw, she turned and appeared to gaze directly at them."

"Oh my stars!" Holly gasped and flung a hand up to her mouth as if she couldn't believe the view. "That's my mother!"

"But where are the others?" Graham asked.

"My sightings are visual only," Plato reported. "Creatures, indoors or underground cannot be seen using the present equipment."

"So the humans could be in a cave?" Suzi asked.

"That is possible. Short-range detectors will be able to confirm or deny their presence in six minutes when life within two hundred metres of the surface will be registered in a radar probe. Live visions at this depth are not possible"

The FanWarrior continued it's silent flight while the anxious passengers waited. Time seemed to slow and every minute felt like an hour until three minutes later when, the vision of the proctor faded and was replaced by a sweeping band of light and a droning noise. The tone changed to a sort of echoing whistle that became louder as the six minutes grew closer. Ten seconds beyond the set time, an elongated patch of light showed on the screen and the whistle turned to a high-pitched hum.

"Confirm the presence of one thousand and eighty two creatures eighty four metres inside the mountain at grid reference..." Plato reported.

Holly bit on her lip and smiled up at Graham who reached forward and clasped her shoulder while George chuckled and slapped Suzi, none too softly on the back.

Only Jaddig continued to stare miserably at the monitor. "But they're squeezed in between the two armies," she whispered. "How can that have happened? My people and the Pulgibr are enemies. They would never cooperate to hunt down humans."

*

A subdued silence filled the inner caves as hundreds of settlers lined up in their sections for breakfast. Clay, allocated to Section 17, carried a four year old while his mother, a young widow of one of the DPF bowmen killed in the initial attack, walked behind with a baby in her arms. Powdered milk had been mixed in large stainless steel vats and rationed to children and pregnant women while eggs and bacon, the usual settler's breakfast, were now restricted to the injured and elderly. Everyone else had to make do with wheat cakes, dried fruit and one mug of coffifake.

"How long can we hold out, Sergeant," the widow asked. "We can't live in here for ever. There is no food, no grass for the horses and our other animals were left behind." Her sunken eyes gazed hopelessly at the white dust that covered everybody's feet and legs. "I never asked to be born on this planet. Why are we being treated as aliens?"

Clay glanced down at the woman and wanted to reassure her but how could he? Everything she said had played on his thoughts throughout the night. "Perhaps Holly Jurjevics managed to get through," he said in a kind voice.

"Pipe dreams, Sergeant," the woman whispered. "Even if she did, how would she find us here deep underground with not one, but two armies hell bent on killing us. What hope is there for my little ones with no father to come home to?" Her face clouded over. "We had everything, Sergeant Farrell; a small farm half way between the river and New Seattle, two gorgeous children; Brett had just bought twenty more dairy cows and our house was complete. But what is there, now?"

"Don't give up," Clay replied. "We have friends who can help."

"A handful of renegade clickers," the woman replied bitterly. "With all due respects to the ones who brought you back, but I doubt if they can do anything." Her eyes turned angry. "And why should they? We have absolutely nothing in common."

"But we have," Clay Farrell whispered, "Far more than you think, Ma'am."

Their line had reached the serving counter so he helped the child in his arms get breakfast, escorted the woman to a table, found a highchair for her infant and excused himself. Though the woman had his sympathy, her attitude somehow annoyed him. He must have looked dejected for at the cafeteria door a small hand slipped into his while a second grasp his lower arm. Bikut was beside him.

"I overheard your conversation with that unfortunate woman, Clay," she said quietly. "Are we so different we can never be friends?"

"We are friends," Clay retorted with anger in his voice. "You are my friend and shall remain so."

"You aren't just feeling sorry for me?" Bikut asked.

Suddenly Clay's tanned face broke into a smile. "No," he replied and squeezed her top hand.

*

High above the ridge that separated the two valleys between New Seattle and the border a patrol of two women sat perched three-quarters way up a giant oak tree. A tiny platform had been constructed between the split in the trunk and crude but comfortable seating provided in Observation Post 217.

Corporal Sheree Gilmore handed the binoculars to her companion, Bowman Deanne Hilton and snorted. "You won the bet and I owe you twenty dollars. They are not friends."

Deanne placed the glasses to her eyes and focused on the road summit between the valleys. Here in the predawn twilight the troops of Vybber and those of The Confederation of Pulgibr met. The stalemate of the last hour had ended and the converging armies both retreated across but not down the ridge. A cloud of smoke rose from a cannon and the distant report ricocheted through the air.

"The clickers are charging," Deanne reported.

The two massed armies became one as the opposing forces moved together. Smoke bellowed into the crisp air across the whole ridge and the pounding rumble of a hundred cannon and smaller sized weapons shattered the quiet morning. For twenty minutes the two humans stared fascinated as little could be fathomed from the movement of creatures below. But there was something happening!

The Pulgibrian motor vehicles began firing. Blazing orange flames shot from raised cannons followed by explosions amongst the clicker troops. Black smoke poured into the air as the vehicles rumbled down into the first valley followed by a sea of foot soldiers. They sliced right through the opposing clickers who could be seen breaking rank and retreating. However, line after line of Vybber clickers faltered and fell, forlorn and still on the snow covered slope.

This wasn't a battle; it was annihilation.

"Perhaps they'll kill off all the clickers and leave us in peace," Bowman Deanne Hilton tried to make light of the battle below.

"No," the corporal replied. "I have a strange feeling the clickers we know are saints compare with that other lot." She reached for her backpack. "Come on, Deanne. We found out what we were sent here for. We are under orders to be back to the inner tunnels by eight hundred hours. We only have a few moments. Let's go."

*

CHAPTER 15

Deep underground, two bowmen crawled through one of many artificial ventilation tunnels that crisscrossed the catacombs. Ian Stainer, the younger of the two men, muttered an oath when he banged his head on the curved rock ceiling above him.

"How's the wire holding out, John?" he panted as the handkerchief he had dabbed on his head came away covered in blood.

"A couple of hundred metres left, Ian," the sixty-year-old at the rear muttered. "We should be above the outer cave now. I'll try a peep hole."

He extracted a thin knife from his belt, switched their only torch off so they were plunged into darkness, and methodically dug into the left-hand wall. The soft substance crumbled and John felt dust falling on his arm as he turned the blade deeper. "Almost through."

There was a slight scrape and a ray of dusty light shone diagonally across the tunnel. As well, noise and fumes filtered through. "Sounds crowded in there," John muttered and lay on the tunnel floor to squint at the scene below. "Have a look, Ian," he continued.

Ian crawled forward and fixed one eye on the opening. "Oh hell!" he gulped.

Huge floodlights lit the outer cave, twice as many as the humans had demolished before their retreat, and thousands of creatures packed the cavity. Three vehicles were using steel blades to scrape soil and limestone from the blown passageways to the inner caves. Other creatures used shovels and wheelbarrows to shift piles of rubble. By the progress made, it appeared that the excavation had been going on for most of the six hours since human engineers had blown the cave.

"They'll be through by mid-morning," Ian whispered.

"Yeah," the older man replied. "It's damn lucky we came to check. Have you the explosive ready?"

Ian slid back from the ray of light and wriggled out of a khaki backpack. He switched the torch on and lifted out a fist full of cardboard cylinders already taped together and fused. Insulation was stripped off the end pieces before the bowman used a small pair of pliers to join similar collared wires together. He examined the tunnel before he decided a small crack in the ceiling was the best place to leave the explosive.

"Right," he whispered with his wide eyes on the other bowman. "We'll set two more on the way back."

John nodded, placed a piece of rubble into the hole he had created and slid back on the seat of his trousers; there wasn't enough room to turn around. Five minutes later, they were back in a subterranean control centre known only to the Inner Council and a selected few DPF personnel.

"Our sounding equipment was correct, Sir," John reported to Commander Evans. "The outer cave is packed with those creatures. There are machines digging the rubble away. I'd say they'll be through in a couple of hours."

"Right!" Evans retorted. "If our ancestors are the engineers we believe they are, your explosives won't be needed but we'll time them to go together. Thank you. You both did well."

"We need to stop the bastards, Sir." Ian whispered. "I doubt if our efforts will more than delay them."

"Stay with us, if you wish," Andrea Jurjevics remarked. "Our ancestors said the inner caves and this chamber are safe."

"Thank you, Ma'am," Ian replied and grinned at John. Their job was over. It was up to the leaders now.

*

Andrea read the sign carved onto the metal console for the third time.

This vacuum bomb has the explosive power to annihilate every living creature in the outer cave, the valley outside to the altitude of hundred metres. The components have been set to collapse the cave and valley walls. Be warned! Do not ignite if friendly personnel are within the danger areas. The area will be free to renter two hours after the discharge but we advise fifty hours before personnel re-enter the destruction zone unless they are wearing protective clothing.

It was signed by a Commander Gerald Kronan, Proctor Stephen Van Schaik and Doctor Malvern Hutchkinson and dated Year 2125 (Earth Time).

Andrea nodded at Toby and stood in front of a grey metal console while the commander did the same. The two cabinets were built so it would be impossible for one person to arm the bomb. The instructions were explicit. If the controls were not operated simultaneously, a time lock cut in and froze everything for twenty-five hours.

She took an ancient key from her zipped pocket and inserted it in the keyhole. "On the count of three" she said and saw Tory nod. "One, two, three..."

Both keys turned and a screen lit up. *Stage one activated. Commander, please enter your code.*

A grim Toby Evans punched in a seven-digit code

A bank of seven red lights flashed on and one turned yellow.

Proctor. Please enter your code.

After Andrea had done so another light turned yellow. Cryptic instructions followed that would only be known by leaders with access to ancient records. Slowly all the red lights turned to yellow and began to flash. *The vacuum bomb is armed. If either party presses the abort button all controls will be frozen for twenty-five hours. Set timing.*

A digital clock flashed on both consoles with the time and date. Andrea and Toby both entered a time fifteen minutes ahead and, after another count down, pressed their own black buttons. A siren sounded and a voice filled the room. "Zero minus fifteen minutes, fifty nine seconds... fifty eight..."

Andrea turned to John, "Set your charges for twenty minutes, Bowman," she said. "If our ancestor's bomb doesn't work at least ours should give us some time."

"Yes, Proctor," the elderly man replied and joined the last wire to an old alarm clock.

*

On board the FanWarrior, Holly had just completed a set of instructions to Plato and the computer was searching for a suitable landing zone with access to the inner caves where instruments had confirmed the humans were hiding. Adjacent to her Jaddig stared, white, numbed and close to tears at the monitor views of her country's army being slaughtered by the invaders. Even in the few minutes Plato had focused on the scene below, hundreds, if not thousands, of Crucnon soldiers had been shot, blown up or crushed under the wheels of Pulgibrian vehicles. Even wounded survivors were shown being slashed down by enemy officers carrying silver machetes.

"Can't we do something?" she asked.

"I'm sorry, Lass..." George replied and was about to continue speaking when the valley below turned white... "What the hell!" he gasped as they were gripped by an unknown force and propelled skyward at a speed so great, the passengers were forced back into their seats by the acceleration.

The monitors went dead and three different sirens sounded. The FanWarrior shuddered so violently Holly bit her tongue and the salty taste of blood filled her mouth. Flesh on her cheeks was forced back and her eyes stung. She couldn't breathe and excruciating pain filled her lungs bloated with unwanted air. She tied to move but her body was held by centrifugal forces that were now squashing her very bones. Her ears blocked out screams around her. She managed to swallow and pop them but by now her throat was so tight no air could enter her body.

Five seconds later, the aircraft stopped and dropped!

If anything, the sensation was now worse. Holly forced her bloodshot eyes open and found her face slapped against the windscreen. Air was howling through her ears and she could see outside. Two monstrous peaks were heading straight for them, sirens still screamed and lights flashed but her companion's screams had halted. Two seconds later the vertical drop became horizontal flight and a safety harness was all that stopped Holly being flung into the ceiling.

"The FanWarrior is under control; altitude one thousand metres," Plato's voice filled the cockpit. "Am initiating a damage check."

"Look outside!" screamed Jaddig.

The white fog they remembered just before they were hit by the energy wave had turned to a swirling mass of brown clouds that were spinning in spirals like horizontal tornadoes. From a centre, not far from where the fighting had taken place, this spiral looked like a gigantic snail's shell with each section a tornado of its own; dozens of them.

There was no noise and the air outside the Fan Warrior was calm, the sun shone overhead and outside this circle of devastation, the world was normal with forests, snow and everything else untouched.

"Maintain height and fly in circles, if it is safe to do so," Suzi Yu directed from the rear seat.

Holly found a handkerchief to hold onto her bloody nose as she gazed at her friends. They all looked blue in the face but were, like herself, only superficially wounded.

"What was it?" Graham gasped.

"The whole mountain range is riddled with explosives set by our ancestors," Suzi explained. "This is more information suppressed by the Survival of Humanity Protocol."

"So we set it off," gasped Holly. "But why would the settlers blow themselves up?"

"I don't believe they have," Suzi reassured. "These explosions are highly directional and accurate. Everything outside the designated area is unaffected."

"But we were!" snorted George. "Explain that, Suzi."

"We were forced up by air being blown out of the bombed area," the scientist continued. "It was like opening a bottle of champaign after you've shaken it up."

"The smoke is clearing!" Jaddig interrupted. "Can we get a closer view?"

"Is that a command?" Plato's monotonous voice sounded completely inappropriate in the circumstances.

"It is," snapped Jaddig.

The main monitors switched to portray the twirling tornadoes close up but they showed little else. It was as if a billion tons of finely ground sand was twisting around.

"I shall artificially enhance the background," Plato reported and the brown swirling sand faded to become transparent. The valley up to the summit where the two armies fought was bare, complete and utterly! There was no army, no road, snow or even forest. Instead was a red surface of liquid rock, oozing and rolling like volcanic lava into the gorge beneath. At one end the lava flow stopped, backed up and solidified. As the seconds rolled by, more molten rock hit the invisible edge, slopped up into the air and retreated back onto itself.

"The other valley!" Holly cried out.

The first valley, filled with Crucnon soldiers and the front of the invading Pulgibrian army was untouched. One could draw a line between the natural green covered valley and the scorched devastation in the second valley. At the other end, the devastation stopped half way up to the border and the rear of the enemy army was unaffected.

"Have our people have survived?" George asked Suzi.

"If they were in the lower caves and I believe they are, they will be safe." Suzi directed the computer to search for human life.

"One thousand, two hundred and twenty one warm blooded and three cold blooded bipeds are alive beneath the surface," Plato reported. "Three others on the surface at grid reference twenty six point three by thirteen point zero five are also alive. Do you wish the FanWarrior to descend and land in close proximity of that reference point?"

"Check for enemy soldiers and, if it is safe, do so," Suzi directed. She grinned at Jaddig. "You mustn't be the only Crucnon to have made friends with us humans," she said.

"More likely there are spies in the caves," the sergeant muttered.

"Shut up, George," Graham snapped. "Stop being such a pain in the butt. If Jaddig came to help us, why couldn't others of her kind?"

"She's different," George retorted.

"No I'm not, " Jaddig replied. "There are thousands like me. Perhaps after this we can prove it."

"The programmed destination is clear of enemy," the computer cut in. "This aircraft can land on a plateau above the forest line within walking distance of the humans and three Crucnon."

"What!" whispered Jaddig.

"Three Crucnon and five humans are proceeding to the surface," Plato added.

Jaddig looked at Holly with tears in her yellow eyes. "We aren't all savages," she whispered and looked directly at the old sergeant. "I hope I can prove it to you, George."

"Aye, Lassie. I'm sure you can," he replied, reached out, clasped the Crucnon in his arms and plunked a kiss on her cheek. "I'm sorry for being a miserable old man."

Jaddig flushed white but squeezed her arms around George's chest and gazed across into his eyes. "For a grouchy old human, you aren't too bad, Sergeant," she whispered and broke into a smile.

*

Snimel, Wunep and Bikut had been in elevators before but the humans were quite nervous. Andrea, Clay, Commander Evans and two DPF officers were pale as the strange metal room shot them upwards in the centre of the mountain. This was another top-secret legacy left by their ancestors and was entered from the control room from where the vacuum bomb had been detonated.

The explosion had gone off exactly on schedule but all they had noticed was a violent twenty-second jolt, objects had crashed to the floor and several people fell over. But that was it! There was no noise or aftershock.

The monitor flashed, *Weapon detonated. Please remain out of contaminated area for fifty hours. Unstable landforms may remain dangerous to walk on after that period of time. Proceed with caution.*

The elevator stopped and the door slid open to reveal a far mountain covered in snow. Freezing air rushed in.

"Well, let's go," Commander Evans grunted. "You can see the damaged area on the other side of that rocky outcrop. This was his second trip up as he had refused to allow the proctor to use the strange lifting device until his engineers had checked it out.

They had moved only three steps when the commander stopped and held his arms out. "Get back!" he hissed.

They all, though, saw the silver flying object hovering only metres above the plateau. Everyone crouched behind a patch of tussock but their eyes were riveted to the alien craft. Evans snapped orders and two armed officers slid off, one in each direction.

"We have nothing like that," Bikut whispered to the proctor. "It must be Pulgibrian."

"Or perhaps more machinery of our ancestors," Andrea replied. "Wouldn't an enemy craft be shooting? I'm sure they know we're here."

"Don't you move, Proctor," Commander Evans replied. "I'm responsible for your safety and should never have allowed your Crucnon friends and yourself up here."

"You didn't Commander," Andrea replied. "I pulled rank on you, remember?"

"Okay," snorted the commander, "but stay down."

*

Tussock immediately below shook in the downdraft of the incoming craft. There was a swishing noise, metal bits under it opened and three sets of wheels swung down. The craft stopped ten metres up and Clay could see tiny white faces in the front window. He was sure he saw a hand wave or was it two hands, two Crucnon hands or perhaps Pulgibrian claws?

My stars! Was it the enemy? He reached across and grabbed Bikut in his arms. She glanced at his worried expression and smiled. "I'm sure it is okay," she whispered. Somehow she looked proud that Clay wanted to protect her.

A metre away Wunep was holding Snimel tightly while even Toby Evans had a protecting arm around the proctor's shoulders.

The wheels touched ground bounced slightly, dust swirled and the faint hum of engines cut off. The craft was more like a circular building than a flying machine. Little round windows along the side showed yellow interior lights and, at the rear flat section lowered to the ground. It hit with a thud and the plateau became silent.

Five beings walked out and stood gazing around. One red headed woman turned and peered towards them.

"Holly," shouted Andrea and stood up. "My stars. It is you?" She stepped forward but the faltering steps turned into a run as she rushed towards her daughter.

*

"Mum!" Holly screamed when she saw the woman rushing towards her.

The humans were all grabbing and hugging then Jaddig walked over to a shy young flying female standing with two other Crucnon at the edge of the humans

146

"I know you!" she gasped and rushed forward to sweep the girl in her arms. "You're Bikut who warned us about the police. How did you get here!"

Holly also spied someone else who was well known. "Clay," she grinned. "So you made it back!"

"But only because of my friends," he laughed. "This is Wunep and Snimel. They rescued me after I blew the bridge and insisted on driving me home."

"And this strange flying craft?" Andrea gasped.

"It's an aeroplane, Mum," Holly explained. "Come inside and look. I'll introduce you to Plato." She shivered. "My stars, it's cold out here."

"Plato?" Andrea queried.

"Just a box of talking wires, Proctor." George grinned, turned to Clay and slapped him on the back. "Glad you made it, Lad," he grunted and winked at the Crucnon standing behind him. "I must say I like your friends, too. I reckon I just lost a bet with Jaddig here."

Jaddig just nodded, walked over and hugged each of her kind in turn. "You don't know how pleased I am to meet you," she said to Snimel and Wunep, "and to know you're safe, Bikut." Without warning she burst into tears, as emotions could be contained no longer.

"Oh Jaddig," Snimel responded with tears in her own eyes.

"Do you wish to establish a security field around our perimeter?" said a monotone voice when they all squeezed past *Charlie* and entered the warm cockpit.

"That's Plato," Holly explained. "Yes, Plato. Set up a force field." She turned to her mother. "A cup of coffifake, Mum?" she asked.

"Sweetheart, I'd love one," Andrea replied as she gazed at the monitors and instruments glowing around. "So our ancestors helped us, yet again?" she whispered.

"That explosion?" George asked.

"Yes Sergeant, we set it off. Our ancestors anticipated this war and had a bomb sitting there for generations just waiting until it was needed. There are others right through the mountains just waiting for our command."

"More information kept from us," Holly added. "Like the information about Jaddig, Bikut and the others."

Andrea frowned. "What about them, Holly?" she asked.

"They're half human, Mum. The original inhabitants are the Pulgibrian."

It was the proctor and commander's turn to be surprised when Holly explained how they discovered Jaddig's genetic background. Of all those present, Bikut, though, seemed the most fascinated.

"So Jaddig had more of the old admiral's genes than you, Holly?" she asked.

"Yes," Holly replied. "Old Plato here still insists on calling her Admiral Jaddig."

"So we're all related," Suzi said.

"But not too close, I hope," Clay interrupted and glanced at Bikut. Holly noticed the young-flying female almost appeared to flush.

A knock sounded on the cabin door. Two DPF officers stood there and stared directly at Commander Evans. "The valley, Sir," the front one muttered. "It's gone!"

"What do you mean…Gone!" he replied.

"There is no valley, Sir, Proctor," the second officer added. "Only a flattened hillside as smooth as a billiard table. It is frothing and steaming like molten steel."

"This, I must see," the commander retorted and turned to Andrea. "If you excuse me, Proctor…"

"Go ahead, Commander. I want to stay with my daughter and friends for a few moments," Andrea replied and smiled at Holly. "Also, I'm still waiting for my mug of coffifake."

*

CHAPTER 16

Holly coughed during the lapse in the discussion, placed a small rectangular instrument on the table, glanced at the other members of the full council. She raised a hand and caught her mother's eye.

"Proctor. may I speak?"

Andrea nodded and all eyes turned to the youngest person in the room.

"We have talked at cross purposes for almost two hours about the evacuation plans, where we should go and how we should get there." Holly stopped and gazed around the make shift council table. "All the three plans that have been tabled have risks as well as merit."

"These are dangerous times, Holly," Ron Cotterell interrupted.

Holly flashed an acknowledgment at the Inner Council lawyer and continued. "I would like to table a fourth plan."

"...But it took us two hours to work out three viable choices," someone moaned from the opposite side of the room.

Andrea glanced at the man. "You are out of order, Councillor," she said in a quiet voice. "Please hear Generation 7 Leader Jurjevics out."

"This is a computer mobile," Holly held up the instrument that was no larger than her hand. "Plato has some suggestions." Holly watched her mother glowered around the table as if she almost dared anyone to object before she began speaking. "The computer answers direct questions or requests, so please forgive my method of approach and bare with me." She pressed a button on the instrument and a green pilot light shone. "Plato, please itemize the chances of success for the three tabled motions?"

"Tabled Motion 1:- Evacuation to Base Alpha. The island has limited facilities and can only support a population of two hundred and thirty humans in comfort. There is only a forty percent chance that the base will be a viable unit after one year."

The councillors glanced at each other and three members shrugged.

"Tabled Motion 2:-Evacuation to the southern continent known by the Crucnon as Tulvar. There is a ninety three percent chance that the local cruck population will not welcome a human presence and attempt to eliminate you."

"Cruck?" Holly asked and hoped the room was listening.

They were!

"The cruck are the native species of this planet," the computer droned on. "The citizens of Pulgibr are crucks. Citizens of Vybber are Crucnon, a hybrid species seventy eight percent cruck and twenty two percent human. The word is a combination of cruck and human, first used by the scientists who transferred human D.N.A into cruck embryo..." The voice continued with technical details as stunned silence filled the room.

Suddenly, everyone began speaking at once until Andrea gave a slight tingle of a tiny bell on the table and the voices halted.

"The facts are true, Ladies and Gentlemen," she said. "I have taken the liberty of removing the secrecy classification on the details so you can all read how our ancestors endeavoured to create a more compassionate native species. The Crucnon are the result of these activities." She stared around the room again. "However, we have a more important item on the agenda at the moment. Holly could you continue, please."

"And the third motion?" Holly asked the computer.

"This is the best to date," Plato continued. "However, the empty lands to the north or extreme south of this planet have very severe winter weather conditions with a maximum growing season of four months. There is an eighty two percent chance of crop failure in the first year with a resulting food shortage."

"So what does my new motion entail?" Holly asked

"The human settlers stay here," the computer replied.

Once again the room broke into a bubble of voices, some curious, others angry. The bell tingled and Andrea raised her eyebrows. It took a few seconds before silence once again reigned.

"Explain the reasons for this choice," Holly continued.

"The new land created by the vacuum bomb is level and highly fertile. It will support vegetables, fruit, cereals and grass. If planted this spring, there will be sufficient food to feed the human population when available reserves run out. Horses are already available to work the land and, once grass is available, other animals can be procured from Crucnon farms..."

"Plato means steal them," Holly explained with a grin.

"The defence shields at Hanger Base Beta can be relocated to border this new land to deflect all intruders," the computer continued.

"Of course..." Ron Cotterell muttered. He tapped a pen on the table as he fixed his thoughtful eyes on the computer mobile.

"Citizens can live safely in the caves until new homes are built. There will be hardships and overcrowded living accommodation but the probability of success is ninety three percent."

"How should the cultivation be done?" Holly asked.

"Every family should be allocated land that will become the family's private property after three years if they produce enough food to feed themselves and have at least a ten percent surplus to distribute to other settlers."

"Why not just give families the land?"

"There has to be an incentive. Humans vary in attitude, work habits and abilities. Some will make a success of this, others will not. Safeguards will need to be incorporated for elderly, families with many children or families with illnesses. The conditions must be fair but firm."

"Thank you, Plato. Sign Off," Holly concluded

The computer's pilot light went out and she held up a pile of documents. "The details of everything the computer reported is here, Ladies and Gentlemen." She waited a moment for her words to sink in. "One hundred and forty pages of notes. I put forward the motion that we all read this document thoroughly and this council makes a decision on the settler's future at our next meeting."

"I second that," Ron grinned at her.

The vote in favour was unanimous but informal discussions continued far into the night as those present discussed the significance of Holly's motion and also the news that the Crucnon were a hybrid species.

As twenty five hundred hours approached, Holly felt a hand touch her. She turned to see her mother's eyes firmly fixed on her own. "You did well, Sweetheart," Andrea congratulated. "I'm sure even the old conservatives who objected to having Jaddig and the other clickers here have something to consider."

"Yeah," Holly retorted and glanced at two elderly men across the room. "They may even be discriminating against their own nephews and nieces." She chuckled. "Not that Bikut, Snimel, Wunep or Jaddig would want them as uncles, anyway".

*

The special meeting of the council began the next evening with another marathon session predicted. The news of the Crucnon's genetic relationship with the humans came to the fore when three members moved a successful motion that the Survival of Humanity Protocol be revised and amendments made so nothing else was hidden from the present and future generations.

Holly also put forward the motion that generation numbers were now unnecessary.

"After all," she commented. "Some of the Generation 6s are younger than myself, a Generation 7."

This was also passed with the amendment than everyone was to be classified as an adult from their eighteenth birthday and a senior citizen after they turned seventy.

"Now, the vote on which of the four tabled motions on the settler's future should be accepted. If necessary we shall have a run off until we obtain an absolute majority. I take it you have all read Holly's notes?" The proctor glanced around the hushed table. "Does anyone wish to make a statement before we vote?"

Ron raised a finger and stood up. "I just wish to thank our Generation 7..." He stopped ... "Sorry, our Young Adults and Children's Representative for the hours of work she put into this fine document." He held it up. "I think every aspect was covered with the risks as well as the advantages of staying here all listed and compared with our other choices. I know I personally spent most of today comparing this option with the other three. Thank you, Holly."

He sat down while the council applauded while Holly felt her cheeks grow hot in embarrassment.

The vote to stay in the inner caves and farm the plateau was won by a clear majority in the first round. Nobody voted against it but two abstentions were recorded from the old conservatives who were now classified as Senior Citizens. Perhaps it was a matter of pride, Holly thought. The two had both voted against removing the generation numbers and the revising of the Survival of Humanity Protocol so their abstentions were progress. She shrugged and wondered what she would be like when she was their age.

"Thank you," Proctor Jurjevics said. She glanced at her watch. " That took less time than I thought. Unless there is any further business, I declare the meeting closed at twenty hundred and ten hours."

*

The attack came two weeks later but the Pulgibrians had left it too late. Like the Crucnon at Hanger Base Beta, the flying females found their explosives slide off the invisible force field and the gigantic wooden towers rolled up against the vertical cliffs at each end of the new plateau burst into flames when they touched the summit. Attempts to descend onto the plateau from the two mountains that contained it also proved futile when the enemy were rendered unconscious as soon as they neared the plateau.

After hundreds of cruck bodies littered the base of the cliffs, the enemy withdrew and bypassed the humans. After a lull of another week a second Pulgibrian army moved into the first valley to attack the Crucnon who had consolidated their hold in the area.

Brutal fighting took place with neither species prepared to compromise. However, through sheer weight of numbers, the Vybber army was forced across the New Columbia River back into their original homeland.

Except for the inner caves and the plateau, New Washington was in cruck hands and their third army opened a new front into Vybber from the eastern mountains south of the river. Vybber cities were being continuously fire bombed by hundreds of flying females.

Meanwhile in The Haven, as the new plateau became known, horse drawn ploughs and half a dozen mechanical tractors cultivated the land. The tractors, another type of vehicle unknown to the humans, were a suggestion of Wunep and a daring night-time raid in the FanWarrior had succeeded in stealing the tractors from unsuspecting Crucnon farmers.

*

It was mid-morning the next Monday morning when Holly and Clay drove their four Crucnon friends along Highway 1, the road that split The Haven down the centre. They turned into Broadway Avenue, a smaller side road and pulled to a stop by a line of small white posts painted with lot numbers. Holly unrolled a map and grinned at Clay.

"Lot 162 is yours, Clay. As you have no family you are allocated a half sized plot."

Clay frowned for a second. "That sounds fair, Holly," he said and attempted to hide his disappointment.

"Lot 162.5 is yours Bikut," Holly added with only a trace of a smile and continued on before anyone could interrupt. "Lot 163 belongs to Snimel and Wunep, if they wish to run it as a family and I shall share 164 with Jaddig. After all she is a distant cousin."

The four Crucnon looked at Holly but she kept her expression serious.

"Holly!" Snimel grinned excitedly at her. "You mean it, don't you?"

"There are the usual conditions. It becomes yours in three years if you can produce a ten percent surplus," Holly replied.

"But we aren't humans!" Jaddig interrupted with her face folded in a frown. "Won't there be objections?"

"All citizens of New Washington are entitled to an allocation. There is nothing in the regulations stating you have to be human to be a citizen of our state."

"And who drew up the regulations," Wunep asked. "You, I suppose."

"No," Holly replied. "Mum did! We also have land in reserve for any other Crucnon who may seek political asylum in our country."

Snimel's eyes glowed and she in turn hugged Wunep while Clay hugged Bikut and Holly together. "Bikut and I will have the best garden in the road," he cackled. "Won't we, Bikut?"

The Crucnon girl grinned. "Now I'm well, I can learn how to plant crops, can't I?"

"You can," replied Jaddig. "I must say you look smart in your new outfit, Bikut."

"And with no wings." The younger clicker girl smiled. "It's so great to be just myself again." She cast as strange look at Holly." Why did you allocate me half of Clay's lot?"

Holly laughed. "I thought you would like it that way but if you'd rather I..."

"...No," Bikut replied. She glanced at Clay who nodded. "It's exactly what we would have asked for. Thank you, Holly."

She grabbed Clay's hand and led him across to their allotment. The tall sergeant towered above the slight clicker girl but they seemed to blend together as her chattering face kept glancing up at him. Wunep smiled, tucked his arms around Snimel and they also went to inspect the hard shell of ground that was their allocation. They knew, though, that beneath the thin crust was a thick loam of soft soil just waiting for vegetation.

"Well cuz," Holly chuckled at Jaddig and gave her an affectionate dig in the ribs. "What say we get the jump on the others and start using *Charlie* to plough our land? I just happened to throw one of those new mechanical ploughs in the back."

"Did you, now?" Jaddig smiled. "A double one, I hope."

"It is," Holly answered. "One of the new ones we nicked when we stole the tractors."

The two opened the back of *Charlie*, placed a plank to the ground and manoeuvred the heavy implement down.

*

All over The Haven, hundreds of humans were also working, the tractors chugged away and a nearby farmer was shouting instructions at his horse that pulled a plough along his half-ploughed allotment. To the east and west, the higher altitudes of the mountains were still covered in snow while, north and south, the land stopped at a boundary fence, beyond which was nothing but blue sky. It was a glorious spring day and almost too hot to be working the fields but nobody had time to let a little heat hinder them. Rain was predicted and they wanted their crops to be in as soon as possible.

Gradually the human settlers settled into a routine. The Pulgibrian now ignored them but were firmly established throughout what was once

New Washington< However, they had not succeeded in crossing the New Columbia into Vybber itself. Patrols in the FanWarrior showed that battles were still continuing on the Vybber eastern border and the Crucnon army had held their enemy off in two mountain passes. If these were breached the plains of Vybber and heavily populated areas were vulnerable and signs of desperate battles were evident.

The spring rains arrived and within days The Haven was a sea of growth with most gardens flourishing and grasses beginning to green the outer edges of the plateau and the roadsides. Several buildings dotted the area and a small village called Zoflum, a Crucnon word meaning hope for the future, began to rise at the base of a new road that wound down from the smaller top plateau where the elevator entrance was situated.

Underground, the Catacombs were being explored. The outer caves were gone but a few more remote tunnels threaded their way around the bombed area and one other elevator was discovered. This rose up a mountainside to a plateau overlooking the deserted remains of New Seattle and gave the DPF an excellent observation post. Other connecting tunnels that could be used by the enemy were blown so human territory became close to being impregnable.

*

Holly grinned nervously at Jaddig, Bikut, Suzi, Clay and Graham, the other passengers aboard the FanWarrior, as they flew across the ocean that spread, horizon to horizon below without even a speck of land in sight. Snimel and Wunep had agreed to stay behind to look after all their properties but the other two Crucnon were keen to accompany their friends on the expedition to the mysterious Base Alpha, three hours flying time from home.

"Most of Delpe is covered in ocean," Jaddig explained to Holly as they studied the deep blue scene below. "There are two other major continents and thousands of smaller islands but little is known about the inhabitants except that are crucks and not Crucnon." She gave Holly a small frown. "It's strange to realize we're as alien to this planet as you are."

"I believe after all this time we all have the right to call Delpe our home," Holly replied, "Who knows what this Earth is like, anyhow? We are forgotten, otherwise contact would have been made with us generations ago. I'm only agreed to make this trip because Mum and the council asked us to check this base out. Personally, I am beginning to lose faith in the value of finding other humans."

"But we need to do something," Graham added. "Even The Haven is only a temporary arrangement. I wouldn't want another seven generations

155

to be stuck on that small piece of land surrounded by enemy wanting to kill our species off."

"I know." Holly shrugged and gazed out at the ocean below. "To think, our ancestors flew light years across space with their lives depending on their machines. If anything went wrong now..."

"FanWarrior aircraft have a ninety nine point three four percent efficiency ranking," Plato cut into the conversation. "Of the three thousand four hundred and fifteen built on Planet Earth at the time of my memory file, only one had crashed causing a loss of life while sixteen others had minor problems that necessitated returning to the point of departure."

"Thanks, Plato, I am reassured," Holly answered and returned to her original conversation. "It's just that I don't think I want to leave my home and travel across a void to a place that probably want us even less than the crucks do."

"What about us?" Jaddig replied in a soft voice.

Holly flushed. "I'm sorry, Jaddig. I didn't mean to be so self-centred."

"You aren't. Here, have a cup of coffifake," Bikut cut into the conversation, smiled and handed a steaming mug across to her.

Bikut had fussed around the tiny kitchen unit at the back of the cabin for the last fifteen minutes and had made a pile of sandwiches. Like Jaddig, she was relaxed and confident while the humans appeared as nervous as Holly felt.

Bikut turned and noticed Clay's white face. "Are you sure you're a warm blooded creature?" she teased and held a plate out. "Here, have a sandwich."

"Thanks," Clay chuckled and reached for one. "I'm glad the proctor let you and Jaddig come."

"Yeah," Bikut laughed. "I don't know how you humans managed before we turned up to look after you."

They both stopped and listened as Plato's voice once again filled the cabin. "Estimated time of arrival at Alpha Base is eighteen minutes. Weather conditions are fine with no wind, a ten percent cloud cover and a ground temperature of twenty eight degrees Celsius. The island will appear on the southern horizon in three minutes."

*

"Go low and circle the island," Holly ordered when a minute speck appeared right on cue in the middle of two worlds of blue; the dark blue ocean below and the lighter blue sky above.

As they flew closer they could see sheer, almost orange cliffs towering above pounding waves that crashed relentlessly between jagged rocks. The island was ellipse shaped, about two kilometres long with a volcanic peak on the northern end that sloped down to rolling hills and a deep saucer shaped valley centred on a small lake. On the southern side, water from the lake crashed down a narrow waterfall into a stream. This, in turn, ran through a narrow gorge that opened out into a small bay of white sand forty or fifty metres below the plateau. This small triangle of beach was the only break in the vertical cliffs that surrounded the island.

"It's beautiful," Bikut gasped.

"But where do we land?" a more pragmatic Graham replied. "The jungle looks impregnable and I doubt if there is access inland from that tiny beach."

"And where is the base?" Holly added.

"If you wish to land the base doors need to be opened," Plato announced. "I can access them, if it is required."

"Where are they?" Clay asked. "Won't the jungle have grown over them?" He squinted at the lush growth of strange tropical plants as the FanWarrior slowed, the wing panels slid back out and the propellers kicked into action.

"The main space shuttle doors will need minor repairs to clear foliage from the access intakes," Plato reported, "The aircraft bay is functional and we can land with a ninety two percent safety margin."

"Open the Alpha Base doors and land," Holly ordered.

The FanWarrior slowed to a hover directly above the lake and turned a hundred and eighty degrees. Like the beach, a narrow strip of white sand surrounded the lake before the jungle encroached. They descended until another cliff on the mountain side of the lake appeared. This was minute compared with the cliffs that edged the island and partly covered with scrubs and creeper so only a small fraction showed exposed orange rock.

Without further instructions, the aircraft flew lower until it was mere metres above the lake before it began to fly directly at the cliff face. Holly paled and gripped her seat but waited. They were less than twenty metres from the cliff when the Fan Warrior stopped so quickly that everyone was slung forward in their seat belts. The aeroplane hovered above the lake below. Downdraft from the propellers sent choppy waves radiating out across the water and spray up towards them as the FanWarrior wobbled on swaying wings.

"The mechanism has to be lubricated," Plato reported. "There will be a ten minute delay."

"Look!" gasped Jaddig as a flock of white and black birds rose from the lake surface and flapped away from them. She grinned. "I bet they haven't had their home disturbed for generations."

Everyone aboard stared, fascinated at the view. The beach glistened in the sunshine but deep shadows and thick foliage on the almost vertical hillsides made them look dank and uninviting. Even the volcanic peak was jungle covered.

"Look!" Graham poked Holly on the arm and pointed to the very top pinnacle that was as sharp as a needle with a strange bowl on the top. "It's man made."

"The mountain?" Holly replied.

"No the point at the top is made of metal. It's some sort of tower."

"You are correct," Plato cut in. "That is the satellite transmission and receiving dish. The dark green colour is camouflage. From a higher altitude it blends in with the natural surroundings."

"It's moving," Suzi spoke for the first time.

It was. As they watched, the bowl at the top began to spin slowly.

"The internal generator and support equipment has been switched on," Plato announced. "Internal electricity supply is operating and equipment is at a sixty one percent efficiency rating. Self repairs will raise this to ninety percent within twelve hours."

"Thanks." Holly grinned. She was becoming used to the percentage efficiency reports by now. No doubt if she required it, Plato would diagnose her own health on the same scale.

"Well here goes," Clay spoke up as the engines increased power and the FanWarrior moved forward.

In front of the slow moving aircraft a black semicircle appeared in the cliff face and increased in size as the entire surface dropped away to expose a curved roofed opening. The floor was level and dark interior flooded into harsh white light as the FanWarrior flew in. The undercarriage swung down and tyres touched a white concrete concourse. No sooner had this happened, when the circular door behind slid up and the view of the outside disappeared.

"Welcome to Base Alpha," an entirely different voice filled the aircraft and a monitor showed the vision of an elderly man dressed in a civilian clothes smiling at them. "I am Admiral Leonard Jurjevics. It is Saturday, the 23rd November 2127, True Time and we have been stranded on this planet for twenty-nine years." He gave almost a sad grin. "I won't convert to Earth time as I guess it will little more than an academic interest to you, one of our ancestors. We are closing this base down and staying on the mainland so I don't visualize anybody returning until the computers release information of our position.

If they do their duty, by the time this message is viewed, Inter-galatical Star Ship 7's fuel supply will have been replenished and a light speed signal could well be on its way back from Earth." He shrugged. "Who knows, they may have even have post light speed communication by your time."

Holly glanced at her companions and saw them all staring fascinated at the screen as her ancestor continued to talk.

"No doubt you are at present sitting watching this video in one of our FanWarriors after arriving on our landing pad. Our scientists have managed to speed up the replenishing of the Star Ship's fuel cells so if the date is beyond 2170, True Time, there will be sufficient anti-matter for a return journey to be made to Earth. The computers will give you full details in due course." He smiled again. "Meanwhile, you'll find the living accommodation here will cater for a hundred people and there is food and supplies in Alpha Base to last a month. Just call my name if you wish to talk. I have programmed the computers to respond in my voice."

He stopped and the viewers saw the admiral's shaky hand reach for a console. However, almost as an afterthought, compassionate blue eyes stared directly at the screen. "If, by any chance, you, Dear Ancestor have four arms and an insect rather than mammal metabolism, please forgive this old man. I tried to stop the experiments but was out voted by my children. May destiny bless you all and have a safe journey back home."

"He knew!" Jaddig gasped as the screen returned to normal monitoring mode.

Holly stared at her and onto Bikut's haunted eyes.

"It appears so," Clay whispered and wrapped his arms around Bikut. "But he never knew the wonderful grandchildren to the seventh generation, that his genes would produce."

"I agree," Graham added and slung an arm around Holly's shoulders. She smiled and turned up to kiss his lips.

Somehow, though, the view of the old man's blue eyes staring out made them all melancholy.

"I wonder what he was thinking when he recorded that message," Suzi whispered. "If I remember my dates correctly, he died only a few weeks later."

"We shall never know," Jaddig replied. "It's a pity, though, that after all these years there couldn't be peace in our world. I'm sure that's what Admiral Jurjevics would have wanted.

Silence filled the cockpit as the engines cut. There was a slight bump as the rear ramp hit the concrete floor. The crew of humans and Crucnon walked out together to see what hope for the future their ancestors had left them.

*

CHAPTER 17

Cool air tickled Holly's nose as she walked away from under the FanWarrior's tail and surveyed the area around. They were in an artificial cave with a curved white ceiling lit by dozens of white lights. Like Hanger Beta, the whole hanger was clean and dust free with only the faint hum of an air conditioning unit to interrupt the silence. Three very ordinary looking metal doors were to the left but it was the scene at the back of the hanger that attracted Holly's attention.

Parked wing tip to wing tip so they stretched right across the cave were two FanWarriors, identical to their craft except that their condition was quite different.

"Someone's been here," Clay spoke in a hushed voice.

The right hand FanWarrior was pristine, almost as if it had only rolled out of the factory, and was completely covered in a white coating of a plastic sealing like a colossal bag while the windscreen and windows had light grey covers over them. As well, stoppers were fitted in all the movable tail and wing sections. This craft was sitting on a metal frame so the deflated tyres were suspended a few centimetres above the tarmac. A bright yellow hose connected a valve on the underside of the fuselage to a similar one in the hanger floor while a smaller black wire ran from the hanger ceiling point to connect with a socket above the aircraft's windscreen. Small interior lights could be seen shining from behind the window seals.

It was the other FanWarrior, though, that fascinated Holly and her friends. Attempts by the automatic cleaning equipment to clean the craft had been partially successful but oil stains and dark blemishes covered the underside, the tyres were flat and one undercarriage had crumbled so the FanWarrior slumped over like a wounded bird.

"Hell!" Jaddig exclaimed as they walked closer. "It's been shot at."

In a diagonal line across in fuselage were twenty or thirty neat holes, each a few millimetres in diameter. Clay and Graham ducked down and examined the underside of the craft while Holly grimaced and also crouched down to examine the underside. Dozens of similar holes peppered the fuselage and wings. The left wing covering had not closed and the propeller stood with the eight blades bent and buckled. Grime had filled many of the joints and black oil stained the concrete floor beneath the wing.

"What happened?" Holly gasped after she crawled back out and straightened up.

"I'd say our army, or perhaps the crucks, tried to shot this FanWarrior down," Jaddig said. "There are bullet holes all over it. By the angle, I'd say one machine gun swept the side as it was parked on the ground and it was fired at from underneath as it took off or flew over."

"Yeah!" Graham muttered. "That one propeller was hit and the engine put out of action, I'd say."

Suzi stared at the damage. "Whoever flew it, made it here, though. I wonder how long ago it was."

They had all reached the rear of the craft to find the ramp was down. The inside was musty and dark with everything crisscrossed with cobwebs.

"No cleaning gear came in here," Clay snorted as he brushed through the cobwebs.

The cargo area was empty and the cockpit lifeless. Like the cargo bay it was covered in cobwebs, dust and grime. Everything stunk of stale air. No computer lit up and there were no responses when buttons or switches were moved. This FanWarrior was just a dead hulk that could tell them nothing.

"Admiral Jurjevics!" Holly called when they stepped back into the hanger.

A voice responded. "I have been programmed to respond to the name Len," the old man's voice filled the air. "Can I be of assistance, Holly?"

"What happened to this damaged FanWarrior?"

"Lieutenant Gordon Dixon flew it in with his crew and passengers. Do you wish a report on their medical condition?"

"Not now," Holly frowned at her friends. "How many passengers were in the Fan Warrior when it landed?"

"Five crew members, one hundred and four passengers and five deceased."

"What!" gasped Suzi. "When was this?"

"At 0300 hours on the 30th of February 2168."

"Over eighty years ago," Clay whistled. "No wonder the old plane is a bit creaky at the joints."

"And when did Dixon leave?" Jaddig questioned.

" At 0700 hours on 8th of March 2168."

"We want a full report," Holly added. Her lips were pursed and eyes curious.

As they expected, the full report that followed was filled with technical details and lists of other data. However, other information of interest to the group filtered through. It appeared three other passengers died from wounds and a hundred and six left together on that March morning. The report continued telling how the base was sealed and maintained afterwards."

"Thank you," Holly interrupted. "Has the base been visited since that date."

"Negative," Len replied. "Lieutenant Gordon Dixon is over due."

"So they were expected back?" Suzi interjected.

"That was their plan. I suggest you consult the flight program. Security rankings have to be checked before I can divulge this information."

"Thank you Len. What do we need to do next?" Holly continued.

"Please proceed to Console Room 2 where identification hand prints will be necessary before personnel can enter Restricted Zone 1."

*

The console room was similar to those in Hanger Base Beta and the usual classifications were issued, once again with Jaddig the only one allowed to continue. As before, she reprogrammed the computer to respond to all those present. Another amusing point was that the computer gave Bikut the same ranking as Holly, one higher than Clay's.

"Well Sergeant Farrell," she teased. "Don't you think you'd better start saluting your superiors."

"No, you're the one in trouble." Clay grinned. "Officers should not fraternize with non commissioned ranks. You'd better stay away from me." As if he realized what he'd said he suddenly flushed a bright red while Bikut bit on her lip and glanced away. It was as if in their jest, inner feelings had been exposed.

Holly, who had noticed both reactions, stepped across, put an arm around the young Crucnon's shoulders and discretely guided her out the door into the main hanger.

"You know," she said in a low voice so the others couldn't hear. "I sometimes go all tingly inside when Graham comes near me but it is perfectly natural."

"But I'm a clicker," Bikut replied bitterly. "I didn't ask to be one, but I am. Clay is human."

"And I'm a human female with ghastly red hair," Holly added. "I did not choose that, either. We are what we are, Bikut. What we do with ourselves is more important. Think of yourself as a woman and be proud." She fixed her eyes on her friend. "We're proud of you, you know."

"But what about Clay?"

"He's more than just proud, Bikut. Just look at his eyes and you'll see the love there."

162

"Love!" Tears appeared in the corner of Bikut's eyes. "Oh Holly, I'm so muddled up inside. What can I do?"

"Nothing," Holly smiled. "Just let everything take its own course and you have our blessing."

"You do," said another female voice. The pair turned to see both Suzi and Jaddig standing there smiling. It was Suzi who had spoken but Jaddig's expression reflected her own approval.

*

Inside the console room, Clay frowned at Graham and shrugged. "I stuffed that lot up, didn't I?"

"Because you're attracted to Bikut?" Graham replied in a blunt voice.

"I guess," Clay muttered. "Now, if she had a curvy figure and long red hair like Holly but..." He kicked out at a small pebble lying on the concrete floor. "Bloody hell, I don't know."

"If we survive the next few weeks, we will all need all the friendship and love we can get Clay. Why care about anyone else back home? There will always be the old bigots like Malone Davidson but what the hell about them?"

"Yeah," Clay grinned. "What the hell!"

He glanced up as the women walked back in and saw Bikut's moist eyes. As she brushed past him he reached out, swung her around and deposited a kiss on her tiny lips. The others suddenly found the instruments on the console needed their attention as Bikut stiffened in his arms before her eyes met his.

"Clay," she whispered. "I didn't mean for this to happen."

"So, what the hell." Clay took a massive handkerchief out of his pocket and handed it to her. "Here, wipe your eyes," he said softly and kissed her again.

This time she responded. Six arms, four petite ones and two, thick and muscular, wrapped around each other and held on so tightly, Clay could feel her thumping heart against his.

"Come on." he whispered a moment later. "Let's go and find our space shuttle."

*

Another semicircular door, large enough to drive a vehicle through, slid open just outside the console room to reveal a long white corridor that disappeared into the mountain. The floor was carpeted and a row of lights stopped in blackness fifty metres ahead. However, as the six moved forward together, more lights switched on and those behind went out. The corridor curved so the hanger door soon disappeared behind. They continued on, always curving right in a continuous oasis of light until, ten minutes later, they came to another door.

It slid open, natural sunlight shone on them and hot tropical air engulfed then.

Holly found Graham's hand in hers as she walked out into a circular concrete enclosure so large it appeared to cover the whole interior of the volcano. Above was the sky and on one side, high above them, she saw the transmission tower noticed when they flew in. In front were six towering frames built in a circle and linked by layer after layer of catwalks, iron ladders and glass-domed elevators.

Four equally large cranes were standing, gaunt and silent with their arms stretched outwards like mechanical monsters ready to reach down to snap up the minute humans and clickers below. The immense area, as big as the interior of an Olympic stadium was filled with equipment and debris, including a small orange tractor with a trailer attached.

But that was all. There was no shuttle or spacecraft!

*

"Oh hell! " Graham sighed and glanced down at Holly.

"Well," she replied with a philosophical shrug. "That's one decision we don't have to make."

"So the passengers in that wrecked FanWarrior used the space shuttle?" Jaddig added. "What now?"

"Ask the computer what happened," suggested Clay. In a strange way he looked relieved as he looked down at Bikut. She met his eyes and smiled.

The group walked around the space ship landing concourse, or whatever it was called, until they came to another control room. Inside, after the usual identifications, Len confirmed their theory that the shuttle had left the base on 8th of March 2168 with the one hundred and three other passengers, joined up with Inter-galatical Star Ship 7 in a stationery orbit above Delpe and departed for Planet Earth.

"What news have you received of their journey?" Holly questioned.

Len replied. "Their journey was successful. News of their arrival was received on 21 November 2245, True Time, at 1614 hours. Inter-galatical Star Ship 7 was decommissioned later that year and replaced by Inter-galatical Star Ship 43."

"They made a few," Clay grunted.

"And the passengers on Star Ship 7?"

Fifty nine were integrated into Earth society."

164

"Fifty nine!" Holly reiterated. "Out of a hundred and four?"

"Three became deceased during the journey and forty two found the social conditions on Earth unacceptable."

Jaddig gave Bikut a tiny frown and added. "Were they all human?"

"No."

"Expand your answer," Holly snapped.

"Out of the forty two, forty were Crucnon and two, human. There were eighteen female Crucnon, sixteen males…

"That doesn't add up," Graham interrupted.

"… Six flying females, fifteen female and eight male humans. Generation 4 humans were…"

"That's all we require on that answer," Jaddig interrupted, "and the ones who stayed on Earth?"

"They were all human."

"So it appears humans are as intolerant with other species as the crucks in this planet were," Clay snorted.

"Okay," Holly whispered and questioned the computer again. " Where are these Crucnon and humans now?"

"Travelling to Delpe aboard Inter-galatical Starship 43."

"In relation to our present time, when will it arrive?" Graham put in.

"At present speed, it will arrive in fifty six years, two months and six days. The time has been rounded for your convenience."

"Another problem solved," Holly shrugged. "If I went on a similar ship I'd be about eighty when I got here."

"Not necessarily," interrupted Suzi and spoke to the computer for the first time. "Tell us, Len," she said in her quiet voice. "How can the journey time be shortened?"

"Details need to be programmed in and transmitted to Inter-galatical Star Ship 43."

A small gleam appeared in Suzi's eye. "What is the shortest possible arrival time?"

"Fifty three hours from this moment."

"What!" gasped Holly again.

Suzi grinned at Holly and continued. "Explain please."

"At post light speed, time is also altered so, in theory the starship can arrive any time in the past, present or future. In practice, though, the starship needs to reduce to sub-light speed and go into orbit. The live creatures aboard have to be brought out of suspended animation and transferred to a landing shuttlecraft, hence the fifty-three hours I quoted. We do not recommend landings before this moment for ethical and social reasons "

"How do we alter the arrival time?" Suzi asked.

"Your two superior offers, Jaddig and Holly need to simultaneously program the arrival co-ordinances in. This is a security protocol built into my programming."

"And can the officers on Inter-galatical Star Ship 43 override our command?" Suzi added.

"Once the craft is in orbit above our planet, they have can reprogram the landing shuttle. However, safety programming will not allow the shuttle to land anywhere except at this facility."

"So what can they do?" Graham added.

"They can remain in orbit but once awakened, their food supplies run out in twenty three days and oxygen supply in fifty six."

Suzi spoke again. "Leave the starship in its present position until we get back to you. That is all for now." She turned to the others. "This is a whole new scenario. Personally, I believe we should return home and discuss it with the council. There are important decisions to be made."

The computer everyone thought had shut down sprang to life. "We have holographic contact with New Washington," it said. "You can talk to the proctor and commander without leaving this room."

*

Andrea was in her outdoor office in Zoflum when suddenly Holly appeared at the table.

"Hi Mum," she said in a quiet voice.

The Proctor gasped in fright. "Holly! When did you arrive? I never heard the FanWarrior."

"I'm not here, Mum." Holly grinned. "This is an electronic holograph. Actually we are all in the control room at Base Alpha. I see you on a screen in front of me."

"More of our ancestor's electronics, no doubt," Andrea retorted. "We are going to get every scientific record and other item opened for scrutiny, warts and all. To think generations of us lived..." She grinned, "but go on, Sweetheart. What have you discovered?"

"Lots Mum," Holly replied. With help of the others and also by sending views of the space station back as a shimmering three dimensional vision in mid air across the back wall of Andrea's office, everything was communicated back home.

"Everything has been recorded in the console room of the inner cave," Holly added. "You can replay it to the commander or anyone else you wish once you have been identified." She grinned. "If the computer doesn't recognize you, just ask Snimel or Wunep to access it for you."

"I'll need to discuss this with the others, of course," Andrea replied, "In the meantime I suggest we should leave their arrival until we get more personnel to you on the island. Can you bring the FanWarrior back?"

"Probably two of them, Mum," Holly answered. "How about tomorrow around midday?"

"That'll be fine, Sweetheart," Andrea replied. In spite of herself she jumped when Holly's vision just vanished in thin air.

*

At eleven hundred and forty hours, the human settlers rubbed their eyes in amazement as two FanWarriors landed on the newly created field on the outskirts of Zoflum. Holly and Graham ambled down the back ramp of one while Clay and Bikut made a more sedate exit from the other.

"We brought back two tractors, three crates of emergency rations, oodles of electronic equipment and some more weapons," Holly told her mother and Commander Evans. "Suzi wanted to stay and research the computer on the island and Jaddig offered to stay with her." She grinned at the pair, "Come and look at FanWarrior 2. It was sealed in protection plastic and is brand new."

However, Andrea hardly had time to welcome everyone back when the old faithful *Charlie* came roaring along the dirt road at the edge of the landing area. Clouds of fine dust bellowed into the air as the vehicle turned and drove up to them. It braked, the passenger's door flung open, Snimel brushed past a small group of bowmen and came running up to the new arrivals.

Her clothes were covered in dust and hands still dirty from working their garden. "Did you see them on the way in, Holly?" she gasped with her blue eyes filled with concern.

"No, we were concentrating on the landing. What is it, Snimel?" Holly replied with a frown.

"We saw a distress flare down in the other valley?" Snimel gasped and her eyes gazed at Holly. "You have to help. They'll be massacred."

Wunep had now come up and continued the conversation. "We went to the edge of The Haven just inside the warning fence in front of the force field. You know the area where you can see right down the first valley?"

Holly nodded and let Wunep continue. "There are three vehicles like *Charlie* down there but they are stalled behind some sort of fixture across the road."

"They're Crucnon. We could see their faces through the binoculars I had," Snimel panted with her eyes still wide with worry, "They are surrounded by crucks. We saw flashes. We think the vehicles were caught in an ambush."

"But why would Crucnon be there?" Commander Evans asked. "They were driven back across the river weeks ago."

"Can't you see!" Snimel retorted desperately. "They must have been trying to get here. There is no other reason. But hurry. They can't last long. Please!" she pleaded and grabbed Holly's arm.

"Take a FanWarrior," Andrea nodded at her daughter. "Snimel could be right."

"Come on," Holly glanced at Graham. "You two as well," she added to the two Crucnon and ran back to FanWarrior 2.

Within two minutes the huge craft was ready to lift off, Toby Evans signalled for the overhead force field to be deactivated and the aircraft accelerated into the air.

"Over there!" Snimel cried and pointed to where the road, wide and muddy after constant use of the two invading armies wound through the forest below.

"She's right," Holly grabbed Graham's sleeve but he'd already seen the cloud of black smoke bellowing into the air. On closer inspection he saw three military vehicles stopped at a bend. The front one was burning fiercely.

"Can you protect the Crucnon in the vehicles, Zeta?" Holly asked.

"Yes," the computer replied and went silent.

"Well do it!" Holly snapped.

"Set the weapon power, please."

Holly remembered the weapons George had at Beta Hanger. "Power four," she said in a calmer voice. "I want the three vehicles protected so we can rescue the passengers."

"Do you wish to activate automatic fire and control?"

"I do," Holly snapped and sat back in the pilot's seat as the engines accelerated.

A shimmering glow encircled the FanWarrior and a bank of lights glowed. The words, *Defence Shield Activated* appeared on a monitor as they moved directly above the three vehicles. Suddenly, without warning they dropped straight down towards the scene. Within seconds, the matchbox sized combos were mere metres below. The FanWarrior hovered above the scene with the downdraft flattening the smoke and flames of the burning vehicle. A gap in the smoke appeared and faces, white were fear could be seen looking up at them from a ditch to their left

Graham snorted. "Look further out!" he snapped.

Also gazing up at them were a score of the brown insect faces and, even as they watched, weapons were raised and orange flashes cut through the air. They were being fired at.

"Hurry!" Snimel gasped.

"The defence shields are holding and no damage is reported," Zeta droned out. "Have ascertained that there are sixteen live Crucnon in the ditch on the southern side of the road and four deceased ones in the burning front vehicle. The attacking force consists of thirty-four cruck infantry. Six are firing weapons at us. If you don't want the attacking force do be taken out this is the last chance to abort the operation."

"Continue!" Holly ordered.

The Fan Warrior never altered course but just hovered on its stubby wings. However, a ring of white rays fanned out around the combos and the ditch. There was a whoosh and red laser beams shot out beyond the white ones. They pulsed like dozens of tiny rockets and the ground; trees and enemy just disappeared in a cloud of brown dust. The fire of devastation continued for less than two minutes but that was enough. Except for the protected oasis in the middle, a two hundred metre circle heat waves vibrating through a hole of bellowing smoke. The ground erupted and buffeted the aircraft with sand that hit an invisible wall several metres outside the windscreen. Nothing beneath that firepower would survive!

"Operation successful," the computer reported a moment later. "All weapons deactivated."

Snimel clasped a window ledge with her hands and squinted through the smoke. "Can we pick them up?" she asked.

"Recommend landing in three minutes," Zeta reported.

"They're safe," Wunep tapped Snimel on the shoulder and pointed. Three of the Crucnon in the ditch were waving at them.

The FanWarrior rotated slowly so the tail was facing the third vehicle and landed with a slight bump on the smoking road.

"Come on," Snimel grabbed Wunep's arm. "Let's get to the ramp."

"Do you mind?" Wunep glanced at Holly and she gave a brief nod of approval.

The two Crucnon squeezed past the crates and one tractor still in the cargo bay to wait for the ramp to lower. Hot air, clouds of brown dust and the stench off burnt wood and chemicals blew in as the gap in the cargo bay widened but as soon as the ramp hit the ground Snimel held a handkerchief to her nose and rushed forward.

"Over here!" she screamed in her home language. "You will be safe with us. We're Crucnon!"

Two dirty-faced clickers appeared out of the dust with apprehensive looks and rifles held ready to fire.

"You won't need the guns," Wunep snapped. "We're friends here!"

The two males stared at Snimel and Wunep and broke into a smile. "Crucnon!" one gasped. "But how?"

At that moment Holly and Graham appeared from around a crate and the clickers shrank back and raised their weapons.

"The humans are our friends," Snimel shouted. "Come on. Get everyone in here."

The clicker in the uniform of a lieutenant studied Snimel for a second, turned and fixed his eyes on Holly and Graham, over to Wunep then stepped forward with arms stretched wide.

"Lieutenant Sirrat Karotor," he said and embraced Wunep in the traditional Crucnon greeting. "This is Sergeant Genowo Cnolyr. We are from the fifth infantry battalion..." He hesitated, "...At least we were."

"Were?" Snimel asked.

"Actually we're Cell 14 of the Blue Watch," he confessed.

"The underground movement," Holly replied. "And were you trying to reach our lines?"

"Yes," replied Lieutenant Karotor "We have wounded with gunshot wounds."

"Well get them in," Graham retorted. "I don't imagine the crucks will be too far away."

Sergeant Cnolyr saw Karotor's slight nod and disappeared into the dust. A moment later a line of clickers walked or staggered forward. Two needed support from their companions while one was carried by the sergeant. All looked at Snimel and Wunep with appreciative eyes that turned apprehensive at the sight of the humans,

"Those who can walk, make your way forward past this crate," Holly said in accented Crucnon. "The others can squeeze in here." She pointed to a space behind where the ramp swung up.

The refugees nodded and moved in. Holly had difficulty telling their sexes but noticed two flying females, both young, timid and looking just like Bikut when they'd first met.

"You'll be safe with us," she said in a kind voice. "My name is Holly Jurjevics. Welcome to our FanWarrior."

One of the flying females looked up at her with a dust stained face and searching eyes. "I'm Jynco Vockek. Thank you so much for coming. You could have just watched while we were massacred."

"That is not our way," Holly replied. "But thank Snimel here. She's the one that saw your flare."

Jynco turned, smiled at Snimel and stepped forward to clasp her arms. "Snimel!" she whispered. "We've heard about you. The government has you on a list of public traitors but your refusal to be called up and take the treatment inspired us all."

"Yeah, I'm a hardened criminal," Snimel replied with a laugh.

"I'll get us home," Graham added and slipped away through the now crowded cargo bay. The clickers moved aside and smiled at the human as he squeezed by. Several touched his arm and a young wounded teenager looked at him with tears in his eyes. Graham reached out and squeezed the youngster's shoulder. "You'll be okay now, Lad," he said.

The ramp door banged into place, engines roared and the FanWarrior began the short journey home with sixteen new citizens and the clicker population increased four folds. A few members of the Blue Watch were safe and with friends.

*

CHAPTER 18

"Jaddig, I need your help," Suzi Yu whispered. She stopped tapping on the keyboard and glanced out the control room window at the empty shuttle bay.

Jaddig, who at that moment was on an observation deck under the transmission tower where the whole island could be seen, had her attention focussed far out on the ocean where something had attracted her attention. A slim black line that, even with binoculars she could not identify was sitting on the horizon. She clicked the small communicator clipped to her blouse and grinned. The equipment available was quite amazing. "I'm at the lookout. What is it Suzi?"

"There is some historical information I have tried to access through Len but I have been denied access. It's like at Base Beta. They both spit out that a Classified 5 is necessary to proceed."

"Be right there," Jaddig chuckled and took the elevator to the main floor.

Suzi glanced up with a worried expression when she arrived and brushed aside two empty coffifake mugs and a half-eaten sandwich. "I don't know if you were told but the Human Survival Protocol was invoked on 1 January, 2166."

Jaddig nodded, pulled a chair up, sat beside the scientist and stared at the mass of data on the monitor. "Go on," she said.

"Well, I discovered there was a secrecy act invoked at the same time. All historical records were classified for eighty years."

"Which takes us to 2246, two years ago so we should be able to access it."

"That's when I ran into the classification system. Can you take over?"

"Sure." Jaddig placed her hand on the identification monitor. After being accepted by the computer, she read the neat notes Suzi had written on a clipboard and spoke "I request the declassification of historical items made before January One, Year 2166, True Time."

There was a burst of data that flooded the screen as reference numbers flashed down the screen. This continued for ten minutes before Len's voice spoke.

"All information has been declassified and is available to all those personnel of Classification 5 or above. Are there any other requests?"

"I want the classification access available to Level 4 and 5 personnel." Jaddig replied.

"This will need to be entered as a written order and authorized by using your hand print."

Jaddig clicked through the keyboard and cursed the design made for five rather than three fingers but finally entered the request, which Len approved. "There you are," Jaddig grinned. "What now?"

"I want to find out everything that was hidden from our generations," Suzi said. "I believe it will affect your people as well as mine."

"A big job," Jaddig replied.

"I know," Suzi replied in a serious voice, "but we need to know about ourselves. There are so many unanswered questions." She fixed her eyes on her friend and relaxed a little. "What were you doing?"

"Looking at the view," Jaddig said. "There was something on the horizon. What say you have a break and come up and have a look? This information has been there for eighty-two years. An other hour or so won't matter."

"Okay." Suzi sighed. "I've been here for a five hour stretch." She turned to the console. "Len, please print out any information now available after declassification on the topics I have listed."

"I shall do that, Suzi. Go and enjoy the sunshine. You need to have some lunch, too. All work and no play, you know!"

"Yes, Len," Suzi broke into a smile and stood up.

Jaddig grinned. The computer programmed with the long dead Admiral's voice almost acted human and often slipped in a comment, suggestion or even an occasional joke. "I reckon the Admiral must have been quite a character," she chuckled.

"Like you," Suzi replied, "but come on. Let's go and see what is out at sea."

*

When they arrived back at the observation post, the black line out near the horizon had increased in size and had become half a dozen objects in the water.

"They're ships," Jaddig adjusted her binoculars and swept her instrument slowly around. "Six, no seven of them. Steamships. I can see smoke from their funnels. They appear to be heading this way. Here, have a look."

Suzi knew little about ocean travel but could clearly see the low lying ships coming towards them. "Who are they?" she gasped.

173

"We used to import goods from Tulvar," Jaddig said. "Their country is in the Southern Hemisphere so has the opposite seasons to us. During winter we'd buy fresh food supplies and fruit from them. Also most of machinery and weapons were imported from Tulvar."

"But do these ships usually cruise along together?"

Jaddig shrugged. "I don't know a lot about them but the few times we visited the ocean and ships came in, there were only one or two at the most. Perhaps Len can help." She switched on the communicator and spoke to the computer.

"They are Tulvar navy vessels. Please wait while we obtain information from SS4." Len's voice came back.

"We do not understand the term SS4" Jaddig replied. "Please explain."

"Stationary Satellite 4. There are seven communication satellites in stationary orbit around Delpe so the entire surface is covered. They can track any moving object greater than three metres in size. We are in contact with SS3 and SS4 that have an overlapping view of this area of the planet."

"What does that all mean?" Jaddig stared at Suzi.

"They're like minute spaceships circling the planet," the scientist explained. "From what I found out from the computers they're used to bounce signals around the planet. When Holly talked to her mother by holograph her image was sent to a satellite then back to a receiving station somewhere hidden above the caves at home."

"So it's like our view here only bigger because of the height," Jaddig scratched her head as she tried to comprehend the technology.

"Exactly," Suzi answered. "We use flags to send messages. Bowmen find the highest hilltops and sent flag signals to someone on the next hill who then passed it down to, say, troops in a valley below."

Len's voice came back through the communicator to interrupt the pair's conversation. "The seven ships you seek information about are Tulvar navy vessels that left the port of Grauncu in northern Tulvar six days ago. Present course and speed indicates they will pass this island to the east and reach Vybber in four days. Two ships are thirty thousand tonnes gross weight troop carriers. The other five are smaller escort ships armed with assorted long range cannons."

Suzi frowned. "I would like a logical explanation for the journey those craft are taking and relate it to the current conflict between the humans, Crucnon and crucks. "

There was silence for a few moments before Len's voice returned. "Lack of detailed information makes the following information problematic with only a fifty one percent reliability ranking. Do you wish to wait until more data can be gathered?"

"No," Suzi replied. "The present information will suffice."

"We consider this is an invasion force from the clucks in Tulvar to support the Pulgibrian in their invasion of Vybber territory. If a second front is opened from a landing in Vybber, the Crucnon will have difficulty in containing their enemy."

"And the humans?" Suzi asked.

"Memory banks indicate the crucks have never formed an alliance with humans and a state of perpetual war has continued between the species. Genocide of humans has only been contained by the superior use of human technology. The flow of radio data being received confirms that the cruck species have an ultimate aim of eliminating humans from this planet. History shows the species has no concept of fair play and cannot be trusted. Individual rights in their species is considered a weakness and the Iblon must always rule."

Suzi paled. "I guessed that," she muttered and turned to Jaddig. "The iblon is an extended tribe. In major battles they combine to destroy an enemy but they do not really have any concept of a country. The place we know as the Confederation of Pulgibr is a human concept. It is, in reality, dozens of loosely arranged Iblon. Every so often there is a feud and a weaker Iblon is wiped out or occasionally a large one splits in two, usually after infighting."

"And their possible relationship with Crucnon?" Jaddig added in a hushed voice.

The computer continued. "As far as we can ascertain, the crucks consider them an inferior species who should also be eliminated. Once again, superior weaponry by the Crucnon and enforced separation by Intergalatical Starxhip 7 kept early generations apart. Later, Vybber and cruck iblon had talks and some trade began between them."

"Enforced separation! Please explain," Jaddig asked.

"The Survival of Humanity Protocol was only one of two agreements that came into being in 1 January in 2166. The other was called The Mutual Survival Protocol for Species of Planet Delpe. Do you require more information?"

"Yes," hissed Jaddig.

"The treaty was really enforced by the humans. It was agreed that the three species should live apart and individuals forcibly moved, if necessary into their own territories. Humans were given the land north of the New Columbia River in what became New Washington, the Crucnon's, Vybber that stretched south of the river and ocean to the mountain passes. The cruck were allocated the rest of the continental land areas. Oceans and unliveable territories such as deserts, frozen lands and islands like this one were declared open for any creature.

The Inter-galatical Starship 7 enforced the divisions with force fields monitored by computers. No creature could travel between the territories. As the years went by the force field was, unknown to any creature, turned off for varying lengths of time until 2200 when it was closed down and kept in reserve to stop any open warfare."

"So why isn't it working now?" Suzi asked.

"When the starship left for Earth the electronic equipment that made the force fields went with it. We still have smaller ones to protect this base and the one now use to protect The Haven but no planetary field. It was only during the last five years that the species realized the force fields were permanently gone. Since then, both the Crucnon and crucks have built up their military forces with the main aim of eliminating the humans. The crucks also wish to continue on to eliminate Crucnon. Without any technological intervention, there is an eighty nine percent chance that humanity will be destroyed and a seventy three percent chance the Crucnon will become an extinct species. The alternative for the Crucnon is enforced slavery for their entire race"

"Oh damn," Jaddig gasped. "What can be done to stop the crucks?"

"This can be achieved by using the superior human weapons and bringing the force field back on line."

"Which needs a starship," Suzi added.

"Yes," Len replied. "Once it arrives the fields can be reinforced but the creatures will need to be back in their own territories before that."

Jaddig stared at Suzi and spoke again. "So we can't leave it out in space for our lifetime, can we? Those thousands of humans and Crucnon will need to be returned sooner rather than later?"

"Yes and with and more assimilation problems," Suzi frowned "When they arrive they will be a majority so we will need to have a very tight system set up that they can join or otherwise." She shrugged. "Of course we have to win a war first."

"And persuade my people to set up a democratic government," Jaddig replied and stared thoughtfully out the window. "If we could persuade my people to join with yourselves we would have a population of hundreds of thousands, not a bit over a thousand. The settlers on the space ship will them have to join us or go their own way." Her yellow eyes switched back to the scientist. "They appeared to be the liberals anyway," she added in a whisper.

"I like your thinking, Jaddig but we will need to very careful," Suzi added. She turned back to the monitor. "There's something else I'm curious about. Len, you stated creatures were forcibly moved before the protocols were invoked in 2166. Explain please."

"A group of humans and Crucnon lived happily together before that time but were forced apart. There were several major conflicts and much ill feeling. Further details are available in the declassified information at present being documented. There is evidence, though, that the group that left for Earth were survivors and descendants of the humans and Crucnon who tried to set up their own country and live together. In later years the Blue Watch was formed in Vybber with the aim of rejoining humans and Crucnon but by then all information on the species' genetic history was suppressed. Humans and Crucnon did not realize they were related. "

"Until I tried to access the force field at Hanger Base Beta."

"Exactly," Len replied and made an abrupt stop. "One moment, please. Information is being communicated to me."

Jaddig stared at Suzi and shrugged. They waited and watched the ships, now visible with the naked eye, far out to sea.

"One ship has changed direction and is heading here," Len's voice came back. "Do you wish to have our presence electronically sealed?"

"Will that protect us?" Suzi was worried.

"Yes. All, except the small beach area up to the waterfall will be protected. We have had and average of two point three landings per year but only one attempt to climb the cliffs was made thirty-seven years ago. The climbers were electrocuted but it was made to appear they were killed in a fall from their ropes," Len continued. "You are safe but we do not recommend using a FanWarrior until the ships leave the vicinity."

"Good. Seal the island, then," Suzi said and frowned again. "Can we be seen here?"

"No this observation deck and all facilities are electronically camouflaged. Flying females or personnel in aircraft will only see a jungle covered island."

Suzi nodded. "Well we'd better inform everyone at home about everything," she said.

"All declassified material and information about the ship movements have been transmitted to the computers in the inner cave in New Washington," Len reported. "The Proctor, Commander and Inner Council will have access. You may wish to make a personal contact but it is not necessary."

"I think we will," Jaddig retorted. "We'll come down to the console room."

"Don't forget to have a bite to eat," Len added. "Remember..."

"I know," Suzi answered with a slight grin. "We will."

After a final glance at the ships, the pair walked silently towards the elevator. Suzi had learned a great deal but the information really only made more questions to answer.

*

"So that's it, Holly." Suzi smiled at the three dimensional monitor. "The computers said we're safe but there are big decisions to be made soon."

"Thank you, Suzi. We'll get a full team researching all the declassified information." Andrea sat beside her daughter, looking serious. Her eyes switched to Jaddig. "We have some news for you too, Jaddig. Personal news."

Jaddig froze. "Go on, Proctor," she whispered in a very formal voice and avoided Suzi's eyes.

"We rescued sixteen Crucnon who were trying to reach our lines today. They were members of the Blue Watch, Cell 14. I had a long talk with Sirrat Karotor, their leader. You may know him."

"No," replied Jaddig. "My group was Cell 6 but there's more, isn't there?"

"I am afraid so, Jaddig. Your partner, Birobi Osyjil was killed a month back. You have my deepest sympathy, My Dear."

Jaddig held her head high but a faint quiver of her chin showed her inner turmoil.

"How?" she stated in a monotone.

"In battle. His unit was fighting crucks in one of the mountain passes. A bullet hit him in the head, I believe."

"I understand that would be quick," Jaddig replied. She turned and faced Suzi but face showed the lines of grief. "There is nobody in Vybber, now. I have nobody." She gave one tiny sniff, stood and was about to switch the monitor off when Holly appeared on the monitor.

"You have us," she said "You have Bikut, Snimel and Wunep. You have Mum, Graham and Clay and even old George. You have Suzi there with you. We all love you, Jaddig and don't you forget it. We can never replace your family and now Birobi but we can be your new family if you want us."

"I do," Jaddig whispered as Suzi placed an arm go around her.

"Holly's right," Suzi said. "Everything we've gone through together will not be in vain."

"Thank you Andrea; Holly. You are my family now." Jaddig said and switched the connection off.

She turned and was about to walk out when her slight frame erupted into sobs, long shuddering sobs with tears that rolled down her cheeks.

"Oh Jaddig," Suzi reached out and held her friend while Jaddig just wept over her shoulder.

"My bloody human genes to the fore," she stuttered when words returned.

"And why not?" Suzi responded tenderly. "I know there are some bottles of wine stored in the pantry. I think we could do with a little, don't you?"

"Yes," sniffed Jaddig. "What a damn day and it's only half over."

"May I add my condolences," the computer's voice filled the room. "I perceive you are distressed at the loss of a friend and mate, Jaddig. I missed Admiral Jurjevics when he died and also having no creatures to communicate with for scores of years. If it is any help, I think I understand."

"I believe do you, Len," Jaddig gave a moist smile. "Thank you."

"One piece of good news," the computer continued. "The ship heading this way has altered direction and has returned to its original course so relax for a while. I'll keep monitoring all frequencies."

Jaddig glanced at Suzi. "We were about to have a wine, I believe, then I'd like a walk outside along the lake."

"Me too," Suzi added. "And you have my permission to kick me if I return to this console room before tomorrow. We'll both have the afternoon off."

*

Sirrat Karotor, who preferred to dispense with his military ranking, and a female introduced as Dold Cimog had been with Andrea and Toby in the proctor's office for two hours discussing the situation back in Vybber.

"Thank you for your frank report of the war in your country." Commander Evans glanced up from his clipboard. "How long do you estimate it will be before the crucks break through you defence line in the mountain passes."

Sirrat shrugged. "It is just a matter of time," he replied in his slow English. "We have superior weapons but they use sheer numbers. Thousands of their infantry have been brought down but every night they reform and a whole fresh battalion attacks at dawn in the morning. Their flying females are very accurate and swarm in. Most of the villages and towns in the area have been attacked and have had to be evacuated."

"And the morale in Vybber?" Andrea asked.

"The military elite and government are still firmly in control," Dold Cimog continued. She was a middle-aged clicker and one of the first who could be described as chubby. However, behind the mother like exterior she had an astute mind and more knowledge of happenings in Vybber than any of her companions. "The fast majority of our citizens are demoralized, food is running low and everybody between eighteen and fifty has been called up for military service." She hit the table with her fist in frustration. "Scores of young girls are being forced to become flying females and sent on almost suicidal flying missions. Their casualty rates are phenomenal."

"And the Blue Watch?" the commander asked.

"We are spreading but fragmented and infiltrated with spies. Many citizens sympathise with our cause but are too afraid to openly support us," Dolt continued. "Without outside help, we have no hope of changing the government."

"What would happen if the crucks opened a second front, say from the sea," Andrea casually slipped in.

"We have very little defences along our coast." Sirrat Karotor replied. He frowned. "That is an unusual question, Proctor Jurjevics. Do you know something we don't."

Andrea glanced at Toby who nodded. "We have reports of a navy flotilla sailing north from Tulvar. Indications are they are heading towards Vybber."

The two clickers were silent for a moment before Sirrat spoke. "Without your assistance, I'd say the Crucnon will be overwhelmed and within a month our country will cease to exist."

He stood up and leaned forward, his four arms rigid and knuckles white. Eyes, his brown in colour, stared at Andrea. "And with our kind wiped out, how long do you think the humans can last, Proctor…one season, two; perhaps even three years before the crucks find a way around your defences and cut you down like flies." He coughed and wiped a small handkerchief across his face. "You may think my kind are ruthless but the crucks have no human traits at all. None." He sat down and his voice became low. "Even our military dictatorship is better than their continuous genocide."

"That's why we came," Dold Cimog continued. "We need your help to prevent being annihilated."

Andrea pressed a hidden button and four DPF guards armed with new weapons brought in from Base Alpha slid discretely into the room.

"You are not from the Blue Watch, are you?" she stated with her eyes like steel. "Please do not shift your hands, Lieutenant and Ms. Cimog I'd like your hands on the table.

The two clickers returned Andrea's gaze and nodded.

"You are perceptive, Proctor," Dold replied. "Yes, you are correct. The other fourteen are genuine members of the Blue Watch and do not know about us." Her face showed no fear as she switched her eyes to Toby. "I have been sent by the Vybber government to ask for the human's help."

"So you can wipe us out when the crucks are removed from Vybber?" Andrea hissed.

"We shall sign a peace protocol, withdraw from New Washington and return the lands north of the river to humans."

"An empty gesture," Commander Evans retorted. "There are no Crucnon in New Washington. The Pulgibrian have already reached the river."

Andrea gave the Crucnon slight grin but her eyes remained tight. They had already anticipated the real motives behind the arrival of the Crucnon and knew everything about them. The Full Council had sat right throughout the night drafting the treaty she produced and placed on the table.

"These are our conditions, General Karotor and Deputy President Cimog," she began. "At least you had the courtesy of using your real names, if not your ranking in the Vybber government..."

The two clickers straightened in their seats but showed no other reaction.

"Congratulations on your security service, Proctor," Cimog replied in a soft voice. "You are correct in everything you say but it does not alter what was revealed here, today. Our situation has not been exaggerated. We need your assistance."

"And you know our genetic relationship?" The proctor asked.

"Our government has known that for many years," General Karotor replied with a sigh. "We felt it would demoralize our citizens if they were to be told the facts."

"Controlled, like everything else in your government." Commander Evans snapped.

"We shall transport you home in our aircraft so you can consult your parliament," Andrea continued. "In two days, representatives of our government will arrive to hear your reply to our conditions if you wish our help. It is written in both our languages to prevent any misunderstanding. We are prepared to compromise on some issues but not on the main focus of our offer."

"And what is that, Proctor?" Deputy President Cimog replied. Her face was grim.

"Within six months of the war being finished, the cruck returned to their territories and force fields reinstated, the Vybber government will resign and democratic elections held. Furthermore, no females will be forced to become fertile unless they wish, individual rights shall be established and political prisoners released. The Blue Watch will be registered as a political party and allowed to participate in the aforesaid elections. Our own constitution is being changed also, Deputy. We are henceforth a human and Crucnon federation. All Vybber citizens who wish to become citizens of our country will be welcomed. In this treaty, your government will allow them to emigrate, if they wish."

General Sirrat Karotor turned over the first page of the document; his two right hands shook slightly when he read the heading written in two languages on the title page.

Survival of Human and Crucnon Protocol, it read.

*

"There is little time General; Deputy President," Commander Evans spoke "Our security services advise me Vybber will be attacked from the ocean the day after tomorrow. The Tulvar flotilla is closer than we originally thought. The troop ships, we heard, carry the elite 3rd Marine Battalion. No doubt you know they are particularly sadistic personal fighting force of the Grand Emperor of the United Lblors of Tulvar."

"We have a vacuum bomb ready to load in our aircraft. The enemy can be taken out any time we wish." Andrea held her hand out. "We shall expect your reply by Wednesday."

The two Crucnon government officials shook Andrea's hand but refrained from making a Crucnon embrace.

"Oh yes," Andrea said softly as the visitors walked to the door. "Will you please leave your handguns on the table. To prevent any misunderstandings, you understand."

The general glowered but placed a small silver gun on the table. Deputy President Dold Cimog's thin smile hid her thoughts as she also place her own black one on the table, swung her shoulders back and walked out through the human guards standing rigidly at attention.

"Thank you," Proctor Jurjevics continued with a flicker of a smile. "Our aircraft will have you home in half an hour."

*

182

CHAPTER 19

As it appeared through the clouds below FanWarrior 2, the city of Dememu two hundred kilometres across the Pulgibr boarder was unlike any Holly, Graham or George had ever seen. It was built on a flat plateau and, in reality was eight hexagonal shaped cities varying in size from a kilometre from north to south to a gigantic one twenty kilometres wide. Linked between them were black highways and fields of cultivated land, all hexagonal shaped and surrounded by small canals linked to a larger waterway that encircled the entire complex, fifty or more kilometres in length. A river flowing from the northern mountains flowed into the waterway.

"Suzi sent me information on Dememu," Holly said. "Each hexagonal town is a different iblon with its own hierarchy of power, the bigger the town, the more powerful the iblon." She pointed to one shaped like two joined hexagons; one section blackened with burnt out buildings. "That is where one iblon has defeated another and has absorbed it."

"And your mother expects us to negotiate with that sort of philosophy," George muttered.

"No really," Holly replied... "Oh my stars...look!"

Rising up towards where they were hovering at an altitude of five hundred metres was a black swarm as hundreds of flying females.

"Will our shields protect us, Zeta?" Graham asked the computer.

"No problem, Graham. Do you want the approaching craft destroyed."

"No," Holly replied. "Retract our force field as close as possible. I'd like a closer look at these flying females."

"It is done. The FanWarrior will remain hovering until ordered to move."

As the swarm of flying females circled up, another swarm approached from a different hexagon below.

"Opposition," George muttered. "Perhaps they'll attack each other."

Holly shook her head and watched as the black smudge in the sky approached. There were more than hundreds; thousands of the creatures approached and, in spite of herself, a shudder of fear gripped the her throat. What if the ancient human technology failed?

"It is scary," Graham confessed and tucked an arm around her.

To their east the creatures blotted out the sun and a gloomy shadow covered their craft. Suddenly the attack came. Wave after wave of flying females dived down from above and dropped small black cylinders onto FanWarrior 2. The sky above turned into a world of orange explosive that must have incinerated the females who dropped the bombs.

The aircraft shook but the force field held and explosive slid, like molasses, off the invisible barrier and tumbled in huge globules to the ground below. Within minutes the town below them was a mass of flames with black smoke pouring skyward.

"Move forward at your slowest possible speed until we're above open land," Holly ordered.

The FanWarrior edged forward but the defiant swarm flew straight at them until they were covered in the creatures. There were two different swarms; one dressed entirely in black body suits and a second swarm in dark green. Yellow eyes stared at them and mandibles crunched while claws tried to grab the fuselage.

"They're hideous," Holly gasped.

"And dangerous," George added. The old sergeant fixed one of the creatures with his eyes as it slid down the invisible shield two metres out from the windscreen.

Their craft ploughed its way through them until they were above a yellow crop. Another attack came with more explosive detonations slid off them until the crop became covered in bellowing smoke. This time the attacking force were dressed in navy blue but the attackers were as suicidal as the first two.

"Have you seen enough?" Graham asked Holly.

"Yes," she replied. "Drop the canister. Historians can't say we didn't warn them."

"Bomb is away," the computer reported.

A small cylinder dropped from the aircraft and, before a flying female could reach it, burst open so a thousand leaflets fluttered out and down to the ground below. On them was a message in the local language telling the Pulgibrian troops to evacuate the valley in the Human Territory of New Washington as a vacuum bomb was to be detonated there the next morning at nine hundred hours.

"Let's go home," said Holly. "I can sympathize a little with our ancestors and see why they attempted to create a more benign species."

"And it worked," Graham said. "Just think of Jaddig, Bikut and the others."

"Yes," Holly turned to Graham, "but was the price too high?"

"They're like us now," George added. "There are the good, the kind as well as the bad and the ruthless; just like humans."

"I know, " Holly whispered. "Zeta, head home."

"And fly high," Graham added. "This place looks better from a distance."

With a growl of increased speed, the propellers gripped the air and the FanWarrior shot skyward through the swarms and into the clouds. The Lightshield motors switched on and within a few minutes the friendly mountains poked through the clouds. The scene was so beautiful it almost seemed impossible that the country below held such creatures.

*

At the same time, in the cockpit of FanWarrior 1 with Andrea; Toby, Snimel, Wunep and Bikut watched the ground as they landed in the centre of Jarta. The capital of Vybber stretched along the shore of the ocean. Around them was a park and two tall administrative buildings surrounded by a wide ring road packed with vehicles and hundreds of Crucnon gathered behind orange tape. Police officers on horseback could be seen patrolling the area in front. Behind the crowds, commercial buildings rose to the sky and beyond them on a low hillside stood street after street of apartments.

The three clickers appeared glum as the FanWarrior touched ground and the engines swished to a stop.

"It's okay," Andrea sympathized when she noticed the trio. "There is a force field around us."

"I know," Snimel shuddered and bit on her lip. "But if anything goes wrong?"

"The force field encircles us to a radius of twenty metres," Plato reported. "We can go out but nothing can enter."

Andrea nodded and waited for the ramp to hit the ground. Forty-one bowmen dressed in ceremonial red and blue uniforms marched out in two lines to ring the aircraft. Their crossbows were strapped across their backs as Clay, dressed in his immaculate new sergeant's uniform shouted commands.

"Squad... Atten...shun!" he shouted. The bowmen's feet snapped together as one.

"On command... Load weapons!" Clay roared.

Together as one the twenty men and twenty women slung the crossbows off their backs and aimed towards the sky.

Clay stood at rigid attention as Andrea and Commander Evans descended down the ramp and walked exactly twenty paces out from the aircraft.

A line of Crucnon guards, also dressed in ceremonial clothes, snapped to attention in front of them.

"Fire!" Sergeant Clay Farrell shouted.

Forty arrows shot skyward curved and plunked to the ground to encircle the Proctor and her Commander. Every arrow was spaced exactly where the bowman had intended so forty quivering feathers vibrated for a moment in the slight breeze. Gasps and murmurs rang out from the crowd. In response, local guards fired a volley of shots into the sky and three Crucnon dressed in golden suits stepped from a tent that had been erected on the lawn. One was Dold Cimog but the other two, unknown males.

The ceremony continued with Andrea inspecting the line of guardsmen before returning to embrace the three officials, Crucnon style.

With no forewarning, something else happened. As Snimel, Wunep and Bikut stepped from the ramp and walked in a line under the aircraft's wing and well within the invisible force field, the crowd saw them and the polite clapping turned to cheers, applause and shouts. Everyone, it seemed was shouting, waving and cheering the three, so-called traitors of Vybber.

"Look at them," Snimel whispered and grabbed Wunep's arm. "They're cheering us!"

"I know," gulped Wunep. "But have you seen the president?"

Snimel glanced to where the male, in his glittering golden uniform had just completed embracing Andrea and Toby. He stood back at attention facing the aircraft but it was his face was contorted in a glare of absolute fury and hate.

"Ignore him," hissed Bikut. "Do nothing!"

"If you say so," Snimel replied but could not resist eyeballing the president with her searching blue eyes. Their eyes held for a second before the Vybber leader glanced away and spoke to Andrea.

The pair turned and entered the tent while the crowd still cheered and waved from behind the barriers across the grass.

Snimel glanced at Bikut, then Wunep and waved back. "Come on," she urged. "Don't be a prude."

The other two followed and waved to the crowd; their countrymen, their kind; and they all felt proud. Meanwhile the two opposing guards snapped to attention and marched off, Clay's bowmen to form two lines out from the FanWarrior and the Crucnon to continue the line to the tent entrance.

*

Inside the tent, His Imperial Excellency Klyl Olcmal III, President of Vybber talked through in interpreter to Andrea. She, though, replied to his brief welcome in accentless Vybber and accepted a seat next to Commander Evans. Her eyes fixed on the man and a slight smile crossed her lips.

"I hope our conditions are to your liking, Your Imperial Excellency," she said when the treaty was set out in front of them by a guardsman. Unlike the humans, the Crucnon guards were all males.

"They are quite unacceptable," the Crucnon leader announced. "We object to having our internal affairs dictated to."

"Then I am wasting both our times," Andrea replied and turned to Toby Evans. "We shall return to the aircraft, Commander."

Toby stood and tried not to smile. "Certainly, Proctor," he replied. "Shall I order FanWarrior 2 back to base."

"Yes." Andrea whispered and fixed the Emperor with her blue eyes. "If you think we are bluffing, Sir, just ask your officers if they can see the flotilla on the horizon. We estimate they'll be in sight about now."

Even though she spoke in English his reaction was immediate. So he only pretended he couldn't speak English! He pressed a button on the table and an officer walked in.

"What have you to report, General?" he snapped in his own language.

The general went to hand a document to Olcmal who brushed it aside and snapped. "You can tell the Proctor the contents, General."

"Very well," the Crucnon replied. "Flying squadrons 5, 17 and 8 have returned from their attack on the enemy vessels, Sire."

"Continue," the leader snapped.

"Fifty six flying females attacked the flotilla and three returned to base."

"Three," hissed Andrea.

"Yes Proctor," the general replied. "The rest were shot down."

"The enemy ships," the president added in a cold voice.

"One patrol craft was sunk, Sire. Two other ships suffered structural damage but the troop ships were not hit." He hesitated. "Concentrated firepower stopped the squadrons getting through."

"So, Your Excellency," Andrea said in a cold voice. "Do you wish to discuss our treaty or would you prefer to have this beautiful city in ruins before you reconsider our offer. I have heard that the heavy artillery the enemy have on their ships is particularly devastating."

"There are some points that need to be explained," His Imperial Excellency Klyl Olcmal III, President of Vybber replied in English and sat down. Except for a slight twitch of lips his face was expressionless

"Go ahead," Proctor Andrea Jurjevics replied. "I am prepared to discuss every clause, if necessary."

Two hours later the two humans walked out to the FanWarrior. Andrea looked exhausted but smiled at Bikut, Snimel and Wunep when she entered the cockpit and sat down in the co-pilot's seat.

"The old bastard signed," she grunted.

"And your compromise?" Bikut asked with a worried frown.

"All minor," Andrea grinned. "I think Holly will be proud of me. As from midnight tonight the States of Vybber and New Washington officially cease hostilities and agree to become allies to drive the enemy from our territories."

"But I wonder what would have happened if his squadrons of flying females were successful," Toby grunted.

"He played his last card but it wasn't big enough," Andrea replied with a shrug. "I only regret the huge loss of life because one man's pride was pricked."

*

Dawn broke, cloudy and cool as FanWarrior 2 lifted off the ground and rose higher than Holly, Graham and Bikut had ever been. The area of Vybber was strangely dark, as was the ocean. Both sides appeared to have blackouts in a futile effort to remain hidden.

"We have reached a safe altitude of twenty thousand metres and shall be over the drop zone in five minutes." Zeta announced.

"Thank you," Holly replied. "I would like the bomb zone restricted to the warships programmed into your memory banks."

"All details are on record. Switch to automatic flight and enter the arm code, please."

"It's all so clinical," Holly commented. "Like some game but because of us, hundreds of living creatures will die today." She shuddered.

"And possibly millions will be saved," Graham answered.

"As well as two countries," Bikut added.

Holly nodded, switched in the code and took her hands off the controls. FanWarrior 2 glided through the air to where the land below became ocean. A monitor flashed on and the diagram of the enemy ships showed as black models on a red grid. They looked like toys on a table. Holly glanced outside but could see only clouds and the black ocean. Above were the few stars still bright enough to compete with the rising sun.

"Locked onto target," the computer announced. "The vacuum bomb has left the aircraft."

Holly could see nothing but mentally counted. She reached fifteen before an oval of orange covered the ocean below, there was another delay, a slight bump and the model ships on the graph disappeared. That was it!

"Target destroyed," the detached voice announced.

"Let's go home," Holly whispered. She reached out and grabbed both her friends' hands. "I only hope the other bomb kills less enemy."

188

"Well," grunted George to Wunep. "They must have some common sense."

With Snimel, they were observing the first valley from the top point near the elevator. The valley below was deserted. Not one cruck was in the area they'd been warned to evacuate.

"Zero minus five minutes," Snimel cautioned. "I think we should head down."

"Right," George replied. He grinned and followed his companions to the elevator and descended to the inner cave where the whole human population had gathered just in case something went wrong.

Like Holly's experience a few moments earlier, the blast was almost an anticlimax. A slow rumble vibrated though the cave and nervous lips smiled. Half an hour later every human who was not doing essential work crowded along the edge of The Haven to gaze across at the first valley. But it had gone! The plateau was now twice it's size with a beautiful green side filled with grass, vegetables and crops. The other was still a wall of falling soil, rock and debris swirling and tossing from hundreds of metres up but it was contained and this time nobody was hurt; not even the enemy.

"And look who has arrived," George said in a quiet voice.

FanWarrior 2 had just landed and their three friends waved. It hardly seemed like a day that altered the history of their planet for generations to come. 17 June 2248, True Time was written in the records as The Day of Destiny. The war wasn't over, enemies would not become friends but the humans on Delpe were to take the first step forward with the future now a little more secure.

*

In the city of Jarta a few hundred kilometres away, citizens gathered along the beaches and gazed out to sea where a wall of water, like an inverse waterfall rose up to the clouds. There was no noise but a wind blew offshore, an unnatural wind as if air was being sucked out to join the water. Police attempted to move the crowd back as it was feared a tidal wave would pound onto the beach. But nobody shifted! Everyone wanted to watch the action.

For five minutes the water appeared to rise then, without warning, it dropped in one gargantuan splash. Water on the edges of an invisible barrier splashed skyward again, fell back, the ocean inside the zone boiled and settled. There was a flash of sunshine on a reflected surface and the wind dropped and eerie silence followed. Everything was normal except the flotilla of enemy ships had gone. Not even debris remained.

"I heard the humans dropped the bomb after an agreement was signed yesterday," a young male Crucnon said to the female beside him.

"Yes," she replied and turned her green eyes up at him. "I also heard we're half human." She shrugged. "Next they'll be telling us the war will be over soon and conscription cancelled."

"We can dream, My Love," the young male replied. "I have a feeling the worst is behind us."

"I hope so," she replied and squeezed her hands with his. "But come on home. Mama said she'd have breakfast waiting." She gave a tiny giggle, ran up the beach, kicked her shoes off and laughed back at her friend. "Come on you slow poke," she laughed.

Her companion laughed and ran up the beach. She could have reached the road before he caught her but then there would be no fun. Even in a totalitarian regime, summer love had a place.

*

Holly stood with hands on her hips and shook her head while Snimel only laughed and wiped a hand across her brow. Whereas, almost every garden had rows of vegetables, Snimel and Wunep had their garden planted in pentagons. One pentagon contained potatoes, tall and green, the next cabbages with heads twice the size of Holly's, carrots next then an area of pumpkin plants that exploded over the tiny path. Right in the centre was a pentagon of flowers with rich blooms in red and yellow. Everything was huge and so healthy, only Bikut and Clay's allotment a few metres away could match it. Holly and Jaddig's was growing well but was only half the size of her friend's.

"It's the fertilizer we used," Snimel explained. "An old concoction that I knew the recipe for. Of course, I've had more time to spend on gardening than you."

"And I noticed you pulled the weeds out of Jaddig's and my garden. Thanks for that."

"Well, you're so busy, I thought it was only fair," Snimel replied, obviously pleased that her efforts were recognized. She bit on her lip, glanced at Holly and her face turned serious. "Can I ask something? I heard all about your trip you're about to make back to Dememu in Pulgibr and their strange conditions."

"Did you now?" Holly replied. "Is nothing a secret around here?"

"I doubt it," Snimel replied. "I just want to ask to come. I know Jaddig is your first choice but..." Her voice trailed off, "I just want to do more to help. That's all."

"It could be dangerous," Holly replied.

"So!" Snimel replied.

"Okay. I'm sure Jaddig won't mind. You'll need a new dress, though. It's very formal."

"I'd like that." Snimel grinned. "And I can look after Jynco."

Jynco Vockek, the young flying female who had come in with the Blue Watch group had adapted to life with humans well and had been selected at the request of the Pulgibr who had made contact with the humans through a newly installed radio system. The details were brief and blunt and merely stated they requested a visit of six representatives of all species they were at war with, including a fertile female from each culture. A time and landing area had been given and that was it.

Suzi had researched the cruck customs and had found that fertile females were often the peace brokers between warring iblon.

"We'll get you a gown tonight," Holly said. "We leave in Fan Warrior 2 at eleven hundred hours tomorrow."

Snimel eyes glowed. "Thanks Holly," she smiled. "I won't let you down."

"Are you sure it's not just because Wunep is going?" Holly slipped in and saw the girl flush white.

"Partly," she whispered, "but I really want to help, too. Does it make any difference?"

"Of course not," Holly laughed. "After all, I have Graham."

"You're a pal," Snimel said. "But who is the sixth person?"

"Mum insisted on Commander Evans."

Snimel screwed her nose up. "Oh well, he's not bad for an old guy," she replied and laughed again so her eyes twinkled. "Actually, I like him. He and your Mum should get hitched. They'd do well as mates."

"Snimel!" Holly gasped. She'd never thought of her mother as ever wanting a partner again. "My stars, you're a scheming young lady "

"Well, why not?" Snimel retorted. "Your mother is still quite young; not like the old geriatrics on the council."

"Careful," Holly warned. "I'm a member, you know."

"Yeah but as the young people's rep. you're different."

"Thanks," Holly laughed and gave her friend a tiny hug. "I'll take that as a compliment."

*

CHAPTER 20

The second visit to Dememu was different from the first in that they were expected and no swarms of enemy attacked. Buildings below, shone in the noon sun as the FanWarrior hovered over one of the middle sized iblon and a voice in crude English came over the radio to direct them to a stadium in the north of the hexagon shaped urban area.

Snimel tugged Wunep's sleeves and pointed down. "The stadium," she whispered. "It's full!"

Wunep gazed down as the FanWarrior descended into a central grassed area. The stadium was filled with thousands of faces that stared up at them. Every seat was occupied and six squads of troops were assembled on the grassed interior around the landing zone. Everywhere, long yellow and white flags were flying. "There'd be thirty thousand crucks there," he whistled. "I hope they don't decide to charge."

"What do you think?" Holly asked Toby Evans.

"If Suzi's research is correct, those yellow flags show their peaceful intentions," the commander replied.

Like Graham and Wunep, he was dressed in civilian clothes with a neat suit and yellow tie. Holly, Snimel and a highly nervous Jynco were all dressed in long flowing dark yellow gowns, similar except for different cuts to fit their anatomy. Jynco had her four wings folded and glistening across her back and her tiny fingernails painted a light pink while Holly let her red hair flow free to her shoulders that were tanned and bare. The temperature according to their computer was a sweltering thirty-six degrees Celsius outside, a stimulating heat for the Crucnon but the opposite for the humans, so no other garments were needed.

The Fan Warrior hovered for a moment before the tail swung around and the craft descended to the ground. There was a faint whir of machinery and a slight bump as the ramp hit the ground.

"Shall we go?" the commander smiled.

It had all been rehearsed. Holly and Jynco stepped outside first, followed by Snimel with Wunep and the two human men at the rear.

As they stepped into the glaring sunlight onto a yellow carpet that had been rolled to the edge of the ramp, music filled the air and row upon row of soldiers in dark green uniforms and holding fierce looking firearms stood at attention with eyes staring directly ahead. Every soldier, though, was wearing yellow gloves.

A command was shouted and, as one, the soldiers moved the weapons across their bodies, bent down and placed them sideways on the ground. Another order was shouted and the solders turned and marched away with their weapons left behind.

"Come on." Snimel whispered. "There's a platform ahead."

As they stepped forward six tiny cruck children stepped forward and gave every visitor a tiny posy of yellow flowers. Snimel realized what was wanted and crouched down so the child, probably no older than six could pin the flowers to her dress. This was repeated with all the visitors.

"Thank you," Snimel said in Crucnon as was amazed when the little boy looked into her eyes and spoke also in that language.

"You are welcome," he said in a slightly squeaky voice and she was sure his bony lips twisted into a smile.

The humans found their youngsters spoke in English and all said exactly the same words.

When they arrived at the platform, two soldiers guided the visitors behind a long table where an elderly male cruck stood waiting. Holly tried not to react to the creature's ugly appearance as yellow eyes watched every move she made.

"Please be seated Miss Jurjevics," the male said in English. His eyes moved on and he named them all in turn. "We are honoured to have your presence here today."

Holly smiled and sat on a soft chair, then realized the thousands of onlookers who had also been standing, sat in unison to the ground while music by a string orchestra filled the air.

"I am Elder Tant Volafol, a professor of cultures at our university and because of my knowledge of your languages have been asked to represent my government at this meeting." He sat and poured a clear liquid from a flask into seven crystal glasses and invited them all to refresh themselves.

The liquid was a sweet tasting honey mixture that, Holly was sure, had a high alcohol content so she prudently took the merest sip.

Elder Volafol took a waxy type document off the table and gazed at the crowds in the stadium around. "You may think of us as a ruthless unfeeling species," he said and fixed Holly with an unblinking stare. "We are not humans nor the hybrid race of Crucnon and our life-styles and values are different."

"And so they should be," Holly replied in a soft voice. "Our present generation realizes that and regret the mistakes made by our ancestors in the past."

"Thank you," the professor continued. "I predict you are about to become one of your species' great leaders, Holly Jurjevics and surmise it was your decision that led to this meeting today."

"I don't understand," Holly replied.

"I shall explain. In front of you, assembled on the stadium floor is the fifteenth battalion of the fifty-third iblon. That is the iblon you are now in. This battalion was until recently based in what you called the First Valley in New Washington. Beyond them on the stands are the extended families, I guess your words are, of the soldiers who were in that valley."

"I see," Holly said slowly. She glanced sideways to see Graham smile.

"Yes, Holly Jurjevics. Without your brave flight here to warn us, these soldiers would now be dead, killed by that foul weapon your ancestors buried throughout your land. Those thousands of children gathered on the stands would be without parents." He stopped and sipped his drink. "Our policy was to cleanse our traditional lands of your kind. To us, your ancestors were aliens who arrived on our planet and attempted to change our species into something to become their slaves, hence the Crucnon who are neither crucks nor humans but some freak of nature in between."

Holly's face clouded and the youngster beside her was on the verge of tears. The professor turned to Jynco and reached across to squeeze her arm.

"Forgive me, child," he said with compassion in his voice. "Please listen to an old man."

He turned back to Holly. "But we were wrong. Many generations have gone by and our creatures have remained separated, The Crucnon and human became enemy and our leaders thought it was a time to attack your nations." He glanced down. "I was one of a few who tried to stop them but the military don't listen to old academics. I personally believe our three species should live in peace."

"So," Holly interrupted. "What happens now?"

The professor's eyes lifted. "Because of your compassionate warning of the vacuum bomb explosion and the consequent saving of thousands of lives, The Confederation of Pulgibr shall be withdrawing all its troops from the countries of New Washington and Vybber." He sort of winked at Holly. "Of course the annihilation of our ally's navy showed the generals the futility of trying to conquer your lands."

Holly broke into a smile. "This news is unexpected and welcome," she replied.

"There can be no formal peace," Elder Tant Volafol cautioned. "Our species are a militant race and..." He hesitated as if he was trying to find the correct words. "Shall we say don't want to lose face or compromise our pride. Do you understand?"

194

"I do," Holly responded.

"We shall return to the status quo as it was before the Crucnon attacked New Washington. Not peace but an agreement to leave each other alone." He stopped again. "When your spaceship returns, perhaps you'll be courteous enough not to reinstate the force field along our mutual border."

"So you know about it?" Holly whispered.

"Oh yes." The professor sighed. "That was something else that frightened our generals into attacking your country. A pre-empt attack, I think your ancestors called it. So you see our little meeting here today can be of benefit to everyone on, or soon to arrive on this world."

"We will see that the force fields are not reinstated," Holly replied and glanced at Toby. "Won't we Commander Evans?"

"I see no problem with that," the commander replied in a very formal voice.

"Good," their host said and stood up. "So go in peace, My Fellow Beings of Delpe." He turned and gazed at the young flying female beside Holly then on to Snimel. "I must add, I think you young ladies look very beautiful in those yellow gowns of peace. You are a credit to your kind and I apologize for the crude remarks made earlier. In our society the females are the symbols of creativity and peace; the males are providers and warriors."

Jynco looked up. "Thank you, Professor," she said in a strong voice. "I was hurt by your comment because I do not regard myself as a freak. I believe every creature on this planet has the right to live here. Our ancestors did some repulsive things but that was not our doing, was it?"

"No, Jynco," the elderly cruck replied and his antennae drooped down in affinity. "It was not."

He stepped forward and embraced the youngster before walking along to do the same with the five remaining visitors while, at the same time, the stadium broke into applause and a thousand yellow balloons were released into the sky.

"So, perhaps now we may now have peace on our planet," Snimel spoke for the first time.

"That is also my wish," Elder Tant Volafol replied.

*

As the FanWarrior rose into the air, Holly looked down at the exotic city with a faraway gaze.

"And your thoughts, My Sweet" Graham asked. He tucked his arms around her and peered over her shoulders as the stadium became smaller and smaller before blending in with the other buildings around.

Holly leaned her head back against his shoulder. "Oh, I don't know," she replied. "When does a society ever become perfect?"

"Never but neither is it all evil."

"True," Holly replied and turned to Jynco. "I was proud of you down there," she said. "Really proud."

"Me too," Snimel added and Wunep nodded. "I was too scared to say what I thought."

"As far back as I remember, I've been scared," the young flying female replied. "As a child I lived in a orphanage and was constantly scared of doing the wrong thing. I was terrified when I received my call up papers and told I was ordered to become a flying female, I was petrified when we were attacked down in the valley. You humans scared me too but were so kind to me I now realize I am what I am and have done nobody any harm so why shouldn't I be proud of myself?" She bit on her lip and glanced at Holly. "Like Jaddig, I have nobody back in Vybber and you have made me feel wanted and even needed. I am so glad I am here right now."

"You are wanted and needed, Jynco," Holly added. "I think you proved that today. Our land is going to become a better place because of Crucnon like yourself."

"What about Wunep and me?" Snimel cut in.

"Yeah," Holly grinned and winked at Wunep's smiling face. "I guess you two are okay, too."

*

Flights over New Washington and Vybber during the next two weeks showed that the Pulgibrian's intended to keep to their agreement. Lines of vehicles were seen returning home. Those in New Washington had followed the New Columbia River east as there were now no mountain passes to the north. In Vybber, local troops followed the crucks to reoccupy land vacated by the retreating army but this nation also kept its agreement with the humans. New Washington was not re-entered and the human territory stood alone and forlorn.

DPF patrols left The Haven and fanned out over the countryside to fine it stripped. New Seattle was gone as was New London. There was no pontoon bridge connecting to the Vybber side and every farmhouse or farm building had been burnt down. There were no animals or even fences. Roads and bridges had been destroyed and the network of power lines gone. Between them, the two armies had managed to destroy a century and a half of human occupation in a few months.

After the council met, a public meeting was held to inform the settlers what to expect if they returned.

"We have made some concessions," Andrea announced to the hushed audience. "The efforts of you all to farm The Haven and produce food for us all is appreciated so each allotment will immediately become the property of the family occupying it… " She waited as the main cave erupted into applause. "Furthermore, all farms and land in New Washington shall be returned to the original owners. Unfortunately, everything has gone and we cannot afford to rebuild the towns of New Seattle or New London. The council has decided to continue development of Zoflum instead and a new south-western road will be built down to the river. This will shorten the distance to our border by over a hundred kilometres."

"What about the Crucnon refugees living with us, Proctor?" a voice called out.

"We need them as much as humans," Andrea replied. "Those who have not been allocated a plot of land will be offered some in the new area being brought in. The rest of the new plateau will be divided up into areas slightly smaller than your allocations and reserved for immigrants from either Vybber or Earth."

A ripple went through the crowd as everyone had heard about the starship returning. Andrea waited until the crowd quieted before continuing. "We have decided on two other important items that will affect us all. So we are not overwhelmed when the new immigrants arrive, we need to have a working system of government and justice system in place. We have delayed the starship's arrival until this happens."

She stopped and waited for the slight murmur throughout the crowd to stop. "As well as generation numbers being abandoned, The Council and Inner Council will be disbanded as from November 1, 2248 and elections called for a new House of Representatives consisting of twenty five members and a president. Anybody in our country over the age of eighteen can put themselves forward as a candidate. Anyone nominated can be a candidate for president." She stopped again so the crowd could digest the information. "I have allowed my name to go forward in this contest," she added in a modest voice.

The cave was silent for a moment before it erupted into spontaneous applause, hoots and whistles that grew even louder when Andrea sat down and Holly stood to face the crowd.

"Stand against your Mum!" someone shouted out and the clapping erupted again.

"I have one other point," Holly added. "The voting is not restricted to humans. We have eighteen Crucnon citizens at the moment and they will be recorded all rights to be nominated to the House of Representatives and also voting rights." She grinned and glanced down at an upturned face in the front row. "Except Jynco who will have to wait until her eighteenth birthday to vote, the same as the human population."

Once again the settlers erupted into applause of approval.

*

The polling booths closed at nineteen hundred hours on November 1, 2248 with a ninety-two percent turnout of eligible voters. By twenty hundred hours most of the population were gathered to hear the result. Commander Toby Evans stood and faced the crowd of expectant faces while the sixty nine candidates for the House of Representatives and three presidential candidates sat in a cordoned off area along the side of the small stage where Toby stood.

"In the presidential race the results are as follows." He paused and grinned at the crowd. "Ronald Cotterell, 227 votes; Malone Davidson, 63 votes..." A groan went through the crowd. "Andrea Jurjevics..." He paused before he raised his voice." 753 votes."

The cave erupted in shouts, whistles and cheers. Blue and white flags, Andrea's campaign colours, waved above the crowd while Ron stood and walked across to congratulate President Andrea Jurjevics.

"I knew you didn't have to worry," he grinned.

"No, but you were a good opponent, Ron," Andrea replied and grimaced. "I didn't want Malone Davidson the pleasure of being the only other candidate."

Toby Evans tapped his microphone and the cave quieted into a gentle hush. "The result of our House of Representatives election in descending order, Ladies and Gentlemen..." Once again he paused... "The highest recorded vote was for Andrea Jurjevics with 856 votes but as president, she is automatically withdraws from this contest and is replaced by the twenty sixth highest polling candidate..."

"Get on with it!" a voice in the crowd shouted.

"In second pace with 827 votes is Holly Jurjevics..."

"Oh my stars!" Holly gasped and tears of joy sprung to her face as Graham seized her in a bear hug placed a sloppy kiss on her lips.

Her other friends around laughed and slapped her back. "You just about beat your Mum," Snimel laughed and Jaddig's smile was right across her face as she waved the blue and white banner just like the ones that filled two thirds of the room.

The commander's voice droned on. Ron won third highest placing and other successful candidates were named and congratulated. Green flags of the second most successful group joined the blue and white ones but the red flags of Malone Davidson's party were conspicuous by her absence. She, though, won a personal seat with 617 votes.

"But listen!" Clay interrupted Bikut and his other friends gathered around him.

"In 18th place with 697 votes is Doctor Suzi Yu."

It was Suzi's turn to be overwhelmed and congratulated by her friends and colleagues around her. Holly and Jaddig hugged their friend and more blue and white flags were waved.

The state of the parties at this point is Liberal Party, twelve seats; Progressive, four, and the Environment Party, two; but there is more to come."

Toby, now obviously enjoying himself, reached for the next pile of results. His voice continued until he came to the twenty-second place when he paused and waited. "It gives me great pleasure in announcing this result, Ladies and Gentlemen," he stated and waited again for the murmuring to stop. "Representing the Liberal Party with 637 votes is Ms. Jaddig Qarte, our very first Crucnon representative."

Jaddig's face turned white as she stared at the commander. It was only after a great deal of persuasion by Andrea, Holly, and her friends that she had even agreed to put her name forward. She'd only consented when Bikut offered to participate as well.

"You did it!" Snimel screamed and rushed into Jaddig's arms. "I knew you could."

Jaddig just stood holding a bunch of flowers thrust into her hand. Her body shook and tears appeared in her eyes as the other Crucnon hooted and cheered. Andrea and Holly both appeared and hugged the surprised Crucnon woman. Three young clicker males snapped a bottle of foaming champagne and squirted everyone within range.

But the results were not over.

"With 598 votes and in 23rd place is Sergeant Clay Fennel."

"Oh damn." Clay grinned as Bikut wrapped her arms around him and stared up into his eyes.

"Congratulations, My Dear," she whispered and, not caring who saw, kissed him on the lips.

Toby Evans smiled at the pair and showed Andrea, who now was beside him on the stage, his list. She broke into a smile but nobody could hear what was said. He read out two more results and waited once more.

"As I said earlier, Ladies and Gentlemen, the twenty-sixth most successful candidate is also elected. Representing the Liberal Party and with 493 votes is Ms. Bikut Kegning, our second Crucnon citizen elected. "

Bikut still in Clay's arms gave a tiny shriek and stared dumbfounded around as the focus of attention moved to her. Jaddig was suddenly beside her and a quad of arms encircled each other. They were bustled up onto the stage to tremendous applause as even more blue and white flags were held high. It was a night to remember with the Liberal Party gaining a clear majority and fifteen seats. Malone Davidson's Environment Party came in third with four.

The celebrations continued until three hundred hours when the tired but happy candidates returned to their homes, some in new apartments or cottages in Zoflum while others to their quarters in the cave.

Across town just before dawn broke on a new era, President Andrea Jurjevics broke her chastity of more than a decade and a prediction of a young Crucnon came true. Commander Toby Evans, her friend for thirty years now became a lover in a tiny room of her newly constructed cottage on the edge of Zoflum, the word that meant hope for the future.

*

CHAPTER 21

It was two hundred hours and snowing in Zoflum when Andrea was awoken by tapping on her bedroom door.

"Mum," Holly whispered. "You didn't answer the telephone. Something important has happened. Could you come to the cave, please?"

Andrea yawned, wiped her eyes and switched the bedside light on. "What is it, Sweetheart," she exclaimed with alarm in her voice. "Is someone hurt?"

She glanced up and saw Holly was not alone "Oh hello, Suzi," she said and her manner relaxed a little. "What have you discovered now?"

"We're in live contact with Earth, Andrea. The president of United States of America on Earth is on Video Vision and wishes to talk to you right now."

"What!" Andrea gasped and flung her blankets aside. "But that is impossible."

"I thought so, too," Suzi added. "You know we have direct communication through Len at Base Alpha to monitor Inter-galatical Starship 43's computer?"

"Yes, but keep talking while I fling something on," She rushed across to her wardrobe and grabbed some clothes.

"Well, I entered all the election results to the earlier program itemizing our new system. Apparently, Len transmitted this information to the Starship. That took a week at post light speed. From there it was transmitted onto Earth. That took another three weeks."

"Here do my zip up, Sweetheart," Andrea wriggled into her long skirt and turned around. "So it is now still December. At that speed, no reply would be due back until the end of January next year."

"That's it," Suzi explained. "Unknown to me, Len downloaded new lightpulse technology that can sent video and sound signals but not holographs at gegalight speed. A signal from Earth takes three seconds."

"Oh my stars!" Andrea gasped and ran a comb through her air

"Up until now, Earth withheld the technology from us," Holly explained as they crunched through the snow to where *Charlie* was waiting, It's headlights cutting through the surface fog, motor throbbing and fumes puffing into the sub-zero air.

"So why the change?"

"We're a democratically elected government, Mum, and as president you're entitled to belong to Earth's United Nations and also United Extra-terrestrial Settlements, They're human settlements on other planets."

"I'll drive," Suzi said after they all jumped in the front seat.

"You mean there are others?"

"Three that we know of," Suzi added. She changed gears and switched on the windscreen wipers. "But they're further from us than Earth itself. I was actually asking Len for info about them when this video flashed through." She glanced at her watch. "That was half an hour ago."

"Half an hour," groaned Andrea.

"Don't worry. The Earth president is quite enraptured with our Vice President," Holly grinned. "She's talking to him."

Andrea smiled and was pleased Jaddig had been nominated the Vice President. They took the elevator down to the inner cave and stepped through the deserted main concourse to the communications room.

Jaddig was sitting at the console gazing at a three-metre high colour monitor where a coloured but only two dimension picture showed the head and shoulders of a middle aged black gentleman.

"Excuse me, Mr. President," Jaddig spoke to the vision. "Mrs. Andrea Jurjevics, President of New Washington has just walked in the room. She turned and smiled at Andrea who noticed her own image on a smaller monitor.

"President Jurjevics," Jaddig smiled at Andrea when she sat next to her. "May I introduce the 96th President of The United States of America; Doctor Peter Arbour." She faced the video screen. "Mr. President, this is President Andrea Jurjevics."

There was a very slight delay, three seconds actually, before the man replied. "Call me Pete," drawled the man. "I must say Madam President, I enjoyed my little chat with your Vice President."

"I am Andrea," Holly's mother replied.

"Ah, yes, Andrea," President Arbour replied and a smile crinkled across his chubby face. "I have had the pleasure of speaking with Jaddig here I apologize for the middle of the night call but we did not know your local time zone." He coughed, "This is, unfortunately more than a social call to demonstrate our new technology. Are you in a secure environment?"

"I believe so," Andrea grinned. "We are only thirteen hundred souls, less a than the population of one of your apartment buildings. The other creatures on this planet have no facilities to intercept this signal, if that is what you mean."

"Inter-galatical Starship 43 is heading for your planet but has not gone into orbit, is that correct?" President Arbour asked.

"Yes. We've purposely kept it away until we've settled our affairs."

"A wise choice. I've been informed of your recent war and must congratulate you on how it was solved. This video vision is to stop you being involved in another conflict. "

Andrea frowned but only nodded.

"To put it frankly, Andrea, that starship is not what it seems. Intergalatical Starship 43 is a hijacked craft manned by a sect convinced humanity is the only form of intelligent life worth preserving in the known worlds."

Andrea paled and glanced at Jaddig who sat emotionless with Suzi and Holly in the semicircle of seats. "How many are there aboard, Sir?" she asked.

"Until they moved into post light speed there were twenty three conscious identities. We assume they are the hijackers. Some are known terrorists or anarchists. We infiltrated their organization but were too late to stop them leaving." Pete Arbour frowned. "Our agent was assassinated."

"Go on." Andrea stared at the screen.

"The last signal we received is that their intentions were to leave the settlers in suspended animation and arrive as friends then forcibly take your settlement over."

"But why?"

"They're wanted people on Earth. They need a base to use to extend their ideology. They know of your ancestors' weaponry and would use it without mercy to wipe out the other creatures on your planet."

"So what do you advice, Mr. President?"

The man gave a twisted smile. "We are involved in another skirmish in another star system at the moment and have no vessels available to come to your assistance. However, the possibility of one of our starships being hijacked or stolen was anticipated in the original design. Doomwatch, a secret computer and communication program is built into all our later starships. It is independent from and unknown by the main inboard computer systems or the crew. By using Doomwatch we have the power to override the main computer system. If it was not for the prisoners aboard we could have destroyed the Starship 43.

"I see," Andrea frowned again. "But tell me? How do I know this call is genuine? You could be an actor sitting in a spacecraft in orbit around Delpe. With all due respects, we have been out of contact with Earth for two centuries so have no idea on what has happened there."

"A good point," Peter Arbour gave a slight grin. "We will send you classified information about the original crew of Starship 7, including personal information about your ancestors that you can check with your historical files. As a sign of our good intentions we are also prepared to download Inter-galatical Starship 43's Doomwatch access code so you can control it."

"But how do you know we're genuine, Sir?" Suzi cut in. "Couldn't we be as bad as the criminals you're trying to stop?"

"With your delightful Vice President?" Pete smiled for a moment before his face turned serious. "You have been under surveillance ever since we switched on this new gegalight technology. There is little we don't know about you all."

"How long?" Andrea snapped.

"Fourteen months. We were monitoring every move made in your wars and how you used the new technology your ancestors left." He smiled, "I must say we are extremely impressed."

"And if you weren't?"

"This discussion would not be taking place, right now and we would have attempted to bring Starship 43 back to Earth. You are a long way away, Andrea and there is another problem as well."

Andrea frowned. "And that is?"

"The Crucnon on board are, as you know, a cold blooded species who, we believe, go into a natural unconscious state when their body temperature drops too low."

"That is correct, Doctor Arbour," Jaddig cut into the conversation, "but we have largely overcome this by wearing artificially heated body suits like the one I'm wearing at this moment. It is winter here and snowing outside. Without the suit or heated quarters I would be in a state of hibernation until spring."

"Yes, That's the difficulty with your species in suspended animation on board the starship."

"But how?" Jaddig replied. "Hibernation is a natural condition for us. Our bodies should be less affected than humans."

"Quite true," the American president replied. "However, the system was designed for humans with in-built safety procedures. The computers read the very slow heartbeat of your kind in suspended animation as being potentially fatal so they stimulate the bodies and bring your kind almost to an awakened stage. Their blood begins to flow as a human's would, the computer decides they are fine and reinstates the suspended animation status. We have tried to issue different safety programs but can't change it too much or the humans in the suspended animation state would be at risk. We cannot isolate the Crucnon and put them on a different program."

"I see," Jaddig replied, "but I see no problems. We often go in and out of hibernation. I, for example, can set my room at a low temperature and sleep for three days before the temperature is raised and I wake up."

She gave a slight grin. "The advantage is that, unlike humans, I can stay awake for three or four days without needing more sleep."

"Yes, but this is happening every few hours. The Crucnon aboard never actually wake up but when their body is warmed the body organs need energy."

Jaddig paled and stared at Andrea before switching her yellow eyes back to the monitor. "I think I understand, Mr. President," she said in a slow voice.

"But I don't," Holly replied.

Jaddig turned to her friend. "Unless they are brought into a conscious state and given something to eat they will slowly starve to death."

"Correct," Doctor Arbour replied. "The intravenous drip the computers inserted helps somewhat but it is losing the battle. They have already lost most of their reserve fat tissue. Once again, the system was designed for humans."

"So wake them up!" Holly snapped.

"We considered that, too but we have never awoken a species travelling at post light speed. We believe it will kill them. If we drop the craft back to sub-light speed it will take more than a natural lifetime for Starship 43 reach yourself or Earth."

"So we do not have unlimited time, Mr. President. How much do we have?" Andrea added.

"Computers predict the Crucnon on board will begin dying in twelve Earth days. We are too far away and, even with time alteration, they would be dead by the time Starship 43 arrives here." The man's brown eyes fixed them in a concerned glare. "However, at maximum operating speed they can be above your planet in six Earth days." The president gave another slight grin. "Of course, this can be any time you choose at your end. We do not really understand what would happen if, say, you chose to make it as year before the craft arrives."

"So it is not worth the risk?" Andrea replied.

"Correct and, to be frank, the sooner you can get those Crucnon onto your planet, the better."

Andrea nodded, "With this new Doomwatch we can operate all of Starship 43's systems?"

"Yes."

"But we already do that."

"Only until the ship is in orbit over your planet. At that time you would lose control. The inboard computer was pre-programmed to bring the crew out of suspended animation before the others. The hijackers would have landed and used new technology to assassinate you all. They are ruthless people, Andrea."

"I see," Andrea replied and made a decision. "We will get them here. You can start uploading every program we need. How can I get back to you?"

"This is an exclusive frequency and your computer already has the coordinates. Any calls you make will be answered immediately by my people. We'll have a twenty-four hour watch"

"And the other hour?" Andrea gave a wry grin.

The American president frowned. "I don't understand."

"We have a twenty-five hour day here, Pete," she replied.

"In spite of the seriousness of the call, Doctor Peter Arbour broke into a broad grin. "You are one astute lady, Ma'am. I'm glad you aren't a candidate here in U.S.A. when my re-election comes up next year."

"Why, thank you, Mr. President," Andrea replied with a smile.

She exchanged a few more pleasantries with the man on the other side of the galaxy before the screen switched to a view of Delpe as one of the communication satellites viewed it, a beautiful planet that was all blue and white.

Andrea turned to Holly Suzi and Jaddig "In some ways our decision to play it safe with Inter-galactic Starship 43 almost killed the very people we're trying to save."

"But we weren't to know, Andrea," Jaddig replied, "and there is still time."

"Len here," the computer's voice interrupted their conversation. "There is a ninety eight point three percent chance that incoming vision was genuine, Andrea. Do you want a more extensive check?"

"No, Len but prepare to receive the downloads the president mentioned.

"They are on file. Do you wish to examine them."

"On file? That was quick."

"The downloading took twenty one hours and was completed four days ago. This included the modernization of all my files and a complete historical record of events and scientific achievements on Earth since 2020. It was, however, classified so you could not be informed until now."

"Of course," Andrea sighed. "And the new communication with Starship 43?"

"Doomwatch is on line. We have direct control over the starship's operations. Earth control have already erased the original computer's programs from the craft's memory banks and substituted direct control by Doomwatch. The rest is apparently up to us."

"Since when?" Jaddig asked.

"Yesterday at six hundred hours."

"And the present condition of those on board?"

"All life species are in suspended animation and shall remain so until we order otherwise. At present speed, Starship 43 will arrive here in forty-six years. That figure is rounded."

"I want the speed increased so Inter-galactic Starship 43 is in orbit around Delpe as soon as possible without affecting the passengers' safety. However, on arrival, the crew and passengers are to remain in suspended animation."

"That shall be done," an entirely new voice replied, a rich vibrant female voice, quite unlike the usual monotonous ones usually associated with electronic speech. "This is Doomwatch 43 speaking, President Jurjevics. My programs have been placed under your government's control."

"Without time alteration, how long will it be before the Starship is in orbit?" Suzi cut in.

"Three days and four hours, Delpe time, Doctor Yu." The voice stopped and Len came back on line.

"Is there anything more, Andrea?" he asked.

"No, thank you," Andrea replied and yawned as the monitors switched off. "I could go with some coffifake and an early breakfast."

"It's on its way," Suzi grinned. "I ordered bacon and eggs on toast ten minutes ago."

"Oh damn!" Andrea retorted. "I'm fast becoming redundant around the place."

"But always wanted, Mum," Holly smiled. "I'm glad you were here handling one of the most powerful persons in the galaxy."

"Yeah," Andrea grinned, "but any of you three could have done it. He was, after all, only a man."

*

Silent crowds watched as FanWarrior 2 landed in a park adjacent to the ocean in Jarta and two Crucnon doctors ran towards the lowered ram.

"Thank you for coming at such short notice," Jaddig greeted them. "I am..."

"We know you, Jaddig Qarte," the middle age male Crucnon gave a slight grin. He turned to his companion, a younger female. "This is my colleague, Doctor Flamy Gelpa and my name is Doctor Hennyn Iwacu." He embraced Jaddig and stared with an amused expression at the interior. It was filled with Crucnon. Snimel, Wunep, Bikut and Jynco were all there as well as the other Crucnon who were now New Washington citizens.

"Our species on board the Starship were badly treated by humans and are in poor physical condition," Jaddig explained. "We thought if they were treated by our kind it would be of benefit to them."

"True," Doctor Iwacu replied. His green eyes fixed Jaddig with a concerned look. "And what is their condition?"

"They will be very weak from malnutrition. We do not know their other injuries but assume there are some. I'll explain on the way. She sat down and introduced the doctors to the group who methodically walked along and embraced every one there. Afterwards, the pair were shown through to the cockpit and met Holly, Graham, Clay and George.

"We're so pleased to have you aboard," Holly welcomed. "Take a seat and watch the view. Your city looks quite breathtaking from the air."

The pair sat down but looked uncomfortable as the engines started and the FanWarrior began its slow rise above the city. However, as the panoramic view spread out below, their curiosity overcame the fear and they chatted away with each other and tried to identify buildings below.

After Snimel gave him a prod and told him to be sociable, Wunep came through and sat beside the two doctors "Our visit wasn't a secret," he commented when he noticed thousands of the city's citizens waving at them.

"No," Doctor Flamy Gelpa smiled up at him. "Our citizens regard you all as heroes who, single-handedly defeated the crucks and saved Vybber from defeat." She chuckled. "According to local gossip, the humans didn't even figure in the fight."

Wunep shrugged his shoulders. "That's a little unfair."

"I know," Flamy replied, "but it gives our people something to be proud of. We saw Jaddig and Bikut being elected as members of your parliament. I think everyone in the city were as nervous as you would have been. When they won seats, thousands cheered."

"How did you know about the results?" Wunep asked. "Wasn't everything censored?"

"We have television now," the doctor said. "Just a few sets in public places like taverns and in shopping malls. It was all televised and our government allowed the broadcast to go out live. I think they are trying to create a more liberal atmosphere with our own elections only six months away. We had screens set up in the main square and there were twenty thousand of our people cheering the pair on."

"Oh my stars," Wunep flushed but looked proud. "Only a few weeks ago we were traitors to be shot on sight."

"Yes," interrupted Doctor Hennyn Iwacu. "Perhaps the government thought you'd both be heavily defeated and the result would make the local citizens realize how selfish and self-centred humans are. They miscalculated the result and the ground swell of affection between humans and Crucnon." He scowled. "I only hope this episode with these wounded citizens arriving doesn't turn the tide. If any are seriously hurt, our government will swell it up to show humans cannot be trusted."

"But what about the suffering in their hands?" Wunep snorted. "Sure there are bad humans but our species have been bloody murderers. Jaddig's family was wiped out simply because she refused to kill herself instead of surrendering."

Hennyn shrugged. "Most citizens have had family members killed or tortured, Wunep. Our nation is still filled with fear. Nothing is said but we can remember."

"Then you'd better see you help the new arrivals," Snimel who had slipped into the cockpit unnoticed said. "The humans in New Washington have been nothing but kind to us. Not one in this aircraft would want to go back to Vybber."

"I guess not," the older doctor replied. "Rest assured, young lady, that is why we volunteered to come. We will do everything possible to help our kind who are arriving from the space ship."

Holly grinned at Snimel's loyalty as she gazed outside. The land had disappeared and only the ocean showed below. It had been a frantic four days since the American president's warning. Almost to the minute the Inter-galactic Starship 43 swung into orbit on the third day, so gigantic it could be seen as a shooting star in the southern sky every night. After Doomwatch advised the suspended animation robotic workers under her control could transfer containers to a shuttlecraft, it was decided to bring the Crucnon to Delpe first while they were still in suspended animation. If there were problems when they woke up, qualified staff could help hence the emergency call to the Vybber government and the agreement for two doctors to accompany them to Alpha Base.

*

Holly who, with Jaddig had been given their first government assignment, that of overseeing the arrival of the space shuttle, stood and stared skyward. A siren sounded and the cranes in the centre of Base Alpha swung outwards so the area became an empty space.

"Arrival time is two minutes, sixteen seconds," Len's voice boomed out over a dozen loud speakers.

"My stars! There it is," Graham shouted and slung an arm around Holly's shoulders.

High above in the blue sky was a sphere, black and shimmering with the surface in constant motion. The only noise was a sort of thumping sound similar to the FanWarrior when the landing propellers were in use.

The craft dropped, grew larger and became a dark green colour of spinning light.

Several gasps filled the air as the noise level rose to a deep rumble like a tumbling waterfall and the craft hovered a hundred metres up. It was huge, almost filled the sky, a perfect sphere like a planet landing on top of them, a hundred metres up ... fifty... twenty until the craft was inside the surrounding volcanic walls that hid the landing area. The spectators were buffeted by a tremendous down draft but continued to stare upwards as four panels slid open on the underside of the shuttle and metal pods, like legs of a stool slid out.

Sirens sounded again, the cranes all simultaneously hinged back forty-five degrees and the craft came in. All the time, the shuttle was spinning like a top and the air inside the landing concourse howled. Holly's hair and clothes flapped and she had to grip a nearby barrier to stop being swept off her feet. But it wasn't all spinning; only the top hemisphere was. The craft was, in reality, a sphere inside a lower hemisphere like a boiled egg in an egg holder.

"Fun, isn't it?" Bikut screamed in her ear and laughed at the human woman's, usually well-combed red hair being blown everywhere.

"If you say so," Holly yelled back. She glanced along the curved platform where everyone else, human and Crucnon, gripped the yellow rails and tried to hold their flapping clothes.

With a crunch, the cranes gripped the shuttle, landing pods squeezed down on shock absorbers before, with a hiss of compressed air; they rose a fraction and held the craft up. The motors stopped, the top sphere whined down until it stopped spinning and, except for two small openings that vented white clouds of condensation, the shuttle became still and silent.

"Shit, it's big!" George snorted.

"The door!" Snimel gasped.

A ramp of similar design to that on the FanWarrior and large enough to drive a vehicle through, hinged out and down directly in front of Holly. She could see the lit interior like a massive circular room. In the middle, a small aircraft with long pointed nose and folded wings was parked while all around were dozens of long dark crates, almost like coffins with glass tops. Yellow tubes ran from each one to wall sockets and a faint hum of machinery could be heard.

"Come on Jaddig," Holly said.

She walked up the ramp and up to the first crate. Inside was a Crucnon flying female who lay asleep on a soft synthetic mattress, dressed in a body suit, boots and gloves. She could have been Jynco except for a bloated abdomen. Jaddig took one look at the scene and gasped.

"Get Doctor Gelpa, Holly. This girl is about to lay her eggs."

"Right," Holly replied and headed away.

Jaddig examined the chamber but could see no latch or manual controls. She knew from experience, though, that as soon as this flying female became conscious she would begin laying eggs.

"Damn," she uttered and was about to move on to examine the second container when a movement caught her attention. The eyes flickered and opened and, wide with curiosity, stared back at Jaddig. For a second the flying female hesitated before her face turned into a smile.

"So it wasn't just a dream," a feminine voice, in English, echoed out through a hidden speaker. "I dreamt a friend called Doomwatch was looking after me. She said our kind will come and rescue us and my children will grow up in freedom again." The tiny chin quivered and tears burst down the sunken cheeks. "Tell me you are real and this is not just another sadistic trick."

*

CHAPTER 22

The female doctor was beside Jaddig within a moment and confirmed that the flying female was about to begin laying eggs. She turned to Holly. "We need to get her into the infirmary immediately, I need at least thirty sterilized containers with five litre capacity and all males, human and Crucnon need to leave the area." She smiled at the youngster still sobbing beneath the glass. "I am Doctor Flamy Gelpa, my friend. You are at Alpha Base on Delpe and in safe hands. None of the humans who imprisoned you are awake."

"My eggs!"

"They will be looked after," the doctor said. "I have cared for hundreds of eggs and they all produced lovely bouncing babies. I'm sure your ones will be perfect. Tell me, my friend, what is your name."

"Pinin Hyrof." the girl gasped. Her sunken face attempted to smile again but instead she gave an utter of pain.

"We must hurry," Flamy ordered.

Jaddig nodded and gave brisk instructions. "Computer, please open the life support cylinder containing Pinin Hyrof."

"Doomwatch remote here, Jaddig. Thank you. I have been keeping a close watch over my charge and have allocated extra nutrients to her. However, her body diverted these onto her eggs. I am afraid she is urgent need of food and liquid. I suggest a honey extract as her stomach will not retain solid food."

Holly rushed back. "We have found forty or more plastic buckets. They've been rinsed with boiling water and are brand new so should be sterile." She grimaced. "I'm afraid there's nothing else."

"That'll do," the doctor whispered. "I now need an intravenous drip set up. We anticipated this condition and have brought satchels of our blood with us but I'll also take Pinin's blood type and ask for donors. "

While the doctor talked, four tiny wheels unfolded out from the cylinder and the glass top slid back. "The chamber can disconnected from life support systems and wheeled out," Doomwatch announced.

"Good," the doctor replied. She reached in and took Pinin's pulse as the youngster gulped for air and struggled to sit up, "No, lay back my friend." Flamy said and placed an oxygen mask on the patient. "Just breathe deep slow breaths. You'll be fine."

Holly was fascinated as she watched the flying female produce twenty-eight eggs, each a small bag of jelly membrane with a minute but perfect two-centimetre foetus inside. Each egg was caught in a bucket and handed to Snimel and Bikut who were in the delivery room to help. Bikut and two other Crucnon of similar blood type to Pinin had all donated a litre of blood and the satchels were suspended above the patient with another intravenous injection placed in the lower left arm.

"What happens now?" Holly whispered as the exhausted mother lay gasping on the bed forty-five minutes later. Her face was grey but her body now a normal size.

"As long as the room temperature is above twenty degrees Celsius, the eggs only have to be kept free of contaminates. They'll grow and hatch in ninety five days."

"And Pinin?"

"If she is fertilised, she will produce another two to three dozen eggs in three months. Fertile females can produce up to a hundred and fifty offspring a year and continue for five or six years with around a thousand offspring before their body is exhausted." The doctor frowned. "Usually they die within a year of this time." She glanced at Holly. "That is how our population became so much larger than yours. I believe human females only bare two or three offspring."

Holly nodded. "We have birth control systems in use." She glanced at the flying female who had lapsed into a gentle sleep. "And if she is not impregnated?"

"If she is free of sperm for six months she enters the retro-metamorphosis stage and loses her wings."

"That's what happened to Jaddig and Bikut," Holly added.

"Oh, so you know about retro-metamorphosis?" the doctor glanced up at the human woman. "I thought humans were ignorant of this stage in a flying female's life. It can be a difficult time."

"I know," Holly replied and told Flamy about the rush to the hospital with Jaddig.

"Yes, if you're going to have more Crucnon settlers in your country, you'll need a women's hospital for maternity and retro-metamorphosis cases."

"It will be of one of our top priorities," Holly replied.

The doctor gazed fondly down at her sleeping patient. "We seldom allow mothers to have more than two egg laying sessions. Their bodies can cope with that and females like Jaddig and Bikut who have been through retro-metamorphosis can expect to live a normal life span of a century or so."

"The same as humans," Holly replied

"There are a few cleaning up procedures," the doctor continued, "She'll be exhausted for a couple of hours but will be fine." She glanced at her patient with sad eyes "Pinin was lucky we arrived when we did. Another day in suspended animation would have killed her. I'm only sorry we were too late to save the other three."

In an adjacent room the other flying females had been wheeled in. Of the original six who had left Delpe in March 2168, three had died and the other two were carrying eggs but not to Pinin's advanced stage. These two had also been awoken and cared for by females, both Crucnon and human. Of those still in suspended animation, two males and one female had died and thirty-one survived. Doctor Iwacu had recommend that in the meantime they all be given intravenous food supplements and kept asleep aboard the space shuttle.

*

After helping remove the bodies of those who never made it, Graham, Clay and George had little to do so decided to examine the other containers in the shuttlecraft.

"My stars," George muttered after they'd opened the fourth container. "Weapons and more weapons, enough to fight a small war."

"Our robotic workers on Inter-galactic Starship 43 removed every item of destruction from on board," Doomwatch's voice filled the interior of the shuttlecraft. "In your hands they may help defend humanity, not destroy it. However, if you wish, we can make them all inoperable."

"No, That's what our ancestors tried" Graham replied. "Leave it in the meantime."

"Very well, Graham."

"But what about the aircraft?" Clay asked.

"It is a FanSpeed, a Mach 4 personal transport with the capacity for twenty three passengers and can be flown by any authorized personnel."

The men had no idea what Mach 4 meant but were impressed when told the three hour journey back to New Washington in FanWarrior would take twenty five minutes in the new craft.

"If you wish to inspect the upper decks and control cabin, please step in the elevator at the Sector C entrance," Doomwatch continued.

The men did and found a self-contained spacecraft with living and sleeping quarters for fifty, storage bays and a control room with lights and monitors flashing everywhere.

"This Space Shuttle Model 157B is capable of maintaining an orbit above the planet's surface but cannot make a deep space journey." Doomwatch reported.

214

"How long can it say in orbit?" Clay asked.

"Indefinitely but this is restricted for living species by food and air supplies."

"And the communications?" George muttered as he stared at three monitors that showed various views of the island they were on.

"All local communications can be monitored and, through Starship 43, all planets with a human or intelligent species known to humans can be contacted. There is a three second time delay to Earth and a twelve-second delay to Spectra 5. However, due to military activities in that zone all messages and contact to Spectra planets have to be cleared through Earth Control."

"I'm impressed," George continued. "And can we view the interior of Starship 43 on the monitors?"

Immediately, the monitors in front showed two identical white circular rooms filled with suspended animation cylinders. They were, though, floating above each other in clusters of nine. Life support tubes seemed to be floating haphazardly everywhere.

"With no conscious beings aboard, the artificial gravity is not functioning. It is brought on line before any creature is awoken." Doomwatch reported. "My robotic helpers are, at the moment separating the settlers from the personnel who hijacked the Starship."

"Then what?" Graham added.

"Starship 43 has been the property of the government of New Washington for four Delpe days, now. All live species aboard will be kept in suspended animation until your government issues an order on what is to be done. "

"That sounds fair," Clay answered and turned to the other two men. "Shall we go and bring Holly and Jaddig up to date on everything?"

"Yes," George replied. "Our friendly computer seems to have everything sorted out."

"Except what to do," Graham added. "Tell me, Doomwatch," he continued. "Does this shuttle have to land here at Alpha Base?"

"It is advisable."

"But necessary?"

"No, we can land on any flat surface if the weather conditions are suitable. Secrecy would be lost if we landed in populated areas."

"That's not important now," Clay added. "I think everyone on the planet knows about the starship, anyway." He turned to Graham. "Are you thinking the same as me?"

"That we should land the shuttle back home? It would save a lot of transportation worries flying back and forth in the FanWarrior."

"That's about itbut Holly and Jaddig could take some persuading," Clay added.

"Let me have a wee chat to Holly," Graham replied.

However, when the men returned to the infirmary they were met in the corridor by Jaddig and Holly who appeared distressed so Graham decided leave the discussion on the starship until later.

"Pinin and the other flying females told us what happened to them," Holly began. "It was sadistic cruelty of the worst kind. If Doomwatch hadn't been activated I have no doubt what-so-ever they would all be dead by now." Her face was white. "I cannot believe humans can act in such a manner. I feel sick at the thought of it."

"What happened?" Graham asked but Holly merely shook her head.

"You don't want to know," she whispered and would say no more.

Jaddig was also tight lipped. "Just turning off their air supply is too good for them," she added in a voice so grim the men glanced at each other with raised eyebrows. "The female humans, from what we heard, were as bad as the males."

"Worse," Holly added. "I suggest we discuss everything with Mum and involve the Vybber government. I know the Crucnon were escaping from their country but officially they are still Vybber citizens." She shrugged. "It might even show them we care about Crucnon as well as humans."

"In the meantime, I think we should concentrate on getting my people who are still in suspended animation back to a healthy condition and wake them up," Jaddig added. "Those monsters can wait."

"But what about the other humans in orbit?" George put in.

"Doomwatch said they're safe. It was only the Crucnon who needed to be rescued so quickly. A few more days or even weeks will make no difference to the humans' health." Jaddig added. "I suggest we help my people first then deal with the criminals."

*

Holly sighed. "Perhaps we are caught up in the emotion of it all, here. A more neutral stance could be needed."

"Possibly but not for those hijackers," Jaddig replied with bitterness still reflected in her yellow eyes, "They deserve nothing!"

"Yes they do," retorted Holly. "A trial and a chance to show their real personalities."

"What!" cut in Jaddig. Her voice rose in anger. "I know I'm not human, Holly but I do have values. These creatures deserve..." she glowered at Holly and turned away unable to complete the sentence.

216

"So they just discretely disappear from the known universe," Holy replied in a soft voice, "and in a few months or years another of group of humans, Crucnon or even crucks decide to do the same thing. What have we gained?"

"I see," Graham grinned. "You think they should be made as an example to others just like using the vacuum bomb to finish the war?"

"Something like that," Holly replied. "We need to show the universe we will not tolerate any species being treated how Pinin and her friends were." She turned to her friend and placed an arm around her. "I am every bit as sickened as you are, Jaddig in the same way as I was when there was a wounded enemy shot down after she attempted to bomb our home and she opened her heart out to us."

Jaddig swung back to face Holly but the anger in her eyes had been replaced by empathy. "I'm sorry, Holly," she whispered. "I should have known you were thinking of us all. I guess I was so hurt and humiliated when I heard how my kind had been treated, I just wanted revenge." She swallowed. "That lowers me to the hijackers' level, doesn't it? "

"No," Holly replied. "You could never be that low, Jaddig. Your morals are so high it makes me feel uncouth at times."

Jaddig fixed her with her eyes and nodded. "Pinin needs another blood transfusion. I promised to donate another litre. I'll need to get over to the infirmary." She turned, touched everyone in the room on the arm and silently left.

*

When the thirty-one Crucnon were brought out of suspended animation, there were mixed emotions. They were all relieved to find themselves rescued and back on Delpe but this was followed by deep despair when they realized that eighty two years had past since their departure so friends and relations would be nearly all be dead. One middle-aged male was heart broken when he discovered his partner had been one of those who'd died while an elderly female did not seem to understand what was happening.

Of more concern for the doctors was the poor physical condition of the group. Besides all being undernourished and covered in filth, many had signs of physical abuse. The females were covered in bruises including welt marks across their buttocks and limbs. Three males had stab wounds and one, a broken arm. Skin sores from rashes to horrible looking boils covered many of the Crucnon's bodies and limbs. Even their clothes were in tatters.

A massive help and cleanup session swung into operation. Alpha Base was well served with bathroom facilities and one storage room contained Crucnon clothes, left by the victims themselves before their departure all those years before. Wounds were cleaned, injections given, five very weak patients given intravenous drips and litres of honey solution distributed. Every immigrant was allocated a bed, provided with clothes and told they were free to choose between becoming New Washington citizens or returning to Vybber.

The twenty-nine who chose to stay in New Washington were informed they would be given full voting rights in their new country and provided with an allocation of land. Lectures were held on the present conditions on Delpe with an honest appraisal of the difficulties the country still had to face.

Pinin and the other two flying females were flooded with female visitors but males, by tradition, were not allowed in the maternity rooms. Late on the third evening after the landing there was another minor crisis when Plugu and Cnac, the other two mothers, began laying eggs simultaneously. Plugu bore twenty-two and Cnac, thirty. A reception room housed the eighty eggs; all colour coded with the mother's name and divided into genders. Of Pinin's growing offspring, fifteen were female and thirteen males.

Holly examined the perfect little forms in amazement. Eyes remained shut but their four arms and two legs often moved around and an embryo chord ran from their tummy out through the jelly membrane that had changed into a darker colour with the surface becoming like toffee.

"The doctor said they're all perfect," Pinin told Holly with pride in her voice as she led her new friend along the rows of yellow buckets. She chuckled. "Normally they are raised in hexagonal shaped hives made of synthetic material but these buckets are fine."

"And what happens after they hatch?" Holly asked.

Pinin shrugged. "I heard the Vybber government has forced hundreds of girls to become flying females but, in my time, only one or two females in a hundred become fertile. The other females don't bare offspring but most have partners or husbands. They adopt a child to become their family. Eight females here have already asked me for a child to rear." She gave a frown. "I'm not sure what will happen with so many fertile females on Delpe now. There could be a tremendous population explosion. I'd like to keep two or three of my babies to raise but I will not be able to afford it."

"Yes you will," Holly replied. "We will make sure you are provided with a home and cared for."

"But I have no husband," Pinin turned serious. "Fertile females without a husband's support are ostracized and regarded as a harlot only fit for offering her services to males for money."

218

"And do you want to continue laying eggs?" Holly asked.

Pinin shook her head. "No," she whispered. "I never wanted to become a flying female in the first place. It just happened and I was removed from my family and forced to live in a government concubine to service the government officials. I had a friend in the Blue Watch and they raided the place and rescued six us. Only Plugu, Chac and myself survived. That's why we left this world. We hoped Earth would be better but we never really had a chance to find out. It was terribly polluted from space with dirty brown clouds covering almost the entire northern hemisphere. The southern part was better but was mainly ocean."

"And when did things start going wrong?" Holly asked

Pinin smiled sadly. "I'll tell you about it all some time but not now, please Holly. I want to think about the future, my babies and life ahead." She looked up. "I want to become a New Washington citizen like Bikut, Snimel and Jaddig."

"You already are," Holly replied. "It became automatic for everyone who chose to stay in New Washington. You're an honoured citizen and mother of the very first Crucnon babies."

"Yes. I beat the other two by three days."

"And we'll have eighty gorgeous babies soon." Holly grinned. "And every one will be wanted and loved."

Pinin stared at her companion, gave a wee shudder and burst into tears. "I can't believe it," she sobbed. She allowed Holly to guide her to a couch where she sat down and found an affectionate arm placed around her.

"You are safe now, Pinin," Holly said. "Safe and amongst friends."

"I know," Pinin sobbed." The trouble is, to us it is only a few months not eighty-two years since we left. I woke up expecting to see the hijackers waiting and the atrocities to start again but instead I found Jaddig and yourself smiling at me." She wiped two hands over her eyes. "I'm not sad, just so happy. There is so much to take in. That's all."

"You weep as much a you wish, Pinin. That's what we all do. Would you like me to go and find Jaddig or one of the others to be with you?"

"No," the youngster replied. She glanced up at Holly and sniffed back more tears. "I changed my mind. I would like to tell you my story if it doesn't bore you."

Holly nodded "Look, come through the cafeteria. I'll get us some coffifake and a muffin. It's pretty late and most humans, at least, have gone to bed. We can talk. I'll tell you how I met Jaddig and the others. You know she was assigned a mission to bomb our town and we shot her down?"

"Did you?" Pinin gasped and managed a smile. "So how come you such good friends now?"

Holly smiled. "I think we both have stories to tell. I've got the time so let's go and have that supper."

Holly began and it was early morning before she'd finished. Pinin, listened with an intense interest, asked a question now and then about conditions in her homeland, giggled when she heard how Jaddig was the only one allowed to access the Base Beta force field but made no comment when she heard of the genetic relationship between Crucnon and humans.

"We knew there was a Base Beta," she commented at the end. "Our shuttle came from Base Gamma. It was further north near the coast."

"Yes, It's still here parked in the other hanger," Holly replied.

"Not next to the brand new one?" Pinin gasped. "We parked it there. I remember someone commenting we could use the new one if we ever returned. Can I go and look?"

"Sure," Holly replied.

She led Pinin out along the deserted corridor. Three DPF guards saluted Holly and a female officer discretely followed them as they made their way through the connecting airlocks and into the outer hanger. Lights flooded on.

The young Crucnon girl gasped. "Except for the flat tyres it's no different," she gasped.

She walked around and examined the bullet holes across the fuselage and stared up at Holly. "I was certain we'd be shot down," she whispered. "We were crowded together inside with bullets screaming around us. We'd never seen guns before. It was the computer that really saved us."

"How?" Holly asked.

"It switched on a force field. We found out later that safety procedures override preset commands. The humans never knew there was a force field. They were as ignorant as we were."

She walked around the FanWarrior once more but refused to go inside. "I've seen enough. Can we go back now and I'll tell you what happened."

Holly was almost asleep on her feet but was very curious about the events all those years before. If she put Pinin off now, she might never learn the truth.

"Some of the story was handed onto me so mightn't be exactly correct," Pinin began. "If it wasn't for my egg mother I mightn't be here now. " She grimaced. "The others, too, of course…"

*

CHAPTER 23

The covered wagon loaded with enough food and supplies to last three weeks and pulled by two sturdy farm horses, headed towards the main highway with two humans, Lieutenant Gordon Dixon and Bowman Nathan McLean, sharing the driver's seat with Tifru Lettug. She was dressed in the warm woollen clothes the Crucnon needed to remain awake in colder climates. The road stretched ahead like a silver line against the blackness of fields beyond, while a million stars twinkled above. Night noises filled the air around them; the clicking of insects, far off hoot of an owl, the constant swish of branches swaying in the breeze, frogs croaking and occasionally a grunt from a krinton, the three metre domestic insect farmed in the area. Periodically they would pass an oasis of light as local farmers' lamps shone out from cracks between curtained windows.

It was close to twenty five hundred hours and in the four hours since they had crossed the New Columbia River into Vybber they had seen no other vehicle. Pine trees now blocked out much of the sky and an eerie blackness surrounded the wagon. Gordon shivered and reached back for a blanket to pull around them all. He rejected a suggestion from Tifru that he have a snooze in the back and watched as the horses strolled leisurely on. The docile animals seemed to be able to follow the road with ease.

"They probably enjoy a night walk in preference to pulling a plough all day," suggested Gordon to Tifru who still held the reins loosely in his hands but there was no reply. The Crucnon was asleep, as was Nathan, snoring peacefully with his head slumped forward. Gordon realized that the horses and himself were the only ones awake in this strange country on the other side of the river.

But he was wrong!

"Do you want a little company, Gordon?" murmured a young female Crucnon who poked her head out from the under the canvas flap behind. "You seemed deep in thought and completely alone."

"Oh, hello, Syleb. Are you awake? Of course you are or you wouldn't be talking to me."

"Well, we don't need to sleep every day," the youngster chided.

The lieutenant grimaced. "I'd forgotten," he replied, "but yes, I would love some company. The others have nodded off."

The refugees spent the next hour discussing their lives, feelings and concerns, while the sedate horses plodded on. Above them, the dark sky disappeared as a faint red and yellow light appeared to their left and the pair lapsed into silence. Gordon jerked awake and realized that he had dozed off, Syleb was asleep beside him and the horses had stopped moving. He shivered and glanced around. The trees were still near the road but spaced further apart. A wide grass verge could be seen in the early dawn light.

"You marvellous beasts," he praised. "You walked all night. I think you deserve a rest." He took up the reins and turned them off the road into a little dip by a stream. After moving forward around a bend so they were away from the road, he jumped down and unhitched them.

"Relax and have some grass," he said. "I'll get our breakfast."

*

For two days the group travelled on through secondary roads. Traffic became heavier as they moved south but they didn't arouse suspicion although at one checkpoint, a guard eyed the humans with suspicion.

"We don't see many of your kind this far south," he grunted. "I hear they're going to close the border so I advise you to get back across the river before the month is out."

"I know," Gordon replied. "We thought we'd get more for our produce away from the border zone." He nodded at the sacks at the back. Potatoes poked out the top but beneath were clothes and their life's possessions.

"It's probably true," the guard muttered. "You heard about our crop failure, no doubt. With this damn drought along the coast, nothing has grown."

He inspected their papers and cast a suspicious eye at Syleb. "Your papers say nothing except you're a student, Young Madam. Why are you riding this farm wagon? You haven't run away from home, I hope."

Syleb smiled sweetly. "No Sir, I'm on my way back to school in Jarta. Uncle Tifru offered me a free ride."

"Yes money is tight," the guard grunted and rubbed his nose," But since you don't have the proper papers…"

Gordon nodded and reached in his jacket pocket. "Would a gold sovereign be sufficient to account for your inconvenience, Sir. After all, having a teenager on your hands…"he shrugged.

"Make it two, human and you can be on your way," the Crucnon snapped.

*

Gradually, the pine forests turned back into farmland and the road zigzagged down a sloping hillside towards a wide plain that stretched away to the south. Far out in the same direction was a line of silvery blue.

"That's where we're heading," said Tifru. "The ocean."

They travelled on in increasingly hot weather with numerous stops to relax the horses who were getting tired and really needed to be replaced. When they reached the base of the hillside their road joined a much larger, well-maintained and used highway. Carts, wagons and stagecoaches were everywhere as well as a number of pedestrians. Traffic kept to the left of the road, not right as in New Washington and Gordon, who shared most of the driving with the Crucnon, had to be careful.

"Stupid country," he muttered. "They don't even know what side of the road to use."

Syleb stretched out her hands and gently dug the human on the leg. "There's nothing wrong in being different," she commented. "The trouble with this country is that the government here want to control everything. They try to make everything the same."

Gordon nodded, "I know Syleb. Sorry. It's just that we seem to have so far to go and I'm tired and fidgety."

Nathan and Tifru, who were sitting on the buckboard with their legs dangling over the edge of the wagon, were also becoming weary and concerned about the length of the trip. They gazed at the traffic around them. A brightly coloured stagecoach pulled by six black horses was approaching from behind. As it moved out to pass, the pair caught a glimpse of a splendidly dressed female sitting inside on puffy cream pillows. Two red uniformed coachmen sat on the front seat urging as much speed out of their mounts as possible while a third clung on to the back.

"Move over," one shouted. "Make way for My Lady!"

Gordon heard the orders and in his haste to get out of the way, pulled the reins to the right instead of the left. Their wagon moved ever so slowly towards the centre of the road rather than the side, straight into path of the coach.

The black horses reared up and dashed further left to avoid crashing into them. Unfortunately, in doing this manoeuvre, they collided with a krinton pulled wagon, carrying logs coming in the opposite direction. The horses avoided the krinton but the coach itself side swiped the logs, plunged forward in front of Gordon's wagon and toppled sideways. With a screech of wood and metal, it slid along the road in a cloud of dust before coming to rest on the grass verge. The horses stamped and snorted foam out of their nostrils but now stood still.

As with many road accidents, events moved so quickly that it took Gordon and the others several seconds to comprehend what had happened.

Their wagon had now stopped in the middle of the road and, luckily, none of them were hurt. Across the road, the krinton were standing still as if nothing happened while the driver stood at the roadside with a terrified expression on his face.

Nathan and Tifru immediately jumped off the buckboard and ran along to the coach lying sideways in a pile of dirt and grass sods with its two topmost wheels spinning in the air. They noticed that Gordon and Syleb were already calming the horses so they concentrated on the coach. Nathan flung open the vehicle's half-door and peered inside. The female had been bounced around like a tennis ball and lay moaning with a sea of yellow blood covering her frock and petticoats.

Tifru bent forward, took the female's pulse and glanced up. "She's alive but is pretty cut up."

"Let's lift her out," Nathan said.

The pair lifted the unconscious woman onto the grass verge. She was still bleeding slightly from a cut across her cheek, there was a swelling bruise on the forehead and several less serious wounds on her limbs. Nathan shook her shoulder gently and the female's eyes flickered.

"I told Priw he always drove too fast and knew this would happen one day," she said in an educated voice as she rose to a sitting position. "May I thank you human and you as well master, for your help..." Her blue eyes studied Nathan and Tifru.

"Our wagon is undamaged, Madam," Tifru replied. "Can we offer you a ride in our humble transport to the nearest village. I'm sure a doctor can be found to help with your wounds."

"Why yes," the female replied. She stood up and brushed herself down. Her coachmen appeared on the bank and stood looking miserable. "Priw and you others. I have been offered a ride to the nearest medical facilities. You are to see to our horses and arrange for the coach to be taken home?"

"Yes, Ma'am." the taller male replied. "There's a wagon driver here who caused the accident. Do you want him arrested?"

"And your crazy speed didn't contribute?" the female snapped. She glowered as Priw had the grace to flush a pale white. "No, let the poor man attend to his own problems." She turned to Tifru and accepted his arms as he helped her along the road verge and into the wagon. Her eyes caught his. "You have strange company," she whispered. "Humans this far south."

"I'm a transporter, My Lady," he replied. "Hired to take them to Jarta to sell their wares."

"With a teenager who just happens to wear the badge of a full moon, symbol of the Blue Watch terrorist group, I believe." Tifru stiffened and glanced sideways at Nathan who had heard the conversation. The female though kept talking. "I am Dilta Hyrof and this unfortunate accident interrupted an important appointment I had."

She squeezed into the covered wagon between the potatoes and touched Syllabi's arm. "Don't worry," she said. "Perhaps it might be prudent to hide your badge, though. Your organization is not too popular this far south of the border."

Syleb nodded, unpinned the offending badge, slipped it in a pocket and gazed nervously at Dilta Hyrof as the wagon, with Tifru in the driver's seat, started moving up the road.

Gordon and Nathan glanced at each other and back at this Crucnon female. Her cut had stopped bleeding but her clothes were ruffled. There was, though, a dignity about the female that was evident even in her present state.

"I believe, Madam," Gordon spoke cautiously, "that you have some sympathy for our organization or your guards would have arrested us by now."

"Call me Dilta, Mr. ... "

Gordon introduced himself and everyone else aboard before he sat back and waited. The horses plodded on and the road became empty again. They were travelling adjacent to the ocean now and lines of breakers curled up, broke and raced up to the golden sand while, on the inland side, parched farmlands stretched away into the distance where the hills and mountains were low in the distant sky.

Dilta glared at him. "I thought you were a bunch of rogues who wanted to foister human values on our society. Two months ago I would have had you arrested." She glanced around the swaying wagon with those large yellow eyes. "The lot of you!"

"So what changed your mind?" Gordon added.

"My niece," the female replied in a hushed voice. "She's a flying female called up to do her duty. I was on my way to the local concubine to try to have her released." She shrugged. "However, I doubt if even my standing in society will be sufficient to help. "

Syleb interjected in a frightened voice. "Thank the Deity I never entered metamorphosis."

"You are young, child," Dilta Terudi replied. "It can happen to any female between fourteen and twenty two. Within a few weeks your wings grow and your body undergoes the changes necessary for motherhood." She sighed. "I know. It happened to me when I was seventeen. I guess it was my genes that were handed onto Pinin. You see she is really my egg daughter, not my niece."

"And how did your egg daughter change your mind about the Blue Watch?" Gordon interrupted as he tried to steer the conversation back to the present situation.

"She was a university student, very bright and had a brilliant future but, after her change, she was forced into this breeding centre. I want her out!" Her eyes turned cold. "I would do anything to help her."

"And the Blue Watch?" Gordon pressed.

"I believe you must be on your way to one of the ancient bases set up by your ancestors in several secret valleys around, probably Base Delta, a hundred kilometres along the coast from here."

Gordon stared at Nathan who gave a very slight nod. "And if that was true?"

"You won't get there," Dilta replied in a blunt voice. "The base is surrounded by the military waiting for an attempt by humans to reach it. With the enforced separation of our species soon to come into force, our military would love to access the base and the secrets it contains. They leaked the information of its position and are waiting for you to arrive."

"We can try," muttered Nathan.

"And end up in a Vybber jail." Dilta smiled. "But all is not lost. There are rumours of another base, Base Gamma, I believe it is called, in the foothills only few hour's journey from where we are now."

Gordon sat up and stared at the female. He wanted to believe her but wondered why she was so loose with the information. After all, humans were not liked or trusted in this country.

"Yes, I do have a selfish interest, Gordon," Dilta Terudi's voice grew hard, "If I help you find this base, I'd like you to use the air machine I have heard is inside to attack the concubine and rescue my egg daughter. We will make a pact. My information for your help."

*

A beautiful rocky beach tucked in the city of Jarta but that was the only positive thing about the place. Hundreds of identical stone houses had been built with no regard to maintaining the original natural beauty. Taverns and inns in various stages of disrepute occupied most corner sites while dilapidated flea markets covered the few open areas fought for attention amongst the litter, garbage and rats.

It was early evening two days later when Tifru and Gordon, dressed as farm workers, ambled into a run down tavern near the wharf. Gordon towered above the local patrons as he slid onto a bar side stool.

"Bar man, bring us a double ale each," he demanded in the local language and slapped two coppers on the grease stained counter.

The wizen barman glanced at him and was about to ignore the request when Gordon stood up to his over metre ninety height and leaned a muscular frame over the bar.

"Are you deaf or something? I said a double ale for my friend and myself and don't fill the glasses with froth and short change me. Understand?" He took a tiny but vicious looking knife out of his belt and started cleaning his fingernails.

"I wouldn't annoy him if I was you. Humans get mean if crossed," Tifru murmured softly.

The bar man gulped and hurriedly filled two mugs with frothy brown ale. "Yes, Sir," he whimpered, "Is there anything else I can get you gentlemen? Some food perhaps. We have some excellent meat pies."

Tifru stared straight at him. "Forget the food but we do need information. We're looking for a man called Spinskin, whom, I believe, frequents this inn on occasions." Dilta had given them the name of a local gang leader who, she said, knew information about Base Gamma.

The bar man paled slightly as he handed over the drinks and wiped his hands on a dirty dishcloth. "You don't want to talk to him, Kind Sirs. He's... what shall we say, not too friendly with strangers."

Gordon reached out and grabbed the publican by the collar and proceeded to lift him off the floor with one arm. The Crucnon's face turned a sickly blue colour as his air supply was cut off. Tifru turned to see a rough looking individual at the table behind reaching for a knife. He touched his friend on the back. Nobody saw how but the human was suddenly holding a long, shiny and very sharp sword in his hand. He glared at the man.

"My advice to you, Sir," he stated so he could just be heard, "is to get on with your drink and look after your own affairs."

The male nodded, wide eyed, and withdrew his hand. Meanwhile, the bar man was spluttering and kicking his feet in the air as Gordon put his nose right up to his face and snarled, "I want information, not advice! You seem to be a little slow at understanding a simple request." He let the male down to the floor before releasing him.

The barman rubbed his neck to help restore circulation and pointed to a door near the counter. "He's playing cards out the back," he muttered in a sullen voice.

"Fine!" snapped Tifru.

Gordon grinned, "We did well, Tifru," he praised.

"Keep an eye on the entrance while I get our man," Tifru replied. He walked to the back room door; pushed it open and continued through to find four rough looking characters arguing over a half finished game of cards. Ignoring the hostile glares, he ambled across until he came to the one nearest the wall, a well-built Crucnon with eagle tattoos on his four arms.

"If you want supplies, I have a human who can access the ancient base," he muttered in the male's antennae. "He wants the flying machine but everything else can be yours. Interested?"

The male glanced up and saw Gordon leaning against the wall, so tall he had to bend to avoid the room's rafters. For someone who had never seen a human before, the lieutenant was quite an imposing sight. The gangster stared back at his cards, picked one out, slapped it on the table with one hand and gathered the pile of coins in the middle of the table with one other.

He then looked at Tifru with watery brown eyes. "Just the two of you, are there?"

"He has a human friend and a girl. Won't go anywhere without them."

"No tricks!" the male glowered.

"A human is hardly likely to be working for the police, is he?" Tifru snorted. "And why do you think he is so far south right at the ocean?"

"True," came the grunted reply. "It'll cost you."

"As I said, you can have the base and everything in it. We'll throw in our wagon and horses, too."

Spinskin nodded. Horses were rare in Vybber and were preferred to the strong but slow krinton.

"Met me out the back here at six hundred hours tomorrow morning. It's a three hour journey inland." He reshuffled the cards and began to deal another round.

"We'll be there," Tifru whispered and gave Gordon a slight nod who, in turn, lifted an index finger to Nathan who was waiting at the bar in case things went wrong.

*

It was zero two hundred hours, coffifake mugs and crumbs littered the tiny table as Pinin completed her story. Holly, Jaddig and Bikut, who had found them in the cafeteria, glanced at each other.

"So what happened?" Bikut sipped the last drop of liquid out of her mug and sat it down.

"It was similar to your experience," Pinin added. " Spinskin was true to his word and Gordon accessed Base Gamma." She gave a chuckle. "The base computer tricked the gangster, though. After two hours, all the weapons they were given became inoperable. There was some self-destruct mechanism in them.

My aunt managed to find me in the concubine, confessed she was my egg mother and told me to bring as many friends as possible and be in the courtyard the following afternoon at fifteen hundred hours. We were allowed outside for three hours in the afternoon. Plugu, Cnac and the others were with me. The Fan Warrior appeared and landed by us, we ran aboard and the craft took off. I was terrified."

"And the bullet holes?" Jaddig asked.

Pinin frowned. "I'm not sure but I think Gordon and Nathan never realized the Crucnon had guns. They only used crossbows themselves. We were shot at as we flew out over the wall, our FanWarrior blasted some ray thing back and the whole wall beneath us disintegrated. There was smoke and junk everywhere. I remember a terrible screaming noise when something hit a propeller and the computer shut the engine on that side down. It took us seven hours but we flew on and picked up everyone waiting for us back at a rendezvous on the New Washington side of the New Columbia River. We finally made it to this island."

"And what happened to everyone?" Holly asked.

Pinin gave a sad look. "I never heard from my egg mother again so I guess she'll be long dead. The others are all here."

"Where?" Bikut gasped.

"Syleb and Tifru are probably in the dormitory asleep. Gordon and Nathan are in suspended animation on Starship 43."

"Oh my stars!" Holly whispered. "And to think this happened over eighty years ago."

"Yes," Pinin replied. "I worked out I must be a hundred and one."

"And have hardly any wrinkles," Jaddig added without even a smile.

Pinin lifted her eyes to stare at Jaddig. "What do you mean 'hardly any', Young Lady?" she retorted. "A few stretch marks perhaps, but…"

The lone DPF on guard at the door shook his head in wonder when the group suddenly burst into raucous laughter and were hugging each other with affection.

"And I thought they were only drinking coffifake," Holly heard him mutter to himself. "Women, no matter what species, are all alike and I'll never understand them."

*

CHAPTER 24

Morning arrived and, with it, the usual scrumptious breakfast provided in the cafeteria. Holly was drinking her second mug of coffifake when she heard a polite cough. Pinin was standing there with a shy grin spread across her face. A step behind, were two Crucnon, a young female of high school age and a middle aged male.

"Holly, meet Syleb and Tifru," Pinin said in a proud voice.

Holly stood, stepped forward and gave the pair an embrace. "Join me for breakfast," she said. "I heard all about your journey across Vybber."

Tifru nodded and slid into the bench. "I hear the place is all cars and combos, electricity and other modern conveniences now. It won't be the same, somehow." He grinned at Pinin. "I beat she exaggerated everything, too."

"I did not," Pinin retorted "Most of the story was what you told me, anyway."

"We all played our part," Syleb added. She had enormous blue eyes that sparkled when she spoke. "In many ways, it's a pity we left Delpe. Earth was awful, you know ... polluted and overcrowded. We were tolerated but were not really made welcome." She grimaced and faced Holly across the table. "The rumour is going around that we're partly human. Is it true?"

"Yes," Holly answered. "It was one of the facts made secret during your time. When they decided to separate the species they also suppressed much of the history and scientific achievements brought in by the original ancestors."

Tifru shrugged. "Even in our day we were told nothing. The bases were secret; we didn't have electricity..." He shrugged. "So what happens now?"

"We want to bring the hijackers down to stand trial. Afterwards, we're moving everyone home to New Washington." Holly smiled. "We decided to leave the rest of the humans until afterwards. There are so many of them. However, if you wish we can wake Gordon and Nathan up."

"Will you?" Syleb squealed in an excited voice. "I'd like that! We went through so much together."

"Sure!" Holly replied. "What about the other humans aboard? Did you know many of them?"

"No," Syleb replied. "When we transferred to Starship 43 before it was hijacked, the settlers were already in suspended animation. They wouldn't even know about the hijackers, or us if it comes to that."

"When we arrived above Earth in Starship 7, a bit over eighty years had passed," Tifru added. "We stayed on the planet six months before deciding we wanted to return here. If we used the old ship to return in, it would have been would be another eighty-year journey. Starship 43 was originally going to take settlers to the Spectra 5 system but there is some sort of war going on so they agreed to come here. We were told that if the settlers found Delpe unsuitable there was another uninhabited planet they could to travel on to. We gladly accepted a ride on the new ship."

"All of us, along with Gordon Nathan, the only humans who volunteered to return with us, arrived on Starship 43 and were preparing to go into suspended animation when the starship was boarded," Syleb added. "I think Pinin and the others told you the rest of the story."

"Yes," Holly replied. "I'm just so sorry about all the suffering you all went through."

"The hijackers stayed at sub-light speed so they could remain conscious. I think they wanted to plan what to do at this end when they woke up. I know they spent hours reprogramming the computer system." Tifru added. "It was after about six weeks of suffering we were forced into the suspended animation chambers and the next thing we knew we were here, rescued by you wonderful people." He chuckled. "Gordon and Nathan are going to be as surprised as we were."

"What say we take the shuttle up to Starship 43 and you can show us around?" Holly continued.

Syleb and Pinin glanced at each other. "Is it really necessary?" Pinin asked. "I'm so scared that when we get there, something will happen and we'll never get back."

"It'll be safe," Holly reassured. "The computer is under our control."

"I know but…" Syleb's lip dropped. "If you really want us," she whispered.

"Not at all," Holly answered. The pair appeared so threatened she felt annoyed with herself for making the suggestion. "I understand."

"I'll come," Tifru offered but he also looked doubtful. "

"Look," Holly said. "I was curious, that's all. Doomwatch, that's the computer that runs the starship now, assured me that robotic workers can do anything we wish so we don't need to have anyone aboard."

"In that case, don't risk going there," Tifru warned. "There may be more in built computers or pre-programmed orders. We thought we were perfectly safe when, out of nowhere, the hijackers arrived. We were never told another shuttle had arrived." He stared at Holly. "I wouldn't trust anybody on Earth, either. Something is wrong there."

"What do you mean?"

"It's just the situation. It was almost like Vybber when we left. On the surface it seemed okay but there are big secrets we don't know about. Even some of the top officials were scared."

"But you trust us?" Holly asked in a curt voice.

"You are just like Gordon and Nathan. I'd trust them with my life. So to answer your question and I'm sure the girls will agree, yes we trust you and hope the feeling is mutual."

"Yes, I do," Holly said softly but her lip dropped. "However, a horrible thought came to my mind."

"And what's that?" Pinin asked.

"Those four thousand settlers on board. You said you never met them. How do we know whether to trust them or not? They could overwhelm us."

Tifru nodded. "Can I make a suggestion?" he asked.

"Of course."

"Download their files and get your computer here to analyse them independent from the inboard computer. If in doubt, send the starship back to Earth with them aboard."

Holly nodded. "I'll need to discuss it with my colleagues but that sounds a very sensible idea. We're definitely bringing the hijackers down and putting them on trial." She smiled. "Thanks all of you. It's given me plenty to ponder."

"Just one other small point," Pinin added and continued speaking after Holly nodded. "One or two of the hijackers weren't too bad. The leaders seemed to have a strange control over the younger ones. Some were almost as frightened as we were."

"We will take everything into account," Holly replied. "Your own statements will be very important."

*

After a busy day, it was late afternoon before Holly found time to relax a little in the small quarters she shared with Graham.

"You know," she said to her companion as she sat in front of a mirror brushing her hair. "I can relate to all the new arrivals. Pinin, Syleb and even old Tifru are like Jaddig, Bikut, Snimel and Wunep. When we're talking I don't even notice they have four arms and, in their body suits I hardly realize they have no hair beneath."

"Yeah, " Graham replied. "Old Tifru just acts like George."

232

Holly nodded but still remained serious. "What I mean is that I trust their opinions. I don't think anyone should go up to the starship, at least in the meanwhile."

"I was keen to have a peep around," Graham confessed with a shrug. "All this advanced technology of our fellow humans fascinates me."

"Yes but what are their motives?" Holly replied, "These settlers may be hardened criminals or renegades as far as we know. Even that president could have his own ulterior motives. Why would he really care about a handful of humans on the other side of the galaxy? Who can we trust?"

"Our friends with the redundant arms." Graham smiled as he slipped his own around Holly and ran his chin across her face.

"Graham!" she retorted. "Don't be racist." However, she gazed into his eyes and responded when he reached forward to kiss her. "So nobody is to go to the starship until we find out more. Okay!"

"Okay!" Graham responded but he appeared to have more immediate thoughts on his mind.

Holly noticed and retreated a step. "Graham!" she retorted with a flash in her eyes. "Not now? It's still daytime. Someone may walk in."

"Lock the door," Graham laughed and grabbed her into his arms. This time, though, she did not step back.

*

The next morning was another hot tropical day, perfect for Crucnon but a little too hot outside for humans who preferred the air-conditioned hangers. After speaking to her mother back in New Washington, Holly asked Doomwatch to prepare the human hijackers as well as Gordon and Nathan for the journey down to the surface.

"You don't want the new migrants?" Doomwatch asked in the usual neutral voice.

"No, you reported that they are safe and being kept in suspended animation in the mean time."

"That is true," the computer replied. "If you can clear the personnel from the launch zone, I'll prepare the shuttle for the launch."

"One other request," Holly slipped in. "I wish to view the settlers in their suspended animation chambers. Can you bring a view up on the monitor?"

"I can show you the hijackers," the computer replied and the floating cylinders appeared on the monitor in front of Holly. It zoomed in to one to show a human girl asleep inside, before moving on to show close up views of four other humans."

"Good," replied Holly. "They look healthy. Now I'd like to see the original passengers on Starship 43."

"That is not possible," Doomwatch replied.

Holly frowned and a spasm of apprehension flooded her body. "Why?" she asked.

"Their chambers do not have a transparent top so cannot be inspected without opening. This would be unwise until the life-form is awoken."

"I see," Holly shrugged and attempted to remain light-hearted. "It doesn't really matter. When can the humans I asked for be back at Base Alpha?"

"Three hours, ten minutes from the shuttle's take off. It takes a while for the robotic helpers to wheel the chambers aboard."

"Good. Do it!" Holly ordered.

She frowned and thought about the conversation. Conversations with computers usually consisted of orders or questions that were answered. This time, though, it was as if Doomwatch was avoiding her questions. Holly wandered out into the corridor to find the base almost deserted.

"Everyone has gone outside into the sunshine," one of the guards commented. "It's pretty hot out there but is a beautiful under the trees by the lake."

That was where she found Graham talking to Jaddig. Further up the small beach their Crucnon friends, all in bright swimming suits, were swimming in the shallow clear water. Shouts of laughter and the noise of splashing water filled the air. Out here it was probably as safe as anywhere on the island to talk but Holly was still cautious.

"Something isn't quite right," she said in a low voice and repeated the conversation she had had with Doomwatch.

"So," Graham replied. "It sounded logical enough."

Jaddig though stared at Holly. "I know what you mean," she whispered.

"What am I missing?" Graham asked.

"The computers; Len, Doomwatch the ones on the FanWarriors, always talk of humans, Crucnon or even creatures but, if what Holly said was correct, this time the term "life-form" was used. I have never heard it speak that way before."

"Neither have I," Holly gasped.

Graham also frowned and scratched his upturned chin. "You're correct, Jaddig," he said. "I think we will need to be careful."

*

"Gordon! Nathan! Over here," Syleb screamed while Tifru stood back with the others as the ramp on the shuttlecraft lowered with a clunk and two men almost staggered out.

She rushed up into their arms and plastered them both with kisses. "You both need a shave," she laughed. "Tifru's here and come and meet Holly, Graham Jaddig and the others Pinin's laid her eggs and ..." The words came tumbling out, her eyes shone and arms swung everywhere.

"Whoa!" the tall, well-built lieutenant laughed at the youngster's excitement. "Slow down a little."

Syleb tucked her arms through both men's and lead them over to Holly.

"Pleased to met you Holly," Gordon held out a massive hand and seemed quite formal after Syleb's bubbly introduction. "You have a famous name." He gave a slight grin, "I knew Gerald Jurjevics, your great, great grandfather, I guess he'd be."

Holly smiled, took his hand and gazed into the warm eyes. "Mum might know of him but I'm afraid the name is unfamiliar to me," she replied. "I noticed you have made quite an impression on Syleb, here."

"Yes," Gordon replied in a soft voice. "We went through a lot together."

"We heard," Graham replied as he also reached for the new arrival's hand. "That bit in the tavern . . ."

"Yes, she's a little gossip, isn't she?"

"I am not," Syleb pouted and thrust her four hands on her hips. "Anyhow, it was Pinin who told that story, not me."

"It was," Holly agreed, "and that appeared a most important meeting. Without it you may never have found Gamma Base."

"So it wasn't just gossip," Syleb added with a satisfied smirk on her face.

With all the greetings and small chat, it wasn't until late that evening that Holly, Jaddig and Graham arranged to speak with Gordon and Nathan in the cafeteria.

"I'm glad you had us awoken onboard the starship," Gordon began. He waved away another sandwich Jaddig offered him. "No thanks. I reckon I've eaten so much in the last three hours to last another hundred years.

"We received your cryptic message and went exploring," Nathan added. "It was funny but we found no access to half the ship. All the corridors and airlocks circle the area facing this planet. No matter how far we went we always ended up in the same area."

"When we asked for access, we were informed the rest of the ship was in a vacuum. The only two access doors we found were firmly locked with different access mechanisms," Gordon continued. "It was as if the ship has two complete and separate environments. "

"So we only have more unanswered questions," Jaddig responded. Holly and Graham both met her eyes and nodded.

"There is a mystery there, no doubt," Gordon replied. "I remember, I was curious about this when we first arrived on the starship when it was orbiting Earth. When we were hijacked, there were more immediate problems and I guess I forgot about it.

"And what about the hijackers?" Nathan asked as he munched into his third sandwich.

Holly grinned. "Our ancestors were prepared for any situation. Base Alpha has a very secure brig in the cellar five floors down. It's a bit filthy and dark. We made sure half the guards are Crucnon and the rest, our toughest DPF men. I guess they'll be waking up about now. "

"Holly does have a sadistic side," Graham added.

"It was Jaddig's suggestion." Holly gave a sweet smile. "I'm merely following the vice president's orders."

"If you're following orders, it'll be the first time," Jaddig responded and turned to the visitors. "We believe Holly has the old admiral's determination," she explained.

"Yes," Gordon replied in a slow drawl. "We were told you're related to him, too, Jaddig. "

Jaddig screwed her face up "There's a skeleton in everyone's cupboard." she answered. "I try to forget about those imperfections in my biological past." She attempted to keep a straight face but her lips cracked into a smile when Holly placed playful hand on her shoulder.

*

After researching historical records on the fairest justice systems, it was decided to base the trials of the twenty-three hijackers on the International Tribunals used on Earth in the late twentieth and early twenty-first centuries. In the whole of New Washington there were only three judges so members of the House of Representatives were nominated to build the number up to seven.

Andrea declined a place on the bench so the government nominated Holly, Jaddig, Suzi, and Rob Cotterell as the government representatives on the tribunal. The trial was held at Alpha Base and lasted twelve days. On the afternoon of the last day, the twenty-three humans, now somewhat subdued after initial ranting and refusal to co-operate, stood to await the outcome. Expressions of the defendants ranged from open defiance to uncertainty and fright.

Senior Judge Hilton Mazarin, dressed in a dark business suit and sombre tie began his deliberations "There are a total of fifty two charges as listed on the charge sheet," he said in a quiet voice and fixed an icy stare at the men and woman charged. "The tribunal has come to a decision and find Thomas Albert Anderson, Beverly Jane Chattersfield..." as so he went on with sixteen names read in alphabetical order. ..." guilty to all charges."

The defendants stood with defiant looks on their faces and one man spat on the floor in a futile effort to attract attention to himself.

Mazarin coughed and continued, "The following have been found guilty to lesser charges. They are as follows..." For twenty minutes the judge read out four more names and went through the fifty-two charges to declare each person's guilt or innocence for each one.

The twenty defendants mentioned shall be transported to the Republic of Vybber that has agreed to..."

"You can't do that!" screamed a woman with long blonde hair and Nordic appearance.

"It has been done, Ms. Liepman. New Washington is a small nation with limited penal institutions."

"They're insects!" shouted the women. "As a human, I demand decent and just facilities."

"And you, Madam are an animal," Jaddig interrupted the judge and glowered at the woman. "You chose to treat innocent victims worse than one would treat rats. You gave up any rights with your despicable behaviour. If I had my way, you'd be executed at dawn." She hesitated. "Luckily for yourself, my colleagues on the bench here have a more humane attitude." Her face turned to a tiny smile that never reached the eyes. "Humane! Interesting word that, but somewhat archaic, as this trial showed."

"The twenty guilty prisoners will leave the dock," Judge Mazarin announced and watched as the line was hustled out of the room to leave three young humans, two men and a woman behind. One youth had a tear stained face and the woman, younger than Holly, stood behind the wooden dock with a trembling lip and downcast eyes.

"Barry Andrew Chetwyn, Janice Vera Paterson and John Cameron Tunbridge; the tribunal has decided that, though acting extremely foolishly at times, you were all placed in a situation that you had little or no control over. Furthermore, the testimony of several of the witnesses spoke of your attempts to make the conditions easier for them. Food and warm clothing was sneaked to the victims and medical help provided." The judge stopped. "You have been found innocent to all charges and will be offered a flight back to Earth on the next available starship. In the meanwhile, you are welcome to join the settlement of New Washington as free citizens."

The young woman looked up in astonishment while the youths merely grinned and shook each other by the hand.

"Thank you, Your Honour," the woman spoke in a quiet voice and fixed her eyes on Jaddig. "I apologize for the treatment your kind suffered in our hands."

"And I accept your apology, Janice Paterson," Jaddig replied.

She glanced up and saw Holly standing at the back of the room. Their eyes met and they both smiled. It had been a difficult time but justice had been done with the result, in many ways, quite different from what either of them had anticipated.

*

At seven hundred hours the following morning the FanWarrior rose into the sky above Alpha Base and headed for a remote city in western Vybber with the well-secured prisoners on board. Holly and Graham were watching the aircraft rise above the observation deck on the island when Janice Paterson, Barry Chetwyn, and John Tunbridge stepped out of the elevator and walked across to the observation deck.

The three newcomers appeared self-conscious and stared nervously at the ocean below until Holly made a point of moving across to where they were standing and started a conversation. "And what are you going to do with your land?" she asked with a small grin.

"Land?" John asked. "What land? We have no land and no money to buy any."

"Every new citizen of New Washington is given an allocation," Holly explained. "It's not large but if you can grow enough food to feed yourself and have a ten percent surplus after three years, the land becomes your property. You're also permitted an interest free loan to build a basic house of eighty square metres or smaller. You three will be able to have first choice of sites before the settlers on Starship 43 are brought down."

"You're kidding!" Barry replied with a slight grin and glanced over at Janice. "Can the allocations be combined?"

"Sure," Holly replied. "Families are given a larger area than single people. Why?"

Barry flushed. "It's just that Janice and I are sort of partners."

"Sort of," the young woman scoffed. "Barry Chetwyn, if you call our arrangement, sort of, I'll..." She tried to appear angry but laughed when Barry stepped across, placed his hands on her cheeks and deposited a kiss on her lips.

"Janice is pregnant," he said with pride in his voice. "We never dreamed we'd ever be free again. Now, thanks to all of you, we have a chance."

"Congratulations," Holly replied. "We need all the new citizens we can get."

Janice smiled. "On Earth there are so many people it would be impossible to buy land, unless you're a millionaire or have a family that is." She slipped an arm around Barry and cuddled in close.

"Is that what attracted you to that organization that hijacked the starship?" Holly slipped in.

"I suppose," Janice replied, "They made everything sound so good but after we'd joined a few months we couldn't get out. They had a hold over us." She stopped and stared out across the island. "They took all our processions and said they'd provide for us. I guess they did. This bit about being against outworlders, as we called them, was a recent idea after aliens began to colonize Earth. There are three or four different species there now and the planet is already overcrowded. It seemed logical that they should be told to go home." She flushed and glanced at the Jaddig at the front of their cabin. "That was before I knew any of you."

"After the starship was taken over by the organization," John added, "we were told if we fraternized with the Crucnon or human settlers we'd be punished. We were little more than prisoners ourselves."

"I've still got scars to prove it," Janice continued and lifted her jersey. Holly stared at three purple welts across the woman's lower back.

"That was for just something minor," she whispered.

"Why didn't you show those at your trial?" Holly gasped.

"In our whole lives, nobody believed anything we said," the young woman continued. "We had no faith in receiving any justice here. We thought our leaders would go free but not us."

"Why?" Holly asked.

"They have money and have used it on Earth to bribe their way to freedom. We had no reason to believe it would be any different here."

Holly nodded, excused herself and walked to the elevator and called Jaddig on the intercom. "Jaddig," she said. "Are you busy?"

"Not really," the Crucnon woman replied. "Just helping in the maternity ward. Why, Holly?"

"I want you to come up to the observation deck and talk to Janice, Barry and John. Their experiences sound almost identical to yours before we met."

Jaddig went quiet and Holly frowned. "You should know me by now, Jaddig," she said solemnly. "I'm not trying to make a point or prove anything. It's just that they're so interesting to talk with and are really quite insecure."

"Oh Holly!" Jaddig laughed. "I do know what you mean. I'll come up straight away."

Moments later she was seated with the three newcomers and engaged in an enlightening chat. After a few moments Holly dropped out of the conversation and stood back to watch the four. Janice had just made a point and flapped her hands around while Barry hardly took his eyes from the girl. They were obviously very much in love.

"Excuse me," Holly said and slipped away along the deck to where Graham had retreated. "I love the view here, My Dear."

Graham grinned and held a pair of binoculars out. "Have a look at those birds on the other side of the lake"

As Holly bent forward he reached across he lifted her hair and deposited a kiss her on the cheek. She smiled and reached for his hand. "We did the right thing with the trial," she said softly.

"I think we did" Graham replied. "Those three over there don't look like hardened criminals to me."

"No," replied Holly. "They aren't. I have a strange feeling they're going to be an asset to our community."

"And the other four thousand to come?"

Holly smiled and bent up to kiss Graham. "There will be a cross section. Some won't cope while others will find everything wrong. Some will bring prejudices with them but I'm hopeful most will become useful citizens."

Graham threw his hands up in mock horror. "Imagine four thousand Malone Davidsons! " he chuckled.

"Yes, there are extremes, aren't there?" Holly replied.

She felt so peaceful inside, sort of proud and confident all tied together in a big bundle. Her gaze met Graham and she saw the same expression Barry was using with Janice a few metres away. Thoughts moved on to Clay and Bikut and she grinned again. She brought the binoculars to her eyes and focused on the lake where five huge white birds were about to land. Their webbed feet extended as they skidded in, plopped down on the water in a perfect line, paddled across to where tall rushes grew out of the water and disappeared in the shadows.

"Perhaps we should turn the base into a holiday resort," she said. "I doubt if the view from here could be surpassed anywhere on Delpe. The deep blue lake, green trees…beach!"

"Yes," grinned Graham, "but look the other way."

Holly turned to where the deep valley appeared covered in thick jungle. "There are only trees below," she commented.

240

"But the view there is faked. In reality, you'd see the space shuttle, cranes and the whole space port, junk and all."

"I know but it's still a beautiful island."

"Like our whole world," Graham added. "Beautiful on the outside but a bit raw underneath."

"I guess." Holly threw back her red hair, smiled and reached out for her partner's hand. "But it is our world, Graham. Nobody can deny us that. It is changing quickly but I'm sure it is also becoming a better place.

*

CHAPTER 25

Holly was dreaming! She tossed in her sleep and an arm slung into Graham, snoring peacefully across the bed. She opened her eyes in the dark room, yawned and focused on the digital clock. Three forty seven!

She wriggled up into a sitting position and attempted to recall the dream. Somehow it seemed important. Perhaps it was something from her mother. She grimaced and, a second later gave a gasp of fright. The voice was still in her head, talking to her as if Mum was in the room. But Holly was awake and her mother, thousands of kilometres away at home.

"Sweetheart, listen," said the voice. "If you hear me in your mind, just think a reply. Don't speak out loud."

"How do I know this is not some alien or computer trick?" Holly thought but subconsciously suspected it was some sort of delusion.

Immediately, though there was a response. "Oh, thank the stars!" Andrea's voice penetrated her brain. "You are awake. I was only receiving your dreams."

"Mum it sounds like you but I need proof," Holly thought.

"Remember your tenth birthday, Sweetheart. We gave you a crossbow and you loved the red and green feathers on the arrows. Later you were frustrated when that boy, Philip I think his name was, beat you in the school crossbow championship for Year 5 children."

Memories flooded back into Holly's mind. It must be her mother. Nothing would have been recorded about that minor incident in her life. "Okay Mum, I'm convinced. What's this all about?"

"This mind probe is coming to you via a space satellite that has arrived in orbit around our planet. I have received a recorded message from Earth. The President of the United States of America, Doctor Peter Zarbor has dire news and there is something you must do within the next five hours."

"Go on, Mum."

"All the computers on Delpe, even Doomwatch, are infiltrated by an alien species and need to be manually wiped."

"How, Mum?"

Holly listened to the instructions that involved how to reprogram the base computer as well as those on the space shuttle and aircraft. The procedure was relatively easy but Holly had to keep everything to herself in case the computer overheard her voice.

"I have already over ridden the computers here," Andrea's voice said. "So the rest is up to you. Take care, Sweetheart. If you wish to contact me by mind probe, think Mind Probe Access Code followed by your date of birth to reconnect."

"Right, Mum," Holly thought and found her mind clear of her mother's voice just as if a telephone had been disconnected.

After a nervous wait until morning, Holly had breakfast and strolled into the tiny base library. She searched through a row of blue covered electronic logbooks and pulled out Number 19.

"Can I help with your research?" Doomwatch's voice filled the room and made her jump in fright.

"No," Holly stuttered, "I'm just curious about those birds on the lake and was told they were introduced unofficially from Earth by an original crew member. I thought the old records might tell me more." This was a story her mother had suggested she use.

"There is nothing on record," the computer continued. "Apparently quite a few species were introduced without official approval. Enjoy your research." The room went silent.

The cover of the logbook opened to show a four by two-centimetre yellow computer disk, similar to hundreds of others in the library. In spite of herself, Holly's hands trembled as she slipped the disk in a slot in the computer and a view of the title page flashed on screen, as well as the words, *Please enter your name and loan number.*

This was it! Guided by her mother's voice in her mind, Holly reached for the keyboard and typed in *Code 54 Manual Override Virus.* She gulped and pressed the enter key.

Without even a flicker, the monitor blanked out and so did everything else! Lights switched off, every pilot light on the base flicked to flashing red, elevators stopped, doors froze, stoves in the kitchen switched off; even people having a morning shower found the water stopped flowing.

An agonizingly slow twenty seconds later, red emergency lights came on throughout the base and a siren began to howl followed by a pre-recorded voice advising everyone to remain where they were and wait for emergency evacuation procedures to be announced. Shouts and calls were heard everywhere.

Holly waited as a test pattern rolled across the screen for another two minutes before words appeared. *Download Successful.* There were three buttons to choose from. Holly avoided the *Cancel,* and *Start Evacuation Procedures* to press *Reinstate Local Service* and everything came on line again. Holly heaved and glanced at the clock. The whole procedure had taken only five minutes.

"This computer is off line to any incoming signals but all local memory banks can be accessed," a metallic voice filled the room. "Please select a voice and name you wish to use."

Holly was so intent on watching the monitor she did not hear Graham walk into the room. He stood behind her and stared at the screen.

"What's happening, Holly," he asked." The whole base blacked out."

Holly leaped in fright and swung around. "Gra... ham!" she yelped. "Don't sneak up on me!"

"Thank you," said the computer in a perfect imitation of Graham's voice. "Please advise all personnel I can be contacted by stating my name."

Graham stared at Holly. "Is that my voice? " he asked with a frown.

"It is," Holly suddenly grinned. "You spoke at the very moment the computer was picking one to use." She turned serious and told her partner everything that had happened.

"This is Grey Ham speaking," the computer interrupted. "Do you wish to . . .

"Oh my stars," Holly cut in. "It has interpreted my scream as the name to use."

It was Graham's turn to grin. "And it even got my name wrong. Talk about being a ham."

Holly grunted and spoke to the computer. "Just use the forename Grey, in future," she ordered.

"Sure Holly," replied Graham's voice. "Grey it shall be."

So Grey became the new voice at Base Alpha. Afterwards, Holly took the same disk and overrode the computers on the shuttlecraft and the two aircraft in the hanger and began a mind probe to report the success to her mother. She was though, flooded with a male voice in her mind.

"This is a recording so I am afraid you cannot reply," said the voice. "This is President Peter Arbour speaking. It is essential you override the computer aboard Starship 43. To stop or replay these messages just think an appropriate command. The creatures on board are the alien life form that we are fighting in Spectra 5. If they are brought out of suspended animation they intend to land the starship in the ocean of your planet. This species can live under the water and will use the ocean to establish a colony. It is essential they are stopped."

Holly frowned and grabbed Graham's hand. He stared at her and gulped "I can hear a voice," he gasped. She let her partner go and the contact to him broke off.

"So as long as I am touching you, you can hear the message," Holly whispered.

"It appears so," Graham replied and grabbed Holly's hand. "Yes. There it is again."

244

"The message continued from where it had left off. "Starship 43 has an infrared heat seeking detection device on board that will detect the presence of humans. Only your native species who, I believe, are cold-blooded can enter the starship without detection. Any temperature over eighteen degrees Celsius is recognized."

"Stop!" Holly ordered and spoke briskly to Graham. "We need Jaddig here."

With their Crucnon friend holding her hand a few moments later the president's voice continued.

"The main computer terminal is on level five of the starship," he said. "Artificial gravity will be on-line, as soon as the shuttle attaches but for security there are no stairs or elevator accessing the room. Once inside, the procedure to override the computer is identical to the one I hope you have used for the Alpha Base computers..." The voice continued until Holly again ordered it to stop.

"Can you do it, Jaddig?" she asked.

Jaddig frowned, "We'll be sluggish at that temperature but as long as our body temperature is above fifteen we won't go into hibernation." She frowned. "Let's hear the rest of the tape." Her yellow eyes looked amazed. "What do you call voices in your mind?"

"I have no idea," Holly replied. "The word tape will be as good as anything."

Holly started the voice and heard the rest of the instructions. From the dates mentioned it was certain that Doomwatch would be overridden in three days, an alien incoming transmission would control the starship, wake the creatures up and prepare it for landing in Delpe's ocean. Once this happened it would be too late for humans to regain control. The president also warned they were to make no attempt to use the new gegalight technology to contact Earth. If it was switched on, the aliens would home in on the signal and regain access to all their computers.

"It is too late for Earth now," President Arbour concluded in a sad voice. "If possible, we shall send another probe to your planet with other information. In the meantime, do not attempt to contact us. I wish you well, my friends. Within the next few months you may be the only ones of our kind existing in the galaxy. This is Doctor Peter Arbour, President of United States of America saying farewell and God Bless You All."

The voice in the trio's minds stopped.

"Oh damn," Jaddig gasped. "I'd better get up there to switch that computer off."

"But not alone," Holly replied.

"Well, you or Graham can't come," Jaddig retorted. "You heard that your warm blood will be recognized."

"True," replied Graham. But we have lots of Crucnon to help you." He scowled. "A flying female could also access the control room without ladders."

"But who?" Jaddig replied.

"Pinin," Holly said. "She's out of maternity and is quite a reliable girl."

"I guess and who else?" Jaddig asked in a whisper.

*

After being asked, Pinin and Tifru both agreed to go and a little persuasion made Jaddig agree to Syleb being allowed to accompany them. Forty-five minutes later the shuttle now, under control of Grey and the onboard computer renamed Admiral, shot into the atmosphere above Base Alpha. It was agreed no voice or vision contact would be made so Holly and the humans had to wait until the craft returned, hopefully in a few hours time.

"I hate this," Holly confessed to Graham. "We might never see them again."

"I know," he replied and wrapped an arm around her. "They're all very brave volunteers."

"But Pinin and Syleb are so young." Holly added.

"They'll be fine," Graham added. "I think we're going to be proud of them all in a few hours."

"I hope so," muttered Holly. "I certainly do."

*

Jaddig gripped her seat and tried to relax as the G-force thrust her back into the seat, the noise of the motor vibrated her antennae and her eyes felt as it they were about to be thrust out the back of her head. She managed to glance sideways and caught a brief glimpse of Pinin beside her. Outside, the world became a ball of blue ocean, green landmasses and white clouds, a beautiful planet backed by a black sky and stars, millions of them everywhere. They had been in blazing light from the sun but now darkness surrounded the shuttle. The shudder of the fuselage stopped and pressure on Jaddig eased. Everything lost weight and she realized she was floating above her seat with only the security belts holding her down.

She glanced outside and saw the planet was now above them.

"We are in orbit," Admiral reported. "Arrival time is twenty one minutes."

"There it is!" whispered Syleb and Jaddig stared, enraptured at the glowing sphere in front. Already, it was twice the size of the moon and growing by the second. Fifteen minutes later it filled the sky and as they moved closer still Jaddig could see that, except for a band around the equator, the starship was spinning.

"Please fasten seat belts. Arrival is in four minutes. On contact, we shall begin spinning and you may experience nausea as artificial gravity is reinstated," the computer reported.

Jaddig clung on and watched a mechanical arm swing out from the equator band and grip the shuttle. They were pulled in until, with a shudder, the two ships joined. It appeared that the starship and themselves had stopped moving and the stars, planet and sun were spinning around them. There was another slight bump and her stomach lurched.

"Air locks are in place. You may enter Starship 43."

Jaddig uncoupled her seat belts and stepped to the floor. Though expecting problems, she found it was as easy to walk as back on Delpe.

"Well, " Tifru commented. "Shall we go?"

The interior of the connection tunnel was like the inside of a yellow tube but this became a metal floor when the Starship was reached. They waited, air hissed around them and Jaddig shuddered. It was cold, well below the twenty-five degrees they had become used to back in Base Alpha or the even higher tropical outside temperatures on the island.

"Please wait until the temperature reaches seventeen degrees and air pressure is stabilized," a different but familiar voice announced. "Doomwatch welcomes you to Starship 43 and hope your stay is a pleasant one."

Jaddig caught everyone's eyes, all apprehensive but not really scared. Pinin was wide eyed and bit on her lower lip, Syleb so serious but determined while Tifru appeared no different than he would be back on Delpe.

A buzz sounded, the airlock swung open and they walked into a room with carpet on the floor, rectangular walls, furniture and even windows with realistic views of a forest behind. A human male dressed in uniform stood waiting for them. It was only on close inspection that they could see he was not real but a robot.

"Welcome to Starship 43," he said in a very normal voice. "My name is Harold. If you follow me I shall take you to your quarters. There you can refresh. Dinner shall be served in Cafeteria 3 in one Earth hour. Unfortunately the main dining room is off line due to the small number of humanoids aboard."

"How many humans are there here, Harold?" Jaddig asked.

"There are no humans aboard at the moment. You four are the only Crucnon on Starship 43"

"And who else?" Tifru asked.

Harold blinked his eyes but remained expressionless. "The suspended animation chambers have an occupancy rate of eighty seven percent. No other species are awake at the moment. I shall advise you if the conditions change."

"Another great evasive answer," Tifru whispered in Jaddig's antennae as they walked through a corridor that could have been in a Vybber office block and shown into an apartment. It had two bedrooms and a small but well set out lounge. There was also a small kitchen and bathroom. Once again it could have been an upper class apartment block reserved for government officials back home.

"Thank you, Harold," Jaddig said. "Do we have free access throughout the ship or do we need your assistance?"

"All living areas and control decks are available for your inspection. You have priority clearance to all decks that have artificial gravity and air supply."

"And the rest of the ship?" Jaddig inquired.

"Space suits will need to be worn in the vacuum but access can be provided if you wish to inspect the cargo."

"Can it?" Jaddig was surprised at this unexpected reply.

"Of course," Harold replied. "It will take fifty hours to adapt space suits for your anatomy. They were designed for humans. "

Pinin caught Syllabi's eyes. For a computer, this Harold could be quite devious.

"It won't be necessary," Jaddig responded without even a change in her tone. "We only want access to the liveable area of the starship. "

"Very well," the neutral voice responded. "Just call my name if you need my assistance. The red line on the corridor floor leads to the cafeteria."

"And the main control room?" Tifru asked.

"Follow the yellow line. For other areas, just state your destination and the route will be displayed in the floor panelling."

The robot gave a slight bow of his head and left their quarters.

"I don't get it." Tifru grumbled. "We were warned about keeping a low temperature and not having humans with us, yet it is obvious we are aboard."

"Perhaps they got it wrong," Syleb suggested.

"An emergency is declared if an alien species attempts to board Starship 14," Doomwatch's voice filled the room.

"And humans are aliens?" Jaddig replied with a frown.

"All mammal and bird species with heated blood cells are foreign to our environment and are an alien presence."

"Since when?" Tifru added. "You had humans aboard quite recently."

"Our security precautions were reprogrammed forty three hours ago, Earth time."

"But we're welcome?" Syleb spoke up.

"You come within the parameters of a friendly species. You are welcome."

"Now that sounds like a computer," Tifru muttered. "It answered your questions, Syleb."

"Yes," Jaddig added. "I think the sooner we get our job down the better." She turned to the flying female beside her. "How are you feeling, Pinin?"

"I agree," the flying female replied. "Let's get it over with. This place is too artificial. I have the feeling it could change any minute"

"Me too." Syleb gazed around at the walls as if searching for a listening post. "I feel every move we make is being watched."

Jaddig nodded and led her small group through a series of corridors. Without the yellow line they would have been hopelessly lost. In the middle of a curved section the line turned at right angles into an alcove with an airlock at the end. When they approached the door slid open.

"This is interesting," Tifru muttered. "We were never allowed in an area like this when we were on board."

They were on a steel catwalk that disappeared in both directions in a gigantic circle. In front was a gap that dropped away hundreds of metres with ladders descending and ascending to other catwalks. A steady hum of machinery could be heard and floodlights above cast a harsh white light over the area.

"This is where the shuttle craft is stored for inter-galatical flight," the ever present Doomwatch's voice commented. "It would be damaged by post-light speed if kept outside."

"And where is the main control room?" Jaddig asked.

"Door 376," the computer replied. "It is opposite and five flights up."

The four peered across the abyss and upwards where a blue light began flashing above a very ordinary looking steel door. As they had been warned, all the ladders to the opposite catwalk levels were gone.

Pinin paled and stared down.

"Can you do it, my girl?" Tifru asked.

"Yes," Pinin felt in her breast pocket to check if the disk was where it had been placed and stretched her wings out. "See you guys," she whispered and leaped off the catwalk.

Jaddig who remembered when she could fly, stood looking confident but both the others gasped as the flying female dropped downwards in a slow tumble.

"She'll get dashed against a lower catwalk." Syleb grasped the safety rail and stared down.

But Pinin was capable and fit. Her wings flapped in a blur and she began to rise up past the three spectators in a graceful flight. She circled higher and higher until she looked like a dragonfly in the white light.

"She's almost there," Jaddig said. "Good on you Pinin. Keep going, that's a girl!"

*

By the time Pinin reached the blue lit door her movements already felt sluggish. She was fit enough but the low temperature was cooling her blood so that extra effort was needed to maintain height. She blinked and for a moment, lost concentration and dropped a few metres.

"Buck up, Girl!" she growled at herself and pumped her wings down a little. But her eyes were like lead and began to shut. "It's too cold!" she cried.

"The temperature is fourteen degrees," the computer boomed out and echoed throughout the vast interior. "Do you require it to be raised?"

"Yes!" Pinin gasped but remembered the preset alarm. "Only up to eighteen degrees. Understand!"

"Certainly," the computer replied.

Pinin nodded and gazed around. Way below, her three friends were waving. They depended on her. Holly depended on her. The whole planet! She had to keep going. Her eyes shut but were forced open and her arms ached, not her wings but her arms.

"That's stupid," she snorted. "My wings are doing all the work,"

Of course, her arms had been motionless! They needed to move to restore circulation. She swung and kicked in a swimming motion and it helped. The pain in the arms subsided and her eyes felt less heavy.

Pinin circled around once more to gain altitude and focused on the blue light above the door. It was below her! With a slight twist she swung her legs down, landed on the steel catwalk and walked into in a circular room that towered up to exposed metal beams. Half a dozen monitors showed views of the planet, space and interior corridors. Jaddig and the others could be seen standing on the catwalk and this gave her confidence.

She searched around until she found the main console. It looked similar to that on Base Alpha. With pounding heart, she tiptoed along and sat in the seat. Yes, there was a slit to push the disk in. She found the object

250

in her pocket, took it out of the tiny plastic container and, holding her breath, poked it into the slit.

The screen immediately in front changed so it was a sky blue and the words asking for her name and identity number appeared. Pinin typed in the words she'd been told and waited.

"You have requested the manual override of all computer controls. All video and radio transmissions to outside resources are to be cut," Doomwatch's voice spoke. "Press *Yes* if that is correct."

Pinin reached forward and touched the button.

Every monitor in the room switched to the field of blue. After a wait of several minutes a white box appeared on the screen.

The manual override program has been corrupted. The only alternative still functioning is the self-destruct sequence. Do you wish to enter this phase? Underneath were two alternative buttons, *Abort* and *Yes*.

Pinin was excellent at speaking and writing English but it was still her second language and she could not really understand the statement. Back on Alpha Base Holly had taken her through a sequence and told her that, if in doubt she should avoid the abort button.

She gulped and pressed *Yes*.

Once commenced, the self-destruct sequence cannot be aborted. Starship 43 will implode thirty minutes after the countdown is commenced. Are you certain this is your wish?

Pinin studied the paragraph but had no idea what implode meant. "Well Holly, I hope I'm doing the correct thing." She swallowed, reached for the *Yes* button. She was so intent on the activity a slight swishing noise from behind was unheard.

Only when a cold slimy snake like object wrapped around her waist did she realize something was dreadfully wrong.

*

"Look," Syleb cried out. "The ladders!"

With a grinding clang, twenty or more ladders swung down between the levels and two steel bridges slid out across the abyss to meet and click together in the middle.

"She did it!" breathed Jaddig.

Tifru, though, grabbed her arms. "Listen!" he hissed.

The other two did. The squeaks and groans of the ladders and bridge stopped and were replaced by another sound. Screams!

"Help me!" Pinin's high-pitched voice in Crucnon boomed out through the loudspeaker system.

Tifru took one look at the females and bounded for the swaying bridge. He reached the opposite side in seconds and, closely followed by Jaddig and Syleb, tore along the catwalk. Screams of utter terror filled the air but more chilling was a weird slurping grunt. Tifru reached the entrance to the control room and stared inside in horror.

A petrified Pinin was on the console wrapped around by silver, pulsing being. There appeared to be no head but an oval jelly like body with eight, three-metre tentacles. Three encircled the Crucnon's slender body while the five others waved around in an attempt to grab her limbs. But Pinin was fighting for her life. Arms and legs kicked and punched with remarkable success while she continued screaming in absolute terror.

"We're here, Lassie!" Tifru shouted.

Pinin's eyes flashed relief. With a well place kick, one of her tiny boots hit the creature in the centre of its body mass. It gave a low-pitched hiss and buckled up. The tentacles relaxed a second but this was all she needed. She heaved herself up, found her wings free and flew into the air, straight up away from the vile creature.

Tifru now took control. He reached in a pocket and extracted an ancient firearm. It was only twenty centimetres long but had a barrel the diameter of a water pipe, an ornate wooden handle and iron firing mechanism.

"Get back!" he screamed at Jaddig and Syleb.

None too gently, he thrust his left hands out to stop them in the doorway. With his lower right hand he raised the blunderbuss while two fingers of his upper hand pulled back a steel lever the third curled around the trigger.

Meanwhile the creature had reached up, two tentacles wrapped around Pinin's ankles and it began to pull her down. She screamed yet again, grabbed the edge of a crossbeam and held on, her wings flapped in a blur but she could not escape the creature's clutches.

Tifru fired! The room erupted in a roar, flames shot out the front of the weapon and a thousand stone-like pellets plastered the creature in the middle of its body.

It flipped over so it's forefront could be seen for the first time. In the centre of the writhing tentacles were eyes and a beak like mouth. For a second, the eyes focused on Tifru with an expression on utter disdain; blood, dark red like that of a human, spurted out from a score of wounds and it collapsed onto the floor in a heap of slithering jelly. For two seconds the moans continued before the tentacles jerked and the creature lay inert.

Pinin dropped, weeping, into Jaddig's arms while Syleb rushed to Tifru who lowered his smoking weapons and kicked a twisted tentacle out of the way. "Bastard!" he hissed.

"What is it?" Syleb gasped. She stood trembling from shock.

"I'd say it is one of the passengers on this starship," Tifru whispered. "We need to be careful. There may be more around."

"I had no warning," lamented Pinin. "One minute I was looking at the monitor and the next thing I knew, this hideous creature grabbed me and began to squeeze."

"But you fought back," Jaddig replied and held her companion close. "You did well." She glanced at the monitor and received another shock.

Starship 43 will self destruct in twenty one minutes. Please evacuate immediately flashed twenty-centimetre high words.

Above them a siren began to wail.

"Come on!" Jaddig screamed, grabbed Pinin's hands and headed for the door.

Tifru saw the screen, realized what was happening, grabbed Syleb hands and followed.

They reached the main corridor in seconds and ran, panting, through the myriad of corridors; all the time following the yellow line. The airlock was waiting, so, gasping for air, they flung themselves inside. Jaddig pulled at the door shut as Tifru took one last glance out.

"Another one," he muttered. He lifted his blunderbuss he'd managed to reload somehow in their hasty retreat, and fired.

Another octopus like creature, mere metres behind, was flying through the air. It uttered a howl of rage, the door shut and the slurping scream cut off. Syleb, meanwhile, ran forward and opened the airlock of the shuttle. They tumbled forward to the sound of Admiral's welcoming voice.

"Detach from Starship 43 and fire emergency retro-power to move away." Jaddig ordered and turned to smile at Pinin.

"You did it, Pinin," she gasped. "Don't tell Holly but I think, in the circumstances, your idea to self destruct the ship was the correct one."

"What," Pinin frowned. "I did what?"

"Don't worry," grunted Tifru. "I reckon we've just done this world a favour."

Their conversation was halted when, without warning, they were flung in a jumbled heap on the floor as the shuttle accelerated away. A monitor came to life to show Starship 43 slowly reducing in size as the distance between them increased. It was the size of the moon when, without a sound, a black zigzag appeared across its equator. It widened before curling in on itself, a second diagonal cut appeared, white condensation clouded out and that was it! Within two minutes the white cloud dissipated and only the beautiful blue and white planet showed behind. The starship was gone! Not even debris showed where it had once been.

"Did I cause that?" Pinin gasped. Her face appeared drained of emotion and limbs shook from shock.

Jaddig replied in a tender voice. "Yes and you probably saved our world from an invasion of those creatures. She smiled at her friend before the yellow compassionate eyes moved on to Syleb and Tifru.

"Head for Base Alpha, Admiral." she ordered. " We're going home!"

*

CHAPTER 26

Andrea glanced across at Toby when Holly and Jaddig handed over their official report of the starship's destruction. It included a graphic account of how Pinin was attacked and a description of the creature involved.

"But why did she destroy the starship?" Toby asked.

"The species aboard had sophisticated computers that would not accept the virus disk but they had not taken into account a hidden self-destruct program. Even though the disk Pinin inserted could not override the programs it went around them, so to speak, and accessed the sequence," Jaddig replied. "She merely set it in action."

"It took some nerve to activate the program, I must admit." Toby grunted.

Jaddig grinned when she thought back to Pinin's explanation of what had really happened. "She is a brave young Crucnon," she commented. "I reckon she deserves a medal."

"I agree," Andrea said and reached for a yellow document with *Top Secret* written in red diagonally across the cover. "This is information for our eyes only, Jaddig and Holly," she continued in a hushed voice.

"What is it, Mum?" Holly asked.

"We're on our own, Sweetheart," Andrea replied. "There was a second message sent via that Earth probe. Those creatures used the gegalight transmissions to home in on all human settlements and finally Earth itself. If we ever use the equipment to transmit, it is believed they'll follow it back to attack us. As far as me know, human life on Earth has been wiped out."

"Oh my stars!" Holly gasped. "But why didn't they use the gegalight transmissions to trace us when the president originally spoke to us?"

"We don't know," Commander Evans replied. "Perhaps they hadn't arrived on Earth at that point. At a guess I'd say those ones in Starship 43 were an advanced party sent to Earth."

" … And sent onto us while still in suspended animation," Andrea interrupted. "It appears the hijackers did us a favour."

Toby leaned forward and glanced at Jaddig and Holly. "My guess is that a few of the creatures were programmed so they would be brought out of suspended animation first to take control of Starship 43. Doomwatch must have been partially successful in overriding that control so the shuttle could evacuate the Crucnon, Gordon and Nathan. Perhaps there was some warning mechanism that woke the ones that attacked Pinin when the shuttle docked." He shrugged. "We shall never really know."

"So we're back where we started," Andrea added. "An isolated community having to cope for ourselves.

"Not quite, square one, Mum" Holly replied. "The war is over, we've found the Crucnon are our kind and even have a kind of agreement with the crucks. We found out about our past, brought in new liberal laws and have modern technology at our disposal. That's not too bad, is it?"

"I don't think you would have liked Earth even if you had managed to evacuate all the humans there," Jaddig added. "From what Pinin and the others said the planet was in decline, anyway."

"True," Andrea sighed. "So what do we do now?"

"Listen to the Vybber election results." Jaddig grinned. "I know I'm a New Washington citizen now, but I'm quite interested."

"Are you?" Andrea smiled. "Then you might like to view the preliminary results. They've just about to come through." She reached forward and turned on the television.

"... And with half the returns in." An earnest Crucnon woman stared at the screen, "it appears that the United Front of Decency, the offshoot of the ruling junta of the last two decades has only managed to draw eight percent of the vote and President Klyl Olcmal III has conceded defeat. There is, however, a tight race between the Blue Watch Democrats and Social Action Parties with the Democrats holding a slender one point lead at the moment . . ."

Jaddig leaped to her feet in excitement. "It's happened!" she gasped and flashed her yellow eyes around the table. "I never believed it would happen in my life time."

"The Social Action Party could still win," Andrea warned.

"That doesn't matter." Jaddig laughed. "They aren't too bad. We have a democracy. That's the important part! Oh my Goodness, I must tell the others." She rushed for the door but stopped, swung around and retreated to her seat. "They'll know." she beamed. "Everyone will be watching the results on television."

"That's right," Andrea smiled. "It is all cable television from across the border so no transmissions go off into space to warn any aliens we're here."

"At light speed signal would take at least eighty years to reach Earth," Holly said.

"I know," warned Toby Evans, "but any invaders could merely adjust time to be here in our time."

"Of course," Holly exclaimed. "I forgot about that."

256

"Suzi was the one who warned us. According to her, we can still use the orbiting satellites to communicate with laser beam signals that are bounced back to Delpe. She warned we should never use radio or television transmissions though the atmosphere."

"Dear old Suzi," Holly grinned. "A scientist to the end."

"Not quite," her mother smiled. "I hear she is dating Nathan at the moment."

"And you?" Holly added with a sly grin.

Andrea flushed and gazed across at Toby. "We're getting on okay," she replied.

"Yeah, not too bad," Toby added but managed to slip a wink across at Holly and Jaddig.

*

Three months slipped by and, with it, the arrival of spring, renewed growth and rebuilding programs everywhere. The largest town was now New London with a population of five thousand, ninety five percent Crucnon who had crossed the New Columbia River and had taken New Washington citizenship. Another three thousand Crucnon were spread throughout the land, taking up farmland and allocations in the first plateau near Zoflum.

It was evening and, in one white painted timber house, a tall male human walked in to the smell of roast meat being cooked.

"What's the special meal for?" Clay asked as Bikut glanced up from the stove. They were not the only cross-species couples in New Washington now but still received ignorant stares at times in town, mainly from elderly Crucnon and humans, not that it worried either of them.

However, this evening Bikut was apprehensive. She on her bottom lip and a slight quiver of her chin could be noticed. "I have a request, Clay," she asked as she placed a steaming plate of food in front of her partner. "You know the new laws?"

"Yes," grinned Clay. "The LSC. I have the papers here. I wondered when you'd get around to asking."

The Love and Security Contract and recently been passed in the parliament by Andrea's Liberty Party but not without strong opposition from the minority parties. Finally, though, the numbers were there for it to be passed. It replaced the ancient marriage laws and allowed any two citizens, no matter what gender or species, to take vows to be partners.

"Oh Clay," Bikut laughed and flung her arms around her partner. "I was afraid…" Her voice trailed off.

"What do you mean?" Clay grinned. "With local Crucnon males outnumbering females, I was afraid one would sweep you off your feet and you'd tell me to shove off."

"Clay!" Bikut snapped. "She sat down and fixed her eyes on her partner. "There's one other thing," she continued in a shy voice.

"What is it, Bikut?"

"In our society we all have egg mothers and mothers. Our mothers are the females who actually raise us and really mean more to us than the flying female who laid the egg we hatched from. I never knew my egg mother but loved my Mum and Dad." She looked sad for a moment. "Neither of them survived the war."

"I know," Clay replied in a quiet voice.

"Pinin's eggs hatched yesterday. Twenty eight gorgeous little babies." Bikut grabbed Clay's hand. "I want to be a mother, Clay. I want one of those babies." Her words all bubbled out in a rush.

Clay rubbed a hand across his chin. "Oh, I see," he replied in mock concern. "You want to adopt a child?"

"Yes," whispered Bikut.

"I don't want a child," Clay replied.

She stared at the wall all hurt and lips pinched. "I know they aren't human, Clay but you can't adopt human babies and only flying female Crucnon lay eggs." She swung around and tears rolled down her face. "It doesn't matter," she cried and went to run from the room when Clay caught her in a massive hug.

"Go away, Clay!" Bikut screamed, squirmed and kicked. "Just leave me."

"I don't want a child," Clay restated. "I want two, one male, one female. I was teasing you."

Bikut stopped, stared into Clay's eyes and saw the twinkle. She sniffed and a smile appeared across her face. "Oh, Clay," she sobbed. "Do you mean it?"

"Yes, My Little Sweetheart," Clay laughed. " I told Pinin a week ago."

*

The new New Washington Women's Hospital was crowded that morning as young families came to collect their babies. In an old tradition, Pinin, as egg mother lifted each child, kissed it once and handed it over to the couple waiting. Clay towered over the Crucnon couples and gave an audible sigh as an embarrassed human woman and man walked into the reception room, received one of Pinin's children and stood in a self conscious manner by the back wall.

258

Clay and Bikut walked up and were hugged by Pinin. "I hand into your care, two of my children," the proud egg mother stated in the formal handing over. She smiled and handed a tiny boy to Bikut, reached back to a smiling nurse behind her for an equally small girl who was handed on to Bikut. "Care for and cherish these children and give them the security they need to grow into dutiful Vybber..." She stopped and flushed... "I mean, New Washington citizens.

"We shall," Clay and Bikut replied together in the Vybber language.

"Oh Clay," Bikut whispered. "Aren't they beautiful?"

Clay nodded but, by mistake, stepped back and bumped someone behind him. "Oh, I am so sorry," he apologized and turned to gaze into the smiling eyes of Snimel who also held a little bundle in her arms.

"You've taken two, too," she laughed and clung to a sheepish Wunep who also held a baby. "We've done the same."

"Oh Snimel!" Bikut screamed. "We didn't know."

"Yes," Windup grunted. "They're going to call our street Diaper Alley. Think of it, no sleep, I won't be able to go to the tavern every night."

"You never do, anyway," Snimel laughed.

Towards the end of the ceremony Holly and Graham walked in and, after formally hugging all the new parents, walked across to where their friends were gathered. The young egg mother held the last child in her arms.

"No, you can't have Sorrel." She grinned at Holly. "I'm keeping him for myself."

"Thanks, Pinin but there's no need," Holly flushed.

There was a pause and all eyes glued on Holly. "You don't mean!" Bikut grinned.

"Yes," Holly laughed. "I'm pregnant. Have been for three months. The doctor told me I have a daughter on her way."

Clay grabbed Graham's hand and shook it so hard the other man almost winced. "You old bastard," he chortled while everyone else gathered around to congratulate the mother-to-be.

Holly turned to face the group. "The celebrations are at our house tonight. Just bring yourselves and your babies, of course. Mum said she would shout."

New Washington on that spring day was in good heart with its twenty-eight new citizens loved and wanted with many more to come.

*

On the Northern Border, George Bereano, as grizzled as ever, focused his binoculars across the border to where a cloud of dust was rising from a newly constructed road.

"Crucks are coming," he snorted. "Three... wait a moment, five heavy vehicles."

Corporal Sheree Gilmore and Bowman Dianne Hilton, the only other DPF officers at the border post cast a worried glance at the sergeant.

"Shall we call a FanWarrior in Sarge?" Sheree asked.

"No, wait a minute. They're trucks not those gun vehicles." He grinned. "The front one is flying a yellow flag. That's their peace sign. I think it'll be okay. Let's go and meet them, Corporal" He fixed Dianne with a glare. "Just stay here by the telephone, Bowman. Just in case."

The five trucks rolled right up to the border and halted, with a hiss of air brakes, a metre from where George and Sheree stood; a window wound down and the insect face of a cruck appeared.

"Information has been received on two matters," the cruck said in halting English.

"Keep talking." George replied. "You're still on your side of the border so can do what you like, there."

The cruck wagged its antennae and gave what could have been called a giggle. "We have no guns, so you can relax," it said.

"I am relaxed," George grunted but had crossed fingers held behind his back.

"We heard a Crucnon female named Pinin Hyrof saved our planet from the invasion of an alien species," the cruck continued.

"You could say that," George relied in a cautious voice.

"We also heard she has hatched twenty eight offspring and other flying females have done likewise." The voice sounded quite formal.

"They're being well cared for," Sheree added with her voice quick to become defensive.

The cruck ignored her comment and continued speaking. "Can you humans drive?"

"Yes," George muttered. "Why!"

"We wish to thank Pinin Hyrof for her fortitude and donate these first three vehicles to your country to keep and use." The cruck almost smiled. "They're filled with containers of honey. It is an excellent food source for the newly hatched. We use it all the time and thought humans who use milk for their offspring may be short of the product. Do you accept the gift from our nation to yours?"

For the first time George broke into a crinkled grin. "Certainly," he said. "I shall inform our president and Pinin. We were finding it difficult to find enough honey to feed our new children."

"Hatchlings," the cruck corrected. "They're called hatchlings."

"Hatchlings," George corrected himself. "Healthy little souls, too."

The cruck nodded and without another word, climbed down from the cab and walked back to the fourth truck. George scratched his chin. In the blue body suit, it was impossible to tell whether it was male or female. When the other drivers were aboard, the rear truck backed around and rumbled away down the Pulgibrian valley without any further acknowledgment of the human's presence.

"My stars, they were right," Sheree commented a few moments later.

The three trucks were piled high with row after row of ten-litre containers; everyone they examined filled with honey.

"Well," George grinned. "I reckon we can leave the border post empty for a while and drive back to town. You can drive can't you?"

"Of course, Sarge," Sheree grinned and waved at Dianne to come down before she headed for the third truck.

A few moments later the small convey headed towards Zoflum with the first gift, ever, from the natives of the planet. Even George was impressed by the significance of the event as he crunched through a gear.

"Damn!" he muttered and hoped the girls behind hadn't noticed his inexperienced driving.

*

Travelling in the FanSpeed was an exhilarating experience. After a final inspection of the security systems, Base Alpha was mothballed and Holly, Graham, Andrea and Toby were heading home. The two FanWarriors, loaded with electronic equipment and other supplies considered helpful in redeveloping New Washington had left earlier and would probably be back at Zoflum by this time.

Now, though, Holly and her mother stared out at the ocean below with their continent in the distance, green and with the whitecapped mountains inland. A wiggling blue line of the New Columbia wound its way to the sea while three patches of brown smudge showed where Vybber cities and New London were placed. Zoflum was too small to be seen from this height but hundreds of rectangles of green, yellow and brown represented the farms that filled The Haven and the first valley.

"That's our home, Mum," Holly said. "You can certainly see the cultivated land from here."

Andrea tucked a hand on Holly's shoulder and was about to speak when the inboard computer, also called Admiral, spoke. "An incoming shuttle craft, a thousand metres behind and above us is closing in. Do you wish to make contact?"

The four on board were momentarily stunned. They had only left the shuttle all clamped down by the cranes at Base Alpha. How could it be here now?

"Stay silent," Toby who was in the pilot's seat, snapped and glanced at Andrea.

"Give us more details of the craft and its destination," Andrea added.

"It is a Model 239 Shuttle craft, manufactured on Earth and used to transport personnel from Earth designed starships." Admiral hesitated. "One moment, please. Information is arriving."

Once again the four humans just stared apprehensively at one another, questions rushed through their minds with only Admiral being able to supply any answers.

"A starship is in a descending orbit over the planet. Speed and angles are too sever for the craft to land. It is estimated it will hit the atmosphere in forty minutes and disintegrate on impact," the computer reported.

"And the shuttle?" Andrea snapped.

"It contains an estimated five thousand life forms."

"What!" gasped Holly. "We'd like more details, please."

"In rounded figures, there are six hundred and fifty mammal species, two hundred bird species, six reptiles and the rest insect species."

"The insects?" Andrea asked.

"They're commonly known as honey bees."

"Any species of the type that attacked Pinin on Starship 43?" Holly added.

"Negative. The shuttle is heading in this direction and will be beside us in five minutes."

"It's from Earth, That's for certain," Toby grunted.

"And there it is!" Graham nodded out the windscreen.

It was! A shiny sphere approached from over the curve of the horizon and headed directly for them.

"I am receiving no voice communication with the craft," Admiral reported. "However, electronic data received confirms it departed from a starship thirty-one hours ago. Since then it has been in orbit around the equator. It fired its motors forty three minutes ago to intercept this FanSpeed."

"So they found us and decided to investigate," Holly whispered. Her eyes were glued on the sphere increasing in size by the second.

"It appears so, Sweetheart," Andrea replied. Only a tiny pulsing vein in her neck portrayed any emotion as New Washington's president reached out to touch the window ledge.

The foreign shuttle was upon them before they really had time to discuss the situation. As they watched, small retro-rockets could be seen sending white smoke from exhaust tubes and the gigantic craft, twice the size of the shuttle they knew slipped in beside them.

"Well, it's not hostile," Graham grunted. "Is there any voice or video contact?"

"Negative," Admiral replied.

"So they're purposely keeping the radio off air," Andrea commented.

"We are being electronically probed," Admiral reported. "Do you wish to cut the outgoing signal?"

"No," Andrea gave a twitch of a smile. "Let them find out what we are."

"Look!" Holly cried. "Up in the top section."

A row of panels slid down in the shuttle to reveal eight dark windows that lit up as they watched as if someone had turned on a light. Movement could be seen inside and three of the windows showed silhouettes, profiles of the upper half of creatures with two arms and flowing hair ... One waved!

"They're humans," Holly sighed in relief. She waved back.

"Wait a minute!" Toby added. "They're holding up some cards in the windows. Can you read them, Holly? Your eyes are stronger than mine."

Holly leaned forward and squinted. The windows were filled with white cardboard with black lettering. *Help us!* it spelled out.

"No voice communication," Admiral reported.

"Can you transmit a signal without using radio waves?" Toby asked.

"At this distance we could send a primitive signal using laser light," Admiral reported.

"Good," Andrea replied. "Tell them to follow us down. When we land they are to come in beside us. Can you get that message through."

"It has been acknowledged," Admiral replied a moment later, "They wish to know who we are."

"Tell them the president of New Washington welcomes them to the planet of Delpe."

"Is that wise?" Graham cautioned.

"Of course," Andrea smiled. "If they're hostile, I doubt if we can do much, anyhow. There are no weapons aboard FanSpeed."

*

When the shuttle dropped vertically down onto the landing field outside Zoflum, hundreds of citizens, both human and Crucnon had gathered to watch. Three DPF vehicles screamed onto the field and Holly could see officers fanning out to surround the craft. Already barriers were being put up to keep the crowds back.

"Well, let's go and meet our visitors," Andrea said.

Jaddig and Ron Cotterell met them on the tarmac, both with serious expressions on their faces. Andrea, though, appeared serene. She grabbed Toby and Holly's arms and walked towards the shuttle that had just powered down and stood on six monstrous landing pads towering above the field.

A car roared in beside the president and an officer shouted out a question.

"No, we'll walk," Andrea replied.

Graham fell in beside Holly and reached back for Jaddig's hand. "Come on Vice President Qarte," he stated in a determined voice. "You are needed here with us."

The five, ringed by a dozen or more armed DPF officers walked up until they were in the shadow of the shuttle and waited.

"Lower the weapons," Andrea ordered. "Imagine how they feel."

The DPF officers immediately complied and a hush fell over the crowd as a ramp lowered down beneath the shuttle and the visitors appeared.

"Oh my stars!" Holly whispered.

Two lines of more than a hundred human children marched out. They ranged in age from kindergarten to teenagers carrying toddlers and babies. There were Europeans, Asians and Africans, girls and boys. Everyone was dressed in a blue and white uniform with the girls in knee length skirts and the boys, shorts.

They circled around and formed into four straight lines. No sooner had they assembled when a second group walked out and another hundred children assembled. A third line followed, a fourth and fifth until six hundred or more children assembled in six groups beneath the shuttlecraft.

Holly, Jaddig, Toby and Graham stood in a line behind Andrea, and waited with mixed emotions. When the last child lined up, a girl of about fifteen with her blonde hair tied back in a ponytail stepped forward and marched towards the president.

"My name is Tania Wilkinson," she stated in a quivering voice. "We are from Starship 67 and were told you would protect us." Her voice broke. "There is nobody else. We were selected as the last representatives of humankind and sent to find the last colony of humans." She glanced up with tears now streaming down her cheeks and plopping onto the grass. "We found you," she cried.

"Oh you poor dear," Andrea replied and grabbed the girl in her arms. "Yes, Tania, we will look after the children, every last one of you."

*

Within two hours the children, and there were exactly six hundred, were taken down to the caves and allocated dormitory space. It was crowded but everybody in Zoflum arrived to help, food was set out, the two dozen tiny babies ranging down to three months old were fed honey solution unloaded from George's convey. Dormitories were allocated and every family, human or Crucnon allocated a group of children to care for.

"We called our ship The Ark," Tania who, with a youth named Xen Chan, an Asian boy, were the two leaders and oldest aboard. "Inside you will find a herd of twenty dairy cows, a hundred sheep, pigs, ducks, chickens, a hive of bees and our pets."

"Your pets?" Holly asked.

"Yes," Xen replied. "We were all allowed to bring one pet per family. Most have cats or dogs but there are also some goldfish, a couple of lizards and a dozen turtles." He hesitated. "I hope you don't mind. We thought it might remind us of Earth. "

"So you're in families?" Holly added.

"Yes," Tania replied. "I have a brother with me. Xen has a sister."

"But no adults?"

"No. There was limited space and the adults voted to just send us," Xen added. Like Tania there was sadness in his voice. "It was thought we deserved the right to continue humankind."

"Very interesting," said Toby who was listening. "I'll get the animals off the shuttle." He turned and issued orders to the DPF officers waiting behind him.

"There are also computers, books, clothes, medical supplies and machines for manufacturing items," Tania said, "but no weapons of any sort. Everything we thought would help humanity is included."

"It really is an ark," Andrea replied. "What could be more welcome than the children, animals and creatures from Earth?"

"Starship 67 was an experimental craft with special cloaking devices aboard," Xen explained. "We circled the galaxy for a century before coming here through a time bridge. Our starship was programmed to burn up in your atmosphere so no trace of our existence would remain. We should be safe from the Darugors."

"They're the octopus type creatures?" Andrea asked.

"Yes." Tania's face creased into a frown. "If they find us here we will be annihilated. They have weapons that can wipe all animal life forms off a planet but leave plant life intact. They then just colonize the planet with their own kind."

"And that happened on Earth?"

"Our computer confirmed it did," Tania replied. "We left and were placed in suspended animation before it happened. All the details are available on board The Ark."

*

The car screeched to a stop outside the little white house. The teenager jumped out with her ponytail flying in the wind and ran across to the back door.

"Bikut," Tania shouted and ran straight inside. "Come on. Holly's on her way."

Bikut came out of the bedroom with her eyes aglow. "Now?" she said. "She's not due until next week."

"Come on," Tania coached, "Hurry! Everyone's there."

"But the babies!"

Tania grinned, picked one of Bikut's children up and grabbed a tiny blanket to wrap around him. "I'll help," she laughed. "Where's Clay?"

Bikut picked up the other baby out of the cot and smiled. "He's down on the bottom farm putting another crop in. We can catch up with him later."

"Right," Tania replied and almost ran out to the car. She flung the back door open and handed the infant in.

"Why me?" her eight year old Scott moaned as she plunked the tiny Crucnon on his lap.

"Because I have to drive." Tania glowered.

"Okay, Sis," Scott replied and cuddled the tiny Crucnon in his arms. "I don't really mind holding the baby as long as my friends can't see me."

Bikut sat in the front holding her daughter and they were off down the dirt road with clouds of dust shooting from the tyres and covering the adjacent fields.

"And don't you say anything stupid to Holly," Tania scolded Scott as they pulled into the curb by the hospital. It was funny how things quickly became the norm. She and Scott had been a part of Holly and Graham's family since their arrival all those weeks before.

Tania opened the back door, relieved Scott of his burden and with the baby on her hip walked sedately indoors. Bikut grinned and followed.

Everyone was there; Andrea with Toby, Jaddig, Snimel and Wunep, Suzi and Nathan, Pinin holding her little boy, all their other Crucnon and human friends and Graham, of course. Even old George stood self-consciously in a far corner and watched the centre of everyone's attention.

Holly lay on the bed in a blue floral brunch coat looking quite beautiful with her long red hair brushed out over her shoulders and a rosy face that smiled at the crowd. Beside her, wrapped up, so only a wrinkled head showed out, was a tiny baby.

"This is Solana Andrea Jurjevics," she said and picked her baby daughter up. "In the old system she would have been our first Generation 8 child but that doesn't matter any more."

She reached up and kissed Graham before her eyes glanced around the room at her mother, Jaddig, her other friends and finally her new family. "Would you like to hold your little sister, Scott?" she asked.

"Ah, Mum," the eight year old went a bright red and glanced at his feet. "Do I have to?"

The End